FATAL TEARS

FATAL TEARS

The Journeys of Rupert Winfield

Stuart Fifield

Marjolaine, Enjoy your trip on the Nile! With best wishes, Stuart Fifield. Oct. 2017.

Book Guild Publishing
Sussex, England

First published in Great Britain in 2013 by
The Book Guild Ltd
Pavilion View
19 New Road
Brighton, BN1 1UF

Copyright © Stuart Fifield 2013

The right of Stuart Fifield to be identified as the author of this work has been asserted by him in accordance with the Copyright, Designs and Patents Act 1988.

All rights reserved. No part of this publication may be reproduced, transmitted, or stored in a retrieval system, in any form or by any means, without permission in writing from the publisher, nor be otherwise circulated in any form of binding or cover other than that in which it is published and without a similar condition being imposed on the subsequent purchaser.

All characters in this publication are fictitious and any resemblance to real people, alive or dead, is purely coincidental.

Typesetting in Baskerville by
Keyboard Services, Luton, Bedfordshire

Printed and bound in Great Britain by
CPI Group (UK) Ltd, Croydon, CR0 4YY

A catalogue record for this book is available from
The British Library

ISBN 978 1 84624 872 6

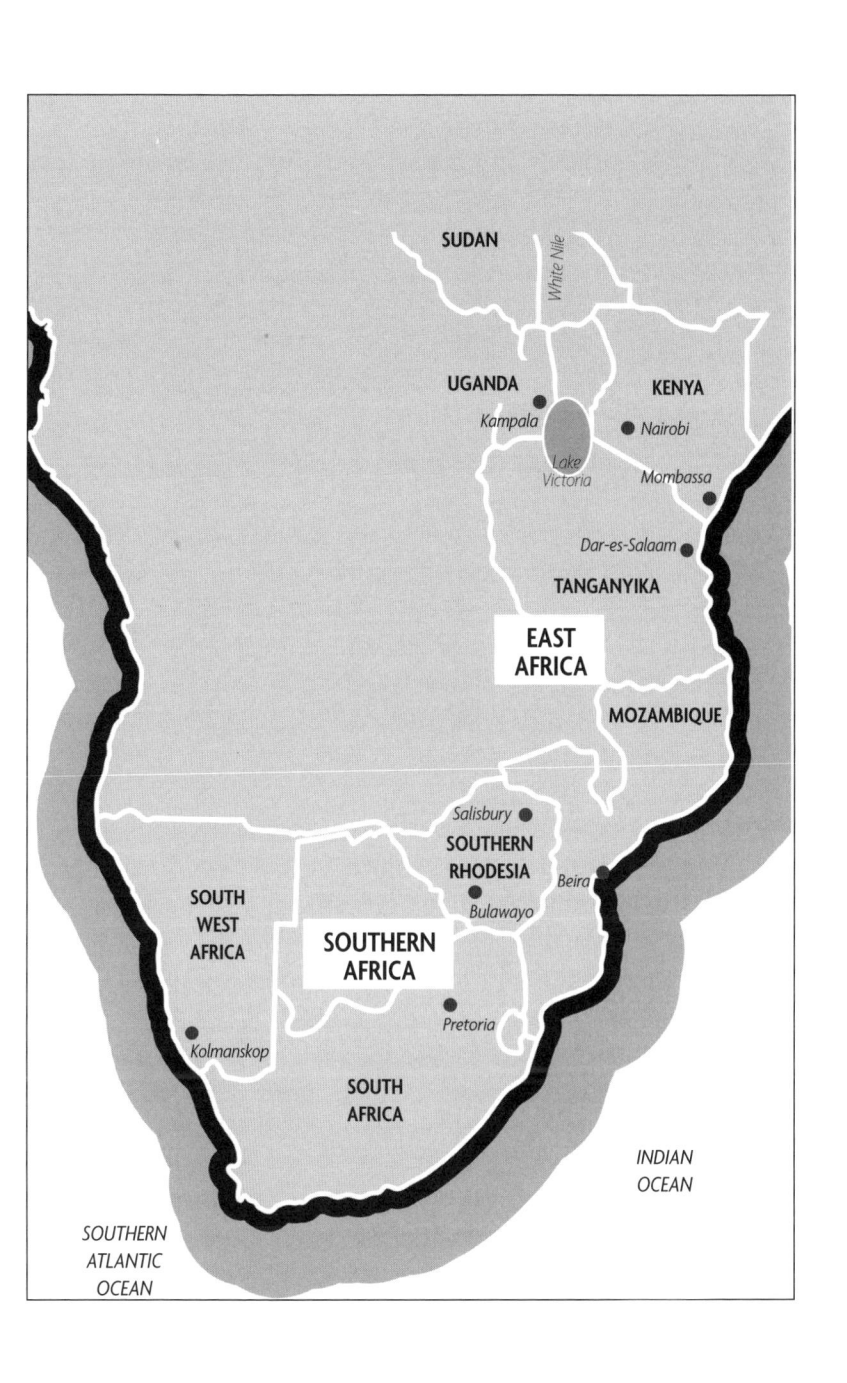

SUDAN

White Nile

UGANDA
Kampala

Lake Victoria

KENYA
Nairobi
Mombassa

Dar-es-Salaam

TANGANYIKA

EAST AFRICA

MOZAMBIQUE

Salisbury

SOUTHERN RHODESIA
Bulawayo
Beira

SOUTH WEST AFRICA

SOUTHERN AFRICA

Kolmanskop

Pretoria

SOUTH AFRICA

INDIAN OCEAN

SOUTHERN ATLANTIC OCEAN

1

South-West Africa

Kolmanskop, near Lüderitz, in the Sperrgebiet – 17th June 1928

Raised by the persistent wind that blew in off the distant Atlantic, the fine sand shifted its position from dune to dune. In the town of Kolmanskop, the clearing gangs were already at work shovelling the ever-shifting sand away from doorways, streets and buildings. Kolmanskop, like nearby Lüderitz, had enjoyed prosperous growth since the area in which both towns lay had been found to harbour a secret. Quite unexpectedly, the soft, sandy earth had yielded unbelievable wealth in the form of very high-quality diamonds. Indeed, it was the Kaiser himself who had given the good people of Lüderitz stained-glass windows for their church, in recognition of the financial contribution their area was making to the wealth of the Reich. This great wealth had come about more by chance than careful planning. Indeed, it was hard to believe that, barely a single lifetime earlier, the old Chancellor, Bismarck, had been reluctant to place the area under German protection at all. He had not been sure if the expense involved would be worth the effort of any likely return. Eventually, he had agreed to the German Eagle flying over the area only in order to prevent the British from laying claim to an even bigger chunk of Southern Africa than they already owned.

Then the Great War had come and, following it, great changes. The unexpected wealth resulting from Bismarck's hesitant decision no longer rewarded the former masters in Berlin. It was now those in Consolidated Diamond Mines in South Africa who, quite literally, reaped benefits beyond even their wildest, expansionist dreams. Excitement grew to fever pitch when the news came through that there were even bigger deposits further down the coast at Oranjemund, where the stones were of even higher quality. This had caused a momentary shudder to quake through the otherwise comfortable lives of the residents of Kolmanskop, but their misgivings soon passed. There were those, however, who were possessed of deeper foresight and who could see the day when their complacent existence would come to an end, as profit drove the mining operations further south.

In the nearby mine compound the outlines of the bulky, heavy machinery and the low-roofed administration buildings had already started their slow, swaying daily dance in the rising heat. Activity was everywhere. It was not yet eight o'clock and, despite the early heat, the morning fog, which rolled inland from the sea every day, still clung to everything. It would only finally lift later in the morning. In this part of the world dawn came early and so did the start of yet another unremitting day of labour in the stifling heat. Only the distant sliver of the cobalt-blue ocean held the promise of some slight relief. Towards the end of the day the temperature would eventually drop and, even if there were to be no breeze from the sea, the land would recoil into a brief period of welcome relaxation, before the temperature of the night plunged towards zero. Work in the *Sperrgebiet* – the old Kaiser's 'Forbidden Zone' at the bottom south-west corner of Africa – was harsh and unforgiving; as hard and unforgiving as the diamonds the zone produced.

'Come!' barked the substantial bulk of the mine manager. The knock on the office door had made him stop writing and look up. His shirt, fresh that morning, was already blotched with sweat.

'Excuse me, Sir...' It was the mine manager's assistant, a slightly built, insignificant man who wore thick lenses on his hawk-like nose.

'Well?' asked the manager, irritated at the interruption, 'What is it?'

'I have a message, Sir. Your visitor has crossed the outer perimeter and should be here within the next quarter of an hour.'

Both men spoke in German. The manager turned his head to stare at the dirty window on the far side of the office. He did not like these visits any more than he liked his visitor.

'Very well,' he said, without looking at his assistant. The sparrow-like man lingered, almost apologetically, barely filling the open doorway. He stood waiting for instructions.

'You can go...' said the manager, as he turned his attention back to the documents on his desk. '... And make sure that you have tidied the outer office this time...' he snapped, as his assistant began to close the door, '... we do not want any further criticism – not like the last time!'

He did not see the face of irritated annoyance his assistant pulled, as the door clicked closed.

The inside of the mine manager's office offered shade from the rays of the sun, but it was stifling – the corrugated-iron roof made sure of that. In complete contrast, the buildings in nearby Kolmanskop had been designed and decorated to be aesthetically pleasing. Transplanted into a harsh, sandy, African wilderness they were reminders of the Old Country. At the mine headquarters, the simple, almost rustic appearance of the buildings understated their importance in the mining operations of this area of what had once been German South-West Africa. Through the compound, of which the office block formed the central structure, passed millions of pounds' worth of diamonds – both legally and illicitly. Faced with such blatant temptation, it was widely accepted that a certain, possibly quite large percentage of the workforce could not be trusted. That much was beyond question and that was why the *Sperrgebiet* resembled more a military zone than a commercial enterprise. The official policy – although never openly admitted – was to shoot first and ask questions later. Anyone caught surrendering to temptation and trying to cream off a stone or two, no matter how small, was dealt with swiftly and mercilessly. That was company policy, tacitly supported by the government. It had been so under the old system of the Kaiser's administration in far-off Windhoek and it remained so under the new South African administration in the even more distant Pretoria. However, despite the rigidly enforced regulations, government policy could only be implemented if the perpetrators were caught.

The mine manager's office was sparsely furnished and – like everything else in the area – sandy. On one end of a large desk stood a battered electric fan, rattling and shaking as it attempted to cut a cooling swathe through the closeness of the air. Somewhere off in the far distance, the dull thud of electric generators rumbled ominously, like distant, perpetual thunder. At the opposite end of the desk stood an old telephone and a wicker tray, which contained some official-looking papers, the top few of which seemed in danger of blowing out of the tray every time the ancient fan rotated noisily in their direction. Behind the desk sat the mine manager, Wilhelm Grunewald, or William Greenwood, as he preferred to be known these days. He was perspiring like a garden sprinkler, but not so much because of the heat, as because of his visitor, who had just been shown in.

'...But we always do what is necessary, Herr Graf. We are aware of our duty...' His chair creaked in protest, as he moved uneasily in it. He spoke quietly and still in German. 'They have become suspicious lately and it is not as easy as we would like,' he continued, making a mitigating gesture in the air with his podgy hands. 'We have lost two of our colleagues recently, as I am sure the Herr Graf is fully aware – that has not helped us in our work.'

Sitting opposite him, in a position which maximized any effect to be gained from the labours of the struggling fan, sat a tall, bird-like figure – ramrod straight – with both hands resting gently on the ornate silver handle of a heavy walking stick. The Graf von Hohenstadt und Waldstein-Turingheim was of the Old Prussian school – used to giving orders and having them obeyed instantly without question. Now, he had much to resent, even to hate. It was a dangerous, resentful hatred, which was focused on the bastard foreigners, who had deprived him of almost all of the lands and possessions his family had held in Germany for centuries. As the Kaiser's Empire around the globe had disintegrated following the war, so, too, had the Herr Graf's overseas assets been seized or confiscated. The losses in South-West Africa had come as a particularly hard blow. In fact, his world had crumbled to the point where he had seriously questioned the value of continuing to struggle his way through it. That had been shortly after the Armistice, in the demoralizing chaos of ignominious defeat. Now, he preferred not to recall that spineless weakness which had given rise to such feeble thoughts. It was not what was expected of a Prussian aristocrat. His outlook had changed when he had been introduced to the manifesto of the fledgling Nationalist Socialist Party. Their policies seemed to him to be sensibly logical; he felt that they spoke both to him directly and to the German People generally, offering all true sons of the Fatherland the chance of avenging the humiliation at Versailles. The Party leader – the future Führer – was someone to be supported – even if he was of lowly Austrian stock. He spoke passionately of a new Greater Germany and that was what had appealed to the Herr Graf.

In the heat of the iron-roofed office almost at the southern tip of Africa, he rose, like some silent bird of prey, and crossed to the solitary window. Through the fly-spattered grime on the glass he stared idly out at a line of sweating black labourers, who were unloading two railway wagons.

'I am aware of what you say, Grunewald...' he used the German form of the manager's name, 'such events are a hindrance. However, we have to rise above such ... inconveniences.' He spoke softly, with a gentle musical voice that masked the steel determination of his purpose, 'I cannot allow myself to fail and neither can you.' He turned steel-grey eyes on the manager as he spoke. The latter shifted again in his chair, but said nothing. 'The Party is aware of the difficulties. Even if we continue to lose people, we must carry on until the successful outcome that is expected of us has been attained. There is no more to be said on the matter.'

He had retraced his steps from the window as he spoke and now resumed his seat, his face steel-like and devoid of any emotion. He turned his gaze onto the mine manager, as a silent signal that that part of the conversation – the attempts to offer excuses – was now at an end. Then he turned and glanced idly down to where his clasped hands rested gently on the ornate handle of his cane and continued.

'Without the stones there can be no question of the Party succeeding in avenging the disgrace we have all had to endure for so long – disgrace which not only affects the Fatherland, but each one of us, as sons of the Fatherland. I need hardly remind you of the loss we have all suffered – His Imperial Majesty, you, I – all of us,' he said angrily.

The manager followed his visitor's gaze to the handle of the walking stick. It was a skilfully worked rendering of a silver-winged bird, phoenix-like, its claws clutching a writhing snake in the flames, its eyes a large pair of port-red rubies.

'Jawohl!' replied the manager almost springing to attention. 'The Party must have our undivided attention and duty. That goes without question!'

'Good. Then we are of the same accord,' came the softly-spoken reply. He allowed himself a short pause before continuing. 'I can inform you that things progress well. The fools of the Old Guard in Weimar and Berlin have started to lose control and the time will soon be ripe for the emergence of our new, single-minded leadership. It is a time which is long overdue – a time when the past will be avenged and the Kaiser will be rescued from his exile and asked to lead the Fatherland back to its rightful place.' The voice had never once risen above the level of a pleasant whisper. That was the threatening thing about it and it was the thing which Grunewald disliked – even feared – the most. 'So now, where is the shipment? I trust that you have assembled only the best-quality stones.' It was more a statement of fact, rather than a question. 'I have orders to leave with them at once, before time runs out.'

The manager heaved himself out of his chair, picking up a sturdy paperknife from the surface of the desk as he rose. He crossed to a tall wooden filing cabinet in the corner of the office, tucked safely away from the window and, with some difficulty, lowered himself to the floor. He started to wheeze as he worked. Using the paperknife, he prized up one of the floorboards. Then he reached in under the floor and drew out a small black-velvet purse. Replacing the floorboard carefully, he returned to the desk and collapsed once again into his chair, sweating even more profusely than before. His wheezing became more pronounced, the rattling of his heaving chest filling the office. His visitor stared at him with a look bordering on disdain. He disliked imperfection almost as much as he despised failure.

'My apologies, Herr Graf, I need a moment,' gasped Grunewald as he removed a large, stained handkerchief from his trouser pocket. He proceeded to dab in turn at the sweat on his face and the saliva around the corners of his mouth. 'It is the heat,' he mumbled, as he upended the opened purse over his desk blotter. Twenty-three cloudy, semi-opaque pebbles, the size of large marbles, fell out.

His visitor eyed them with appraising, practised eyes. From his pocket he drew a jeweller's magnifying glass, quickly selected some of the stones and studied them carefully, one after the other. Once cut and polished, these innocuous pebbles would be worth more than a king's ransom. Eventually, he replaced the magnifying glass in his pocket and resumed his upright posture, hands once again resting on the handle of the heavy cane. The mine manager had stopped wheezing, his chest now more regular in its movement.

'You have done well, Grunewald. Your methods and bribery are obviously still to be relied upon and you have secured a good return for the funds you were given. So much for any loyalty this black scum might feel for their new English masters,' he said, turning to once again stare in the direction of the window.

In the compound outside, the sweating lines of labourers continued to swarm around the railway wagons, but they were only the tip of the iceberg; the vast majority of the labour force was out of sight – dispersed under heavy guard for miles around in the sea of sand dunes, which held the gravel beds in which the stones were easily found.

'A few stupid English shillings in exchange for a diamond worth maybe millions – and all done right under the noses of the British!' He chuckled softly. 'The arrogant swine!' he whispered, his voice suddenly taking on a sinister, chilling tone.

As far as he saw things, he had more than enough reason to hate the English. It was they who had deprived him of everything following the war. It was *they* who had killed most of his family and – by far the most important to him – *they* had stolen a good deal of his self-respect. Only his own foresight in placing a considerable portion of his personal fortune in a Swiss bank in 1916 had saved him from penury – a fate suffered by far too many of his fellow aristocrats, following the fiasco of the signing of the Peace Treaty at Versailles.

'Herr Graf...' Grunewald's voice interrupted the visitor's vehement recall, '... we will, of course, continue with our duty, but the Herr Graf must be aware of the pressures and suspicions which we have had to deflect over the last few months ... since the Herr Graf's last visit...'

'Of course I am aware of the situation!' snapped the Herr Graf, dismissing Grunewald's protestations with a wave of the hand. He glared at the mine manager with a look of intolerance. 'As it is your task to deflect difficulties associated with the procurement of the stones, so it is mine to ensure the smooth transport of the shipment. And how do you think that I accomplish this? Do you think that it is easy? Do you think I simply walk up to the gates of the *Sperrgebiet* and just ask to be let in? If it weren't for the fact that the fog seems to be on our side, I would probably not be able to get in at all.' The visitor despised stupidity with the same intensity as he loathed the English. His cheeks had become tinged with the faintest suggestion of colour – it was the crimson of anger.

Grunewald blushed profusely, realizing that he had said the wrong thing. He puffed out an attempt at a placating apology. 'No, no, Herr Graf ... naturally not ... I merely wish to sug...'

'None of us would be able to operate without each other – never forget that. Some of us lead and the rest follow, but we are all treading a common path to a glorious future. If we had not managed to keep ourselves together as one

Volk, for the sake of the Fatherland, none of what we are doing would be even remotely possible. The English think they have beaten us into submission, but they are too full of their own arrogance to even realize that they are being undermined, both from without and within. We are not the only people to have lost under the English. We have friends around the world who also have reason enough to hate them. But enough of this eulogizing! I must go. These stones have a long journey ahead of them and I must leave before the benefit of our friend, the fog, is lost.'

He twisted the ornate bird handle of his cane and withdrew a razor-sharp stiletto blade the length of a knitting needle. The silver phoenix was its hilt. As the mine manager watched, he placed the deadly weapon carefully on the edge of the desk. Then, he took the uncut stones and carefully dropped them one at a time into a hollow chamber that ran down the shaft of the cane, parallel to another, smaller, off-centre chamber that housed the stiletto blade.

The entire operation was over in no more than a minute. The two parts of the cane were reunited with a click and once again the visitor sat bolt upright in his chair, both hands resting gently on the silver handle of a deadly, solid walking stick that was worth millions.

Five minutes later Grunewald was blocking most of the window with his bulk, gazing out through the dirty glass at the rapidly receding shape of his visitor, who seemed to melt away like a dark shadow flitting across the ground. Whilst Grunewald was without question fully aware of his duty, he was, nevertheless, always pleased to see the departure of the Herr Graf. The man's icy coolness made him more than just a little nervous – it scared him.

The fiery disc of the sun was hovering low over to the west, resisting the enticing arms of the cooling Atlantic, which would, nevertheless, soon devour it. To the east, the distant Schwartzrand range of mountains would hold on to the heat that had scorched the sand for most of the day, until long after the sun had disappeared. Another day was well on its way to being over. As he poured himself a small shot of *Jägermeister*, Grunewald anticipated his evening meal with growing pleasure. The visit was now safely behind him and there wouldn't be another for several months – assuming their activities were not discovered in the meantime. Despite his unease at having had yet another visit and dressing-down from the Herr Graf, the handover of the stones had proceeded smoothly and without hitch. He smiled to himself, as he thought that his duty to the Fatherland – his part in the rebirth of his defeated homeland – was now over, at least for the foreseeable future. He downed the clear liquid in a single gulp, poured himself another, put the bottle back in the bottom drawer of the filing cabinet and took the glass back to his desk. Then he sat down, the chair creaking in protestation as he did so. Yes, he thought, with a glow of satisfaction, it had gone well.

Grunewald raised the glass to his eager lips. Suddenly, the mine compound was full of noise, movement and people. He turned his sweating head to look towards the window – towards the direction from which came the unexpected noise and commotion. The movement had been too sudden and most of the contents of the glass spilled down the front of his shirt, adding yet more wet patches to the two that had spread generously, throughout the day, from his armpits. Before he had the chance to lift his bulk from the chair, the office door burst open and several uniformed men entered unceremoniously.

'I am sorry, Sir, I couldn't stop them.'

The mine manager's assistant stammered an apology, as he followed the uniformed men into the room, weaving easily between them to reach the front of the little group.

Even in the unexpected confusion of his new visitors' arrival, it occurred to the mine manager that his assistant seemed over-enthusiastic in his excuses for the sudden interruption. Something did not ring true. It all seemed to have been rehearsed.

'They pushed right past me and I...'

'That will do,' barked the officer in charge. He spoke English and was obviously a man used to being obeyed. 'You can go – for the moment.'

As Grunewald's assistant retreated to the outer office, closing the door purposefully behind him, the mine manager thought he detected the slightest flicker of recognition between the officer and the hawk-like assistant – an understanding that the one was the secret servant of the other. He suddenly felt as if he was caught in a trap, into which he was about to be further drawn, and from which there would be no chance of any escape. Something also silently warned him that there would be no help from the outer office – for a fleeting second he had seen the look of satisfaction on his assistant's face, as the ineffectual man had turned to leave the office.

'We have more than just a fleeting reason to believe that there is something more than diamond gathering going on here,' said the officer, pausing to let his words resonate around the dry, sandy office. As he did so, he crossed casually to the window. 'Something which cannot fail but to involve *you*,' he said softly, throwing the words over his shoulder without turning his head.

Outside, the worst of the day's heat was over, but the corrugated iron of the office roof seemed reluctant to surrender the high temperature it had stored. Underneath the roof, in the office, Grunewald had started to sweat even more profusely than usual.

'I'm afraid I don't really follow you, Sir,' he said rather lamely, in a voice that was very slightly accented by not being English. 'You can check all the records if you wish – you will find everything is in perfect order.'

'Yes, I'm sure that we will find it is,' continued his accuser, all the time staring idly out of the window, 'that'll be the famous German efficiency for you.' He smiled – more a dangerous leer than anything remotely friendly or reassuring. You see, Mr *Grunewald*,' – he emphasized the German version of the man's name – 'we're not really concerned with what you have shown in your records – it's what you might *not* have put into your records in the first place that is of real interest to us.'

'I'm afraid I still don't understand what point you are making,' replied Grunewald, his sweat dripping in big blobs onto the front of his shirt, as he made to stand up, 'I can assure you that...'

'Sit down!' snapped Major Ashdown, turning around to face the manager. Grunewald's bulk did as it was commanded and collapsed back into the long-suffering chair.

'Don't play us for fools!' snapped the Major, 'we've been watching you for some time.'

Grunewald was showing signs of discomfort and his breathing was becoming shallower.

'Yes, Mr Grunewald. We, too, have a useful network of spies and informers. Do you really think you have the monopoly on information?' Major Ashdown, head of counter-insurgency in Military Intelligence, Southern Command, enjoyed the chase, but he was rapidly growing impatient with this one. 'You buy your diamonds from the natives the same way we buy our information – except that we pay them more.' He was looking at the closed office door as he spoke. 'Then again, not *all* of our information comes from the natives. Money attracts Europeans every bit as much as it does the blacks. We simply pay them more. So you see, whether you answer my questions or not, it is really quite immaterial ... we already have our answers. Most of them, but not quite *all* of them...' He was silent for a few moments, staring fixedly at the closed office door, before turning quickly, to look out of the window again. 'It's very difficult to know whom you can really trust these days ... black or white...'

The sentence hung unfinished on the still, hot air.

Ashdown paused and took out a gold cigarette case from his tunic pocket. He lit one and exhaled the smoke in a long, steady plume. 'So, Mr *Grunewald*,' – he was playing with this man now – 'I was hoping you could help us with those one or two missing pieces of our puzzle. Who knows, if you do we might be able to put in a good word for you at your trial in Pretoria.' He turned and crossed slowly, menacingly, towards the large desk and the heavily sweating man behind it. He took another draw on his cigarette: '...Before they hang you for High Treason.'

The mine manager had started to wring his hands under the desk and his complexion had turned deathly white under the blood pressure blotches which now covered his cheeks and neck. His breathing had become even shallower and he was wheezing again – softly. He was running scared and it was showing.

'But wa...' He stumbled over his words and coughed. Then he began again. 'But what makes you think I would even contemplate anything less than my duty as manager of this mine?' He was buoyed up by false bravado. 'I have grave responsibilities which...'

Ashdown cut across him.

'So do we,' he answered, in a voice that was a whisper almost as menacing as that of the Herr Graf. 'That's why we're not leaving until you see the sense of assisting us with our enquiries.'

He indicated his two uniformed soldiers, who filled a considerable area of the floor space of the office. They were muscular, armed and used to obtaining answers.

Grunewald had barely seconds to decide on a course of action. Should he implement the plan he had often thought through in the event of just such an emergency? Surely there was no need, because the diamonds were gone from their safe hiding place under the floor. There was nothing untoward with the mine's records; everything could be accounted for. There *was* no evidence to destroy, not that there would have been any time to destroy anything – these men had burst in so suddenly that he had almost had to pinch himself to make sure that he wasn't dreaming and that his worst nightmare had not suddenly become grim reality. Unfortunately for him, it had.

'Now,' said the Major, leaning across the desk, ominously, 'we've spent enough time on the niceties. We need to press on to the really serious part of our discussion.'

He paused to let the tone of his voice, which had become very threatening and much softer, sink into Grunewald's hopelessly perspiring head. 'Who was the tall visitor you had this morning?'

The manager had to work hard to hide his surprise at the question. How did this man know that?

'Tall, rather aristocratic, dressed in black...' Ashdown paused to let the extent of his knowledge unsettle the mine manager. 'Tall, like a marabou stork. Carrying a large walking stick and yet striding in a very forceful manner, as if he had no need of it.' He paused and smirked. 'Odd that, wouldn't you say? Walking off like a person who really had no need of a stick at all – so I'm told...' There was another pause. Grunewald's breathing was noticeably shallower than before and he had started to wheeze much louder. 'So, Mr Grunewald, what have you done with the stones? I assume that you gave them to your visitor? Maintaining your old ties of loyalty, foolishly ignoring where your new ones should lie?'

The light had started to fade, but the atmosphere in the

hot office had become highly charged and dangerous. Major Ashdown flicked his eyes, as quickly as a lizard, at one of the burly troopers who had occupied the office with him. Despite his formidable physique and stature, the trooper moved across the office with an eland's grace and speed. Before he knew what was happening, the mine manager was held in a muscle-numbing grip, his arms twisted around and up behind him, almost wrenched out of their sockets. At the same time, the other trooper moved to Grunewald's side, slipping a fine silk bag over the struggling man's head and tying it around his undulating jowls. In his panic, Grunewald's large cavern of a mouth gulped in the loose folds of the fabric, as he struggled for air, trying to relieve the agonizing pain in his shoulders and the burning in his heaving lungs.

'It really is quite hot and stuffy in here, isn't it?' said Ashdown, more by way of statement than question. 'Finding it hard to breathe? Tell you what, I'll let him take the bag off if you tell me who you gave the stones to … and exactly where they're going. How's that? Let it not be said that we British are not fair in our dealings.'

He watched for some sign of acquiescence, but the hapless mine manager was moving about so much that detection of any form of answering agreement was out of the question.

'What was that? Do you want a drink? Well let it not be said we are not even-handed in our treatment of suspects,' and with that he flicked a finger towards the large carafe of water which stood, incongruously, on a doily-covered table at one end of the mine manager's desk. As the water soaked into the thirsty silk cloth, a few precious drops at a time, Grunewald's struggles became ever more frantic, as the air was blocked by the saturated fabric. As he struggled to free himself, the pain in his shoulders grew worse. To his discomfort was added a knee, thrust through the flimsy cane back panel of his chair and into the small of his back.

This extra leverage gave added agony to his aching arms and shoulders. The creation of this desperate situation had not taken more than a couple of seconds; the troopers were well-drilled in the method. They had had recourse to use it on previous occasions – not that the Major's superiors in Pretoria would have sanctioned or even condoned such a procedure for a single second, had they any idea of it. It just was not cricket. But, then again, it was end results that counted and Ashdown had a very impressive string of those to his credit.

The Major motioned to the trooper and the bag was suddenly removed. Grunewald thought his lungs would burst as he gulped in the hot, welcome air.

'So, *Mister* Grunewald – you don't mind if I call you by your real name? You are *German*, after all is said and done. It's a bit silly calling yourself Greenwood, wouldn't you agree?' The Major laughed, but it was a humourless gesture. 'So, Mr Grunewald, now you must tell me to whom and to where...'

The office was filled with the rasping sound of the manager's erratic, shallow breathing.

'I know not ... nothing of what you ask. I am only the manager of th...'

In a flash the bag was once again over his head and the water was splashing into the already soaked fibres of the cloth. The knee seemed to have buried itself even deeper into his back.

'You really are being hard on yourself,' continued Ashdown, 'which is both unnecessary and very foolish...'

Ashdown straightened up and, turning his back on the scene of the struggle, he walked back across the office to the window. Outside, in the mine's central compound, the lines of black miners had been fruitlessly body-searched and sent back to their accommodation, out of the way. As he peered into the fading light, he saw Sergeant Vos standing at the far end of the compound, beyond the railway trucks. Ashdown opened the window and let out a short, piercing whistle. Alerted by the noise, the Sergeant stepped forward and waved his arms over his head.

Of course there was nothing to find out there, Ashdown thought. *The key to it all is in here somewhere, probably locked in this fool's head.*

He closed the window and turned back to Grunewald.

'It is getting late and you are causing me to lose my patience.' The Major's voice was calm, friendly and full of restrained menace. 'We have other methods – none that leave any sort of marks, you understand – that would never do. We can be far more subtle than that, Mr Grunewald, but I'm sure you would not like us to demonstrate just *how* subtle, would you?'

Again, there was a slight flick of the eyes and the silk bag was removed from the desperately moving mouth.

'I ... you can...' The rest of the conversation was unintelligible, interspersed as it was with the wheezing and the desperate, retching heaving of the tortured lungs.

'Der ... Gr ... af ... wir ... d... ge ... win ...'

'What was that?' asked Ashdown, unable to make out what the manager was trying to say.

'Speak up!' barked the trooper who held the wet silk bag in his hand. 'The Major didn't hear you – what did you say?'

Grunewald stared blankly in front of him, his eyes already glazing over. The Major gave an impatient flick of his hand. For the third time the bag covered the now-frothing mouth cavern, but this time, as the water started, Grunewald's ample body suddenly arched itself into a series of spasmodic tremors, which rapidly became more and more violent – almost as violent as the creaking of his protesting chair.

'Shall I take the sack off, Sir?' asked the trooper.

'Possibly,' replied Ashdown, leaning across the desk and

staring intently at the writhing figure, 'he could be putting it on. Still, we wouldn't want any suspicion of foul play.'

Even with the bag removed and the pressure on Grunewald's arms and back relaxed, the spasms continued. His eyes were rolling up in their sockets and he was foaming at the mouth.

'Christ,' said the trooper who had been pinning his arms, 'I have a cousin who does this – epitelsy or something they call it.'

'It's called e-p-i-l-e-p-s-y, but I think this could be something to do with his heart,' said Ashdown. 'Blast it!'

Although his voice did not betray it, for the first time since his arrival the Major was now concerned – things were not going the way he'd have liked them to go.

'Grunewald!! What did you say?'

Moving nearer to the manager's bubbling mouth, which had started to spew vomit, Ashdown repeatedly barked his question.

'Grunewald, what di...'

As suddenly as they'd started, the tremors subsided and the mine manager was still. The chair also suddenly ceased its creaking protests. As the last air rattled through the vomit and foam in his mouth, Grunewald's grotesquely distended features subsided into the suggestion of a smile.

'D...e...r...Gr...aaaa...f...ein...ein...'

The lips sagged and twitched, but there was no further sound.

'Bastard!' spat the Major, as he swung his hand up and struck the mine manager across the face. The lifeless muscles offered no resistance and the head lolled to one side under the force of the impact. The two troopers looked on dispassionately.

'Sounded like "griffin" or something such, Sir,' muttered the trooper who had pinioned the manager's arms.

'Griffin?' repeated Ashdown. 'Griffin?'

For a second, the office was still – even the ancient fan seemed to be continuing its rattling, noisy rotation in unreal silence. Despite its best efforts, it could not blow away the cloying stench of vomit, sweat and death.

'Bugger it!' said Ashdown, as he crossed to the window, in search of fresh air.

Outside, the shadows continued to lengthen.

'Right,' said Ashdown, 'the usual – get the lads in and take it all apart.' He paused for a moment, taking another cigarette out of his case, 'and if you don't find anything, when you've finished put it all back together again the way you found it.'

What has a griffin got to do with all of this? reflected the Major as he strode out of the office and onto the veranda, cigarette clamped firmly in his mouth. He was far from pleased. *I wouldn't have thought someone like Grunewald would even know what a Griffin is. Is the heat getting to me, or are they flying the diamonds out using a half-lion half-eagle mythical bird?* He looked up at the bleached, blue cloudless sky. *Don't be so stupid! Just focus on what has to be done next,* he thought, as he angrily flung the cigarette onto the dirt and marched purposefully down the steps.

What neither Ashdown nor his men in the mine manager's office had understood was that Grunewald's last gasping mumble had been "*Der Graf wird gewinnen*": The Graf will win.

2

Two Months Earlier

Whitehall, London – 20th April 1928

'You've been out there and you know the country ... and the people.'

'With respect, surely you cannot be serious, Uncle? I might have been out there for some time, but I know absolutely nothing about Military Intelligence...'

'Perhaps not, my boy, but you are intelligent and have common sense, and that's what we are looking for.'

It was an evening in early spring, but it was unseasonably cold. The memory of the recent winter still lingered. Beyond the comforting warmth of the large office, the streets of London were enfolded in an obliterating blanket of thick, damp, fog. In the distance, the striking of Big Ben was barely audible beyond the precincts of Parliament Square: it was shortly after eight o'clock. Feeble lights heralded the imminent approach of vehicles, as they picked their way slowly along the congested, shrouded roads. The streetlights, many still gas-fired, spluttered valiantly against the cloying atmosphere, managing only to cast feeble pools of watery light onto the pavements.

Inside the wood-panelled office, a much brighter pool of light was being thrown onto the leather top of a large desk. Apart from this warm circle, the rest of the room was lost in dark shadows.

'As I say, my boy, you know the place quite well and I dare say that you've used your time out there to make some contacts that may prove useful to us,' the Uncle continued, 'so I want you to keep an eye and ear open for me. That's all.'

'But open for what, Sir...?'

'Anything and everything you think might be a bit odd and out of the ordinary ... that sort of thing.'

'I'm sorry, Uncle, but this becomes more and more confusing by the second. Can you at least give me an idea of what you might consider to be "a bit odd"?'

'Anything and everything that does not look quite like cricket, Stephen.'

His uncle only used his nephew's name when he wished to emphasize the finality of a point of discussion, as now. For his part, although he knew perfectly well what the man's names were, Stephen had only ever addressed his relative by the term 'Uncle'. Considering the power his relative wielded, it would not have been unreasonable to consider him as the Uncle of the Nation, not that Stephen would ever do so. The thickset, elder man leaned forward in his chair, still keeping himself largely out of the pool of light cast by the desk lamp.

'This situation in the Middle East is potentially volatile at the moment – politically unstable and a breeding ground for Arab nationalism. Added to that, there is this vexing question of diamonds,' he said in a hushed voice, somewhat dramatically, 'from old German South-West Africa.'

'Diamonds?' repeated the younger man, surprised.

'Yes, diamonds. We think they are being smuggled up through Africa. Our chaps out there are on to it, of course, but an extra pair of eyes and ears never goes amiss, even if they do not belong to Military Intelligence,' – a smug smile crossed his mouth as he spoke – 'and besides, there have been many instances where we have benefited directly from information received from sources other than the official ones. All I want you to do is to carry on as normal and just look and listen. Don't go looking for trouble – just cast your eyes around as you go. You know the sort of thing...'

Stephen was not at all sure that he did.

'We'll make all the necessary arrangements to back you up,' the Uncle went on, 'should the need arise. And if it should not, then at least you have the satisfaction of knowing that you will have done your bit for your country – for the second time.' He leaned back in his chair, one hand unconsciously fidgeting with his black bow tie. 'If you come up with anything,' he continued, 'just let the Embassy know – tell them the message is for Cecil – they'll know what to do and they'll be able to give you any instructions, should that prove necessary.'

The nephew stared at the dim shadow of his uncle, through the pool of light.

'Well, Sir ... I'm a bit lost for words ... but, of course, if you want me to, I'll do the best I can...'

'Of course you will, my boy. I knew we could rely on you. Another brandy?'

A short while later Stephen realized that this visit to his uncle had drawn to a close. After their pleasant interlude the elder, thick-set man had to return to the business of Empire, a fact that was confirmed when, following a discreet knock on the door, his uncle's private secretary entered the room. The hours this man kept, as a result of the position he occupied, were in no way dictated by the hands of the clock. It was already late, but the Machinery of Empire was a hard taskmaster and paid little heed to the passing of time or to the needs of the private lives of the individuals who were charged with its maintenance.

'Ah, Collingwood, show my nephew out, would you?'

As Stephen disappeared into the darkened outer office,

the private secretary silently closed the heavy teak door behind him.

'Good boy, that,' said the Uncle, as the secretary returned to the shadowy glow that surrounded the large desk.

Collingwood did not feel it his place to comment.

'The latest communication from Pretoria, Sir,' he said quietly, placing a buff folder on the desk in the pool of light in front of the Uncle. It was tied up with red ribbon and stamped *'Top Secret'* in large red letters that had smudged. 'I thought it best to bring it to your attention immediately it was convenient, rather than to wait for the morning.'

The elder man, who had stood up as he watched his nephew leave, sat down again. He opened the folder and read the contents.

'Good ... very good. It is possible that they could be making modest advances ... at last...' he said.

Meanwhile in Nuremberg, Germany

There was a soft, but confident knock at the door. The short man turned slowly away from the large window as he heard it. He was tired – again.

'Hermann,' he said softly, as a well-built, dapperly dressed man entered the room. He did not smile and his voice bore no tone of welcome.

'We have good news,' said the visitor, as he closed the door, 'our sources report very favourably on progress following your speech last night.'

'Do they?' replied the other, distantly, 'and what of the People? What of *them?*'

'They begin to realize the wisdom of our...' Hermann paused and, with a slight nod of the head, corrected himself, '... *your* ideas for the future.'

The shorter man clasped his hands behind his back, but said nothing. The veins were showing in his temples.

'They continue to buy your book – that is another indication of our growing success. And with the increased sales comes the spread of your vision. The people need the example of your firm leadership – the fools in the Reichstag cannot deliver what their parties promise – but *you* can deliver what *you* promise in your vision of the future.'

'Hmm...' replied the man at the window. When he was tired he found Hermann's fawning particularly irksome. 'And where are we with the authorities?' he asked, turning his head to once again look out of the window at the square below.

'More and more of them are joining us – secretly, naturally. When the time is ripe we will enjoy an easy victory, of that I am certain.'

Hermann spoke with conviction, his eyes blazing intensely like two small embers.

'Yes ... good news...' muttered the man at the window, as he folded his arms across his chest. He repeatedly smoothed down the edges of his little black moustache – a sure sign that he was tired and fidgety. The continual effort of his politicking and the endless preparation for that necessary speechmaking at the rallies had started to drain his energy. Neither did he sleep well, as his mind continued to compute and plan long after the rally and its carefully rehearsed oratory had finished.

'As I said ... it continues to go well...' continued the visitor, pausing.

To the man at the window, the pause seemed a little uncomfortable and it caused him to stop smoothing his moustache.

'Except for one small thing...' continued Hermann, in a way that presaged bad news, '...a message from The Phoenix...'

The shorter man turned abruptly to face his visitor full on.

'What about The Phoenix?' he snapped, suddenly energized.

'He reports that collection of the stones is proceeding as planned, but that the net is being drawn tighter all the time. He thinks that the British suspect our operation and that the route could well be cut at any time. He says that he is not yet ready to depart with the shipment, but fears that time will run out before he can leave with *all* the merchandise assembled. He asks: should he leave as soon as possible with what has been collected, or should he wait until the full shipment is ready?' There was a pause. '... And run the risk of discovery and capture?'

The shorter man turned his head away and stared out of the window. He felt the weary emptiness begin to enfold him once again; it was a feeling he was finding harder and harder to keep at bay these days.

'We cannot stop now,' he said softly, as he sank deeper and deeper into his thoughts, 'we are not yet ready ... we cannot stop now...'

The room was filled with the electricity of expectancy, but neither man spoke for what seemed like minutes. At the window, the shorter man was thinking – weighing up the options. From experience, Hermann had learned not to be so foolish as to attempt to pre-empt the other's thoughts. He stood and waited in respectful silence, his own considerable ego held in check.

'Tell The Phoenix to bring the full shipment ... now', said the man at the window, softly, his voice rimmed with steely determination. The veins in his temples were now standing out markedly, pale blue lines against the oatmeal pastiness of his skin. By contrast, his eyes burned with an intense energy, which would vanquish the weary emptiness, as it attempted to smother him.

'As you wish, I will instruct him to do so as soon as practically possible,' replied Hermann. There is al–'

'No!' exploded the shorter man. 'I said tell him to bring them *now*! All of them...' He displayed the temper and energy he usually reserved for the more animated moments of his rally speeches. '*Now*,' he repeated with a voice only marginally less violent than before. 'Tomorrow may already be too late. What he brings us is vital to the funding of our work. We cannot afford to lose them...'

Hermann did not relish discussing such issues with his Leader when he displayed such irrationality and contradiction. Had he even heard what Hermann had told him? And if he did, had he actually understood it? Such behaviour was infrequent, but it did happen. He had experienced it before but, in the interests of self-preservation, had never dared mention it to anyone. He had no way of knowing that others had witnessed this behaviour, too.

As the other man spoke, he moved away from the window and took two steps into the room. His voice trailed off and he once more subsided into his calmer self.

'We need the full shipment, Hermann,' he said quietly, 'even if the net is closing. Tell him to bring the full shipment and tell him to leave immediately...'

Hermann gratefully left the room. He would tell Phoenix to bring what he had and to bring it now, even if the full shipment was not yet ready. Despite his Leader's last, confused instruction, Hermann decided that it was best to set The Phoenix on his way with the diamonds, just in case the net did close on him. The Leader did not take kindly to having his instructions questioned. Any future outburst on his part over misinterpreted instructions would have to be dealt with in due course.

As Hermann gently closed the door behind him, the shorter man, alone in the opulence of the large room, crossed once again to the window and stared at the square below. He clasped his hands behind his back and let out a sustained sigh. He was alone with his thoughts; thoughts which, he had begun to realize, were becoming heavier and heavier. The realization of the burden of the responsibility he had taken upon himself, to lead his people to a glorious new future, was a heavy load to bear. It was a load which he knew he could not share with anyone. The veins in his temples were less obvious now, but his head had started to throb. The energy which, a few minutes before, had filled his being with invigorated power had started to drain away again. He would have to take some of his pills.

He was suddenly tired again.

3

The Nile, Cairo

Early morning – 15th July 1928

The little white paddle steamer lay snugly attached to the quayside. From the top deck, under the large canvas awning, Rupert Winfield gazed lazily over the railings. On the quayside below him, the tourist machine had long since started its frenetic, daily activity.

A little over half an hour before, a small band of tourists had exchanged the quiet, colonial luxury of Shepheard's Hotel for the rowdy noise of Cairo, as a small fleet of cars had carried them through the teeming streets and upriver towards the waiting steamer. Their arrival at the quayside proved difficult as the cars were blocked by a mingling crush of humanity, all desperate to sell their wares. Despite the best efforts of several burly policemen and the company representative, himself an Egyptian, it took some time before the cars were able to deposit their passengers near the steamer.

High above this sea of activity, from the safety of *Khufu*'s top deck, Winfield watched the new arrivals. They appeared ant-like, as they struggled through the throng, until they finally managed to clamber up the gangway and disappear beneath him into the welcoming cool of the steamer's main foyer. On the quay, their place had been taken by a team of porters, who struggled with the mountain of luggage.

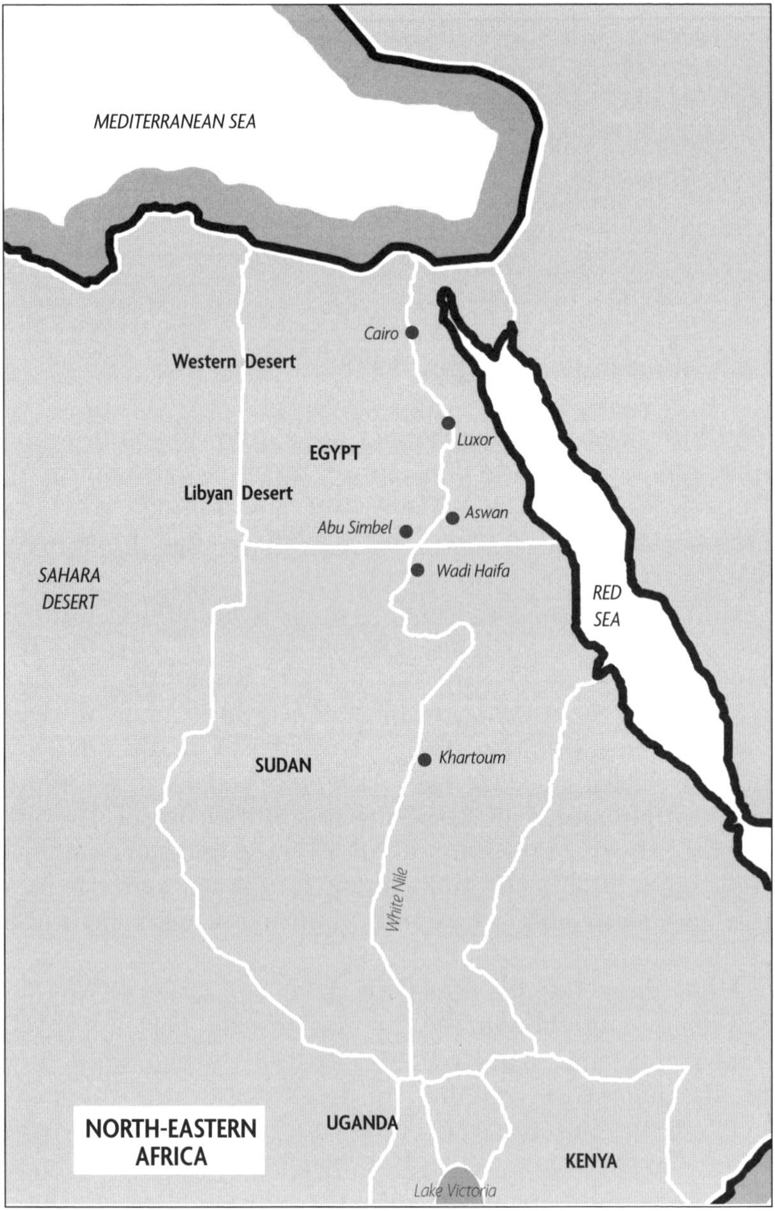
MEDITERRANEAN SEA
Cairo
Western Desert
Luxor
EGYPT
Libyan Desert
Aswan
Abu Simbel
Wadi Haifa
SAHARA
DESERT
RED
SEA
SUDAN
Khartoum
White Nile
NORTH-EASTERN
AFRICA
UGANDA
KENYA
Lake Victoria

The hawkers had no interest in selling their antiquities, most of which were of dubious origin, to these humble porters and so they moved off *en masse*. Accompanied at a discreet distance by the policemen, who seemed to be waiting for their share of any prospective sales, they had reassembled downriver, next to the only other steamer moored alongside the jetty that day.

Here we go again, thought Winfield to himself, as he flicked the used match expertly down into the water between the steamer and the quay. *And it looks as if there aren't many under sixty years old!*

The cloud of cigarette smoke he exhaled hid his smile. They might be a bit past it, these 'Explorers eager to discover the glories of ancient Egypt', as it said in the promotional brochure, but they had healthy wallets and the tips were usually well worth the effort of his being charming. He had become well practised in the subtle art of interested indifference. Strong white teeth, a broad smile and disarming dimples were a combination that usually won over even the most disengaged tourist without too much effort on his part. Even now, during the heat of summer – the wrong time to be travelling in Egypt – his charm offensive would still be reasonably well rewarded, even if his new flock had taken advantage of the reduced rates offered by the company for their out-of-season holiday. As it was, he would earn far more in a year out here in Egypt than he could ever have hoped to earn back in England teaching in a stuffy university. As an eager, newly graduated archaeologist with a passion for all things ancient Egyptian, he had given that a go – and had soon regretted the predictable boredom of it all. On balance, he much preferred what he now did for a living.

Only trouble with this line of work is the bloody heat, he mused to himself, from the shade underneath the upper deck awning, *particularly at this time of the year.*

On the banks of the Nile, just up river from Cairo, it was barely 10 a.m. and already the heat was becoming unpleasant. In the three years he'd been shepherding his flocks up and down the Nile, Rupert Winfield had still not been able to get used to the sapping heat. It wasn't so bad once the steamer got moving on the river, but, without the benefit of the soothing river breeze that the motion of the ship usually created, visiting the temples and other sites of interest could become quite unpleasant. And then there was the matter of the Valley of the Kings. Carter's recent discovery of the tomb of the Boy King, Tutankhamun, had added a new excursion to the 'Nile Exploration Tour' offered by the company. There was actually nothing to see at Carter's excavation, save for a large hole in the ground, the occasional archaeologist, scurrying Egyptians in their flowing galabeas, armed guards everywhere and piles and piles of sand and rubble. And yet, some people wanted to make the visit, enchanted by the romantic mystery of the Boy King and hopeful of catching a glimpse of ... of what? There *was* nothing to see. Unless he managed to get his flock in and out by eleven in the morning at the latest, they would be prisoners of the extreme heat there – temperatures in excess of 120 degrees Fahrenheit on a bad day. Given the physical condition of some of his charges, getting them into the Valley at all was something of a miracle in itself.

As the noise from the quayside below him filled his ears, he was suddenly reminded of the time in the Valley when several of Carter's men were actually in the process of removing something from the tomb. On that single occasion, he had felt like abandoning his charges to the heat and pushing forward for a closer look, but the armed guards had quickly put that thought out of mind. He never discovered what the object was. Despite that, he knew that his real interest lay in the dry, preserving sand of Egypt, where these marvellous things had been discovered. He thought enviously of Carter. Then he thought of himself – what was *he* doing acting as a cultural shepherd to a flock of over-pampered, wealthy tourists, who were generally not *that* interested in what he had to share with them? Where, he thought, was the archaeology in it all – where was the fuel for his own all-consuming passion?

He took in a lungful of the strong Turkish tobacco and smiled again. The heat of the Valley was several hundred miles upriver; at least here, near Cairo, it was a little cooler. The thought of some desk in a dingy office in a bleak outpost of archaic academia, lecturing to a class of students who either thought that they knew it all or were only there because their parents had thought it a good idea, made him shudder inwardly.

'Sorry, Mother,' he said softly to himself, his voice lost in the hubbub, 'I really couldn't have stuck something like that. I know you wanted me to become a professor, but I'd have died of boredom long before that happened...'

For a moment, he retreated into that part of his being which was strictly private, where he sheltered the thoughts that only he knew and where nobody else, not even his mother, was ever invited. Here he kept his special feelings and memories. Deep down, he knew that he had made the right decision: even if he was thousands of miles from home and had no one to share his experiences with, on balance he preferred the present to the past, but that didn't stop his mind from occasionally returning to his earlier life.

He had a couple of draws left on his cigarette. Most of the luggage had been manhandled up the gangplank and had disappeared below decks, to be delivered to the respective owners' cabins. Some of the crew were already making ready to swing the wooden gangway up away from the quay and to secure it against the steamer's gleaming white side. A short while before, the narrow quay, which was now almost deserted, had been crowded. Now, the unaccustomed silence was broken by just two traders, who were earnestly trying to convince somebody down on the lower promenade deck to buy their overpriced 'artefacts'.

Standing on the top deck, Rupert's mind once again returned to the day of his graduation. He heard his mother tell him how proud she was of him, as well she might have been, for he had passed out of his years of study *cum laude* with the prospect of a brilliant career at the university before him.

That happy day of achievement had been marred by the absence of his father, who had not come back from the war. Captain Stephen Winfield, Territorial Army, had set off with his men for France. He was too old, but had insisted on doing his bit. Towards the end of the conflict, a faltering war machine needed everyone it could get, so age had ultimately proved a negligible obstacle. All that was left of his life were a couple of faded photographs, the letter from Haig and the Military Cross. Of these, the photographs were by far their most treasured memory.

'Your father would have been so proud of you, Rupert,' his mother had beamed from under her carefully arranged coiffure and stylish, broad-brimmed hat.

'Yes ... Father *would* have been very proud, even if he *was* wrong about trying to get me to join the family firm!' he had replied.

Mrs Winfield had winced at that – she had always regretted her husband not being more insistent on the subject. Their son was, after all – and not for want of trying – their only child. The fortunes of the family's successful business would henceforth lie firmly upon her brother-in-law's shoulders and not those of her son.

'Well, never-to-do, dear', she had continued in that almost patronizing way which sometimes got on his nerves, 'but at least you can now excel at the university and become a professor.'

She had sounded more hopeful than totally convinced, but he had made no comment. For his part, he had wanted to get out into the field and get his hands dirty. He had excelled at the book learning – now he wanted to get going with the hands-on part.

The entrance to his private place was suddenly and automatically slammed shut, as his senses became aware of someone beside him.

'They are all present and corrected, Mr Rupert, Sir. I have checked most scrupulously through our list and they are all being here – all except one, who is being absent – a lady, Mrs Printon,' said the man, indicating his passenger manifest with a flourish. Rupert smiled. Mohammed was the company representative and the steamer's manager. He was always very eager to please and was generally far too enthusiastic, which often pushed him to verbosity.

'I have now straight away sent a message to be telegraphed to Head Office with the news that we are all being presenting and corrected – except for the esteemed Mrs Printon – and that we will shortly be casting ourselves off and into the river – *insha'Allah.*'

Rupert smiled at the flow of information, so genuinely meant, but so torturously expressed: everything in excessive, unnecessary detail and always 'At the will of God'. His own Arabic was embryonic – a word here and a sentence there – but he marvelled at the command of English which people like Mohammed possessed. Rupert had never had an ear for languages. He remembered his father lecturing him on the need for greater effort when he had started school at Blatchington College; he had scored quite badly in his first English examination. That had alarmed his parents.

'More application needed. Academic ability evident, but perhaps not in English', the report had read. 'Definitely more effort required.'

He had shown them, though – by the time he had reached

university he excelled in the language – just the one. He had also managed a rudimentary grasp of Greek and Latin, but that was it. Foreign languages had proved to be something of a closed book to him.

'So there you are having it all. Most satisfactory and Bristol fashion,' continued Mohammed, as he adjusted his fez to a more rakish angle, 'we are being most truly prepared.'

'Indeed, Mohammed,' replied Rupert. 'Well done. So here we go again, eh? Off into the wild blue yonder!'

Mohammed stared at him, somewhat blankly, his confusion suspended on his face.

'Up the river, I mean,' added Rupert. 'It is a saying we have. It means to set off again.'

'Ah yes, indubitably, up the river,' answered the Egyptian, his face breaking into his broad smile. 'I must now make sure that our guests are all having their correct cabins and are happily comforting themselves.'

Rupert watched the receding figure stride off towards the companionway and then quickly disappear down it into the cool depths of the little ship.

Nice chap, he thought. *A decent type.*

As he flicked the stub of his cigarette into the water he felt the dull thud of the gangway swinging home against the iron side of the steamer. From above his head came the throaty wheeze of the whistle – three long blasts. Far below his feet, he felt the release of power, which had been confined in the steamer's boilers – horsepower that would soon churn the Nile into white, bubbling froth as *Khufu*'s paddle wheel clawed its way up the Nile, pushing the little vessel against the current, on its way towards Luxor.

A sudden burst of activity down on the quayside caught his attention. Now that the threat of the burly policemen had passed, a gaggle of waving, shouting urchins had suddenly appeared, as if by magic. Despite the smiles, these street children conveyed the more serious message of the poverty that was the reality for the mass of the Egyptian population. Rupert had seen these twin faces of Egypt almost as soon as he had arrived in Cairo to take up his post with the company. He had seen the doorman at Head Office chase away another group of urchins, who had descended on his motor vehicle the moment it had stopped outside the company's imposing offices. He had been genuinely taken aback by the experience and, when his new superior had offered him the chance, he had passed an appropriate comment about his feelings. From behind the comfort of his large, mahogany desk, his superior had simply dismissed the incident.

'That's life out here, old chap', he had said indifferently. 'You'll get used to it quick enough. It's a bit like one of those old gods they had – the one with two faces – have and have not. You'll know the one I mean better than I, being the expert,' he'd explained and then laughed. 'Don't take it to heart – it's the way out here. You just need to accept it, that's all.'

Rupert had winced inwardly at the man's indifference and ignorance, but made no comment.

It was a Roman *god called Janus, you ignoramus...*, he had thought, ... *not an Egyptian one.*

Back on the quayside below him, far away from Head Office in Cairo, this same contradiction was once again being played out – the *haves*, in the comfort of the steel-hulled Nile pleasure steamer and the *have nots*, on the shore in their grubby galabeas.

Rupert became aware of a conversation from immediately below him, which rose in opposition to the noises of their departure. Some of the newly embarked tourists had gathered on the lower promenade deck – no doubt in response to Mohammed's exhortations to 'View the magnificent River Nile as we depart upon our watery voyages' – and had become the targets of the smiling group of urchins, all with outstretched arms and grimy hands.

A few coins glinted in the morning sunlight and there was muffled laughter from the lower deck in response to the scrambling and fighting on the quay that resulted from the display of largesse.

A steadily widening gap had begun to open up between the shimmering side of the tall steamer and the compacted earth of the quay. Deckhands were scurrying across the deck, letting go mooring cables. On the bridge – perched in a wheelhouse set just back from the bows – the engine room telegraph rang steadily, confirming the orders from the *reis*, or captain – 'slow ahead … medium ahead.' The paddle wheel had started its endless rotation and the grey-blue of the Nile erupted into a mêlée of bubbles. With practised ease, the last rope was cast ashore, three more wheezing blasts escaped from the steamer's whistle, a large cloud of puffy, black smoke suddenly belched from the single funnel and *Khufu* pointed her beak-like bow into the river and moved slowly forward.

'Here we go again.' said Rupert Winfield quietly to himself, as he straightened up and turned to descend the companionway.

4

The Nile, Cairo

Afternoon – 15th July 1928

'Well, I'm not at all sure if that *is* all right...' whined the large, ruddy-faced woman in the dowdy dress and over-large sunhat, '...you expect everything to be just so and – well, it just isn't. Mr Grassmere will have something to say about this... won't you, dear?'

She stabbed a podgy finger at the shoulder of the diminutive figure sitting to her right. Mr Grassmere, an elderly man with thick lenses, stared back at her with mouth half-open, as if to speak. He had been subjected to over thirty years of his wife's belligerently aggressive attitude and the experience had taught him to think twice before acting. He closed his mouth, removed his heavy spectacles from his lean nose and grimaced.

'Yes, dear...' he mumbled for the millionth time, rubbing the bridge of his nose in suppressed resignation, '...anything you say, dear.'

Following their noisy arrival on board *Khufu*, the tourists had been shown to their cabins. After having been served a light lunch they had been allowed to recuperate from the exertions of the morning. Now, as the day began to prepare itself for dusk, they had been assembled in the forward observation lounge for the formal greeting.

From the back of the room Rupert surveyed this latest

group of travellers into his treasured, sacred world of ancient Egypt. If truth be told, he felt a little resentment at them trespassing into what he regarded as his territory. He felt very possessive about the culture that had once ruled most of the then-known world. Tourists! What did *they* understand? What interest did *they* have in any of this glorious record of a civilization now vanished? He couldn't remember the last time one of them had shown any real interest in the ruins and monuments. He tried hard to do so, but just couldn't. By the end of the trip it was usually all most of them could do to remember one of the ancient gods' names or even the names of some of the places they'd visited. He strolled over to a nearby table, stubbed out the smouldering end of his cigarette in an ashtray, and, with a final glance around the room, took a seat at the rear of the assembly. He let out a barely audible sigh. Yet another invasion of his Egypt had very definitely begun.

For her part, Mrs Grassmere was not about to give up the attention she fancied she had secured for herself. She seemed to have some sort of issue with the lunch she had been served, or was this just the preamble to something else? They hadn't been on the river more than a few hours and there were those amongst Rupert's flock who had already been marked out as potential troublemakers. It was always the same. He could never fathom quite why they were so bent on unfurling their colours and nailing them to the mast almost before the mooring ropes had even dried out from their dunking in the river. Both he and Mohammed had met the Mrs Grassmere type before; both disliked them intensely from behind a mask of necessary, polite civility.

'Why are we sitting here, waiting?' asked a gentleman in a light cotton suit. 'Surely we should be up on deck watching the passing parade, or the parade as we pass *it*, if you will.'

He laughed at his own witticism. Nobody else did.

A military type, who thinks he's still on a charger giving orders at Omdurman, thought Rupert, as he glanced at the way the man held himself upright in his chair. The man's upright military bearing reminded him of his father, who had always carried himself smartly, as if he had been a general on parade. Rupert remembered his father as a kind and polite man; it seemed to him that Colonel Ponsworthy, retired, had the potential to be quite the opposite.

The observation lounge was lined on both of its longer sides with large picture windows. Through one of these, Rupert caught a glimpse of Mohammed walking briskly along the promenade deck towards the stern. He seemed to be in his usual purposeful hurry. Inside, the room was filled with the subdued, yet animated chatter of those with little to do and a great deal of time in which to do it. Mrs Grassmere was still picking on Mr Grassmere, while the Colonel was attempting to engage the man to his left in conversation.

'Wasn't like this in my younger days, y' know', he said, in his pompous manner, 'we were a lot more organized – that's the secret, y' know – organization.'

He snorted his approval at his own utterance. To his left sat Mr Rotherham, widower and owner of Rotherham's Patented Relish, who nodded in agreement.

'I couldn't agree with you more. You don't get the jars packed and despatched without it,' he replied, laughing quietly as he did so, which seemed to temporarily stop Colonel Ponsworthy in mid-charge.

'Er ... yes, exactly,' mumbled the military man, knocked a little off his stride.

'We didn't get the company to where it is without it ... organization, I mean.'

'Really ... er, company, y' say ... what company would that be then?' asked Ponsworthy, looking around imperiously at the rest of the assembled tourists in a way that suggested he neither had any real interest in his question, nor expected any answer to it.

'Rotherham's Patented Relish,' replied the widower. 'We've just started exporting to Australia – South Africa will be next. Believe me, I know exactly the value of organization...' He paused and then suddenly changed the topic of conversation completely. '...You know, when my Edith was alive we always said that we'd do the Nile Trip one day...'

Colonel Ponsworthy, his face fixed into an expression appropriate to the receipt of news of some dreadful defeat, turned his gaze back to Rotherham. He was unnerved by not being in control of his conversations, and he felt that he had just lost control of this one to this funny little man and his jars of relish. He clamped his jaws firmly shut, whilst Rotherham continued to tell him of his late wife, Edith.

For the rest, the steady hum of chatter continued to fill the room.

'Stephen Hopkins,' said a well-dressed young man to the bearded man sitting next to him, as he extended his hand, 'don't try to remember – we all tend to forget a name almost as soon as we hear it,' he continued, chuckling.

The bearded man laughed apologetically.

'Yes, that is very true,' he said, shaking the proffered hand in greeting.

'Is this your first time?' asked Hopkins, with a twinkle in his eye at his use of the old cliché.

'Eric Kormann,' smiled back the bearded man, who looked a few years younger. 'Yes, I have a passing interest in ancient Egypt,' he continued in a clipped accent, which was definitely not home-grown English. For an inch or so along his right jaw ran a small scar, caused by a childhood skiing accident, but now barely visible behind the beard.

'German?' asked Stephen, smiling.

'Swiss,' came the reply, 'I come from Switzerland,' he said self-effacingly.

Hopkins tried to engage Kormann in deeper conversation, but soon formed the opinion that the Swiss was of the timid type and afraid of his own shadow.

Behind them sat an elderly couple, with whom Rupert had attempted to start a conversation earlier in the afternoon, when they had been standing on the top deck. His efforts had been rewarded with non-committal, monosyllabic answers, and he had made a mental note not to bother with the Manningtons again. Now they sat impassively, staring ahead of them like a pair of ancient funerary statues – devoid of conversation and, it seemed, possibly even of life itself.

He must have put the fear of God into his customers at the Shire and Counties Bank, thought Rupert, as he stared idly at the backs of their heads from the rear of the room.

Before his recent retirement, Mr Julian Mannington had been the manager of the Central London branch of that august institution. Apart from this one fact, Rupert had been unable to prise anything else out of him. Mrs Mannington had said absolutely nothing during the failed attempt at conversation and had just looked on, a pained smile affixed aimlessly to her mouth.

Mohammed, who had been busy attending to matters in the steamer's kitchen, suddenly appeared in the observation lounge doorway. He strolled into the cool shade of the room, relieved to have escaped from the afternoon heat outside.

'Greetings, most honoured guests! Welcome aboard the most excellent steamship *Khufu* to you all and everyone.' There was a shifting of positions, as everyone turned to face him. Conversation stopped and the room became silent, save for the sound of scraping chairs.

'Most grateful thank you to everyone for attending our

first meeting of your *River Experience*,' beamed Mohammed, his fez tassel swinging energetically, as he crossed through the chairs to the front of the lounge and took up a position perilously close to Mrs Grassmere. There was a second shifting of chairs, as the tourists altered their positions and turned to face the front of the lounge. 'I, myself, will be informing you of our outstanding expedition and the esteemed Mr Win–'

'Excuse me, Mumed,' said the voice under the sunhat. 'It just won't do, you know – will it, Mr Grassmere?'

There was a momentary pause, as Mohammed first lost the thread of what he was saying and then, with a discreet sideways glance at the source of the interruption, regained it before continuing.

'... And then I will ask the excellent Mr Winfield, himself a graduate of your famous Oxford University, to tell us most interestingly about the sights and sounds we will be visiting, indeed.' Mohammed tried to carry on, politely ignoring the irritation of the fat, wheezy woman as best he could. He had given the same speech many times before and disliked being interrupted in mid-flow, especially by over-large ladies wearing sunhats indoors.

'I said it just isn't good enough, Mumed,' continued Mrs Grassmere, with greater emphasis than before. She raised one of her large, podgy arms in his direction. It was plainly obvious that she was a stranger to the polite niceties of good manners.

'I think you'll find it is *Mohammed*, actually', said the stout, scholarly-looking woman seated behind and to the left of Mrs Grassmere. 'It is the name of the Prophet of Islam, you see – they all seem to be called the same out here – very confusing!' And she gave a horse-like whinny of a laugh, which made her glasses ride up her nose. Whereas Colonel Ponsworthy snorted at his own witticisms, Marjory Cuttle had an unfortunate tendency to whinny at hers.

Unmarried and with not much chance of catching anyone, I shouldn't wonder, thought Rupert, from the back of the room. *Hardly surprising, I suppose ...*

Mrs Grassmere, who had half turned in her seat to look behind her in the direction of the irritating noise, had been deflated – but only for a moment.

'What...?' she mumbled, realizing that her bulk would prohibit her from ever turning around sufficiently to see who owned the voice. She gave up in mid-attempt and turned back towards the front of the room. 'Yes ... well, Mumed. As I was saying, this just will not do at all,' she continued, fixing the little Egyptian with her pig-like eyes. 'Mr Grassmere and I chose your company on the advice of Lady Renton, who spoke very highly of her recent trip. Do you remember her at all? Lord Renton is very big in heavy machinery.'

Mohammed nodded benignly, raised his shoulders slightly and flashed his gold-toothed smile. He had not the foggiest idea what this large, obnoxious woman was talking about.

'Well, I can tell you that Lady Renton would not be impressed ... would she, dear?' continued Mrs Grassmere, ignoring her husband completely. 'The crowds on the quayside were bad enough, but, when we finally reached the gangplank and boarded the boat, what do I find? We are on the wrong side. We can't possibly travel on the right side of the ship going *up* the river...'

'Starboard, dear', muttered Mr Grassmere, *sotto voce.*

His wife ignored him again, if, indeed, she had heard him at all.

'Port out, starboard home. That's the way you must travel when on a sea voyage – anyone can tell you that. We're going "up" or "out", so we must have a cabin on the left side.'

Mr Grassmere, already weary at the very start of his *Nile Experience,* sighed once more, removed the thick lenses from his nose and shrank a further inch or so into his chair.

'It just won't do! And this tea you served me – it's far too weak. And it was more cold than hot! Cold tea won't cool you down – has to be hot, you know – like we used to drink in India.'

Colonel Ponsworthy turned to her and allowed the faintest smile to turn up the corners of his mouth, although the action was largely hidden by the lush, Kitchener-style moustache on his upper lip.

India, eh? he mused to himself, *Now where did she learn that from, I wonder? Wouldn't have thought she'd seen more than a couple of sunny days in her life, judging from the pasty complexion ... She wouldn't have lasted five minutes in the Indian heat.*

'Honoured ladies and gentlemen,' continued Mohammed, desperately trying to regain control of the assembly and return to his prepared script, 'please, with your permissions we will continue...'

Mr Grassmere, who had started to feel the all too familiar feeling of other people's irritation at his wife's behaviour, put a tentative hand on her arm.

'Dear...'

She shifted her bulk and silenced him with one swift glare – a movement perfected over many years of practice and, despite her considerable size, executed with the grace of a ballet dancer.

Mohammed shot Rupert a broad smile, which was really a plea for rescue. Each knew the other's signs and they worked very well together as a team. Between them, they had considerably experience of controlling some of the less pleasant characters they encountered from time to time on board *Khufu*.

'Ladies and gentlemen,' said Rupert, as he stood up and strode leisurely to the front of the lounge, 'may I introduce myself? I am Rupert Winfield and I am your Egyptologist, as Mohammed said.'

He took in the assembly with a sweeping glance and made a point of saying *Mo-ham-med*, very carefully, as he gazed at Mrs Grassmere. She was oblivious to this subtlety.

'May I suggest that we continue with our introductory welcome, as we have rather a lot to get through and we don't want to be late for your first high tea on board?'

Mrs Grassmere made to open her mouth, but Rupert fixed her with a beaming, yet threatening smile and continued speaking.

'Afterwards, I am certain that *Mo-ham-med*' – again he emphasized his colleague's name for her benefit – 'will be only too pleased to attend to your every wish. So, with everyone's permission...' There was a general murmur of assent. Even Mrs Grassmere fell silent.

'Thank you very much,' Rupert continued. 'Firstly, I, too, would like to welcome you aboard the steamship *Khufu*, which will be our floating home for the next few days. *Koo-fu*, also known as *Cheops* – that's *Key-ops*,' Rupert repeated both names carefully, 'was the pharaoh for whom the Great Pyramid at Giza was built, nearly four and a half thousand years ago. Our modest vessel was named in his honour.' He looked around the lounge and pressed on with his introduction before anyone could interrupt him. 'Secondly, I would like to tell you a little about our first stop ... Then there are a few basic points on how to look after yourself in the heat ... Has anybody ever been to Africa or Egypt before?' He looked around the room.

'During the war – Mesopotamia, actually,' said the Colonel, raising his hand and glad to have escaped Rotherham's seemingly endless recollections of married life.

'Kenya' contributed a bohemian-looking woman sourly, a cigarette clamped firmly in her mouth. 'My father had a farm outside Nairobi. I was brought up there.'

That must be Ruth Kirby, thought Rupert. Earlier in the day, he had noticed the name tag on several items of luggage. The suitcases had also carried old Union Castle Steamship Company labels, so Rupert had assumed there to be an African connection.

'Thank you. It's Miss Kirby, isn't it?' he asked.

'Mrs, actually,' she replied offhandedly, removing the cigarette and tipping the ash off the end with a practised movement. Her nails were chewed and her expression set hard. She replaced the cigarette in her mouth and folded her arms across her chest.

'I was born in Malaya,' said a third.

'Good, good,' continued Rupert. 'It's er...' This one had him foxed.

'Sylvia Baxter,' replied the woman with a smile, 'Miss Sylvia Baxter.'

'Thank you,' continued Rupert, 'so some of you are not strangers to this heat. You'll find that the Egyptian sun, whilst offering the ideal geographical conditions for the creation of the marvellous civilization we will be visiting over the next few days, is also a very unforgiving sun. You will need to ensure that you drink plenty of water, which must be boiled – the boys will make sure we have plenty, even when we are away from the ship. Ladies, you should also make sure that you cover your arms and heads as far as possible – sunstroke can spring upon you from nowhere and ruin your expedition. Sadly, it can also kill...'

He paused. There was some throat clearing. From deep within the steamer, the pianissimo background thud of the engines pulsed on reassuringly – like the heartbeat of the river. It was loud enough to be comforting, but not loud enough to be distracting, which was something which could not be said of Mrs Grassmere. Rupert was beginning to positively dislike the woman and that was not really in his character, which was generally tolerant by nature. He continued.

'Our first call will be at Luxor, which we should reach

the day after tomorrow. Going upriver, Luxor will only be a refuelling and provisioning halt. We *will* be visiting the great temple of Karnak, as well as the smaller temple in Luxor proper, but these we will only include on our return trip, when we travel back down the river from Aswan.'

He was surprised to see that the passengers had all focused on him – even Mrs Grassmere seemed to have paused for breath and then subsided into a passive heap. Mr Grassmere looked relieved, but still receded into his chair, having recovered none of his lost stature.

'After we leave Luxor, our first real exploration will be the Temple of Khnum at Esna. This is from the Graeco-Roman period of Egyptian history and has very interesting column capitals. You'll also be very surprised to see that some of them still have their original colours, and the paint is almost as bright today as the day they were painted, over two thousand years ago.'

'Temple of whom?' asked Mr Arling, a middle-aged man with a close-cropped beard.

'*Kh-nu-m*,' repeated Rupert, splitting up the name into syllables, 'the ram-headed god who modelled the destiny of all human beings on his potter's wheel. So that made him the patron of all potters,' he added lightly. *That's the first name forgotten already*, he thought, as he looked around the rest of the party.

'Will we have to walk much?' enquired a middle-aged woman in a lightweight cotton blouse and skirt.

Rupert thought her an interesting contrast to Mrs Grassmere.

'A little,' he replied, smiling, 'Miss Eggerton, isn't it?'

Miss Eggerton blushed in amazed confirmation that someone actually knew who she was. She wasn't to know it, but both Rupert and Mohammed usually tried to learn the passengers' names on arrival, as they were being processed through the reception area on the main deck. It was not a difficult task, given the select number carried on each of the company's tours.

He had also learned from past experience that it did not do to tell them how much 'a little' actually was. He usually found the news of having to endure a donkey ride into the Valley of the Kings quite enough to deter all save those who might be genuinely curious. The thought of the discomfort, a belligerent donkey, the flies and the heat was more than some of his flock could tolerate.

'You'll also have the opportunity to sample a genuine Egyptian souk on the way.'

'That's the market, isn't it?' asked Mr Arling. The young woman next to him smiled in tolerant sympathy at the question. Mrs Esther Arling had little interest in Egyptology. Her passions lay elsewhere.

'Indeed it is,' replied Rupert. 'Remember that barter and bargaining – haggling in other words – is all part of the Egyptian way of doing things – so be prepared to argue over the price of anything that takes your fancy. I'll give you some bartering tips a little nearer the time, so don't be too concerned about it for the moment. We'll have the opportunity to go into more detail about each archaeological site before we visit it and there'll be plenty of time for questions.'

'And whatever you do, don't trust them at all!' added Colonel Ponsworthy with a gruff guffaw, as if to disguise his remark. 'Count your fingers and watch your wallet!' he snorted.

There was a mixed reaction to this remark. Miss Eggerton looked a little shocked; Mr Arling shot his wife an apprehensive glance, eyebrows raised; for her part, Esther Arling admired her red fingernails and adjusted the opening of her blouse to reveal more cleavage; Mr Grassmere stole a glance at his wife, but elicited no response other than a vacant gaze.

'It never hurts to be cautious,' continued Rupert, by way of diffusing the Colonel's remark, 'but it would be wrong of us to assume that all Egyptians are cheats, any more than it would be wrong to assume that most Englishmen are less than honest.'

Ponsworthy scowled at him.

He's trouble, that one, thought Rupert, *I swear that the ends of his moustache twitched!*

Rupert had always found those Egyptians with whom he had had dealings to be much as himself – honest and quite trustworthy. Naturally, he had heard anecdotes to the contrary, but they were second-hand and he remained uninfluenced by them. He resented Ponsworthy's uncalled-for insinuation.

'So there we are for the moment, then,' continued Rupert, 'a real adventure awaits us and there is a lot to do and to see.'

'Well, now, I certainly intend to see it all,' boomed a loud voice, which made Mrs Mannington start. 'That's what Elias B. Grupfelder has come here for – yes, ma'am,' he continued in his American drawl, turning to smile broadly at the woman who was sitting on his left.

Mrs Lydia Porter, widow and retired schoolteacher, glared back at him through her steel-rimmed spectacles.

'Well, yes,' she replied, 'I suppose that *is* a good enough reason for coming here,' she said, with ill-disguised disdain, the barb of which seemed to go completely over Elias B. Grupfelder's head. In the short time since leaving the Cairo quayside, she had decided that the man was odious and to be avoided. If the truth be told, she harboured a passionate dislike for all Americans anyway – something she had inherited from her late husband, who had spent a lifetime blaming the Americans for just about everything.

'Made my money in cattle ranching, ma'am,' he continued, oblivious to the woman's open hostility, 'three dollars apiece.

Those little beauties are my sacred cows, if you like, ma'am,' and he roared with laughter at his own wit. 'So I thought I'd get me over here and take a look at them Egyptian ones – also sacred so I'm told – but not to the tune of three bucks a piece, I bet!' He let out another explosion of laughter. 'Ain't that so, Mr Winfield?'

Rupert smiled tolerantly at the large, good-natured American, and simply nodded in answer. Mohammed had slowly glided towards the back of the room and was now standing in the doorway at the rear of the lounge. He was tapping discreetly on his wristwatch, a souvenir of the British Army in Egypt during the recent conflict.

'I think we should adjourn for the moment, as my appetite and Mohammed both tell me that high tea is very soon to be served. Let me hand you over to Mohammed with a reminder that I am more than happy to answer any questions you might have regarding your expedition. Thank you.'

'Esteemed ladies and gentlemens,' began Mohammed, as he launched himself through the lounge, deftly avoiding the tables and chairs. He was also careful to give Mrs Grassmere a wide berth. 'Mr Winfield is, of course, correcting, and I, myself, can be informing you that even now Faisal, the esteemed maître-d'hôtel, is eagerly awaiting your presences in the dining room, which is being directly supine to our present position.' He made a sweeping gesture down towards the floor, beamed angelically and then smiled disarmingly, revealing his large gold tooth. 'Even now I can be detecting the most appetizing aromas of the labours of our kitchen, can you not be?'

By the time Mohammed had finished his torturous explanation of the culinary delights awaiting them, Rupert had retired discreetly to the rear of the lounge. He studied the assembly as he reached for his cigarettes.

The numbers are more or less balanced this trip, except for the absent Mrs Printon, which puts the women in the minority, he thought to himself. *Average age: well past it and with interests probably very uninspiring.* He took a cigarette from his case and reached into his jacket pocket for his lighter. From outside, on the promenade deck, came the metallic bonging of the three notes of 'Three Blind Mice', over and over again, summoning everyone to the dining room. *Spot on, Mohammed*, thought Rupert, *timed to perfection.*

The assembly began to break up. Chairs were pushed back, bags and hats collected and cigarettes stubbed out in the brass ashtrays. Rupert stood politely back from the entrance door, watching his flock collect themselves. He took a draw on his cigarette and exhaled, watching them idly through the gently curling smoke. There were those who had said nothing throughout the entire gathering, as if they did not want to get involved. Then there were the others who had – like the Arlings, Colonel Ponsworthy, Mrs Kirby and the rest. And there was also the loud American and his cows.

Despite her earlier withdrawal into herself, at the promise of food, Mrs Grassmere was amongst the first to reach the door. No mean feat, given her considerable stature.

'Right then...' she said, waddling past Rupert and off down the passageway towards the dining room. '...And Mumed, I do sincerely hope that the tea is hot this time.'

5

Cairo

Late afternoon – 14th July 1928

'Sit down ... please...' said Siegfried Holtzecker. High up on the ceiling, a fan drew lazy circles through a plume of wispy bluish smoke, which he had just exhaled. 'Cigarette?' he asked the tall man opposite him. His visitor had just been shown into the office and was now settling himself into a comfortable leather armchair.

'Thank you, yes,' replied the man, as he reached out and took a cigarette from the gold case. The flame flared from a heavy silver desk lighter and the visitor took a deep draw as the end of the cigarette glowed into life. He did not relax – it was not in his nature to relax. He never relaxed. 'A mixture of very good Rhodesian tobacco with a suggestion of some good Turkish,' he said, before pausing to correct his comment. 'No ... Egyptian tobacco I believe. An impressive change from the usual run-of-the-mill...' he continued, as he felt the warm smoke fill his lungs.

Between the two men stretched a large desk, the surface of which was covered with papers and folders, all arranged in meticulously neat order.

'I am impressed by your powers of deduction,' said Holtzecker. 'Your reputation, which, of course, has preceded you, is not exaggerated. You are quite correct. It is one of the finest Rhodesian blends – a little luxury to make up for being stationed on the fringes of civilization. Of course, it goes without saying that our first duty is to the Party and Fatherland, but such little pleasures do tend to add an extra sense of value to our efforts.'

He allowed himself a slight grin, which was accentuated by the creased lines around his austere mouth. Across his left cheek, running down and forward from the bottom of the earlobe to the jaw line, was a white wheal that stood out angrily against the brown, tanned skin.

Most probably a duelling scar honourably won representing some university fraternity, thought his visitor. *Many of the old school have such a souvenir of their student days. Quaint, but rather pointless.* But he said nothing. It was part of his job to assess people and situations – and quickly. He did so from behind a neutral smile, which gave away nothing.

'A drink?' asked Holtzecker. 'Have you managed to acquire a taste for the local coffee yet?' The question was merely a tool of conversation, as he had no idea of how long his visitor had even been in Egypt. In fact, following the usual operational procedure, he had been told almost nothing about this man, other than the reason why he would suddenly appear in Egypt and that he was one of the best operatives the Party had. 'Or perhaps you would prefer something more homely ... a little schnapps ... ?'

'Thank you,' replied the visitor. 'Schnapps.'

Holtzecker got up from behind his desk and crossed the large office to a cabinet, from which he took two glasses and a tall bottle filled with clear liquid.

'You seem quite at home in the import business,' said the visitor, as he took another draw of his cigarette, '*Kohler & Zehler, Importers of Fine Gourmet Consumables,*' he said, remembering the details displayed on large brass plates to either side of the main entrance to the building. 'And do I have the honour of addressing Herr Kohler ... or Herr Zehler ... ?'

There was the hint of a knowing smile on his lips, as if he already knew that his host was neither. In fact, he even doubted if this man's name really *was* Holtzecker and he cared even less. In his line of business everything was best camouflaged or hidden – even names.

'It was not always thus ... it has been a hard journey, but our masters seem to be content with the result,' replied Holtzecker, ignoring the question as he handed a glass of the clear liquid to his visitor. 'We have now been here nearly ten years, since just after the tragedy of 'eighteen.' His voice was tinged with bitterness. 'Please help yourself to a refill, if you wish,' he added and sat down behind the desk again.

For a few seconds the two men stared at each other in silence, the fan swishing around on its endless journey above them. Then the visitor, who had not taken his eyes from the other man's face, spoke.

'Your efforts are spoken of very highly,' he said, making a gesture with his hand, 'and I am impressed that you have managed to create such an effective station right in the midst of our arrogant, stupid enemies, who would as soon have you shot as have you as a friend.'

Holtzecker sat fingering the scar on his cheek with the index finger of his left hand.

'Arrogant, yes. On that point we are agreed,' he replied, 'but stupid, no. The British are foolish, rather than stupid. Think back to the war in South Africa. For them, it proved to be a crippling campaign against the Boers. Despite the Fatherland's support the Boers lost, but were fortunate in that the British were too foolish to stamp their authority on their newly acquired lands.' He reached across the desk and stubbed out the remains of his cigarette in a large alabaster ashtray. 'No, my friend, instead of that, they spent vast amounts of their money re-establishing the Boers in their own homelands. We have many sympathizers down there – when the time is ripe, the British will regret such generous foolishness.' He took another cigarette, but this time did not offer his visitor one.

Is this man nervous, or is he simply addicted to the nicotine? wondered the visitor. He noticed such things – that was why he had survived for so long.

'The same holds true here in Egypt,' continued Holtzecker, once he had lit his cigarette, 'we have learned two facts to our advantage. The first is that loyalty can be easily bought. The second is that human greed can be one of our strongest allies,' he said, blowing smoke up towards the rotating fan. 'The high society of Cairo has a taste for the good life and so do most of the British officials here. Of course, on the one hand the British are deadly serious about playing the game fairly, but, on the other, even *they* are not against the acceptance of the occasional *gift* ... ' – he accented the word, hinting at the significance of such an action – '... especially if that same *gift* is of very high value and the price ticket is – shall we say – missing. None has ever been returned...'

He smiled at the other man, who reached out to refill his glass from the bottle, but it was a cold smile – deadly serious and devoid of any mirth. 'We have also learned that to donate expensive delicacies to official receptions, not to mention the officials themselves, can bring worthwhile returns. Egypt runs on a mixture of corruption and patronage: that is the Arab way. The British like to see themselves as the arbiters of honesty and fair play, but they are only fooling themselves. Some of our best results have come from government officials ... mainly Egyptian, but there has been the occasional British source as well. Large cash donations to charities – especially those concerning children – are also highly beneficial to one's credentials in the end. The British are well known for their uncontrolled concern for the welfare of animals and children...'

'So it is all about fair play and good cricket, what?' replied the visitor. He laughed softly, but showed no signs of relaxing into the armchair. Although they hardly moved, his eyes missed nothing – every detail of the office and even of Holtzecker himself, had been captured and imprinted on this visitor's memory.

Holtzecker smiled inwardly to himself. So, what he had heard about this man via the rumour mill seemed to be quite true: charming on the surface, but underneath like a dangerously coiled cobra, ready to strike at any moment. He suddenly felt a little uncomfortable with this man sitting opposite him, whose face gave away absolutely nothing. He felt slightly unnerved. Since their meeting had commenced, it had been he who had done most of the talking – it had been he who had given away the most information. His visitor had shared practically nothing with him in return. He had entertained the Party's agents before, but they had not been like this man. This one was different: cold and – just possibly – potentially as dangerous to himself, as he would no doubt be to the enemy.

'Ah, yes – their interminably boring game of cricket. A good analogy – yes, indeed, you could put it that way,' continued Holtzecker, eyeing his visitor with carefully concealed apprehension, 'their foolishness is in not being able to exert their authority without first constantly correcting themselves over their ludicrous notions of morality and fair play. You know as well as I that nothing is achieved by paying any heed to the disorganized lunacy of a committee. Firm leadership and control, with the minimum of discussion or input, is the only true recipe for progress. Our Leader and the Party have proved that, and will continue to do so to the rest of the world.'

Of course, he believed implicitly in what he had just said, but caution had automatically obliged him to say the words out loud. It also suddenly occurred to him to wonder exactly who – if anybody – was in control of his visitor.

Holtzecker got up once again and crossed the office, but this time to the large French windows. They stood open, overlooking the busy street outside. He closed them gently.

'We should, however, never allow ourselves to become complacent,' he said softly. 'In Egypt everything has ears ... and a price.' He crossed back to his desk. 'I am aware of your role and why you are here, and, I am pleased to say, we have had a little unexpected good fortune.'

His visitor put down his glass and sat forward in his chair.

'You are to proceed to Aswan and await the arrival of The Phoenix,' said Holtzecker, his arms balanced on the arms of his chair, his fingers touching, 'You have perhaps met him before ... ?'

'No, never. I have been informed of his contribution to the Fatherland, of course, and of his organizational abilities, but I have never had the honour. We will meet in Aswan through the sign of The Phoenix – his family crest.'

Nothing further was said and the room fell silent. Outside, behind the closed French windows, the chaos on the Cairo streets was little more than a faint rumble in the distance. Holtzecker knew only too well that it was pointless attempting to ascertain any further information. For his part, he had been informed directly of exactly what it was his masters wanted him to know – no more. No doubt his visitor had also been fully briefed on the role he was expected to play. It was undesirable that both should know the other's business. That was the way things like this were done.

'As you say,' he said, waving his hand in the air in a small, circular gesture, 'in Aswan and by the sign of The Phoenix. Your quickest way to reach Aswan would normally be the railway, but our foolish friends are suspicious of the Arabs' growing desire to govern themselves and so they suspect everything. They have police watching the railway stations and have even placed troops on some of the trains. This could possibly make the journey difficult, even for someone of your capabilities...' He smiled and waved his fingers in the air again, in the same circular gesture, but continued before his visitor could make any reply. 'Here, I allow myself to reflect modestly on their foolishness again,' he said, almost wistfully. 'They seek they know not what, nor do they know why they seek it, yet seek it they do, with the utmost dedication and focus of purpose. There are all sorts of stories going about: fears of a new Arab Revolt, the Zionist question, military intelligence trying to sort things out, police on every corner and everyone a potential subversive – everything being watched. But for what reason, no one is quite sure...' Holtzecker's voice trailed off and his words faded into the distant corners of the office. 'Naturally, we do what we can to ferment these stories. We have true allies and, as I have said, there are those who can be easily bought. We also have ways of silencing those who displease us. Sometimes our strongest asset can be that ridiculous notion of great British fair play...' He paused to reach across the desk and stub out his second cigarette. 'How very foolish they really are.' A slight, begrudging smile once again thickened across his chiselled features. 'I am grateful they do not follow the same methods and game rules that we do.'

His visitor smiled his understanding of the situation, but said nothing.

'As I mentioned, Fortune has smiled on us once again,' continued Holtzecker, when it became obvious that the visitor had absorbed everything, but was not about to offer anything in return. Getting up from behind the desk for the third time, he crossed to a large, heavy iron safe in the far corner of the room, 'I have something for you,' he said, over his shoulder.

Back at his desk, he opened the ornate wooden box, which he had removed from the safe, and extracted a small bundle from it. It was wrapped in a piece of white cotton cloth.

'Yesterday, there was a truly unfortunate accident,' he continued, opening the cloth bundle and removing its contents. 'A gentleman of European extraction had a most regrettable meeting with a lorry. Sadly, he did not survive the encounter and is no longer with us.'

The visitor kept a steady gaze on the contents of the bundle, as Holtzecker continued to undo the cotton wrapping.

'Apparently, he did not see the lorry approaching, nor did he hear the warning horn, because, for some reason, he was clutching his chin with both hands. Following the collision, he was dragged along by the running board of the truck for several metres, almost face-down on one of our rough Cairo roads. When he finally rolled free, the truck sped off into the anonymous distance. I am pleased to say that the nature of the accident resulted in this poor man's face becoming unrecognizable.'

'I am impressed at the detail of your information,' said the visitor. 'Is this public knowledge?'

'Not yet, but I dare say it very soon will be. Incidents such as this, involving Europeans, are often quite touchy affairs.' He paused, looking earnestly at his visitor. 'No, my information is first hand – remember, I told you everything in Egypt has a price. No sooner had the unfortunate gentleman rolled into the gutter, than the locals descended on the corpse, like so many hungry vultures, and picked it clean of any object thought to be of value. A few pounds to the right people, plus commissions, of course...' He smiled at the thought and then continued, '...And I now have those same objects and details in my possession.' A look of competent triumph flashed across his face. 'In the present political climate you can never be sure when – or even if – such items might come in useful. I would venture to suggest that these objects will be very helpful to *you*, given the task ahead of you. You never can tell...' Holtzecker left the sentence open as he handed the items to his visitor, one at a time. 'A wallet; an appointment card for that same day with a Dr Abdul Wacheem, dental surgeon; a passport and a ticket up the Nile on the paddle steamer *Khufu*, enabling you to start "Exploring the Wonders of Ancient Egypt",' he read from the printing on the front of the ticket folder.

'So ... how fortunate,' said the visitor, studying the documents slowly and carefully. 'I now have an identity – solid British touring stock.'

Both men allowed themselves a smile at the thought of the ridiculousness of this last remark.

'And I don't even *like* cricket!' added the visitor, but there was still very little humour behind the remark.

'One of our people has many contacts out there in the city...' said Holtzecker, as he thrust out his chin in the direction of the window, '... and these contacts, whose loyalty is easily bought, are skilled. They can do almost anything asked of them, usually overnight. This gentleman's timely demise, and the happy coincidence that you match the details in the passport rather well, has saved us the necessity of having to invent an identity for you. Afterwards, you'll be able to leave Egypt quite legally and simply disappear. They will have no idea of who you really are or what you have been doing here...' Holtzecker continued to look straight into his visitor's face, but was unable to detect any emotion or response in the impassive façade. 'Your profession is given as an engineer. Would that prove to be a liability?'

'Not in the least,' replied the visitor, somewhat icily. 'I have a passing knowledge of several things mechanical. More to the point, is he known to anyone here?'

'No. He was travelling alone – my man has already checked that. You have no danger of meeting an unexpected wife or companion. It will only be you and I who know that you are not at all who you claim to be.'

There was an awkward pause, during which Holtzecker, for the briefest of moments, suddenly wondered if he had gone too far. Too much knowledge was a dangerous thing – even for an extremely competent station head. 'My man will be here shortly to take you with him. You will need a photograph and then he will arrange for the passport to be altered. Our contacts work very quickly, but something like this is very specialized and could be tricky. The job has to be done thoroughly. Even our foolish British friends are not that gullible to be easily fooled by shoddy workmanship. You might not be ready to leave with the steamer, but you can always travel by train up to Luxor and board it there.'

'Excuse me for asking,' said the visitor, 'if I am now a thoroughly respectable Britisher touring part of my Empire, why should I not simply continue on the train to Aswan? That would be much quicker, surely...?'

Holtzecker sat back in his chair. He did not even know when this man was supposed to meet the Herr Graf in Aswan.

'I said that Fortune has smiled on us. I did not say that she had laughed,' he said, smiling. 'Unfortunately, there are sections of the line between Luxor and Aswan which are presently undergoing repair. There have been one or two derailments in recent months and the authorities, always slow to recognize that there is a problem in need of a solution, have now been obliged to admit that the need for more permanent repairs is somewhat pressing. Repair gangs often work on sections of the line, which have to be closed. The delays are sporadic and of indeterminate length.' He sighed, once again bringing his fingers together in front of him. 'We have some very good customers in Aswan – they greatly value what we can supply them and are prepared to tolerate the slight delays.' He made the circular gesture in the air with his fingers again. 'We even have an office in Aswan – very small – but it caters for their needs. We often find it more expedient to send their consignments by river – as the Ancients did before us. River transport is usually very reliable, if a little slower,' he concluded, 'no interference from sandstorms. Besides which, commercial expansion is seen as a sign of confidence and business respectability.' And he smiled, as if to underline the implications of his remarks.

'Thank you for your information,' replied the visitor. 'After I have taken charge of the merchandise I might well have to consider exactly how The Phoenix and I are to return from Aswan...'

'And it is best to be prepared for any eventuality,' added Holtzecker, 'as I am sure I need hardly remind anyone of *your* abilities.'

There was a soft rapping on the stout office door. The visitor quickly and silently put the documents he had been given out of sight, in the inside pocket of his suit jacket.

'Come!' said Holtzecker, looking at the door over his visitor's shoulder. A smartly dressed European woman entered, closing the door softly behind her. She crossed to the desk and, politely ignoring the visitor, spoke to Holtzecker in the same well-educated German the two men had spoken.

'Excuse me please, Sir. He is here,' she said softly.

'Good,' replied Holtzecker, 'Frau Webber, kindly inform this tour company that Mr Printon will be joining *Khufu* at Luxor,' he continued, handing her a small piece of paper, on which he had scribbled the details from the ticket .

He turned again to his visitor.

'Come then, Mr Sebastian Printon. Let us get on with things, shall we?'

6

The Nile, Luxor

17th July 1928

'Good morning, Winfield,' called Simon Arling, as he saw Rupert Winfield approaching.

'Good morning. How is Mrs Arling today? Will she be joining us in time to watch the docking at Luxor?'

'Please, I'm Simon and my wife is Esther. You can drop the formalities if you like. Take a seat,' he said, gesturing to the cane armchair opposite his.

'Thank you', replied Rupert, as he settled himself into the chair.

Arling rested the newspaper he'd been reading on his lap. There was a slight breeze blowing off the water and the edges of the paper, crisp from exposure to the late-morning sun, crackled as they were caressed by it.

'Very pleasant, isn't it?' he asked, more by way of statement than enquiry. 'Thank goodness for the awning and the breeze – and the iced water.' He smiled at Rupert, the open mouth revealing flashes of pearl-white teeth, framed by the dark, close-cropped beard. Rupert felt easy in his company.

The upper deck of *Khufu* was almost completely covered by canvas awnings, under which were laid out assorted tables and armchairs for the convenience of the tourists. Towards the bow, a wooden wheelhouse extended for almost the entire width of the steamer. A painted sign announced that access beyond this point was for crew only. At the stern there was a bar, from which cooling libations were regularly despatched to any of the occupied tables. It stood just in front of the railings, quite close to the top of the revolving paddle wheel, but not threatened by it.

Although he was having a conversation with Simon Arling, Rupert kept an eye on the rest of the deck. Several of the guests were seated at the various tables, drinking and chatting. He fancied that they might be anticipating their arrival at Luxor, but the reality within told him they were probably talking about nothing more exciting than the small things which occupied their daily lives back home. How could they not be as passionate about the Ancients as he was? Why on earth did they spend a small fortune to come on the trip in the first place, if they were not? Tickets for two weeks of luxurious river cruising and idle chatter – even at the reduced, off-season rate – equated to several years' pay for a factory worker back home. Then, during a lull in the conversation, he smiled gently as he noticed that, at least for the moment, they had been spared Mrs Grassmere. She had still to put in an appearance.

From her table on that first night out from Cairo, the woman had dominated the conversation of the entire dining room. Everything about the woman was to excess, from her physical appearance to her dress, and that evening had been no exception. She had constrained the ample proportions of her flabby neck within a circle of bright, sparkling diamonds, which, she quickly informed everyone, had been a recent birthday present from her husband. As bright and flashy as was the necklace, so Mr Grassmere was dull, dominated and uninteresting – he was also spineless.

'Mr Grassmere thought these would suit my complexion to a tee,' she had brayed, as she repeatedly patted them and adjusted the strands. The rest of the dining room had simply sat and stared at the tasteless spectacle, seemingly lost for words.

At a neighbouring table, and from behind the safety of his spectacles, Eric Kormann had eventually offered polite conversation in response.

'Diamonds have been discovered for over four thousand years,' he had said, 'and the ancient Greeks thought they were the tears of the gods. When they were saddened by the stupidity of mortals, they shed them and they dropped from the sky. Then the "stupid" mortals discovered how to cut and polish them – making them gleam like sparkling stars. We have early records showing how valuable they became. Cleopatra and Julius Caesar were particularly interested in them, as were all of the Ptolemies in ancient Egypt.'

'Such insignificant lumps of carbon, and yet they have had the power to create mayhem and death in their wake, often because of man's greed. Perhaps a better name for them would have been "the fatal tears",' Simon Arling had muttered, looking with disdain at Mrs Grassmere. 'There were also those who thought that they were an aphrodisiac,' he had added, softly, 'except that to ingest diamond powder is lethal, so quite how that one worked remains an ancient mystery, I would say.'

'Surely, darling, they were an aphrodisiac only when a woman was prepared to do *anything* for them?' Esther Arling had cooed, her red lips lingering on the word. 'And then, surely, only when they were sparkling, and in one piece.'

There had been a muffled response of subdued laughter from those who were close enough to have heard this. Mrs Grassmere had not, and so continued singing her own praises and that of her somewhat tasteless and expensively vulgar accessory.

'I always say that you can see when a person has the correct idea of polite society,' she had babbled, patting the necklace once again, with a flabby, ring-bedecked hand, 'especially if they have the ability to carry jewellery correctly – especially diamond jewellery, like this. I remember...'

And, at that point, she had made her mistake by making a remark about her memories of touring in India. The Colonel, who had managed to avoid being seated on the same table, had interrupted her from across the room by asking her a question about Simla – the cool, mountain retreat which he had often visited. From the nonsense of her garbled answer, it was glaringly obvious that, despite her claims, she most definitely had not visited the place. At last she had fallen silent and had turned her pig-like eyes back to her plate. The Colonel had beamed the smile of the victor – he had succeeded in shutting her up. The relief of the other diners had been palpable and the pleasant chatter of people enjoying their meal had grown steadily out of the previously frigid silence. It had been only the first evening meal of the trip...

Now, as the small gleaming-white iceberg neared Luxor, in the hot sunshine of the top deck, Rupert was suddenly aware that Arling had refocused his gaze on the newspaper. He had turned the page and folded the paper in half and now pointed to a lengthy article about the state of Germany.

'Hmm ... it looks like things are getting better, but they are still in a bit of a mess. He seems a good chap on the surface, but it's always the same with a reformer – scares the Establishment to the point of nervous recognition of their own incompetence and they react badly – "hammer to crack a nut" syndrome, as it were. What do you think?'

'Sorry, I didn't catch that one ... You were saying?'

The question had taken Rupert by surprise because his mind still lingered on the pleasant memory of Mrs Grassmere's recent, ignominious silencing.

'In the newspaper...' said Arling, throwing it onto the low cane table between their chairs, '... quite interesting

… what they have to say about Germany. This Hitler chap has some reasonable ideas. He's already been locked up with some of his followers – for subversive activities against the security of the State, which seems to be in a terminal mess, anyway. I was there a couple of years ago and it was in an awful muddle. Do you know that they had a banknote for one hundred million marks?'

'Er, no, I didn't actually', replied Rupert, his mind now refocused on the conversation, 'but I do remember reading about their economy – almost collapsed, hadn't it?' He might be fascinated by the Ancients, but he did live in the modern world and tried to remain as up-to-date as possible.

'Indeed,' replied Arling, 'they couldn't pay their war reparations. We and the Yanks were happy to renegotiate, but the French and Belgians said "*Non!*" and that was that. Can't blame them, I suppose, all things considered. Still, Hitler didn't waste his time behind bars. He's written a book called *Mein Kampf* – some of it is racial rubbish, but there are some quite inspirational bits in it. He's quite charismatic on the page – must be electrifying in the flesh, I shouldn't wonder.'

'You seem to have a great interest in Germany,' said Rupert. 'You pronounced the book's title very well, at least to my ears!'

Languages were not Rupert's strong point. Arling laughed – the teeth flashed again.

'I know that *mein* means "my", but the other bit's got me, I'm afraid,' continued Rupert.

'*Kampf* means "struggle",' answered Arling, 'so the title is *My Struggle.*'

'Do you speak German?' asked Rupert.

'Yes. I'm from the English branch of the family, but the rest of the tree is spread throughout Europe, mainly Germany, Amsterdam and Vienna. They are bankers,' he said, his tone changing as he did so, 'capitalists with a capital C and

I despise them for it. They make millions whilst millions are penniless. Ironic, isn't it?' He stared out across the river with a vacant look on his face. The veins in his temples stood out against the tanned skin of his face, an outward sign of some inner struggle. 'If I had been taken in by their capitalist claptrap', he eventually continued, 'I'd be just like them – stinking rich with no conscience. That would bother me – I'm all for a bit more equality.'

Rupert felt it was not his place to say anything. He made it a policy not to get involved with the opinions of his fellow travellers, political or religious, but he couldn't help wondering about this man. A member of a family of extremely wealthy bankers, yet he seemed to have ideas that would be quite at home in the new Russia with that Lenin character.

'The worst rubbish in *Mein Kampf* is against the Jews,' continued Arling, 'but he isn't going to be able to sustain that one for very long if he gets the go-ahead to take power. He won't be able to do much without money and most of that comes from us – or them, I suppose I should say. It's a well-known fact that it is Jewish money that makes the world go around.'

The deck was still slowly filling with passengers. Across the broad expanse of the river, through the haze, small white blotches hugged the bank. The outlying buildings of Luxor staggered gently from side to side through the heat. Even the cooling effect of the river couldn't defeat that.

'So, *mazel tov*! – it's a boy! Shimon Ehyrling – the hope of the English branch of the family – turns out to be a radical thinker – Simon Arling. Not quite what the family wanted...'

'That must put you in a very difficult position,' replied Rupert. 'Families are not the easiest of things at times, are they? It's even worse if you think differently from the way they do.' He remembered his own experience.

'Ah … here's Esther,' said Arling and the mood was immediately changed.

'Hello, Mr Winfield', she said in her deepish voice, 'are you and Simon having a good chat – boys' talk?'

Rupert made to give up his chair, but Arling waved him aside. Esther reached across to the table next to theirs and pulled up her own chair.

'Lovely with a little breeze, isn't it?' she continued, 'but we do seem to be getting there very slowly.' She took a pair of sunglasses from her bag and put them on. 'Is there much to see in Luxor? Will we have enough time to go and look?'

'Well, yes there is, as a matter of fact,' replied Rupert, conscious that she had pulled her chair unnecessarily close to his. 'There's the temple itself and then there's the Great Temple at Karnak, which is just a couple of miles further away, but we won't be doing any of that until we get back to Luxor from Aswan, towards the end of the trip. Then there's the Valley of the Kings on the western side of the river, over there,' he gestured across his shoulder. 'That's where Carter found King Tutankhamun back in '22. They're still digging things out – fascinating treasure trove. We won't be able to see anything, though, but at least we can see the spot.'

'That sounds very exciting, Rupert', she butted in, patting his knee, 'you're so knowledgeable about these things. So what will we be able to do this afternoon, then, after we've docked I mean?'

She was not an unattractive woman, late twenties, perhaps, and a little younger than her husband. The large lips, painted delicately with red lipstick and the round, almond-shaped eyes, even when hidden behind the sunglasses, spoke of sensuality. The aquiline nose spoke of her ethnic origins in an age before such things became a defining badge of misery. The light cotton blouse she wore, with the top buttons undone, was amply filled by the full roundness of her breasts. She still had her hand on his knee, although it had moved a little higher.

Although he had never really had the time to think about it, Rupert had never been comfortable in the close company of women. He had long been seduced and dominated by his books and the insatiable desire for the intimate knowledge of the Ancients. The Esther Arlings of this world were, as yet, an undefined quantity to him.

'We should only be in Luxor for a few hours,' he replied. 'We have to report back to Head Office in Cairo and see if they have anything for us, then the boys will load fuel and provisions and then we'll be off – probably late afternoon. Then it's on to our first real stop at Esna. The Temple of Khnum.'

'Oh yes,' she said, 'the ram-headed potter god.'

There was emphasis on the 'ram-headed', which even Rupert did not fail to notice.

'You could always have a drink or take tea at the Winter Palace Hotel,' offered Rupert. 'It's a grand old building and the service is very good – as one would expect, naturally.'

'A thousand regrets ... please to be excusing this most regrettable intrusions of your conversation.'

It was Mohammed, who had walked up behind Rupert's chair and was now standing at his side, hands clasped in the same self-deprecating gesture he always employed when talking to persons of a much lighter skin colour than his own.

'May I be having a short discussions with you, Mr Winfield, Sir?'

'Yes, of course, Mohammed,' replied Rupert, almost relieved at being given the unexpected opportunity of escape from the hand on his thigh. 'Excuse me, please, Mrs Arling ... Simon.'

It was only as he got up and turned towards Mohammed that Rupert realized he had used the informal form of address with Arling, as invited. He had not done so consciously.

'We need to be going through our Luxor procedures, as we will very shortly be making landings on the bank,' continued Mohammed.

Rupert smiled inwardly at this little man's misuse of English – it was quite endearing in its own way. He had decided to reserve the opportunity to offer correction only when his own Arabic was on an equal footing with Mohammed's English – and that would not be for quite a while yet.

'Right you are, Mohammed,' said Rupert, as the two of them strode off across the deck towards the companionway and the office, which was below them on the main deck.

In the wheelhouse, the engine room telegraph jangled its instruction to the engineers to reduce revolutions. Out across the water, the buildings of Luxor continued their soporific, heat-induced dance.

Elias B. Grupfelder had asked Eric Kormann if he would like to go with him to explore the market. The idea had not really appealed to the little Swiss, but he had not been able to think of a convincing excuse quick enough to avoid the invitation. The Arlings had gone off with Stephen Hopkins who, despite his limp, was keen to 'have a look around'; the Manningtons had decided to stay on the top deck and watch the passing parade from there; Colonel Ponsworthy had wandered off on his own and Mrs Grassmere, to everyone's relief, had retired with a bad headache.

As for the rest, a small group had decided to take up Rupert's suggestion and had adjourned to the nearby Winter Palace Hotel. In Marjory Cuttle's glass, ice cubes clinked invitingly as she put it down on the brass-topped table in front of her.

'Quite refreshing, really,' she said, as she fanned herself

slowly with the menu card. 'Chopped mint, crushed ice, lemon juice and a dash of sugar. But I must say that I *do* prefer a G&T.'

She picked up and opened her handbag, which stood on the floor next to her chair.

'Cigarette?' she asked, as she held out her gold case towards Sylvia Baxter.

'Thanks' came the reply.

The lighter flared and, almost immediately, the freckled and not unattractively plain features of the younger woman were shrouded in a cloud of white smoke.

'Pleasant here, isn't it? Don't know why Miss Eggerton didn't want to come, I'm sure,' said Miss Cuttle. 'Better here than being cooped up on the ship.'

From the shaded expanse of the terrace of the Winter Palace Hotel, the two women gazed lazily out across the broad expanse of the river. White feluccas, like so many polka dots on a rich blue background, glided noiselessly across the still surface. On the far side of the river, the necropolis of ancient Egypt shimmered in the searing heat, waiting for the tourists – most of whom were indifferent to the glories of the past. There, the Boy King Tutankhamun, the pharaoh about whom history had very little to say, was still rubbing shoulders with the twentieth century, as Howard Carter, the intruder-excavator, unearthed one fabulous royal treasure after another. Each was to give new life to the other. It was almost as if three thousand years had made both men equal; there were even echoes of the ideology of Marx and Lenin: the 'new way' of the twentieth century; the levelling of man to a common denominator of timeless equality. And it was there that Rupert would march his charges following the steamship's trip back down the river. They would experience the surreal atmosphere and chronic heat of the Valley of the Kings – this meeting place of millennia.

FATAL TEARS

From their position on the terrace, the two women could clearly see *Khufu* moored alongside the riverbank. The activities of the crew resembled an army of ants, scurrying up and down the gangways, carrying the essential food, wine and fuel needed for the trip. On the bank of the river buzzed the inevitable swarm of urchins and beggars, selling anything they could to make a few coins. On the ordered expanse of the boulevard, which ran along between the hotel and the Nile, the throng of carriages, carts and the occasional motor vehicle went about their business in seemingly contented confusion.

'I suppose they do have rules about traffic out here,' commented Sylvia, 'but it does make you nervous trying to cross the road, doesn't it?' She had become quite at ease and sat easily with the smoking cigarette held between her fingers.

Marjory laughed her whinnying laugh. Although she had to fight hard to disguise the fact, Miss Sylvia Baxter was highly amused to see that the elder woman's teeth were heavily flecked with shards of green mint leaf. Not only had the flecks adhered to large areas of the enamel, they had also become wedged between the teeth, giving her usually warm smile the appearance of that of a semi-toothless crone from the back streets of Luxor. Sylvia's suppressed mirth suddenly evaporated, as two things crossed her mind simultaneously. The first was a fond remembrance of Aunt Hetty, who had been so fond of roast lamb with mint sauce. The second, and possibly more important, was that her own teeth, were probably equally as liberally decorated with the pungent green flecks as were those of her companion. In a panic of insecurity, she set about trying to brush her teeth with her tongue, whilst trying not to make things too obvious.

'I think the chaos makes it all the more exotic. I suppose that they will have to put in some of those new-fangled traffic light things to control the traffic if it gets any worse,' continued Miss Cuttle, as she took another sip from her drink and waved away an annoying fly.

'What sort of lights?' asked Sylvia blankly, trying not to open her mouth too wide as she spoke.

'You know – they change colour and control the movement of traffic, or so I've read. In London, they had to put them in last year – the traffic was out of control.'

'Aah, in London,' mumbled Sylvia. 'We don't really get much news of London, and when we do it's really rather out of date.'

Marjory looked at her companion with a quizzical, yet not unkind frown.

'Well, come on now, my dear. Malaya is hardly the moon.'

'No, I know it isn't, but we seem to keep ourselves to ourselves a bit much. That's why my Aunt Hetty insisted that my father allow me to come on this holiday – it was for my twenty-first birthday, you know...'

Aunt Hetty had been a formidable figure within the social bubble of the European rubber planters out in Malaya. It had been at her instigation that a world trip had been booked to celebrate Sylvia Baxter's coming of age or, as Aunt Hetty put it, her emergence into the character forming 'real world of Life'. She would take her niece away from the cosseted safety of the plantation and return her as a fully fledged mature woman with a well-developed character, something which, in her opinion, her niece had so far lacked. Three weeks before their departure, Aunt Hetty had suddenly died in her sleep. Already in her mid-seventies, she had made it perfectly clear to everyone that the trip *would* go ahead, no matter what and despite any unforeseen eventualities. She, herself, had arranged everything and it had all been paid for. Following the sudden shock of her passing, even in death, nobody had found the courage to ride counter to her clearly expressed intentions, such was her formidable reputation. The trip *would* go ahead, no matter what.

'Aunt Hetty felt that I had to try and just find myself – become a little more adventurous and so I came on this trip alone. Back home it's always the same thing – the Club in the afternoons, polo in the season, sometimes a garrison dance and staying at the coast in summer – and that's about it.' Marjory thought she detected a touch of resentment in the younger woman's tone. 'We never seem to do much or meet many interesting people, stuck out where we are. Aunt Hetty insisted that I come on this holiday – she had taken others on similar trips before and thought it was just the thing. She always said that such an experience made you a "noticeable person".'

'And did it? Did these other people return as "noticeable persons"?'

'Well, I don't really know, to be honest – I couldn't really stand my cousin Bronagh much before she went away. When she got back, she was so full of her new self that I found her positively painful and I went out of my way to avoid her.'

Marjory whinnied out loud. Her teeth, save for one or two of the more stubborn shards, had now largely recovered from the mint's onslaught.

'You funny thing,' she snorted, between whinnies. 'Here, have some of these nuts – they're delicious.'

Sylvia took a couple of cashews from the bowl, grateful that chewing them would help to clean her teeth. She popped them into her mouth, where they mingled with the smoke from her cigarette. She was starting to enjoy cigarettes, although she was not too sure what her family would say if they could see her puffing away contentedly.

'We'd best keep an eye on the time,' said Marjory, after a companionable silence. 'Remember that we have to be back on the ship by four.'

There were another couple of mouthfuls of the refreshing lemon-and-mint mixture left in each glass.

'You seem very confident,' said Sylvia. 'I really am very lucky to have found you on a trip such as this.'

'Me? Well, let me tell you, it's a case of having to learn to be confident in this world. If you don't, you'll just get trodden on and ground into the dirt – just like this butt end,' she added, as she ground the stub of her cigarette into the ashtray. 'Don't stand for it, that's what I say. You're just as important as the next one – so stake your claim on life and hang on to it.'

This was obviously a topic dear to her heart and her cheeks reddened slightly with the excitement of it.

'When I went to university I really had a rough time of it – it was just something a woman wasn't supposed to do – quite why, I don't know. Perhaps it's some male conception that an enlightened woman is a dangerous thing. We're all right when it comes to sex, but anything else...'

Marjory Cuttle noticed that her companion had also reddened at this last comment, but whether through excitement or, more likely, embarrassment, she wasn't sure.

My poor little innocent, she thought. *I'm going to have to take you even more firmly under my wing.*

As the final ice crystals melted into the bottoms of the now empty glasses, Luxor continued its frenetic passing parade on the broad boulevard below the terrace where they were sitting. Sylvia was about to start a new line of conversation when a horse reared up and flailed the air with its hooves. Within a split second the movement on the boulevard had become even more chaotic than before, as horses, carriages, pedestrians and the odd automobile jostled with each other in an attempt to resume the normal flow of movement. From the confusion at the centre of the blockage emerged the solitary figure of a woman. She was walking determinedly across the street towards the bank of the river and, further on down the boulevard, to *Khufu*. As she did so, she held her own in the argument, which had blown up around the gridlock.

'Wait a minute,' said Marjory, adjusting her glasses, 'isn't that our Kenyan friend, Mrs Kirby?'

Both of them stared down at the scene.

'She's an odd one,' pronounced Marjory Cuttle, who fancied herself to be a good judge of character.

'I've just thought of something,' chipped in Sylvia, 'it's that big hat of hers. When we walked here from the ship, we arrived at the hotel and then you said you had to go and powder your nose – remember?'

'Well, a perfectly natural thing to do, but yes, actually I do.'

'I waited for you in the foyer – they had a copy of *The Times*; it was quite a recent one – quite a change from receiving them back home, really,' she said, with a little chuckle.

'And the point of this conversation is?' said Marjory, her curiosity aroused.

'While you were busy and I was reading the newspaper, I saw Mrs Kirby with her big hat at the reception desk. She was saying something about if they couldn't read her writing then she would read it for them – or something.'

'Read what?'

'Well, I'm not sure, but I think it was a telegram she was trying to send. Anyway, she took the paper back from the desk clerk and read it out – something about she would need more at Esna – or such like.'

'Need more?' repeated Marjory. 'More what?'

'I don't know. Perhaps I heard it wrongly. But it did sound something like that.'

'I tell you, she's a bit unusual, that one,' muttered Marjory conspiratorially, '*Mrs* Kirby ... So where is Mr? And she doesn't seem to encourage any sort of conversation, either.

Bit of a loner, I'd say – I wonder if she realizes that she's actually left the outback of Kenya, "somewhere near Nairobi", as she put it? That's the trouble, I suppose – if you live out in the middle of nowhere, you turn out a little *strange* in the end.'

She suddenly realized what she had said and took Sylvia's hand in hers.

'But not you, my dear, we'll get you sorted out before too long.'

'That would be nice,' whispered Sylvia, 'yes, that would be quite nice,' she repeated, speaking as if from the tranquil yet stifling depths of the terrace of her lonely prison, way out in the bush on one of her father's rubber plantations in Malaya.

'But now, we had better get a move on. Let's see if we can get across the street with less disruption than did our Mrs Kirby.'

Earlier that same afternoon, back on board the little steamer, Mohammed had found himself more than a little annoyed. Just when he thought the trip was well under way something had happened to upset his ordered thinking. A simple thing in itself, but enough to cause him considerable annoyance: despite his picturesque English, Mohammed was a very methodical person and liked everything 'tickety-boo', as he kept saying. He had accepted the job just after the war and it was precisely because he *was* so organized and methodical that he had risen rapidly through the ranks of the company over the last eight years. No mean feat for an Egyptian.

In the cool confines of the little ship he had sat at the desk in his office and drummed his fingers. He had stared at the telegram in front of him. It was from Head Office in Cairo and it told him that there had been a mix-up in procedure, due to a typographical error in the outer office.

FATAL TEARS

The Mrs Printon who had missed the boat in Cairo was, in fact, a Mr S. Printon. He had had to seek the services of a dentist, due to a painful and dangerous abscess on his jaw, or so it was surmised by the staff in the outer office in Cairo. When Mr Printon had called to collect his ticket, he had been almost unable to talk because of the discomfort and pain in his lower jaw and had spent most of the time holding it with both hands. Later, someone had telephoned to say that Mr Printon was well, but would only be able to join the steamer at Luxor. The upshot of the missive, and the source of Mohammed's annoyance, was that Mr Sebastian Printon would be arriving in Luxor on the 6 p.m. train from Cairo and Mohammed would have to make the necessary arrangements to meet him at the station. That would mean at the very least a two-hour delay in *Khufu*'s departure. It had been this seemingly insignificant fact that had annoyed him. The well-oiled machine of his Nile Exploration Tour had been thrown into disarray and he didn't like it one little bit.

Now, he stood on the station platform, smartly turned out with his company name badge pinned to his lapel, his fez tassel swaying gently from side to side. As he looked alternatively at his watch, the station clock and the empty track, he was becoming impatient. It was almost 6 p.m. and there was still no sign of the train.

I hope Mr Winfield has managed to placate our guests, he thought to himself, as he paced slowly across the narrow width of the platform, his hands clasped loosely behind his back. *Such a poor display of timekeeping is really most inexcusable – even if it is not our fault.*

He waited a further ten minutes, but there was still no sign of the train from Cairo.

'You stay here and wait for the train,' he said to Achmed, his underling from *Khufu*, 'I will take tea in the waiting room. Call me when you see something coming.' He used the familiar Arabic of his birth.

Some thirty-five minutes later, as he was finishing a second pot of hibiscus tea, Achmed appeared at his table.

'*Effendi*,' he said respectfully, 'it is coming.'

Mohammed drained the last of his tea, wiped his mouth and stood up.

'At last!' he muttered, straightening his fez and looking at his watch. 'One cannot be setting the watch to the railway. Most inconveniently unreliable!'

It was past eight o'clock before Mr Sebastian Printon found himself and his single small suitcase safely on board *Khufu*. By that time, the chimes of the first three notes of 'Three Blind Mice' had summoned everyone to the dining room, which was the undoubted domain of the maître-d'hôtel, Faisal. As a result, Printon had been received on board into a deserted foyer. He showed no sign of awareness that his late arrival had caused a delay in the steamer's departure, despite the fact that the board at the top of the gangway still proclaimed that the ship would sail that afternoon at four o'clock. Had he done so, or even offered an apology, Mohammed – all smiles, beaming gold tooth and with practised theatricality – would have waived it aside. As it was, Printon offered none. During the trip from the station, his only comment had been a brusque criticism of the questionable reliability of the Egyptian railway system.

'Please, not to be concerning yourself with the subject that is you are late,' Mohammed had said, all smiles, as the cabin steward carried Printon's bag down the cabin corridor, which led off the entrance foyer. 'You are comfortably accommodationed in Cabin 10. Please to follow me,' and with that he had bobbed past Printon and walked off down the same corridor. *This man is very cold – like ice*, he thought to himself, as they reached the open door of the cabin.

The truth of the matter was that Mohammed could quite

happily have berated Printon for the disruption he had caused to his timetable, but his professionalism prevented the thought from manifesting itself further. Behind his fixed, golden smile, Mohammed was not impressed. And, besides, this Mr Printon seemed to have made a remarkable recovery from an infliction so serious it had caused him to miss the start of the trip in the first place. Mohammed thought that odd.

'If you will be pleasing to follow me,' said the little Egyptian, after Printon and his suitcase had been settled in his cabin. 'We will be enjoying an evening meal.'

They entered the dining room, where the evening meal was already in full swing.

'Honoured guests,' said Mohammed, flashing his familiar, gold-toothed smile from the centre of the room, 'may I with your permissions be presenting Mr Sebastian Printon, who has joined us here in Luxor.' There was a pause in the sounds of eating, as heads turned in Printon's direction. 'If you are pleasing to sit over here, Sir,' beamed Mohammed, motioning him to an empty seat at a corner table.

As they crossed the room, a tall, well-built man of about Printon's age turned to his wife.

'I say, that's a coincidence,' he whispered very softly, 'I used to know a Printon back in the war. He was seconded to us for a month or so. Decent chap, too.'

Richard Lampton was ex-military, late a lieutenant in the Royal Engineers, now in charge of railway expansion and bridge building in the Gold Coast.

'Really, dear?' said his wife, as she cut a roast potato in half with her knife.

'I wonder if that's him? It was a long time ago – can't really remember what he looked like. Mind you, we all look different in civvies.' He chuckled at his own observation. 'Printon used to have a problem with the sun, as I recall – used to burn bright red if he wasn't careful – something to do with his skin's reaction to the sun's rays. Seems to have gotten over that, judging from the look of him... He's quite tanned, isn't he? I must have a chat with him later ... see if he *is* the same Printon, eh?'

I will never understand these Infidels, thought Mohammed to himself, after he had made the necessary introductions and deposited Printon into Faisal's care in the dining room. Once back on the promenade deck he leaned on the rail, on the opposite side of the steamer to the city of Luxor, and let the soothing evening breeze wrap itself around his face. The sun had long since set, and the cool of the evening was now upon the river and city. He lit one of his little cigarettes and relaxed into the strong Turkish tobacco – 'dynamite' Rupert called them. As the wisps of smoke eddied and blew away from the security of the little steamer, Mohammed returned to the question of this cold and aloof Mr Sebastian Printon. In his remote village, when he was a boy, Mohammed had sometimes seen donkeys and camels with abscesses on their jaws and, he recalled, they took some considerable time to heal, if at all. During the war he had seen British Army veterinarians treat horses for the same thing – admittedly, they did recover – and sometimes quickly, too: but not in as short a time as this Printon man seemed to have done...

He pondered this vexing question for a short while longer, then, glancing up at the massed array of brightly twinkling stars that filled the sky above the Valley of the Kings on the far side of the river, he suddenly addressed another question. It was one he found equally vexatious. Earlier in the week, in the dining room, he had heard the Kormann gentleman say that diamonds were like the stars sparkling in the sky; they were jewels called the 'tears of the gods'. But why did these tears stay up in the sky and not fall to earth? Sometimes, he found what these Europeans said in their English very confusing. He would have to ask Mr Winfield to tell him what it all meant. Mr Rupert understood these Europeans far better than he, himself, did, which was hardly surprising, as he was one of them. Mr Rupert would know what they were talking about.

And with that thought in his head he flicked the butt end into the smothering arms of the Nile and turned towards his office and his own food.

7

Esna

19th July 1928

It was just before first light. *Khufu* was slowly and carefully nudging her way towards the western bank of the river and the town of Esna. The settlement was strung out along the bank and consisted of shops, mosques and the occasional substantial villa, usually the residence of some expatriate or Egyptian official. Here and there the occasional street light glimmered very feebly in the gathering dawn and the sounds of a settlement coming to daily life could only just be faintly heard – as if from a long way off. As in Luxor, a boulevard ran along the side of the Nile above the bank where the steamer was to tie up, but it was on a far less impressive scale.

Down on the main deck, moving in and out of the pools of light cast by the ships lights, Daoud and Khatose, two deckhands, were busily engaged in preparing the ropes, which would shortly lash the steamer to the riverbank. In the hush of the dawn the steady throb of the engines offered a comforting reassurance of safety. The metallic ring of the engine room telegraph tinkled gently and the throb slowed, perceptibly. From the bridge, *reis* Tarek, the master of the steamer, shouted something down towards the deck and Daoud went strolling off towards the bows.

Through the hazy smoke of his first cigarette of the day,

Rupert Winfield watched with contented familiarity. He had made the trip many times over the last couple of years, but had never grown tired of the impressiveness of a dawn arrival along the way. Leaning on the rails of the top deck, he regarded this as *his* time of the day; *his* time to soak up the atmosphere and to think of *his* Egypt. He thought of what was happening back down the river, in the Valley, at Karnak and, elsewhere, at Philae, Dendera, Kom Ombo and a score of other sites. What had so far been uncovered and recorded had led archaeologists to believe that they were dealing with only the tip of the iceberg, compared with what was still to be discovered. In the strange, almost surreal tranquillity of the pre- and early dawn, he could think on these things without interruptions from his flock, free from their often all too inane questions and pointless comments. This chilly, isolated period of recharge prepared him for the day ahead.

'Almost immediately we will soon be ready at the quayside,' said a quiet voice at his elbow.

'Hello, Mohammed,' replied Rupert. 'Cigarette?'

'Oh, most thankfully no,' replied the little Egyptian, with a polite wave of his hands. 'It is almost time for being praying.' And with a slight bow, he was gone.

Good old Mohammed, with your picturesque English. You can usually be relied on to exaggerate and call a raindrop a flood, he thought, as he looked down at the flattened bank of smooth, compacted earth that served as a landing stage. *'Quayside' indeed? 'Riverbank' is more like it!*

There was another metallic ring, more shouted commands and Daoud was scrambling over the rail and up the riverbank towards a metal bollard, which surmounted the bank like some modern statue of Rameses the Great. The throbbing had died away completely now, and the gentle splashing of the enormous paddle wheel had stopped with it, to be replaced by the sloshing and gurgling of the water, rudely awoken from its slumbers, which was now squeezed between the steamer's white hull and the shore. Despite the considerable activity on the bank, which had resulted from the docking manoeuvres, something made Rupert turn away, towards the stern. He was not alone on the top deck. There was someone else standing in the far corner of the deck, someone else who had watched the paddle wheel come to rest – someone else who now stood watching the awakening town.

That has to be the first time that's happened, thought Rupert, from behind his smile. *They usually only just manage to make the early breakfast call, let alone five in the morning.*

'Good morning,' said Rupert, acknowledging the other man with a nod.

'Good morning. Beautiful, isn't it?' answered the other in reply to Rupert's greeting. 'It's so still and calm, yet just under the surface you can feel the energy of the new day about to burst forth.'

He was right. In the slowly decreasing darkness, figures were already scurrying about heralding the start of yet another cycle of the eternal Ra. The same solar disc that had shone upon the thousands of years of the ancient kingdoms of Egypt was about to do so again upon the twentieth century.

'Indeed,' replied Rupert, smiling, 'I think this is really the best time of the day.'

The other man moved away from the rail and walked down the length of deck to where Rupert was leaning. He walked with a limp, which Rupert had not noticed before.

'Hello,' he said, 'remember me? I'm Hopkins ... Stephen Hopkins. We haven't really met properly yet, and if you're like me, names take a bit of remembering before they stick,' and he held out his hand. 'I did enjoy your talk. I find everything about Egypt quite fascinating.'

'Ah well, there we instantly have something in common,'

replied Rupert, his smile widening, 'and I completely agree with you. Egypt is a fascinating place. Is this your first visit?'

'Well, strictly speaking no,' replied Stephen, leaning on the hand rail next to Rupert. 'I was out here during the war, but I didn't really have a chance to see much, apart from the pyramids and such around Cairo. Just the sights that were close by and could be seen on a short pass – army style.'

'Yes, I know about the way the army works,' replied Rupert. 'My father was in the war, too.'

There was a pause.

'Does he talk about it much?' asked Stephen.

'No, not at all. He never came back,' answered Rupert, flinging his butt end down into the rapidly narrowing gap between *Khufu* and the riverbank.

'I'm sorry,' replied the other man.

'Thank you. I'm forgetting my manners – here, would you care for a cigarette?'

'No thanks, not before breakfast.'

The engine room telegraph tinkled and the huge paddle wheel began rotating once again, very slowly and this time in reverse. On the bank, Daoud had secured the rope around the metal bollard and was waving at the bridge. At the stern, Khatose had also scrambled up the bank and was waiting for the paddle wheel and the current to finally bring the steamer alongside before tying his rope around a second bollard. They were both shouting orders to other crewmen, who were hurrying about absorbed in their allotted tasks. At that moment, it seemed as if the little steamer was the noisiest thing in Esna. Above, on the boulevard, shadowy shapes were moving – people, carts and donkeys, peddlers and the occasional suited businessman. And the police – two of them standing idly watching the docking procedure, with their hands grasped casually behind their backs. There were three things that could always be relied upon in Egypt: flies, heat and the appearance of the police.

'Well, best be getting back to my cabin,' said Stephen, straightening up.

As he did so, as if to announce that she had finally arrived, the little steamer bumped gently, but unexpectedly, against the bank with a dull thud. Hopkins lost his balance and fell against Rupert.

'Steady on ... are you all right?' Rupert asked, as he held Stephen by the arms.

'Yes ... yes. Sorry about that. It's the leg – sometimes little things cause me to lose my balance for a bit.' He was looking straight into Rupert's eyes. 'Thanks – I'm fine ... now.'

Rupert smiled, a little embarrassed.

'Good. Sometimes even the most experienced *reis* can get it wrong – the thump, I mean. He must have misjudged the distance.'

'*Reis*? I don't know what that means,' said Hopkins.

'*Reis* – it's Arabic – it means a captain or leader – someone of experience and who is respected. Tarek is our *reis* – he's the captain – *reis* Tarek.'

Rupert had begun to feel a tingle – almost a kind of electricity. It was an exciting, very pleasant feeling and, he suddenly thought, it had caused him to ramble.

'That's my first word in Arabic,' replied Hopkins, 'and thanks again. I'll see you at breakfast, then.' He gave Rupert's shoulder a pat and turned away.

As Stephen walked away towards the stairway, Rupert felt the tingling continue. He had read books in which this sort of feeling was mentioned – in the classics of English literature and, occasionally, in one of those cheap novels, the sort his mother used to call derisively, 'trashy penny dreadfuls'. He watched Stephen's head disappear down the stairway and then he turned to once again look at the bank.

He stayed there, thinking, for a long time – until the familiar chimes of 'Three Blind Mice' called him to breakfast.

'This is the Temple of Khnum, the ram-headed potter god who fashioned the fortunes of all humans on his wheel.'

Rupert's voice echoed around the hypostyle hall and reverberated between the massive stone columns.

'You can get a really good view of the column capitals from here – look, you can still see the paint on most of them.'

There were pockets of workmen busy working and digging in various areas around the building, overseen by one or two archaeologists. Some of them Rupert knew, but not these two. They were new to the site – probably graduates from back home – or from some American university.

'Why was this allowed to fill with sand?' asked Marjory Cuttle.

'It's what happens when there is no interest in the past and rulers are too busy protecting themselves to spend money on restoration projects. That's the story of Egypt for the last thousand years or so,' answered Rupert.

'It was the French who found the Rosetta Stone and a Frenchman who broke the hieroglyphics code,' commented Simon Arling, 'not an Egyptian.'

There was a ripple of laughter.

'And there were others,' corrected Rupert, 'not just the French. Champollion did sterling work, but don't forget our own Alan Gardiner – he was an expert on hieratic.'

'What's that?' asked Esther Arling. 'Something you burn at the stake?'

There was another ripple of laughter. Rupert looked at her with patient tolerance.

'Hieratic is a kind of shorthand hieroglyphics, used for documents written on papyrus scrolls. Actually, there are three different types of writing in ancient Egypt. The hieroglyphics you can see all around you on the stone walls and columns; then there is hieratic; and finally demotic – no, not a devil,' – there was yet more laughter – 'but an everyday handwriting that the scribes used, a bit like our handwriting as opposed to the formal type of something that's been printed. That was from about 650 BC, even before this temple was built.'

Rupert had shepherded his flock around the monument as he had been speaking. Now, they were near the entrance again.

'How much of this is still under the sand, then?' asked Mr Rotherham, who had managed to manipulate his way to the front of the party.

'Quite a bit, I'm afraid,' replied Rupert. 'When we get back to *Khufu*, remind me to show you some pictures of the ruins drawn by David Roberts way back in 1839. That'll give you a good idea of how much sand has already been removed. But look up there,' he pointed to several areas on the ceiling, where the remains of the paintwork had disappeared under a blanket of black soot. 'See that – areas of smoke damage, which tells us that the floor level we're standing on was much nearer the ceiling not so long ago and people lit fires in here – hence the soot deposits.'

There was a general murmur of comment and opinion as he led the group on, until they emerged from the darkness of the hypostyle hall and into the blazing sunshine outside. It was only just past ten o'clock, but already the morning heat had established its control over the day.

'Careful as you go back up the steps to street level,' called Rupert, as he shepherded his flock towards the rickety stairway, which led from the sunken level of the temple up to the street level above.

'Why is the temple so much lower than the street?' asked Sebastian Printon, now seemingly fully recovered from his jaw abscess. 'It is illogical to think that the building was planned in such a way.'

The first members of the party had already reached the steep flight of steps and were slowly making their way up.

'Possibly subsidence in part, but mainly because the ruin filled with sand and rubble over time and the town around it was built on successive layers, so it just kept going higher and higher. And that was that.'

'Excuse me, please,' said Kormann, 'is that the same as in the city of Herculaneum, near Vesuvius? I have read about that place.'

'I have not yet visited Herculaneum or Pompeii,' replied Rupert, 'but I would imagine that any difference in levels there, such as we have here,' he gestured up towards the street, 'would have been as a result of the devastating volcanic eruption which destroyed both towns and of the deposit of ash and such material following the disaster.'

Rupert hoped that his answer would keep the Swiss happy, as his own knowledge of the excavations around Vesuvius was purely book-based. A short while later, the last of the group had gathered at the foot of the wooden stairs, which led precariously back up to the street high above.

'Did you enjoy that?' boomed a voice from the street. The ample features of Mrs Grassmere leered down over the protecting wall, gravity seemingly bent on dragging her jowls down to the temple level. 'All those stairs!'

Next to her, Mr Grassmere, dominated in stature and spirit by his wife, stood under his solar topee. Next to them stood Mohammed, who had been obliged to stay at street level and act as guard, when Mrs Grassmere announced that she couldn't possible go down that many stairs. Over half an hour in her company had left him far from amused, but he smiled warmly at the vanguard of the party of tourists, who were about to emerge from the stairway onto street level.

'That was really interesting. It's been there since the second century BC,' said Sylvia Baxter. 'Can you imagine that?'

'They all look the same to me,' continued Mrs Grassmere, warming to her slowly assembling audience. 'I don't know how you tell the difference.'

'This one is Graeco-Roman, apparently,' said Mr Rotherham, as he reached street level and started mopping his brow with his handkerchief. 'That means it is quite a new building in terms of ancient Egyptian history. Mr Winfield explained it to us.'

'Really?' replied Mrs Grassmere, a silly grin covering her face. 'You really have been listening then, haven't you?'

Mr Rotherham looked crestfallen, replaced his hat and moved once again to the back of the group. He fixed Mrs Grassmere with a frosty stare.

Ghastly ghoul, he thought to himself.

Hopkins reached the top of the stairs and swayed slightly, as he corrected his footing on the step.

'Are you all right?' asked Rupert, as he put out a steadying hand in the small of the other man's back. He had found himself coming up the stairs behind Hopkins. He was also very aware, once again, of the tingling he had started to feel.

'Fine, thanks,' answered Hopkins, smiling warmly, 'we can't blame the *reis* this time.'

Richard Lampton, who was coming up behind them, cast a furtive glance in Printon's direction. He had introduced himself to this man at breakfast and had been coldly rebuffed at the suggestion that their paths might have crossed through army service.

'I am sorry,' Printon had replied, 'you are mistaken. I have never been in the army.'

A frosty stare, ice-bound in its determination to prevent

any further conversation, had taken the wind out of Lampton's sails.

'I'm sure that should be him,' he whispered to his wife, resplendent under a sun hat that had a protecting veil balanced on the broad brim, 'after all, it's not *that* common a name, is it? And the funny thing is that when I went to Mohammed's office to ask about some stamps, he was filling in the details of our Mr Printon's passport in his ledger.'

'Do you think that it was the right thing to do, dear?' replied his wife, 'I mean, it isn't really the done thing to pry, is it?'

'I'd hardly call it prying – it was just open on the desk. And it said that he was born in Melton Mowbray. Now there's another thing,' he continued, his voice sinking to a conspiratorially low level of mystified excitement, 'old Printon's people came from Melton Mowbray and in the Mess he was ragged about being born in the town where the pork pies come from.'

He sat back with a look somewhere between triumph and confusion on his face.

'Why would being born in Melton Mowbray matter?' asked his wife.

'Really, Susan! Printon was Jewish, so mention of a *pork* pie was amusing to some...'

'...And highly offensive to others,' cut in Susan Lampton. 'No wonder he didn't want to renew your friendship. In any case, as you said, perhaps he looks different in civvies, and you just *thought* it might be him,' she replied.

Richard's revelation about the passport seemed to have gone over his wife's head.

'I seem to recall that he wore a moustache,' continued Lampton, 'but I suppose that he could have shaved it off...'

There were still a couple of the tourists who had only just set foot on the very first steps of the stairway, and still had to make the steady climb to the top.

'Just a couple more to come,' said Rupert, looking down over the protecting wall, 'then we'll have some time to look around in the market before we rejoin *Khufu*. Remember that we sail at one o'clock and that it's going to get even hotter, so we should aim to be back on board by...'

He broke off in mid-sentence as a scream made everyone nearest the retaining wall turn around and look down the stairs. At the bottom lay Rebecca Eggerton, her leg pinned under her. She was crying out. At her side was Marjory Cuttle.

Rupert turned to make his way back down the stairs and saw that Kormann and Elias B. Grupfelder, who had both been a couple of steps in front of Marjory Cuttle, had turned and had almost retraced their steps back down the stairs to the prostrate figure.

'Hang on, we're coming!' shouted Rupert.

'Please not to be too distressing at this events,' said Mohammed to the rest of the party, most of whom were, by this time, gaping over the retaining wall at the spectacle on the sand below. 'This has happened an event of the most profound misfortune, but the gentlemen will, as soon as even possible, have the unfortunate lady rescued. Please remain being calming.'

'It's my ankle, I think; I've broken it and it really, really, hurts,' said the unfortunate Eggerton, through clenched teeth. Marjory Cuttle was trying to comfort her, dabbing at her brow with a cologne-soaked handkerchief.

'Don't fret yourself, m'dear,' said Colonel Ponsworthy, who had reached the unfortunate girl before Rupert. 'We'll have you playing polo again before you even know it.'

'Where does it hurt?' asked Rupert, as he and the Colonel carefully moved her and freed the pinned leg, 'Your ankle, you say? Please ... Miss Cuttle ... would you mind ... ?' said Rupert, motioning her out of the way. With a look of concern on her face, she did as she was told. Rupert gently ran his fingers over and around the girl's ankle. She had started to cry and was blood-red with embarrassment.

'Does this hurt?' he asked.

She shook her head.

'Not really – any more than the whole thing just throbs,' she whimpered through the tears.

'Doesn't seem broken to me,' announced Rupert, 'but then I'm not a doctor.'

'I am,' said a voice from above them, as Stephen Hopkins' shadow fell across them. 'Let me have a look.'

With practised skill he quickly felt for breakages and confirmed Rupert's amateur diagnosis.

'Your diagnosis was quite correct – nothing's broken,' he said, looking at Rupert with that smile on his lips again. 'I'd say it's just a bit of a twist and a wrench. We'll need to bind it, so I must ask for a couple of gentlemen's handkerchiefs please. It's best to bandage the ankle to guard against swelling – just to be safe. In the absence of real bandages, the Mother of Invention will have to suffice,' he continued, as he was offered the requested large cotton squares.

Marjory Cuttle gave a sigh of relief. 'Thank goodness,' she said.

'I feel so stupid,' whined Rebecca Eggerton. 'I just wanted a last look back at the temple and didn't look where I was going. Next thing I'm down here with a throbbing ankle. I'm so embarrassed...'

'There's no need to be,' came the soothing voice of experience. 'We'll get you back to the ship and get some ice around it. With a bit of luck you'll be right as rain in a couple of days. All right?'

Hopkins stood up.

'If you and Arling can help her up the steps? I'm a bit wobbly...' he said, patting his leg.

'Now don't you fret yourself none,' boomed the big

American. 'We're used to this sort of thing back home – especially during the calving season.'

There was a momentary hiatus, as they turned to look, blankly, at Elias B. Grupfelder, as he advanced towards the crumpled figure lying on the sand.

'Not that I'm saying you're like a calf, ma'am,' continued the American, realizing what he had just said and feeling slightly embarrassed at the way it could be misinterpreted.

He bent down and easily picked up the slight form. Then he carried her towards the foot of the stairs, as if she had been no heavier than a bunch of flowers.

'Strong fellow,' muttered Colonel Ponsworthy.

'Miss Cuttle, perhaps you could carry Miss Eggerton's bag?' said Rupert.

It took no time at all for them to reach the street level, where Rebecca Eggerton was welcomed with expressions of sympathy and comfort.

'We must haste to the ship most quickly,' said Mohammed, who had recovered somewhat from his initial alarm at seeing one of his charges flat on the sand at the foot of the stairs. 'Mr Winfield, I will arrange for some excellently strong sailors to come and carry Miss Eggerton back to our steaming ship. Immediately, I go now. I will return. This I am saying.'

'Now hang on, there, fella,' said the American. 'I'll just carry the little lady back to the boat myself.'

'Most kind, Sir,' replied Mohammed, 'but you are most surely not troubling yourself. We have strong people who will do the job. Thanking to you the same.'

And with that the little Egyptian pressed his way through the sizeable group that had gathered around the commotion at the top of the stairs and swiftly disappeared into the throng, until only the top of his red fez was visible.

As if by magic, a chair had appeared.

'Are you an England...?' said a voice in broken English. 'Please to sit...'

An Egyptian stallholder, resplendent in a heavily embroidered galabea, had suddenly appeared as if from nowhere. With a disarming smile that would have made Mohammed envious, he gestured to the small chair before barking a string of instructions to several young boys who leapt about like animated cheetahs, eager to carry out his bidding. An aged parasol, stained and with a rip in one of the sections, also appeared, together with a small glass of steaming, dark-brown liquid.

'I say, Winfield, I'll stay here and watch him,' said Colonel Ponsworthy, glaring disapprovingly at the Egyptian. 'You can't be too careful with these chaps, y' know. They're always after something.'

Rebecca Eggerton had been deposited on the chair, which proved to be quite sturdy, despite its rickety appearance.

'Me ... Abdullah,' said the owner of the chair. 'You looking ... me shop,' he said, indicating several shops, which lined the route through the souk and onwards, back to the riverbank.

Having been assured that everything was well in hand, some of the party began to drift away in the direction of Abdullah's shops.

'Not long now,' said Hopkins reassuringly. 'Have some of this tea – it's boiling hot, so be careful, but the sugar will do you good.'

There was so much sugar in the tea that the liquid had reached saturation and the undissolved sugar formed a thick layer at the bottom of the glass.

'It was lucky for us that you're a doctor,' said Rupert, as he offered cigarettes to Grupfelder, Colonel Ponsworthy and Hopkins.

'Oh ... well...' replied Stephen, 'you do what you can, when you can.'

'Do you have a speciality in medicine?' asked Rupert.

'No, not really. General practice for nearly a year before the balloon went up. Joined the RAMC and...' He paused, and blew out diaphanous wisps of smoke. 'Well, you see it all then, don't you?'

Ponsworthy was being very gallant and saw it as his gentlemanly duty to defend Miss Eggerton from the unwanted attention of several street urchins.

'No, no,' he barked, 'Go – *jaldi, jaldi.*' He could not speak Arabic, so in a moment of fluster he unthinkingly resorted to his Gujarati vocabulary. Not surprisingly, this had absolutely no effect.

The sudden appearance of Abdullah from out of the throng did. The urchin, who had been given the responsibility of shading the White Lady with the parasol, had allowed it to droop, exposing most of Rebecca Eggerton's face to the bright sunshine. Abdullah's flood of Arabic engulfed the surprised mite and the parasol was hastily restored to its correct position.

'This is all very kind,' repeated Rebecca Eggerton for the tenth time. She had stopped crying and was slowly regaining her composure. 'It is very kind of you to hold the parasol like that,' she said, smiling at the urchin. He returned a grin, but the otherwise vacant questioning stare confirmed that he had understood not one single word, other than Abdullah's tirade of Arabic. And he had no wish to be subjected to that twice in the same day.

'There, there, m'dear,' said Colonel Ponsworthy, patting her gently on the shoulder, for he thought that the remark had been aimed at himself. 'It's no trouble.'

Rupert, who was enjoying this unexpected opportunity to talk to Hopkins, was about to ask for more details about his army career when Mohammed reappeared.

'We have in the last returned,' he began, out of breath from his exertions, 'and you are well looking after.'

He let fly in Arabic at the throng, who finally began to

disperse at the sight of Daoud, Ali and the other muscular crew from the paddle steamer.

'We have brought this chair and our mens will carry you back to *Khufu*. You do not need to use or think of the foot in the journey. Now we go.'

With almost no perceivable effort, Miss Eggerton, seated on the chair brought from the ship, was raised to shoulder height, but not before she had taken a few coins from her purse.

'This is for you,' she said, holding out a few coins to the urchin with the parasol, 'for being so kind and shading me from the sun.'

Rupert slipped Abdullah a single banknote and, with much handshaking and many gestures of goodwill, the little procession, complete with chair, picked its way through the throng, Miss Rebecca Eggerton swaying in semi-regal estate, like a maharani in her howdah atop an elephant.

Sebastian Printon, who had kept largely to the background, remarked that it was like something out of the seventeenth century – sedan chairs and all. That raised a laugh from those who had stayed with Eggerton.

'Anyone fancy a spot of shopping?' enquired Rupert, as they moved through the throng of the souk. There were no takers. 'Right, then let's meander back to the river,' he said. 'Straight ahead – just follow Miss Eggerton.'

'Winfield, can I ask you something?' asked Hopkins, as they neared the exit from the souk. Without waiting for an answer, he continued. 'Don't turn around too obviously, but isn't that Mrs Kirby over there, behind us ... to the right?'

Rupert managed a hasty glance under the guise of turning his head to scratch his neck.

'Er ... yes, it is. Why do you ask?'

'Who's that chap she's talking to – the Egyptian in the smart suit and sunglasses ... in the shade of this covered souk?'

'Haven't a clue – I've never seen him before.'

'A bit odd to be involved in so deep a conversation in the corner of a passageway through a souk, wouldn't you think? I wonder what he's got to sell – or what it is she wants to buy.'

'I'm afraid I don't follow you at all,' replied Rupert. 'Perhaps she's just looking for a souvenir or something.'

'Then why not try a stall or a shop – she's surrounded by them, after all. Why have a conversation in the corner? And another unanswered question is where has she been whilst we've been viewing the temple?'

'Well, they do say that you can buy almost anything and sometimes anyone in a souk,' muttered Rupert, as they emerged from the souk. The broad expanse of the Nile lay before them.

'And that Swiss fellow, Kormann, do you remember seeing him since the fall?'

'Oh, we saw him when Grupfelder put Miss Eggerton down on the chair. He went off this way – must have gone back to the ship before we did,' said Ponsworthy, who had missed the first part of the conversation because of the babble of noise in the souk.

'Curious, though, wouldn't you say?' said Hopkins.

Back on board, an early luncheon had been served. After the exertions of the morning, a sense of tranquillity had descended on *Khufu*. After Hopkins had confirmed his earlier diagnosis that it was just a minor sprain to the ankle and not a break, Miss Eggerton had been made comfortable in her cabin with her foot up. In his office Mohammed had allowed himself to finally calm down. He was much relieved that everyone had been brought safely back to the ship and that his routine had been restored. During the meal Rupert had given considerable thought to the sense

FATAL TEARS

of elation he felt in Hopkins' company. This was a new experience and he was not sure what to make of it, but he knew that he couldn't wait for the next opportunity to talk to him again.

On the bridge, *reis* Tarek was impatient to get going. They had to cover the distance to Aswan before mid-afternoon, otherwise they would arrive late, the heat would be up and so would Mohammed's temper, if his precious tour schedule was to be thrown into turmoil once again. *Reis* Tarek preferred the cool atmosphere of his bridge and a timeous departure instead of Mohammed's ranting. There was almost a full head of steam up – another few minutes and they would be off.

One or two of the passengers were on the sun deck, behind the bridge, relaxing under the awnings on steamer chairs. The rest of the tourists were either taking a nap in their cabins or were lining the rail on the main deck. Three deep-throated booming and yet wheezy blasts on the steam whistle, signalled the start of their departure.

'This is all so exciting,' said Sylvia Baxter. 'I've taken several photographs already.'

'And there will be many more to come before we're finished,' replied Rupert.

There was a general air of excitement on the decks, as the steamer prepared to leave the bank. Despite the unexpected events of the morning, everyone seemed to have had an enjoyable excursion – even the odious Mrs Grassmere had pronounced positively on the morning, not that she had actually done much.

Perched on the bank, next to the metal bollard, Daoud stood ready to slip the bow mooring rope. On the bridge *reis* Tarek rang down to the engine room for slow ahead and gave two more short blasts on the whistle. The paddle slowly started to turn, churning the murky water into a white froth. Daoud gave a heave and the rope slipped over the bollard and coiled down the bank, to splash into the water. On the foredeck, Ali had already pulled in enough of the rope to be able to begin forming it into a neat coil on the deck. Slowly at first, the bows began to swing silently out into the river, as if they were reluctant to leave the security of their berth at the bank.

'They'll leave the stern tied to the bank until the current turns the bows out into the river a bit more. Watch the gap between us and the shore widen. Then, when the *reis* thinks it's time, they'll cast off the stern rope and off we go.' Rupert had addressed these remarks to nobody in particular and everyone within earshot in general. 'They've done this so many times they could probably do it in their sleep, I shouldn't wonder,' he said.

Mr Rotherham was looking over the rail at the gap, which was slowly starting to open up as *Khufu* started to move.

'I find it fascinating that one wheel – big as it is – can push this entire ship through the water. What a marvellous invention that Mr Watt had with his steam engine – it's truly amazing, when you think of that power – and all from boiling water. We used to have steam power in the factory in my father's day. It's all electricity now...' His voice trailed off leaving the sentence unfinished, as if longing for something which was no longer there.

'Come along, dear, quickly now – let's get a photo as the boat leaves the quay ... over here will do nicely – next to the rail...'

Marjory Cuttle marshalled Sylvia Baxter into position just to the left of the section of rail where the gangway was usually positioned, but which was now closed. Sebastian Printon was leaning on the rail, next to the closed gate, watching the activity on the quay.

'Mr Printon, would you mind being a dear – can we join

you for a photo? Odd numbers of things always work best, I find – including people. We'll squeeze in around where you're standing.'

She laughed and Sylvia Baxter giggled excitedly.

Printon continued to lean on the railing, ignoring them.

'Mr Lampton, perhaps you could do the honours for us? The shutter is primed ... All you have to do is to push ... here...'

Printon straightened up.

'I am not photogenic,' he said, in a voice somewhere between detached disinterest and icy rudeness. 'I will take the photo for you. Perhaps Mr Lampton can join you in your picture?' he continued, motioning Lampton to where he, himself, had just been leaning on the rails.

With a lot of laughter, Lampton joined the two women and they bunched up, smiling at the camera.

'Move a bit further back,' said Printon, waving for them to do so. 'Look relaxed – try leaning on the rail and think of a cooling...'

He got no further. A cry rent the air, followed by a loud splash.

'What the hell?' cried Simon Arling.

'Man overboard,' shouted someone up forward, nearer the bows.

'Richard!!' screamed Mrs Lampton, ramming her fist into her open mouth, her eyes wide with terror.

'Where?' shouted someone else.

Grupfelder and, surprisingly, Eric Kormann, rushed to drag the women away from the railings where they had been standing. Richard Lampton had fallen through the gangway gate, which now swung free, out from the ship's side, leaving a gaping hole in the railings.

In the midst of the confusion the paddle wheel slowly continued to turn, beating the river, and the metallic jingle of the engine room telegraph, oblivious to the drama unfolding below, floated melodiously out from *reis* Tarek's domain on the bridge.

'Stop! Oh stop! Look, it's Mr Lampton,' cried Sylvia Baxter, 'Stop! Stop!'

'They can't – not that quickly,' shouted Ponsworthy, 'the backwash will take him towards the paddle – if he's not crushed by the boat first.'

Alerted by the noise and commotion, Mohammed appeared amidships and, immediately aware of the seriousness of the situation, for the second time in a day, sped off to effect a rescue – this time to the bridge. Lampton, overcome by the sudden, unexpected shock of falling through the railings, was in difficulty and was flailing around in the water, adding to the froth. The gap had widened considerably and the current was pushing him astern towards the paddle.

'Hang on,' screamed Sylvia Baxter, who seemed on the verge of hysteria.

'There's nothing for him to hang on to,' shouted Mr Rotherham, who had released a life-ring from its holder and was about to throw it into the water.

It seemed as if all of this had taken several minutes but, in reality, it had all happened in little more than a few seconds.

Rupert turned to the bows where Ali had pulled in Daoud's rope.

'Ali – the rope! Give me the rope,' he shouted in a mixture of English and pidgin Arabic. 'Take this,' he said, as he threw his jacket at Ali in exchange for the latter's coil of rope.

He leapt into the river and struck out towards the flailing body in the water. He had always been a keen swimmer and had excelled at sport at school, not that his father had been impressed that much; he had wished for more academic progress. Suddenly that didn't matter at all – it was unimportant. Within a couple of seconds he reached the struggling form.

'Can't swim ... can't swim,' gasped Lampton, as he fought to spray out the mouthfuls of water he was taking in.

'I can! – I can!' shouted Rupert. *If the paddle doesn't get us, we'll be fine*, he told himself, in an obscene moment of calm amidst the chaos.

He struggled to get the rope under Lampton's arms and up around his shoulders. Then he struck out for the bank, towing the flailing man in a combination of doggie paddle and treading water. He saw that he was losing the battle. He had to get the other end of the rope around the bollard; otherwise they would both be for the chop – literally.

'Take the rope! – Take the rope!' he shouted at Khatose, who was still on the bank. He had not cast off the stern line and had run towards the bows and the gaping gap in the railings. 'Take the rope!'

Winfield had abandoned any attempt to use what little Arabic he had. With his free hand, he tried to throw the loose end of the rope to the bank. It fell short and splashed into the foam of the water. Khatose scrambled further down the bank, but could not reach the rope before it sank rapidly into the churning water. Rupert tried to gather it in with his free hand to try throwing it again. They were being sucked backwards, toward the paddle. He also realized that he was starting to tire and lose ground in his battle with the river. For a split second a voice in his head told him it was hopeless.

There was a lot of shouting from the steamer and Rupert was suddenly aware of how close to the water's edge Khatose was standing. If he could just be thrown the rope one more time ... he might be close enough to catch it and ... Without warning a dark-skinned arm emerged from the turbulent water and folded itself around both the rapidly tiring form of Rupert Winfield and the struggling Lampton. It was Daoud.

'Daoud! The rope! End of the rope – to Khatose! There!'

shouted Winfield above the noise that seemed to be enfolding them with as much determination as was the water.

'I have it done, Sir,' said Daoud in very passable English. He seemed calm in the mist of the chaos. He was also a very strong swimmer. 'He already has the rope,' he shouted again, this time over his shoulder, as he held the Europeans with one arm and struck out against the suction of the paddle with the other. 'We will move backwards no further until they pull us out. See, the rope is already taut...'

'Nothing to worry about,' said Hopkins reassuringly, as he folded his stethoscope away and put it back in his bag. 'Just a bit of a shock, that's all. Lucky escape, really. Anyway, I've given you something to make you sleep. You'll waken tomorrow morning and feel as right as rain.'

Lampton smiled up at the doctor.

'Thanks for that, Doctor,' he said.

'That's me done,' continued Hopkins. 'I'll drop in before bedtime to make sure you're sleeping as restfully as a baby.' He flashed his smile again. 'With Mrs Lampton to keep you company, you'll be back to normal in no time.'

They both muttered grateful thanks.

'We were very lucky to have you with us, Stephen. Thanks,' said Rupert, who advanced from the back of the cabin, from where he had been watching. He was suddenly conscious that he had used the other's Christian name for the first time.

'That was a very brave thing you did, back there,' said Lampton, who was starting to feel drowsy. 'I owe you my life.'

'Not me as much as both of us owe Daoud,' replied Rupert. 'He's the brave one.'

'Oh, I ... didn't realize ... That he also...' continued Lampton, but his speech was becoming slow, blurred and very quiet.

'Yes – apparently Daoud thought that, as I seemed to be next to useless in the water, something more decisive needed to be done,' continued Rupert, smiling. 'So that's why he shot along the bank, leapt across to the ship – they hadn't cast off the stern yet – and fetched a coil of rope. He's a quick thinker. He tied the rope around himself, threw the other end to Khatose, who scrambled back up the bank to the forward bollard and secured it and ... Well, the rest you know.'

'Yes, brave chap ... that. Must thank ... him ...'

The voice was almost inaudible now, as sleep took control.

'We'll be off then,' said the doctor, motioning Rupert towards the door. 'I'll drop in to see how you are a little later.' He walked to the cabin door. 'Don't feel too bad about things – "accidents will happen", as they say.'

In the passageway outside the Lampton's cabin, Rupert turned to Stephen.

'Mohammed is upset again about this – it's not going to look very good at Head Office, I'm afraid. I can't believe that they didn't secure the railing properly before we left – they've done it so many times before; it should be automatic by now.'

'Perhaps it was just one of those things. At least nobody was *really* hurt...'

Later that evening, a first-class dinner had been followed by detailed analysis of the day's events. Later still, a few of the passengers were taking a final stroll around the deck before turning in for the night. Within a short time the decks cleared, leaving a solitary figure standing next to the railings, quite near to where the accident had happened. The red pin-prick of a cigarette end glowed in the shadows and then arched gracefully out into the light Egyptian night before sinking into the water. The figure moved along the railings and looked idly at the hinge that secured the gangway gate section to the fixed part of the rails. Necessity had prompted running repairs and the two halves had been linked together and secured with heavy wire. A faint smile of success, tinged with annoyance at temporary failure, crossed the figure's face. From the deep pocket of his evening jacket, he drew a heavy steel pin of considerable thickness, slightly longer than the hinge. It was flattened and curled around at one end, forming a kind of handle. The sound of *Khufu* slicing her way through the water hid the sound of the splash, as the pin struck the surface of the water and disappeared. As it did so the figure turned and walked silently off, back to his cabin.

8

Pretoria

23rd June 1928

'It was unfortunate, Sir, an opportunity lost,' said Major Ashdown. 'We were convinced that he would be the one to close the gap in our chain. Regrettably, we had no information to the effect that Grunewald, alias Greenwood, seemed to have had a heart condition.'

'Indeed,' replied the older man from his large, padded leather chair. 'So ... do you think we are any nearer to "closing the gap in the chain", as you put it?' He stared earnestly at Ashdown. 'There are those higher up whose demands for tangible results grow louder each day. They see the prevention of this diamond smuggling as an essential part of proving that we are on top of things – not to mention demonstrating our ability to implement current foreign policy. Are you aware of the present situation regarding Whitehall's stance on foreign policy?'

Ashdown was a little taken aback by the sudden change in direction his superior had taken.

'I have *something* of an idea, Sir, following the details you revealed at our recent briefing, but that was some weeks ago.'

'Yes, it was...' replied the older man, as if trying to recall the exact date when the briefing had taken place. Seemingly, he could not. 'Well, nothing's changed since then,' he continued. 'It seems that Whitehall continues to be concerned about many things, not least of which are the possible threat to the Suez Canal, the expansion of the new ideologies in Germany, the threat of the Russian Bear smacking its lips covetously on the Indian border and the aggressive, expansionist tub-thumping of this Italian chap, Mussolini.' He waved his hands in the air and shrugged, as if to indicate that the perception in high places was that the enemy was already at the gates. 'All of that, plus several other minor issues – it's all behind their current thinking.'

He shifted his position. 'To put it bluntly – and this is for our ears only – Whitehall is concerned about the possibility of the Empire unravelling, with the consequential loss of trade and territory.'

He paused and stared even harder at his subordinate, but Ashdown revealed no emotion. After what had happened to his father and brothers in Tanganyika during the war, he often felt that he had no emotion left to feel.

'Mussolini in Italy is starting to rave on about a new Roman Empire and seems to be set on expansion, probably southwards – they can't really go anywhere else. If that happens and he tries anything in North Africa, it could well provoke another Fashoda incident – especially if it's anywhere near Suez. That would draw us in to protect our interest in the Canal and the link to India. Germany is also causing concern … again.'

'I have read the reports on this Hitler fellow,' said Ashdown. 'His ideas of National Socialism seem to have caught on somewhat in Germany and annoyed the Russians.'

'To Hell with the bloody Russians – wouldn't trust them an inch,' thundered the elder man, 'Not after what they did in '17. Anyway, as far as Whitehall is concerned, the real concerns at the moment are shared between Rome and Hitler.'

'They could have a point, Sir. This Nazi Party that Hitler

leads ... there were reports of rabble-rousing rallies in Nuremberg recently. Apparently our man Hitler is quite an orator. Anyone who has charisma and can use it effectively in public speaking should find it easy to persuade the masses ... sheep-like as they are.'

The elder man smiled at this last remark. Ashdown might have been born and bred in the wilds of Kenya, but he was not totally uninformed when it came to the worldly matters of foreign policy and of human nature.

'Over time I suppose Hitler could become a problem, which could get out of control if not checked,' said the Major.

'London appears to think the same,' replied the other figure. 'Trouble is, short of assassinating him, there doesn't seem all that much we can do about it. You'd think the Germans would have learned their lesson after the last drubbing, but they seem to be re-arming – League of Nations or not! The lessons and consequences of the folly of going to war don't seem to interest them much. At the moment, Whitehall thinks that the only way we can block them is by cutting off as much of their source of income as we can. Possibly a quite brilliant idea, but absolutely like trying to find the proverbial needle in the haystack, wouldn't you say?'

There was more than just a hint of sarcasm in his voice.

'I shouldn't think they have any of their assets lodged with the Bank of England, Sir,' said Ashdown, smiling at the thought, 'so exactly *how* does Whitehall propose that these sources are identified and cut off?'

'Don't ask me!' replied Ashdown's superior, with a dismissive grunt. 'Some bright young spark in London has come up with the idea that the diamonds are being smuggled from under our very noses and then ending up in Germany – to fund the political machine run by these Nazi chaps. On the whole, they seem to be a rather unpleasant bunch, from the reports we've received. Cigarette?'

He reached across the wide expanse of the polished mahogany desk and offered the Major a cigarette from a large silver box. After both cigarettes had been lit, the elder man continued, once again changing the subject. Ashdown began to wonder why. Could it be that his superior, a man many years his senior, was having difficulty remembering the thread of the conversation?

'You lost family in the fighting in Tanganyika, didn't you, Ashdown?' he asked, as the smoke wafted up into the higher recesses of the office ceiling.

'Yes, Sir. My family have farmed coffee in the highlands of Kenya almost since the day the Protectorate was declared – over ten thousand acres. Only my sister and her husband are left there now. He was disabled in the same campaign that took my father, two elder brothers and cousin – down on the coast, near Dar es Salaam.'

'Fighting Lettow-Vorbeck's lot, were they?'

'Yes, Sir. That was in '17 – we'd had no real bother up in Kenya, but the Germans had thumbed their noses at us and by the time the war ended, they were leading everyone a merry dance through Mozambique and across into Northern Rhodesia.' There was angry resentment in his voice. 'My family had gone off with a contingent of the King's African Rifles. They were to act as trackers and guides, as we were all used to the bush and could easily read its language. Their column was ambushed by the German colonial troops.' He paused and, in his memory, stared at the sudden endless infinity of the desk in front of him. 'Very few survived to report the disaster – my family were not amongst them.'

The elder man looked at Ashdown – there wasn't much that seemed appropriate to say, given the circumstances.

'You mustn't dwell on it, old chap,' said the other figure, almost paternally. 'These things happen in war.'

'Indeed they do, but it doesn't excuse carelessness or

lack of intelligence, Sir. I had been sent back to base for more ammunition and supplies, whilst the column moved forward and walked into a trap...' He paused, recalling the events. '...A trap that could easily have been avoided if our chaps at HQ had got their facts straight.' His voice rang again with the steel edge of barely suppressed resentment. 'If they'd walked out of it again, that would have been one thing – as it was, most of them did not, including my own people, Sir. That's what I find hard to live with – they were sacrificed to someone else's gross incompetence.'

'Quite so, old chap.' Lieutenant-General James Shorrocks (retired) leaned back, rested his arms on the arms of his comfortable, padded chair and stared intently at his subordinate. 'So that's why you opted for Military Intelligence, then?' he asked, more by way of a statement of fact than a probing question.

'Yes, Sir. With respect, if we could perhaps return to the matter of Grunewald and the mine...'

Shorrocks looked at his subordinate, but the man's words seemed to grow dimmer and dimmer, the more his mouth moved. The older man had occasionally come across men like this Major – young men eager to avenge some past grievance, or to win promotion or to just make some sort of a mark on life – and he judged the Major to be a mixture of all three. Perhaps that was why this young man managed to deliver results to the extent that he did, driven by the fire of an inner zeal which was uncommonly rare. Shorrocks then allowed his thoughts to drift to his own past. He had enjoyed a long and illustrious career and had survived the fiasco of the Gallipoli campaign, emerging with a Military Cross to add to the impressive medal ribbons he already had attached to his now seldom-worn uniform. He was a career soldier who had always taken his responsibilities very seriously. It had irked him that sometimes his fellow officers were callous, incompetent or – at worst – just plain stupid.

He had taken the interests and welfare of his troops to heart: the fact that this had all too often not been a shared emotion with the other senior officers at HQ had been one of the reasons that had driven him to hang up his uniform and move into the anonymous mechanics of Military Intelligence, Southern Africa Command. From his top-floor office in the newly built Union Buildings he administered a secret empire of intrigue, information and – frequently – death.

'... So we managed to get something out of him before he died, but it doesn't really make much sense, I'm afraid, Sir.'

The Major was still talking. Shorrocks was brought back from his reverie, not having heard much of the Major's conversation.

'Not a complete waste of effort then, eh? So tell me, what did you manage to get out of him?' he asked, hoping that Ashdown would repeat some of what he had just said.

The Major looked a little surprised at the question. Perhaps his earlier observation regarding the state of his superior's mental health had not been far off the mark. He repeated part of what he had just said.

'It was very hard to hear, what with the foaming at the mouth and the spasms brought on by the heart attack. And he was speaking German, which was hardly surprising. We knew that Grunewald was German and that his family had lived in the old German South-West Africa for years. They lost everything after the war.'

'As did so many others,' murmured the Lieutenant-General, 'on both sides.'

'What he said sounded like "griffin", but we couldn't be totally sure.'

'"Griffin"?' repeated Ashdown's superior slowly, looking thoughtfully at the Major. Then he reached across to his in-tray and took out a small pile of manila folders.

'Yes, Sir – "griffin". That's what it sounded like,' repeated Ashdown.

Shorrocks put the folders on the desk in front of him and opened the top one. His eyes had become sharp and shone like black jet. He was thinking.

'We also know that Grunewald was visited earlier on the same day that we visited him. Our source reported that his first visitor was a tall, aristocratic figure dressed in black and carrying a cane. Our chap did think it odd that this mysterious man in black carried a cane in the first place because he strode off at such a pace as to suggest that the aid of such a thing was not necessary,' continued Ashdown.

'Gentlemen often carry a cane,' replied Shorrocks distractedly. 'It is not dependent on the physical state.'

'As you say, Sir – but they are more likely to do so strolling along the paved streets of London or Cape Town than they are around a sandy diamond mine in the middle of nowhere.'

'Possibly ... you could well have a point there,' said Shorrocks, opening the third folder. 'Ah ... here it is. This might be of interest ... it came in with the other reports first thing this morning. I thought it was routine when I read it, but, after what you have just said, I'm not so sure. It might take us somewhere.'

He picked up a sheet of paper on which was typed a short report. Holding it in his hand, he proceeded to give Ashdown the gist of its contents.

'This incident took place up on the Southern Rhodesian border late yesterday afternoon, just before the crossing closed for the night – a car broke down just this side of the bridge. Apparently the police at the crossing had to go and help. The passenger was quite irate about the "incompetence of the idiot driver", as he apparently put it. Eventually, the police managed to get the car going again – something about a broken distributor cap or some such thing – anyway, the gentleman in question was extremely authoritative, rather tall, dressed in black and he carried a heavy walking cane...'

Major Ashford, too, was suddenly alert and very interested.

'It seems he wielded the thing more like a rapier than a walking stick, according to the officer in charge, who says that he nearly got hit by it,' continued the Lieutenant-General.

'And that was yesterday afternoon – at Beit Bridge?' asked Ashford.

'Yes,' replied the elder man, 'quite routine in itself, but this is the interesting point. The handle of the cane was silver and was fashioned into a big bird...' He adjusted his half-round, tortoiseshell glasses, before reading out loud from the sheet: ' "Dragon- or bird-shaped head with unfolded bird's wings and what looked like red rubies for eyes." It obviously impressed the chap who wrote the report,' he concluded, with a chuckle.

'A dragon-type beast with wings ... that could ... well, it's possible it could be...'

'A griffin?' Shorrocks completed Ashdown's sentence for him. 'Could there be a link, I wonder? Greenwood – griffin – the stones? It's all rather tenuous.'

Ashdown's face was lined with acute concentration.

'Possibly, Sir...' replied the Major slowly, more to himself than to his superior. His mind was trying to fit together the as yet unmatched pieces of an unknown puzzle. '... Greenwood – griffin – Beit Bridge – a heavy cane with an ornate handle – and the stones...'

The Head of Military Intelligence replaced the sheet in the folder and closed it. Then he spoke to Ashdown in a tired, but firm voice.

'I suggest you get off straight away and see if you can make anything of it – try and find a trail – if there is one. Get on with it before things go cold.'

'What about the driver of this vehicle, Sir? Any description ... ?'

'Nothing, except that the police thought he might be Asian. They didn't even think to take down the number plate – they must have been simply relieved to see the back of them, I shouldn't wonder.'

Shorrocks pressed the button on a large wooden box, which stood on the desk conveniently at his left elbow. The front of it was covered in a circle of fine wire mesh.

'Could you come in for a moment, please?' he said into the mesh, before letting go of the button.

'I'll have a letter of introduction drawn up for you – look after it. If your investigation leads to anything further afield, it will get you all the assistance you need – right the way to Whitehall, if necessary. You'd better get straight off – if there is a trail it might still be warm. Good luck.'

9

El-Bisaliya Qibil

The Nile, at El-Bisaliya Qibil – 20th July 1928

Khufu was moored alongside a wooden jetty that thrust along the rocky, boulder-strewn bank of the Nile at the little town of El-Bisaliya Qibil, halfway between Luxor and Aswan. It was early evening and the lights of the little town were bravely attempting to hold back the advancing tide of dusk. Osiris and the countless hosts of his faithful departed would soon begin their ancient journey over the west bank of the river and onward through eternity, shrouding everything in the cooling cloak of the darkness of the night. From the tall minaret of the solitary mosque, the muezzin called a different host of the faithful to different prayers.

'Some say this is where it really took root, you know.'

'Oh ... hello. You took me by surprise.' Rupert turned his head and smiled at Stephen Hopkins. 'What took root here?' he asked.

'Christianity,' answered Hopkins, 'the Copts – the earliest sect. We call it Coptic Christianity now. Look – over there. See the twin towers of faith – one is the mosque and the other, the shorter one right next to it, is the local church. They're nestled in quite comfortably next to each other.' He pointed in the direction of the buildings. 'It's been like that for centuries; the Islamic crescent seems to get along with the Christian cross well enough ... despite the mess the Crusaders made of inter-faith relationships when they blundered into the Middle East.'

Rupert did not seem to have heard the other man's comment on the Crusaders.

'I'd noticed that before – it's the same all over the place, wherever there's a large enough settlement you'll see the spire and the minaret. I never gave it much thought...'

'Is that because you were stunned by the "savage beauty" of the scene which lay before you?' asked the doctor, not looking at the other man, but repeating one of the phrases Rupert had used earlier in the day.

Rupert wasn't sure if he was being sarcastic or not.

'What did you think of our excursion today?' he asked.

In an attempt to beat the heat, they had set off that morning before dawn on their journey to the temple and pyramid of Hathor, the mother goddess, the Mother of Kings.

'Hmm ... quite interesting, in its own right ... the belief patterns and all that,' replied the doctor enigmatically.

'Well, you must admit that the site really is quite beautiful – and it *does* possess a savage beauty – and being off the beaten track has also helped preserve it,' said Rupert. 'Hathor was one of the most important of the ancient Egyptian gods. She was the deity who welcomed the dead into the afterlife, so Pharaoh and commoner alike paid her due respect in equal measure...'

'...And with equal enthusiasm, just to hedge their bets,' murmured Stephen, with a chuckle.

'Most amusing,' replied Rupert, who took his love of Egyptology extremely seriously, even if others did not. 'What we visited today is one of the best preserved of the monuments of the New Kingdom, from about 1450 BC.'

'You're right,' said Stephen, suddenly becoming more serious, as he realized how intense his companion had become. 'It *is* quite an achievement to have survived three thousand-odd years and still be that well preserved.'

They were leaning on the rails of the top deck of the little white steamship, gazing out into the fading, oriental exoticism which spread itself before them. Beneath them, from the dining room, they could hear the sound of cutlery and crockery being prepared for the evening meal. They were comforting sounds, which gave the feeling that everything had returned to normal, following the incidents of the previous day. In the companionable silence, which now descended between the two men, Rupert recalled that he had suggested to Mohammed that perhaps it would be a good idea to extend their stay at Esna for twenty-four hours, just to give the passengers a chance to settle down after the unfortunate incident in the river. The little Egyptian, as punctilious as ever, had found all manner of reasons as to why they should not. He wanted to press on with the schedule. Rupert had diplomatically pointed out that delaying their departure, even briefly, would show Head Office that they were fully in charge of the situation and, most importantly, attentive to the welfare of their charges on the tour. He was at pains to point out that some of them could still be suffering from shock.

'We don't want to rush them off up the Nile until they've settled down a bit. That business in the water has really upset some of them. The last thing we want is to have Mrs Grassmere making any sort of complaint to Head Office about her nerves, now do we?'

At first, even the mention of Mrs Grassmere had not managed to persuade Mohammed to delay their departure from Esna, although he had discreetly voiced his opinion that he found Mrs Grassmere almost more than his limitless reserve of polite good manners could cope with. Nevertheless, Rupert had persevered and, eventually, Mohammed had come around to his idea.

'Well, most agreeably, Mr Rupert, when we consider the position from such an angle, we must first put the welfare of our guests before our desire to be remaining on time with our table.' (Rupert had insisted that Mohammed use his Christian name when they were alone. Announcing himself to be very honoured, the little Egyptian had agreed but, he had said, he would feel far too uncomfortable with such familiarity if the title of Mr were to be dispensed with as well.) 'And you are right. We have, ourselves, to be searching with intensity for the reason of the open railing gate. That itself will be needing to be explained to Head Office.' His face clouded with the visible signs of puzzlement. 'I am not understanding how such a things can happen, *insha'Allah*, but, Mr Rupert, I am thinking it is of the best to press ahead as soon as is being possible, nevertheless.'

And so, after further discussion, Mohammed had agreed to an evening sailing instead of an afternoon one. According to his reasoning, this would allow for passenger calming, where necessary, and – assuming a clear river passage during the night – not too much of a serious deviation from the timetable.

On *Khufu*'s top deck, the lighting, such as it was, was slowly bursting forth upon the rapidly encroaching darkness. Stephen shifted his position slightly to relieve the pressure on his stump. They had done a lot of walking at the temple that day and the heat and chafing had begun to bother him.

'So,' he said quietly, 'what about the business on the stairs with our little Miss Eggerton? An accident...?' he left the sentence unfinished.

'Pardon?' said Rupert, surprised at the line of questioning.

'Little Miss Eggerton and her fall. An accident, do you think?' repeated Hopkins.

'Well, of course,' answered Rupert. 'Don't you think it was?'

'In all probability, yes,' replied Stephen. He paused. 'What about Mr Lampton and his unexpected encounter with the waters of the Nile, then?' His eyes were alert, but there was no hint of a smile on his lips, as he turned and looked at Rupert.

'Er ... I'm not at all sure if I should be discussing that with a passenger – no offence intended. I am afraid it is purely a company matter,' replied Rupert.

'And quite right, too,' replied Hopkins, smiling broadly, 'but you and I are kindred spirits, and if we can't talk about such things, then who can?'

'Are we?' replied Rupert, who was not quite sure if he understood what the other man was saying. '...Kindred spirits? In what way?'

'My dear chap,' continued Stephen, 'of course we are.'

Rupert was suddenly aware of the tingling and electricity that seemed to once again course through his body. He was at a bit of a loss as to what to say next and stuttered over his reply.

'I don't quite ... How do you ... You could possib...'

'So, what about Mr Lampton, then?' asked Hopkins again, turning his gaze back to the bank.

'Well ... naturally ... it shouldn't have happened – the gate just swinging out like that, I mean. Mohammed was quite annoyed – no, he was *very* upset by that bit of carelessness. He says he's going to find who it was that had been *that* careless and...'

Stephen cut gently across him.

'My dear fellow, have you stopped to think about the mechanism involved? Three metal eyes welded onto the vertical upright of the opening gateway and another three welded onto the upright of the fixed railing. Close the gate, the eyes line up, you slide the steel fixing pin through the lot and gravity does the rest.' He acted out what he had just described. 'A bit odd that one of your crew should *forget* to put the pin through. You know how proudly possessive they become when they get given a bit of responsibility ...

It's one-upmanship or pure pride over the rest of their chaps.'

'Well, Mohammed finds it hard to believe that Khatose just *forgot*. I have to say that, knowing how hard-working the chap is, I have to agree,' answered Rupert.

'Exactly my point,' said Hopkins, 'so, considering the scene of the crime, my dear Watson, who can we recall as being in the vicinity? Most of your tourists were strung out along the railings, watching the departure. Of interest, there were the Misses Cuttle and Baxter – they were standing quite close to the gate. And next to them...?'

'Richard Lampton ... before he fell into the river,' answered Rupert.

'No, old boy, he was standing *behind* them, with his good lady wife. Next to the Cuttle/Baxter duo was our friend with the jaw problem – Sebastian Printon.'

'How do you know all this with such certainty, Stephen?'

'Eyes in the back of my head, old chap. It was Printon who took the photograph and Lampton who took his place in front of the gateway. It was also Printon who kept telling them to move further back towards the rails ... until Lampton finally went clean through and landed in the river.'

'Hang on, are you suggesting Printon was responsible?' asked Rupert, somewhat taken aback. He had no experience with this Sherlock Holmes-like detective business.

'Well, think about it. He could well have had the time to remove the pin before getting Lampton to take his place next to the railings. The whinnying Miss Cuttle had to ask him a couple of times to join them in the photo, before he refused and then suggested Lampton do so instead. He'd have had a couple of seconds to think up something like removing the pin. No one would have noticed – there was such a lot of activity going on and, in any case, most people were watching the shore.' He turned to look at Rupert. 'He could have done it. Question is, what would be his motive for doing so? Why would he have it in for Lampton?'

'Well, they are a bit of an odd bunch, this trip,' said Rupert. 'There's Mrs Grassmere – ask old Mohammed about her! – then the Arlings – she's a strange one, although he seems quite pleasant – Miss Eggerton, Marjory Cuttle, Colonel Ponsworthy... Mr Grupfelder, that quiet Kormann fellow...'

He continued counting off the other passengers on the tour. 'I can't see that any of them would have any reason to do anything to anyone.' He paused for a moment. 'Except possibly to Mrs Grassmere...' he added in a half-whisper.

Hopkins chuckled at this momentary lapse of etiquette from Rupert. He took his silver cigarette case from the inside pocket of his jacket. He smoked far too much, but he found it helped the throbbing in his stump. He took one and offered Rupert one.

'In several respects, she is a little on the large side,' he said, as he replaced the cigarette case in his pocket. 'When referring to her one could even be forgiven for using the term "over-inflated", both in girth and assessment of her own importance,' he added, with a chuckle.

As the lighter flared into life, the light cast the doctor's features into sharp profile. For a split second, Rupert felt giddy at the attraction he had started to feel for this man – and then the image was gone. As suddenly as the light had blazed forth, it died away; Rupert took a deep lungful of tobacco smoke and exhaled it in a continuous cloud, over the side of *Khufu*.

'Printon hasn't been on the trip from the beginning either, has he?' asked Hopkins. 'He joined us in Luxor.'

'Yes, so he hasn't been on the tour as long as the rest of them – it's not as if he's had time to make enemies. Perhaps he knows someone from before ... on another holiday?'

'For someone who was late joining our happy little band

and who then had to settle in and get to know the others, his name seems to pop up with considerable regularity, would you not say?'

'Remember that he had a problem with his jaw,' replied Rupert, who had not fully grasped the implication behind the other's remark. 'It seems that when he collected his ticket, the booking clerks at Head Office in Cairo could hardly understand a word he was saying. Anyway, that's what their telegram said. Mohammed showed it to me when we were in Luxor.'

'Not *our* friend Printon's jaw...'

'Pardon?'

'Not *our* friend Printon,' repeated Stephen, his voice barely raised above a whisper. 'Did you notice what he ate for dinner last evening? There's nothing wrong with *his* jaws or teeth.'

'But how can that be? He's supposed to have had an abscess or something equally as unpleasant. I also know that Head Office made a silly little typing mistake with his name on the passenger list ... a full stop in the wrong place.' Rupert's face suddenly lit up. 'You don't suppose that we've got the wrong person?'

'I can't see that happening myself,' replied Stephen, 'but the lack of a convincing explanation for so trivial a conundrum doesn't make things any clearer, does it? Our man Printon speaks, eats and drinks normally ... I'd say his jaws are quite satisfactory.'

He flicked the end of his cigarette over the side. It fell to the water, a glowing ruby extinguished by the greedy waters of the river.

'I begin to feel that two and two are not making four,' said the doctor.

Dinner passed off uneventfully. There was a considerable

amount of conversation – the usual social inanities, interspersed with the occasional discussion of Egyptology, the Stock Market, world events or, in the case of Mrs Grassmere, herself and her legion of ailments and dissatisfactions. After the meal, most of the party dispersed to their individual pursuits – some to play bridge in the lounge, some to promenade around the deck before turning in and others to tables in the forward observation lounge for coffee and brandies. Rupert had managed to seat himself at a table with Hopkins. They were joined by the Arlings. In the far corner of the lounge sat Colonel Ponsworthy with the Misses Cuttle and Eggerton, the latter of whom now seemed totally recovered from the excitement of the previous day. With them sat Susan and Richard Lampton. Although he had spent much of the day in bed, he had felt well enough to join everyone else for dinner. Kormann and Grupfelder were sitting talking and Mrs Kirby was trying to get rid of Mr Rotherham, who was sitting at her table and obviously annoying her intensely.

'It's been very pleasant having that little extra time yesterday – I was able to go wandering around on shore,' smiled Esther Arling. 'I've bought a few little things – nothing too expensive.' She smiled in her husband's direction.

'Hmm...' muttered her husband, who did not look too pleased.

'Are we back on schedule, Rupert?' asked Arling.

'Absolutely – *reis* Tarek did well to get us to El-Bisaliya during the wee small hours last night. Did you enjoy your excursion to the Temple of Hathor?'

'I did,' answered Esther Arling, 'I find it all so sensual,' she purred, 'when a god is dedicated to sex: the Egyptian Hathor, the Greek Aphrodite and the Romans with Venus and Cupid – man and woman. How remarkable that there should be deities to personify what we all discover for ourselves ... sooner or later.' Rupert noticed that she was pouting at him; it made him feel just a little uncomfortable. 'The Mother of Kings – didn't you say Hathor was called the "Womb of Horus"?' She ran her hand, which had been resting on her shoulder, inside her evening dress, down towards the curve of her left breast as she spoke. She patted Rupert's shoulder with her other hand, the brilliant red of her fingernails showing up starkly against the black of his dinner jacket. 'They were not afraid of showing off their sexuality, were they?' she asked.

'My dear...' said Simon Arling, quietly, to his wife.

'No ... she's quite right, they were not in the least squeamish about such things – certainly nowhere near as touchy as we've become in our own time,' replied Rupert, turning a little in his seat towards Stephen, in an effort to discreetly distance himself from Mrs Arling. 'You'll see that they were not in the least embarrassed about procreation either – we'll see the temple engravings that show that, when we visit Karnak and some of the other places.'

Esther Arling was about to say something else, but was prevented from doing so by her husband.

'So, you were saying, Rupert, we're back on schedule, then?'

'Oh yes. We'll set off before midnight and should be in Edfu within a couple of hours – it's not that far from here. There are interesting things to see at Edfu. I'll be giving a short talk after breakfast. I'll fill you in on the details then.'

A waiter appeared carrying brandy balloons on a tray. Esther Arling reached up to take one from the tray, partially exposing the curve of her breast as she did so. Rupert flinched inwardly – she had, undoubtedly, made the provocative gesture on purpose. He thought her attractive in a flashy sort of way, if that was your taste, like one of those pictures of a female model you sometimes saw on a cheap calendar. He also found it hard to see anything in her that would appeal to her husband. He was the intellectual; in Rupert's assessment she was the trollop, for want of a better word.

'So, how is our patient doing?' asked her husband, turning to the doctor.

'Very well – almost as good as new, I shouldn't wonder,' replied Hopkins. 'It was more the shock of it all, rather than anything broken,' he added, smiling. 'He's sitting over there, actually.'

'Excellent ... fine,' said Esther. 'That's good.'

'So far, quite an eventful trip,' said Simon, breathing out smoke from the cigarette he had just lit. 'Anybody else fancy one?' he asked.

Half an hour passed in pleasant conversation about generalities and the political state of the world. Esther Arling continued to push her feminine charms, which Rupert found increasingly irksome. In fact, he was beginning to find that, like Mrs Grassmere, but for totally different reasons, Esther Arling was tolerable only in small doses. He had never felt any real attraction to what he considered to be 'normal' women: prolonged exposure to Esther Arling's company he found disconcerting.

'That's me done for the night,' said Hopkins. 'I think I'll do a circuit around the deck and turn in – early start tomorrow.' He stood up with ease, disguising the limp which everyone had noticed on the first day.

'I think I'll turn in, too,' said Rupert. 'Don't forget there's a pre-visit talk on Edfu tomorrow morning at seven. Sorry for the early start, but if we don't get going by nine it'll be far too hot to do anything, except wilt!'

The others laughed. Esther took a pouting sip from her second brandy and smiled at them both.

'Good night, then.'

'Good night. Don't forget, tomorrow morning at seven.'

As they walked out of the room, they passed the Lamptons,

who were deep in conversation at a table by themselves. Stephen was aware of Richard Lampton saying something about having known somebody in the army, but they passed the couple too quickly to hear any more.

'Well, Susan, I'm telling you that I did know *a* Sebastian Printon for a while – back in the Royal Engineers – during the war. Fair enough, I *hardly* knew him, but he was a hell of a nice chap and left a deep impression on me. From what I remember, this Printon *could* be about the same build and height ... Besides which, I've seen his passport.'

There was a silence as Lampton silently investigated the records of his past, whilst his wife smiled patiently at him, saying nothing. Her husband was a man of fortitude and considerable resilience. He had weathered the experience in the river, sleeping off the effects within a couple of hours and now, after a day of taking things easy, he was restored to his usual self. Refreshed, his mind was now centred on the question of Mr Sebastian Printon.

'I think he'd grown up in South Africa ... or am I getting him muddled up with somebody else?' His wife smiled, tolerantly. 'I remember he had a degree – in Civil Engineering – and he was always talking about dams and bridges – that sort of thing.' Susan Lampton looked calmly at her husband. Sometimes he could be as tenacious as a fox terrier.

'Perhaps that was another man with the same name, dear,' she said patiently. Her husband's obsession with Printon was beginning to become tedious.

'Well, it's not that common a name, is it now? I haven't come across it again since the war,' replied her husband, still trying to recover from the non-committal response his earlier, well-intentioned enquiry had elicited from Printon.

'You have to face the fact, Richard, that if the man doesn't want to be your friend, there is nothing you can do to make him change his mind,' retorted his wife, eager to move on to a less boring topic of conversation.

At his table, Printon was sipping a brandy, avoiding any eye contact with Lampton.

'And there was something about him – I just can't remember what ... Blast it! But there was something about him ... I read it somewhere ... after the war...'

Once again leaning on the rails of the upper deck, the two men looked idly through the smoke of their last cigarette for the day, out into the dark stillness of the sleeping town.

'Is it just my imagination, or is Mrs Arling what we would call in polite society a *femme fatale*?' asked Rupert.

Hopkins laughed.

'Yes – you can't really fail to notice, can you? She can be quite pushy, can't she?'

'Her pushiness doesn't seem to upset Mr Arling that much, though,' said Rupert. 'Perhaps he's used to it.'

'To be honest, I should think he's far more interested in the politics of Europe than in his wife's performances. It takes all sorts...'

Stephen inclined his head slightly.

'So he's a political person?' asked Rupert.

'Indeed, I had a long chat with him when we first set off – he seemed to be impressed by what that Stresemann chap has done to get Germany back on its feet. He shared the Nobel Peace prize a couple of years ago. Arling was very impressed with him. He even admitted having some initial thoughts that Hitler had one or two sound ideas, too. That I thought was a bit odd, considering that the Arlings are Jewish and some papers are carrying reports about the increase of anti-Semitism over there. Mind you, their Foreign Minister was assassinated a couple of years back, if I remember correctly ... and he was a Jew. From what little I've read, this Hitler does not like the Jews at all. If Stresemann and his chaps can't achieve a really stable Germany in the long term there's no telling what might happen in the vacuum such a failure would create amongst the masses.'

Something in his tone made Rupert turn and look at him with curious interest.

'Do you think there could be trouble?'

'It's quite possible, old chap.' Stephen lowered his head and stared even harder into the river's darkness far below. 'If the Weimar Republic collapses because it can't achieve a stable Germany, the field could be well and truly open to anyone else who thinks that they can. And that includes our Mr Hitler. As I see it, the problem is that anyone who can do that is going to be difficult to influence in the future: mass popularity, saviour of the people and all that sort of thing.'

'I didn't realize you were so well up on current affairs, Stephen.' Winfield had use the other man's Christian name again, almost automatically and with great ease.

'I've quite a keen interest, old chap. Humans are like sheep en masse – they need a leader, particularly one who makes them believe they have *self-worth* and that they actually *count* for something. When that happens, blind obedience often turns the leader into a god or a tyrant – or both. Either way, they learn they can afford to pay little or no interest to foreign opinions. That makes them difficult to control – if you understand my meaning.'

'Yes, I think so,' replied Rupert, 'and I am in awe of your understanding. It's very impressive.'

Hopkins turned and smiled at him – and Rupert felt the tingling and electric shocks race yet again through his whole being. There was also something in the smile, which suggested that the feeling might just – possibly – be mutual.

'Arling said he would wait and see about Hitler ... Funny though, him being Jewish and Hitler being anti- ... I wonder if friend Arling has a Zionist connection with Palestine? That's a thought...' muttered Hopkins to himself. After a few seconds of silent pondering, he continued. 'And he says he comes from a wealthy family, too; not that you'd think it to look at him.' The doctor smiled at Rupert. 'Which does not hold true for Mrs Arling, who seems to be a real painted tart with expensive, somewhat sensual tastes – as she could well have shown you tonight, my dear fellow, if what I saw was anything to go by…'

He chuckled and gave Rupert a friendly punch on the shoulder, by way of admonition.

10

Salisbury

Southern Rhodesia – 29th June 1928

Against the backdrop of a pale-blue, cloudless sky, which promised a pleasant morning, the city was slowly coming to grips with the birth of a new day. In the streets, motor vehicles jostled noisily with African carts, some of which were towed by objecting donkeys, some of which were simply pushed along by their owners. It was market day and soon the open-air space set aside for the trading and bartering of goods would begin to fill up with the produce and merchandise of the outlying settlements. Although quite modest by Western standards, Salisbury was, nonetheless, the pulsating hub of colonial Southern Rhodesia. Indeed, it was a usual topic of conversation in the 'Whites only' clubs, as to which city pulsated more: Salisbury, the capital, or neighbouring Bulawayo, down to the south.

One point in favour of Salisbury was the existence of the Rhodes Hotel. Each of its two storeys was heavily decorated with intricate, wrought-iron tracery, which had been imported at outlandish expense from a Scottish foundry when the hotel had been built in 1898. The investment had been a wise one and the establishment had never failed to deliver on the luxury promised by such an outward display of opulence. Its clientele were the wealthy and well-to-do, not only of the Rhodesias, but also of the rest of British Colonial

Africa. They were wined and dined; their every need catered for under the benign supervision of the large bronze bust of Cecil John Rhodes, founder of the Rhodesias, which had place of honour in the main entrance foyer. Indeed, there were those who put The Rhodes on a par with Shepheard's in Cairo or even The Savoy in London.

As was usual each morning at this time, the chairs on the hotel's spacious verandas were nearly all occupied. At one of them sat a tall, hawk-like individual. He stared out over the scene, which was slowly animating before him. Out in the street all was movement and commotion. Within the confines of the Rhodes Hotel, divided from the masses by wrought-iron railings, all was quiet, measured grace and comfort. In the reality of the world beyond, things were far more hectic.

'*Bwana*'s coffee,' murmured a waiter, as he deftly placed the hot drink onto a small round table which stood next to the hawk-like guest. The waiter was ignored completely, the *bwana* displaying an indifferent arrogance which showed his belief in the opinion that the lesser races were destined to serve the more advanced ones. As the waiter withdrew, the large black tassel on his tall red fez swung around dramatically as he turned away, as if in a gesture of defiance.

The tall guest picked up his cup and quietly sipped the hot, refreshing liquid. He was quite pleased with himself. So far things had gone very well; even that fool of a driver and those bungling police at the border had presented no real obstacle. The driver had been silenced; the authorities would eventually find the body and wrecked car. He smiled inwardly to himself – by then he would be long gone and the trail would be cold. He drained the contents of his cup and replaced it on the tray before taking out a white handkerchief to wipe his mouth. In the corner of the square of fine linen was the figure of an animal, a phoenix-like bird, embroidered in silver and red thread. Deftly, he refolded the square of fabric and returned it to his pocket.

In the street, the driver of a motor vehicle was impatiently sounding its horn at an elderly man pushing a handcart that was piled high with cabbages. Moving much slower than the vehicle, he had tried to cross the road in front of the truck. His misjudgement of the distance and time had brought the vehicle to a standstill and given the Indian driver the opportunity to further highlight the slowness of the African carter by loud shouting and angry waving of his fist. It was almost a perfect demonstration of what some would regard as the need to perpetuate the pecking order of advanced races over the lower races. The Indian driver was not about to let the African forget that it was he who was in the latter category.

'Fools!' muttered the tall man, as he retrieved his cane from between his legs and rested his hands on the ornate handle. The ruby eyes of The Phoenix sparkled in the reflected morning light.

On the other side of the city, Major Jeremy Ashdown was waiting in the outer office of the Commissioner of the British South Africa Police in Rhodesia.

'I really am sorry about this delay, Sir,' apologized the secretary. 'The Commissioner hates to be late with his appointments. I am sure the delay won't be much longer. Would you like more tea?'

'No ... thank you,' smiled Major Ashdown, 'very kind of you.'

The walls of the office were panelled in dark wood and hung with a display of photographs. The Major rose from his chair, smiled faintly at the secretary, and crossed the large space of the outer office to look at them. They recorded the early days of the British South Africa Police in pictures, which, despite being carefully mounted behind protective glass, were now starting to show their age. As Ashdown looked at the photos, he was reminded of his own background, growing up on the family farm in the Kenya Highlands. Here, too, in these fading photographs, were tough frontiersmen, standing around in front of settlers' wagons. He read the captions – details about the Force having been formed back in 1889 to protect white settlers coming up from South Africa, to the promised land of the soon-to-be-named Rhodesia. Also displayed were photographs of lines of smartly turned-out troopers at the celebratory parade in Pretoria at the end of the Boer War in 1902.

'The Force really has the most splendid history,' a voice said quietly from behind him. 'They have been through a lot and today guarantee the security of all Rhodesians.'

He turned to look at the woman, who had silently crossed the highly polished floor of the office and now stood next to, but respectfully slightly behind, him. She was middle-aged, smartly dressed in a white blouse and pale-grey skirt and she wore glasses. Her hair was gathered gently into a bun on the back of her head, but it did not make her look severe in any way. Ashdown appraised her and lustfully thought that when she had been a young woman in her twenties she would have been an absolute stunner. Judging by her soft accent she almost certainly had grown up in this part of Africa. Now in her mid-forties, this still-attractive and elegant woman seemed to symbolize the very age, grace and beauty of Southern Rhodesia itself.

'The First Settlers probably wouldn't have survived without their protection,' she continued quietly. 'They had a really hard time defending themselves against the natives.'

Little wonder, Ashdown reflected. *They were trying to take their land from them.*

The Major was first and foremost a colonial, but he regarded himself as a 'new' colonial – one who had arrived at the conclusion that the only way of ensuring the continued prosperity and happiness of all was to work together to ensure stability. These had been radical and highly dangerous views to hold in the pre-war social whirl of the Kenyan 'White' Highlands and he had learned to keep such thoughts private. Only once had he dared try to steer the conversation towards the topic of greater equality between the races. Unfortunately, it had been during a dinner party hosted by his family at their farmstead. There were neighbours present and his father had only just managed to control his outburst of embarrassed rage; afterwards, he had avoided his eldest son and heir for most of the following week.

Ashdown moved further on along the row of pictures.

'Presumably these are of the Boer War?' he asked, more out of politeness than curiosity. He had already read the printed inscription underneath the photographs.

'Oh yes,' replied the secretary, 'two VCs won in that struggle. The first was at Spionkop and the second at Ladysmith.'

'Really?' he replied, 'I wasn't aware that the Force was actively involved that far south.'

'Oh yes, they were all volunteers and fought as small, contained command groups – "cells", I think that's what they were called. Like the Boers, who called theirs *Kommandos*. But we thought of it before the Boers did.'

'Indeed? You are remarkably well informed on the topic,' he said, turning to smile at her.

She removed her glasses. A look of fond loss, mingled with deep affection, crossed her features.

'My late husband was in the Force. He was a young man in that conflict,' she pointed to the Boer War photograph, 'and he survived that one,' she continued, pointing to the Great War photographs. 'That's him there,' she said, pointing at a tall, bearded man. 'It was at the surrender of the Army of German East Africa – in Tanganyika – at Abercorn in 1918, after the war in Europe had ended.' She adjusted her glasses, the better to focus on the photograph, a look of melancholy clouding her eyes. 'He was always proud to have fought that German general – something Vorbeck, his name was, I think...'

'Lettow-Vorbeck,' said Ashdown quietly.

'Yes, that's him. John always said that he admired him – he was a good soldier, he said, to have lasted the entire war with his little African army. He caused us a great deal of trouble and loss, you know.'

That same general's outstanding military ability had also caused Ashdown a great deal of trouble and loss, but he said nothing.

'And then, after all of that, John was killed when he was hit by one of those noisy motor vehicles.'

Her voice had a bitter tinge to it now. She reached out again and touched the figure in the photograph lightly with her finger. Ashdown had no wish to dwell on the woman's emotional memories, so he moved on to the next photograph.

'That one is a column that was sent up into German Eas...'

A buzzer sounded twice from somewhere underneath her desk.

'There you are,' she said quietly, all trace of bitterness gone from her voice, 'The Commissioner is ready for you now. Please...' she said, crossing to the heavy door, which separated her from the centre of Rhodesian security and power, '...do go in.'

The Commissioner looked up from reading Ashdown's letter – that, at least, had been taken straight in, even if Ashdown had been asked to wait. Over the top of his glasses he stared with new-found respect at the young, tanned and, on the strength of the letter, obviously highly competent young Major standing opposite him.

'I am sure you are acquainted with the contents of this letter, which has come from the highest authority', said the

FATAL TEARS

Commissioner. 'Of course, we will do all we can to assist you in your investigation, Major. Please, sit down.'

'Thank you, Sir,' replied Ashdown. 'I only wish I had a clearer idea as to exactly what it is that I am investigating. We have one or two ideas, but nothing concrete as yet.'

He was playing his cards very close to his chest and had long ago learned that information was best dispensed on a need-to-know basis. At present, all the details the Commissioner needed to know were contained in the letter the Major had presented to him.

'As I was saying,' continued the Commissioner, 'I apologize for the delay you experienced earlier on. We have had rather a serious matter to contend with, I'm afraid. Here in Rhodesia, crime is usually a pretty low-key affair. Almost invariably, the blacks are both perpetrator and victim. We still have a problem trying to civilize most of them – they don't seem to have much of an idea of what we expect of them, I'm afraid.'

Ashdown winced inwardly at the patronizing tone. This man was definitely not a 'new' colonial; in the Major's opinion, he was of the bigoted 'old school'.

'Of course, there has been the rare occasion in which one of our own Rhodesians has been involved, but such instances are extremely rare,' continued the Commissioner. 'I am pleased to say,' he added softly, almost as an afterthought.

The Major thought of the Commissioner's secretary and of her loss.

Had the Commissioner included her husband amongst his list of 'extremely rare' instances? he mused.

'So that is what makes this report I've just received all the more serious,' continued the Commissioner. 'One of my constables raised the alarm just after dawn this morning. The body of a white man was found slumped in a doorway in the main street. The doctor thinks that he'd been killed by a single stab wound to the heart,' he opened a file and

141

continued, 'it says here in the post-mortem report, that death was probably caused by a very thin blade of about twelve inches; something like a stiletto or a rapier.'

The Major's interest was suddenly very much aroused.

'That's a very specific type of blade, Sir,' he said. 'Somewhat anomalous in the centre of Salisbury, I would have thought.'

'Indeed,' replied the Commissioner, replacing the sheet of paper in the file. 'Not something we would associate with the *modus operandi* we come across in such matters. Usually it's a very gory affair with a panga or some blunt, heavy instrument. We have a large Indian population here – left over from the railway-building days, you know. They can be quite vicious with the strangler's cord – the Goddess Khali – quite messy, sometimes. We even have the occasional spearing out in the Tribal Lands, but those instances are usually quickly sorted out by the district commissioners,' he continued. 'I'm afraid to say that I see a European hand in this, more than an African or Indian one.'

'Do you have any evidence to support your opinion, Sir?' asked the Major. 'Were there any witnesses … any clues of any kind … anything for us to work on?'

'Apparently not,' replied the Commissioner, sitting forward in his chair. 'The doctor places the time of death somewhere between midnight and four o'clock this morning. No witnesses, no reports of any disturbance of any kind – nothing, actually, apart from the body.' He looked at the Major enquiringly, but Ashdown sat impassively looking back, waiting for something more concrete to emerge from the report. The European connection was interesting, given the Commissioner's explanation of the usual crime patterns on his patch, but it was probably a totally unconnected incident and, at best, would probably do no more than cloud the water of his real investigation.

Once the Commissioner realized that there was no input forthcoming, he continued. 'We think the body is that of a local petty thief, a Portuguese. He came in over the border from Lourenço Marques a couple of years ago. Since then, he's had several run-ins with the law. I suppose that this could have been one of his illicit dealings that went fatally wrong. People like that have no friends and usually spend most of their time squabbling amongst themselves. I'm sure that this business will turn out to be a local matter. I don't see how it can help you in the broader picture.'

'Possibly not, but you never know, Sir.' said Ashdown, non-committally.

'What exactly *do* you have to work on?' asked the Commissioner, as he closed the file on the desk in front of him. His visitor had given nothing much away and the Commissioner found the level of authority behind this man's letter intriguing.

Ashdown realized that he was quite possibly going nowhere with his investigation and so decided to fill the Commissioner in on some of the more general details of his case, but only as far as he judged the Commissioner needed to know.

'Really?' replied the Commissioner when Ashdown had finished, 'and this is obviously thought serious enough to involve the really top brass, then?' It was more of a statement than a question. 'Of course, we will offer you every assistance we can, but I'm not sure that I have anything that will help you, I'm afraid.'

He folded the letter, returned it to its envelope and then gave it back to the Major.

'That's the problem I have, Sir,' said Ashdown, more to himself than to anyone else. 'We have a vague description of a suspect, some second-hand information from sources who were easily bought, and a single report of an incident at Beit Bridge, which could or could not be linked to my investigation.' He paused and then added, '*Quo vadis*?'

The Commissioner smiled. '"Where to?" indeed. Are you certain that you're looking for diamonds?'

'That's the only thing we *are* certain of, given the information we have. We know that they originate in South-West Africa, but we've drawn a blank trying to apprehend the people who traffic them to Europe. There are forces out in the wider world that have serious ambitions and require considerable funding to make progress.'

He was giving away a little more than he would have liked to, but he deemed it necessary. Truth to tell, he was beginning to feel a little foolish, chasing the proverbial needle in the haystack. Despite the fact that he had little else to work on, Ashdown felt that he needed to keep the Commissioner's interest.

'Do you think they could be taken by sea? On the mail boat from Cape Town, for instance?' asked the older man.

The Major was momentarily taken aback by the Commissioner's suggestion. He had never even considered that possibility, for some inexplicable reason always focusing on the overland route up through Africa, instead of around it. He thought it best not to answer the question.

'With particular reference to this case, Sir, the powers-that-be are convinced that the diamonds are destined for a political party in Western Europe.'

'In Europe?' echoed the Commissioner, 'Where in Europe?'

'Germany. Or it could be ... Italy or even Spain.' Ashdown had added the last two by way of a smokescreen.

'Germany? They're supposed to be in a mess, aren't they? They haven't really recovered from the last war.'

'They are recovering, or so it would seem, Sir. There are those, however, who would see such a political situation as highly fertile ground to capitalize on mass discontent – the promise of something better for the discontented masses: "under new management", as it were.' The Major raised his eyebrows slightly, to emphasize his point.

'Are you referring specifically to Germany and Hitler?' asked the Commissioner. 'But he's in prison, isn't he?'

'He was, but that was three or four years ago. In any case, so were many of the leaders of the Votes for Women campaign, but they succeeded in their ultimate aims, eventually ... notwithstanding the spells in prison...' *For someone of your rank you certainly appear to be out of touch with world affairs,* thought Ashdown. *You are far too comfortable in your colonial paradise.*

'Indeed they did...' muttered the Commissioner. 'Indeed they did,' he added more softly than before.

'Well, Sir, I really must thank you for your time. With your permission I would like to take a look at the scene of this murder. There might be something there that could point me in the next direction.'

Ashdown thought it worth a try. After all, he had absolutely nothing else to work on.

'By all means have a look. My people have already been over the scene very carefully and I doubt that they would have missed anything, but please ... be my guest.'

The Commissioner rose as the meeting ended.

'Good luck,' he said, as he extended his hand. 'Mrs Richards will arrange for a car – the driver will know where to take you.'

'Thank you, Sir,' said the Major. 'I'll report back to you if I find anything. In any case, I will most certainly extend you the courtesy of informing you of my next move. Failing the discovery of anything resembling a clue, that move could well be back to Pretoria,' he added, chuckling softly, but it was an empty sound.

Major Ashdown duly visited the scene of the crime and, very much as expected, he found nothing by way of a clue. He began to feel a wave of resigned pointlessness claw at him. He was getting nowhere with his investigation – no, that was far too grand a name to give it – his wild goose chase, except that nobody had actually seen the goose that was being chased. He laughed out loud at this last thought. Two white women, smartly dressed for the afternoon's socializing, turned and looked at him as they strolled past. Sitting on the edge of the pavement, an African woman did the same as she idly swatted the flies off the pile of paw-paws she had for sale.

Ashdown spent the rest of the afternoon wandering around Salisbury. He had no reason to return quickly to the hotel. If he did, he could well find his thoughts drifting back to his family's farmhouse in Kenya and these days that was usually quite a painful experience. Eventually, as the sun teetered above the line of the distant horizon, he reached The Rhodes. Before getting dressed for dinner, he luxuriated in a hot bath, but, as the warm, comforting water washed away what he regarded as the fruitless activity of the day, he became more disenchanted with his present task. His thoughts strayed back to the Commissioner's office and the photographs on the wall, to the faded images of the tough frontiersmen who had pushed up north from South Africa to establish an outpost of Western civilization in an Africa that was then seen as very dark. More to the point, he remembered his father and brothers and how they would now never be captured through the miracle of chemical interplay that was photography. They deserved to be, but they were prisoners of the earth of a heartless Mother Africa instead; the same earth that had been so kind to them in Kenya now blotted them out, just across the border in neighbouring Tanganyika. He closed his eyes and allowed himself to sink lower in the water. The vision of his sister's face, smiling at him, made him feel suddenly cold and uncomfortable, so much so that he got out of the water and dried himself. As he did so, to clear his sister's face from his mind, he thought of the waiting dinner, which, he anticipated, would be up to the usual high standard of the hotel. Afterwards, he would enjoy a brandy with his after-dinner coffee. And why not? He was, after all, allowed the occasional modest expense. The case wasn't totally without its little perks. Besides, the alcohol would help to banish his sister's face from his mind.

The following dawn, Wednesday 30th May, broke warm and sticky. Ashdown was up and packed early. The previous evening, over his brandy, he had decided that the only sensible course of action was to return to Pretoria and just wait and see.

'Good morning, Sir,' said the attractive girl behind the reception desk. She had the bloom of a transplanted English rose, but, he thought, tinged with the faintest hint of ancestry from the Indian subcontinent. Her teeth were pearl white and flashed in a broad smile.

'Good morning,' he replied. 'Could you please prepare my bill? I intend to return to Pretoria today. I'm going to the railway station to enquire about trains and to purchase a ticket. I'll then return and settle up with you.'

'I can help you with the information you require,' she said politely. 'I have a train timetable here.' She leant over sideways and reached down under the counter top to retrieve a box file. As she did so, he was aware of her shapely hips and small, rounded breasts, which pushed against her white blouse as she bent forward. It had been a while since he had indulged in the luxury of the flesh and he felt a sudden pang of desire.

'Here we are, Sir,' she continued, as she opened the file and withdrew the couple of pages that served as the train timetable.

Cecil John Rhodes had pushed hard to join Cape Town to Cairo along thousands of miles of British railway line, but the size and scale of the undertaking had proved too great, even for someone of his business acumen. New sections had been added, but the iron rails through the scrub and bush were incomplete. Although well advanced, there were still sizeable gaps in the projected thin black line on the map of Africa, which was to have symbolized the twin, continuous ribbons of shining British steel.

'Beira trains, via Umtali, every Thursday and Saturday afternoon, and Pretoria trains every other day from Mondays, excluding Saturdays and Sundays. Two a day, departing at 05.30 and 14.30. I hope that is of help to you, Sir?' said the receptionist, her pearly white teeth flashing again.

'Yes, thank you,' he replied absently, 'most helpful.'

If that afternoon's train was full, he would have to wait until Friday to catch the next one to Pretoria.

'You will still have to visit the railway station to purchase your ticket,' she continued, 'I am afraid we cannot sell them here in the hotel.'

She spoke in a very precise manner.

Convent school education? he thought.

'Oh, that's a pity,' he replied, smiling back at her. 'In that case I will go to the railway station straight away. It's probably best not to do my bill just yet. I may not be able to find a seat on the train for this afternoon,' he continued smiling, but the thought of having to spend yet more time in Salisbury was not an appealing one. *Please God let there be a seat on this afternoon's train,* he thought to himself, behind the smile.

By the time he reached the station, the sun was climbing towards its zenith. It seemed as if half of Salisbury had congregated around and in the modest building. In the cool of the ticket office, the buzz of conversation was only once broken by the shrill ringing of a telephone bell. The Major was impressed, as it seemed that civilization had well and truly reached this far out into the Empire. Outside, a goods engine was pushing and then pulling its load up and down the shiny tracks, which had already started to dance in the haze. How anyone could work on the engine plate, stoking the fierce furnace in the African heat was a mystery to him.

'Good morning. I'd like a single to Pretoria for this afternoon, please,' he said, in response to the greeting offered by the enquiring face that watched him through the circular opening in the glass window of the ticket counter.

'I am sorry, Sir, but this afternoon's train has already been fully booked,' came the reply. The face spoke the English which, delivered in that clipped, precise way, had evolved on the Subcontinent through two hundred years of the Raj.

'I can provide Sir with a ticket for the train on Friday – that would be at two-turty.' The way the time had been pronounced confirmed the official's Indian ancestry.

'Are you absolutely certain there is nothing available before Friday afternoon?' asked Ashdown, frustration once again threatening to impede his progress. 'What about the first train on Friday?'

'No, Sir, definitely not' came the reply, polite but firm. 'The five-turty is mainly a goods train with very little passenger space, and most certainly nothing of first class, Sir.' And that was all that the ticket clerk had to say on the matter. The early train was not meant for Europeans.

'Thank you, then, the afternoon train on Friday will have to do,' said the Major, with a hint of resignation in his voice.

He retraced his steps back to the hotel, idling as he went. He had time to kill and had decided on doing as little as possible during the afternoon, before enjoying another soak, an early dinner and bed. He had no idea what he would do the following day. On Friday, he would report briefly to the Commissioner during the morning and then get himself back to the station in good time to get settled in, before the train pulled out into the bush on its journey southwards.

The following morning, the last day of May, he was one of the first in the dining room. After breakfast, as he crossed the foyer towards the entrance doors, he found himself regretting that he did not have any excuse to stop at the reception desk. Once again the young girl was on duty. The teeth flashed as she saw him crossing the floor space. Once again he was aware of the stirrings of his desire.

'Good morning, Sir,' she called, as he walked, 'there is a message for you. It was received whilst you were in the dining room having your breakfast.'

She gave him a sheet of folded paper. He opened it and saw it was headed with the hotel's crest and address. It was headed simply 'Telephone Message' and read: 'Please telephone this number...'

He knew no telephone numbers in Salisbury and was immediately suspicious.

'Did the person not leave a name?' he asked, looking up from the note.

'No I'm sorry, Sir, just a telephone number. It was a lady's voice,' she said, smiling at him. 'You may use the telephone in the cubicle over there,' she said, gesturing to the far corner of the foyer.

'Major Ashdown?' asked the voice on the other end of the line, 'Thank you for telephoning so promptly. Can you be ready in a quarter of an hour? The Commissioner wants to see you as soon as possible and wants me to send a car for you.'

Suddenly, he remembered the voice – it was Mrs Richards, the Commissioner's secretary.

11

Edfu

The Nile – 21st July 1928

Rupert had not been far off the mark with his prediction: *Khufu* had docked at Edfu shortly after 3 a.m. Even at that time, when the night air could be as coldly unpleasant as the heat of the day, there were people milling about. The occasional shadowy shape could be seen, dimly moving between the pools of light cast by the lamp poles dotted at intervals along the road which ran alongside the quayside. It seemed as if Egypt never slept.

That was more than could be said for the tourists on board the little white steamship. Awoken reluctantly from their slumbers, their start had been an early one, rising even before the first fingers of the true dawn had clawed their way across the eastern sky, vainly trying to catch the souls of the pharaohs as they journeyed eternally westwards on their solar boat of ancient belief. On *Khufu,* the boat of earthly reality, all had been muster and bustle in an attempt to rouse the tourists from their slumbers and feed them. Everyone had been warned of the necessity of an early start, if the heat was to be avoided, and most had responded to the sharp rap on the door at 5 a.m. Most, except for the odd few – Mrs Grassmere, not unexpectedly, amongst them.

'Why do we have to get up at this ungodly hour? If it's that hot, why bother going in the first place?'

Mr Grassmere was heard to mumble something by way of riposte, but his voice was incapable of intelligible penetration of the cabin door – unlike that of his wife.

Outside, in the passageway, Mohammed stared fixedly at the door of their cabin. He was determined that not even a woman as profoundly irritating as Mrs Grassmere was going to wipe the practised smile off his face. He stared at the door and allowed himself a moment of improper thought – how much the number on the door looked like Mrs Grassmere – a generous figure 8!

So much is she like her number, he thought, smiling.

Mohammed repeated his smart wrap on the door of Cabin 9 and was about to move on to the tenth cabin, when Sebastian Printon came unexpectedly around the corner of the passageway, taking the little Egyptian somewhat by surprise.

'Good mornings to you, Sir,' he beamed. 'Are you being in need of anything?'

Mohammed had not failed to notice that the man was already fully dressed and that his polished leather shoes were tarnished around the toecaps by a layer of fine Egyptian earth. He had obviously already been ashore. He also carried a small, parcel-like object. It was wrapped in a short length of decorated rush matting, from the ends of which protruded a piece of dirty cotton cloth. With a single, swift, fluid motion, Printon made to casually hide the parcel behind him.

'Did Sir not repose successfully?' continued Mohammed, his curiosity aroused.

'Very soundly, thank you' came the curt reply. 'I felt the need to walk on dry land for a while. The motion of the water makes me feel uneasy.'

'Then we must be truly grateful we are not on the openings of the sea with the bad stormings,' continued Mohammed, trying to get a better view of the object, but without making his curiosity too obvious. 'We are truly happy with the peace of the river, *insha'Allah.*

Printon made no reply, but simply looked at the little Egyptian with something between revulsion and disdain before unlocking the door of his cabin with his free hand.

'Please not to be forgetting that breakfast will soon be serving,' called Mohammed, as the door was closed in his face. He found some of these Europeans very hard to understand. Some of them seemed to make rudeness an art. Even before he had completed his round of door knocking he made a mental note to tell Rupert of this encounter.

Mohammed's efforts were rewarded, as everyone was finally assembled in the dining room by 07.00. The still-protesting Mrs Grassmere had decided to appear after all, attired in a pair of baggy pantaloons and an open-necked blouse, garishly decorated with a series of tiered flounces. The unsuitability of her outfit, which made her look ludicrous, caused a controlled titter to flash around the still-sleepy dining room. Sitting next to her, Mr Grassmere seemed to cringe over his toast and marmalade.

'Isn't this exciting?' whimpered Sylvia Baxter, almost apologetically. 'I mean going to where others have trod for the last four thousand years.' She giggled in her immature way and set about her poached eggs with enthusiasm. Marjory Cuttle smiled approvingly, but said nothing. She did not cope with an early-morning start at the best of times.

Across the room from the Grassmeres' table, Mrs Arling had just lit another cigarette and was admiring her bright-red fingernails. Sitting at the table opposite, Colonel Ponsworthy disapproved.

'Look at her,' he whispered in his parade-ground manner, 'painted-up like a tart and smoking like a furnace – and at this hour of the morning, too.'

Sitting to his left, Mr Rotherham, owner of Rotherham's

Patented Relish, had more important things on his mind. He was more concerned with an idea he had had, which was to convince the company to purchase his range of products and offer them to their tourists. If, as Mr Winfield had said, Nile cruising was just the tip of the emerging travel iceberg, the potential for a considerable increase in sales was very enticing. Perhaps not surprisingly, he had not been at all impressed with the quality of the limited range of condiments that were on offer in *Khufu*'s dining room. He turned to Ponsworthy and was about to launch into a lengthy exposé of his business plan.

'Er ... crumbs, Colonel,' he said softly, instead.

Colonel Ponsworthy looked down and flicked a few crumbs of toast off his shirt front. Mr Rotherham smiled to himself – he had meant the marmalade-encrusted crumbs, which had somehow become lodged at the ends of Ponsworthy's moustache, but he said nothing further, deciding that, for the moment at least, he would keep his plans to himself.

Elias B. Grupfelder had already been served his second plate of bacon, eggs, kidneys and almost anything else the kitchen could produce. The man had a prodigious appetite, which was more than in keeping with his considerable personality.

Of Sebastian Printon, there was no sign. Although giving the impression that she was still half asleep, Ruth Kirby turned to Simon Arling and was just about to comment on Printon's absence, when Rupert appeared, closely followed by Stephen Hopkins.

'Ladies and gentlemen ... if I can have your attention for a moment, please?'

Stephen smiled a greeting to everyone and crossed to sit at the remaining space at the table occupied by the Lamptons and Mrs Lydia Porter.

'Feeling better?' he mouthed to Richard Lampton.

He was answered with an enthusiastic grin and a thumbs-up sign.

Rupert remained standing at the door.

'I hope you slept well and are ready for our excursion today. We shall be visiting the Temple of Horus, which is almost the same size as the great Temple of Karnak, near Luxor. Remember, we will be visiting that one on our return from Aswan. At Edfu, there is quite a lot of archaeological work going on at present, so I must ask you to be very careful during our visit. Mohammed and his excellent team will cater to your needs and comfort and will be sending our picnic lunch on to us at the temple, later in the morning. In the meantime, please don't forget to take your water canteens with you – there's no water at the temple and you need to guard against dehydration. We must set off in about twenty minutes, so I'll remind you of the points of interest to be seen once we reach the temple. I'll meet you all down on the quayside shortly.'

Even though it was still very early, not yet seven thirty, activity on the quayside had rapidly increased with the dawn light, until it was now alive with the sounds and smells of Egypt. A convoy of horse-drawn carriages had been assembled to transport the tourists to the temple. To the uninitiated, there seemed to be no plan or method to the way in which they had congregated next to *Khufu*. Dust wafted up from the stamping hooves of the waiting horses and was swirled into mini-cyclones by the gently moving air, which floated in off the river. There was a crisp nip to the morning, but this would fool only the unwary, for soon the heat would exert its authority over everything and banish any cooling zephyrs. The early-morning air and diminishing darkness were also filled with the shouts of the numerous drivers and other quayside merchants, all eager to sell something or find the most advantageous spot to park. Tourists were not the only people who could afford the luxury of transport by carriage. Arabic from the quayside mingled with the English from the ship.

'Why do they always have to shout and carry on so?' Sylvia Baxter asked.'I think the ruins are ever so exciting, but I don't think I'd like to live here – all that dust, noise and the flies.'

Miss Cuttle gave her a steadying grin and patted her arm.

'They do what they can with what they've got,' she said and then added mysteriously, 'and they are who they are.'

'Typical,' growled Colonel Ponsworthy, as he stood next to the rail and observed the outward chaos on the quayside. 'Absolutely typical!'

'And yet, they seem to manage to reach the final destination, wouldn't you say?' said Mr Arling, smiling at the Colonel.

'Harumph!' he replied. He did not much care for Mr Arling. For Mrs Arling, the 'tart', with her alluring curves and tantalizing breasts – yes, for Mrs Arling he could really make an effort – even at his age. But he had no time for the husband.

Mohammed was standing at the top of the narrow wooden gangplank, which connected *Khufu* to the quay, like an umbilical cord.

'Ladies and gentlemans, please to be so immediate as to walk this way. This manner of proceeding, if it please you ... yes please.' He gestured down the gangplank towards the waiting horses and carriages, now tightly grouped on the little quayside, like the survivors of the Charge of the Light Brigade.

'Really!' thundered Mrs Grassmere. 'Do we have to risk life and limb by crossing that thing yet again?'

'Most certain you are,' replied Mohammed, his patent grin plastered firmly to his face and the figure 8 firmly planted in his mind. This woman was not going to get the better of him. 'It is but the shortest of walkings and then you are in the carriage. No problem, madam, it is most safe – I will be showing you,' and with that, to avoid any more of this obnoxious woman, he swept on down the gangplank ahead of her.

Within the space of a few minutes, the seeming chaos on the quayside had miraculously disintegrated into an organized procession of plodding horses and carriages, full of chatting tourists. Mohammed had remained behind on the quayside, waving to the departing carriages. He would follow later, with the lunch hampers and several of the crew. They would also bring collapsible tables, umbrellas and chairs, which would be set up in some shady spot within the temple.

'Oh yes me, we think of every one of your comforts indeed,' muttered Mohammed to himself in his quaint English, as he turned on his heel and walked smartly up *Khufu*'s gangway, 'even you very fat ladies, who go off dressing like chef's cake when he makes it wrong, do we care for. Oh yes!' By the time he crossed the deck and disappeared into the foyer, he had a large grin, almost from ear to ear, plastered firmly on his face.

Shortly after eight o'clock, the extended procession of carriages had reached the outer perimeter of the ruins of the temple. After a short delay, during which the carriages disgorged their cargoes, Rupert assembled his flock for a short briefing. Stephen stood a little behind him, to his left. He had decided that, as some of the party could well be liabilities, he had better bring his black medical bag with him, just in case.

The now-empty carriages, drawn by emaciated horses, some of which were already partly exhausted by the first ride of their day, slid off, gratefully, to find shade. The sun had broken through, and was dispersing those few clouds, which had tenaciously clung to the low eastern horizon. Already there were pools of heat, shimmering on the ground.

His briefing now safely delivered, Rupert began shepherding his flock towards the temple. As they moved towards the towering edifice, the rays of the sun began to strike the high side wall.

'We'll walk around the side of the complex and view it from the main entrance, looking north,' he said, as they moved along. 'The pylons are quite well preserved and they'll give you some idea of how grand a complex this really is, even allowing for the excavation work.'

'It's so big,' said Esther Arling, emphasizing the 'big' unduly. 'Are all the old temples like this?'

'Most of them are,' replied Rupert. 'Some are even larger, as you'll see when we return to Luxor and visit Karnak. That's really a complex of three temples in one – it was added to over several hundred years. Don't forget that the ancient Egyptian religion lasted for well over three *thousand* years. It was central to their lives – and it held the promise of an afterlife.'

The group was in motion now, ambling along towards the sandy yellow bulk of the entrance pylons like a mini, brightly coloured caravan out in the desert, little eddies of dust, disturbed by their feet, rising into the air as they moved.

'Be careful once we are inside the complex. Please remember that it is also an archaeological site and that there are loose chunks of masonry everywhere.' Rupert was warming to his passion. He patted a large chunk of stone, lying crazily on its side and covered in finely carved characters. 'This fellow came from up there,' he said, pointing to the top of one of the pylons. 'Look, here is Seth, brother of Osiris and his murderer. And here, this looks like part of Isis, the faithful wife of Osiris. They're the good forces in the pantheon of the gods. Seth is the black sheep, as it were. Don't worry if you can't remember the names, we'll keep coming across them as we continue the trip.'

'Where will we be taking luncheon?' asked Mrs Grassmere.

Rupert was taken aback for a second. She couldn't have been listening to his talk at all.

'Pardon?' he said.

'Luncheon ... we've been going for simply ages and I'd like to know when and where our luncheon will be provided.'

Mr Grassmere, ever obedient to his wife's slightest whim, was having a problem trying to remove the stopper from her canteen of water. The heat had started to increase noticeably, even in the short time since arriving at the temple complex, but Rupert felt another kind of heat cross his cheeks. He was starting to contemplate the possibility of losing patience with this woman.

'Mohammed and some of our crew will provide that,' he replied, somewhat tersely. 'They will erect awnings for us in the Central Court, which is the open space we can see in front of us there – through the pylons. And it will be more of a picnic lunch than a luncheon,' he added, smiling at having been able to correct her.

'May it please you, m'lud,' chimed in Colonel Ponsworthy, in an over-pompous impersonation of a barrister in court. He dissolved into laughter at his own wit, his appreciation of which was not generally shared by the others, save for Mr Rotherham, who thought it best to simply smile, although he was not totally sure as to the reason why.

Thanks to Mohammed, Rupert had also now started to think of Mrs Grassmere as 'The Lady 8'. Turning away from her, Rupert tried to return his concentration to the next stage of his talk.

'... Walk straight up through the temple complex, through both hypostyle halls, the Offering Chamber and on into the Central Hall. You won't be able to go further than that, due to the excavations. When you have had a look at the

Central Hall, retrace your route to the Second Hypostyle Hall and I'll meet you there in, let us say, one and a half hours' time. There really is an enormous amount to see, so please take your time. Ask, if you have any questions. I'll be circulating.'

But, by that point, most of the travellers in his group had already wandered off.

'Then I'll tell you about the next stage of our exploration of the complex,' he added, softly, more to himself and to the emptying court than to his flock.

Back on the quayside, the well-drilled procedure for forwarding the picnic to the temple was well in hand. Mohammed had supervised the initial stages of the operation and had then passed overall command to Daoud. Like Achmed, who was on duty behind the reception desk, Daoud had begun to display leadership qualities which Mohammed thought worthy of fostering and developing further. The still-unexplained matter of the unbolted gangway rail had not really shaken Mohammed's faith in his protégé's ability. Perhaps there *was* nothing sinister about the man falling through the railings; perhaps it was just one of those things that was meant to be – *insha'Allah.*

The kitchen had provided each of the passengers with their own individual wicker basket. Each was about the size of a small picnic hamper, and contained the picnic lunch, prepared according to any special dietary requirements they might have. Each basket was neatly labelled with a manila ticket and had a carrying handle on the top of the lid. The lid itself was tightly secured with a leather tongue and simple fixing pin. Inside was all the equipment necessary for a picnic, including the food and a small canteen of chilled water. The problem of keeping the water cool and the food fresh, even for a short time, had occupied Mohammed's mind for years and he felt justly proud of his solution, for he had devised his own, simple cooling system. This involving covering the hampers with a tarpaulin, once they had been loaded onto a cart, and giving a few coins to some local urchins to continually flick water over the cloth, the evaporation of which tended to have a cooling effect on the picnic hampers and their delicate contents. Once at the temple, the cloth would be removed and any remaining water on the hampers would evaporate in seconds in the heat.

Sitting on the driver's bench, the cart owner looked resolutely ahead, not wishing to get involved in the loading work, which was in full swing behind him. His horse stared equally blankly ahead of itself, but due more to tiredness and lack of food than lack of interest in the activity going on behind it. Times were hard and the fares his owner received for hiring out his cart were modest.

'Be careful with those, you sons of a mangy camel!' shouted Daoud, as two of the crew busily stacked the baskets within the narrow confines of the hired cart. Speaking Arabic, he had no fear of offending the sensitive ears of any Europeans who might be passing.

'How many times do I have to show you how to load the baskets?' he thundered, 'And still you make a mess an idiot would be proud of! Get them off the cart – look, the bottom ones must be flat...'

Daoud proceeded to rant against the unfortunate crew, as they unloaded and then reloaded the baskets to his satisfaction. As he did so, he happened to notice one of the kitchen hands standing at *Khufu*'s stern, in the deck area set aside for the crew's use. The man, an Egyptian, was idly wiping his hands on his apron, as he watched the loading operation with detached interest. Daoud recognized the man immediately – he was bad and took no pride in his work. There had been a couple of incidents, over the previous days, which Daoud had reported to Mohammed.

And now, why was this man just standing there watching and doing nothing, when there must be plenty of work in the kitchen? Before Daoud could shout to the man to stop lounging and get back to work, Mohammed leaned over the rails of the promenade deck, high above everyone's heads, and called down to the quayside.

'Are you ready yet? The time of the meal approaches and you still have to load the chairs, tables and umbrellas.'

Speaking his native Arabic, Mohammed was devoid of the syntax of his peculiar brand of Egyptian-English.

'At once, *Effendi*, we are almost ready to proceed,' called back Daoud, waving a reassuring hand.

Mohammed waved back, more by way of exhortation to get on with things rather than greeting, and returned to his office. Daoud turned back to the cart to be greeted by the larger of the two crewmen who was holding two of the hamper name labels in his hand.

'And what is this?' he enquired 'Fools – look what you have done!'

'We found them on the ground,' stammered the crewman. 'They must have come off with the movement of the baskets.'

'They have come off the baskets due to you having a brain the size of a single sheep's dropping,' thundered Daoud, as he snatched the labels from the extended hand, 'and now you have made us late, because you have to find which baskets have no names. Do it now!'

He threw the tickets back at the crewmen and stormed off to attend to packing the picnic equipment into the second cart.

The two tickets fluttered to the dusty earth delicately, like two butterflies, before the fumbling crewman could catch them. They landed on the dusty quay, writing uppermost.

'Miss Sylvia Baxter' read one and 'Mr Richard Lampton' read the other.

12

To Beira

Saturday, 30th June 1928

Major Jeremy Ashdown sat in a first-class train compartment, staring idly out of the window. The whistle had blown and, almost to the second of the departure time, the journey had begun. Twenty-four hours earlier, he had faced the prospect of the long haul back down south, along the line to Pretoria. The train would have rattled through Que Que and Gwelo and then, before the Matopo Hills and Bulawayo, it would have branched out into the veld, heading for Beit Bridge and on, over the border into South Africa. Now, he was going in the opposite direction – out to the west towards Umtali and the coast, to cross a different border into Portuguese East Africa.

Funny how things turn out, he mused to himself. *A couple of days ago I'd have gone straight back to Pretoria.*

The two powerful steam engines had hauled the long train up the slight gradient out of Salisbury. Puffing steadily, they had gradually picked up speed. Outside the swiftly moving train sprawled the panorama of the real Africa. A broad vista of scrubland and trees, the occasional collection of African huts, enclosed in their protective thorn bush hedges and always, or so it seemed, knots of smiling, waving children. As the Major waved idly back at one such group, seeing his own image reflected back at him in the window glass, he pondered on how far removed these smiling little faces were from the events of the previous day.

The moment he had entered the outer office, Mrs Richards had shown Ashdown straight into the Commissioner's inner sanctum.

'...And coming as it did on top of the murder, I thought it best to get hold of you and let you know, Major.' The Commissioner sat behind his large desk looking somewhat ruffled. 'This seems to be becoming something of a habit...' he said, more to himself than Ashdown, '...first that stiletto business and now this. We like a quiet, orderly existence here...'

Ashdown thought it appropriate to murmur some words of consoling agreement.

'Anyway, that's as may be...' continued the Commissioner, appearing to pay no heed to Ashdown's remarks, '...there was some sort of a fracas at the railway station first thing yesterday morning. It all got quite ugly and my chaps were called in to sort things out. Quite routine, you might think...' He paused, as if to underline his displeasure at the disruption to his normally placid existence, then he continued: 'But it really is not. We get disturbances all the time. As I have said before, they're usually caused by the natives, not the Europeans. Since this business with the stabbing, my chaps have been extra vigilant.' He sounded tired. Close to retirement, he could hardly be expected to appreciate any increase in unsolved violence – not before he could hand over to his successor and make a dignified retreat to his farm in the tranquillity of the cooler highlands. 'See what you make of this.'

He handed Ashdown an official report folder, printed with the crest of the British South Africa Police and marked for the attention of the Commissioner. Inside were a couple of report sheets, neatly typed:

> *In the early hours of Thursday, June 28th last, I was called to the railway station in response to a disturbance. Apparently, a European gentleman was standing on the platform waiting to board the 06h30 Beira train, when a porter accidentally bumped into him from behind, causing him to drop his cane on the platform. This seems to have been a genuine accident, but the European gentleman flew into a rage, which seemed uncontrollable. He picked up his cane and proceeded to lay about the unfortunate porter, who was obliged to shield his head against the blows with his arms. A passenger attempted to assist the porter, but was also set upon by the tall gentleman wielding the cane. The unfortunate porter took this opportunity to escape. Eventually, the Station Master was summoned and, having failed to placate the gentleman, he summoned the police. We managed to diffuse the situation, due to the fact that the European gentleman had to board his train and depart the station. He spoke with the faintest trace of a foreign accent, although his command of the English language was faultless. He also had the bearing of an aristocrat. The porter seemed to have escaped any serious injury and was more shocked than anything else. When asked, he said that he did not wish to press charges, as he thought he might lose his job in consequence. He was, however, very agitated about the way he had been set about with the heavy cane. He was particularly concerned that the heavy handle of the cane, in the form of a silver bird-like animal with red eyes, might do his head an injury. He also vividly remembered the way the red eyes of the bird flashed in the electric lights, as it was being wielded about his person.*

'Griffin...' muttered Ashdown, '... is this "The Griffin?" – it's that cane again – with the same description – the heavy handle of the cane, "in the form of a silver bird-like animal with red eyes".'

'Eh? What's that?' asked the Commissioner, who had crossed his office to the large window, which overlooked the well-manicured lawns and bushes outside, whilst Ashdown had busied himself reading the contents of the file.

'The cane, Sir,' replied the Major, 'it could be connected.'

The Commissioner's shoulders seemed to sink slightly, and his facial expression looked both tired and more than a little mystified by Ashdown's remarks.

'If you recall, Sir, the cane was referred to at Beit Bridge. The tall chap with the aristocratic bearing – "The Griffin", as we seem to have begun calling him – well, we've come across him before – he was connected to the incident in the mine manager's office in Kolmanskop – in the Forbidden Zone in South West Africa.'

The Commissioner resumed his seat behind the desk. What on earth did any of what this Major had to say about far-off South-West Africa have to do with him? What on earth did a griffin have to do with anything?

'Could any of this be connected to the murder, d'y' think?' he asked. He was beginning to wish that this Major would move on – and soon.

'Possibly,' replied Ashdown, 'but this report is really all we've got to go on. It says he got onto a train. Today's Friday, so yesterday would have been the train down to Beira...'

The Commissioner looked blankly at him with raised eyebrows. He was not *au fait* with the railway timetable. Besides, the report had *said* it was the Beira train. There was nothing new in that, even if it did seem to suddenly excite this Major.

'...And the next one is tomorrow afternoon. Thank you very much, Sir. This has been the most promising turn of events so far. With your permission, I'll make arrangements to follow our man down to Beira.'

The Commissioner nodded his agreement, barely concealing his relief at the imminent departure of this Major and his own sudden reprieve from any further involvement. The Commissioner liked straightforward policing – he had no time for this cloak-and-dagger stuff.

'That is, of course, if your man actually intends to go to Beira,' said the Commissioner slowly. 'Perhaps he's going back to South Africa and is laying a false trail?' He looked at Ashdown with a questioning expression on his face. 'He could give the impression of going to Beira, but it is possible for him to get off somewhere along the way, return here, and then catch the next train to Pretoria?'

'Possibly, Sir, but I think it highly improbable.' The Major was impressed with the older man's sudden suggestion, although he put no real credence on it. His gut reaction to what little information he had so far managed to assemble told him that his quarry was heading for the coast. 'Our man – "The Griffin" – could be just a link in the chain, and he could pass the stones on to someone else, in which case we'd be heading in the right direction, but chasing the wrong man. We'd be back to square one.'

'On the other hand, if he *does* go back down south – by whatever route – he'll be spotted – the border crossing into South Africa is being carefully watched,' said the Commissioner, refusing to let his idea go.

'One would hope so, Sir,' replied Ashdown, 'that is, *if* he doubles back on himself and *if* he chooses to cross the border legally. Remember, many do not, as there are a thousand places where you could slip across, without anyone seeing or even suspecting.'

The Commissioner looked crestfallen – he had thought his suggestion rather clever.

'If I carry on to Beira, at least we'll have both possible avenues of escape covered.'

'As you wish, Major,' replied the Commissioner, once

again animated at the thought of the departure of this man, who seemed to have brought trouble with him since his arrival in the capital. 'The language could be a bit of a problem, though,' continued the Commissioner. 'How's your Portuguese?'

'Non-existent, I'm afraid, Sir,' replied the Major.

'Hmm,' grunted the Commissioner, 'I know one of their chaps in Lourenço Marques. Good fellow, actually. I'll have a word with him – see if he can get someone with passable English to help you when you get to Beira.'

The Commissioner got up, pushing his hair back as he did so. 'I'll have you driven back to your hotel – or anywhere else you might need to go. Just tell the driver. Keep me posted as to events,' he added, as he extended his hand.

Sitting in the back of the official car, Ashdown smiled to himself. The pretty young thing behind the reception desk would, indeed, be making up his bill. But first, he had a railway ticket to exchange.

Major Jeremy Ashdown was brought back to the confined reality of the swaying carriage by a loud knocking on the compartment door. It opened to reveal a white-jacketed waiter carrying a tray of tea and biscuits, which he placed on a fold-up table under the window. As he smelt the refreshing aroma of freshly poured tea, Ashdown, at last, started to feel more confident. It seemed as if, at last, the first few pieces of a jigsaw had fallen into place. The fact that there were only a couple – in a puzzle which contained an unspecified number of pieces – did not concern him. At least, now, he had something a little more concrete than just vague suspicions and sketchy descriptions to follow. Perhaps the needle would not be as difficult to find in the haystack, as he had come to think it might be. As he munched on one of the biscuits, Ashdown looked down into his cup and saw that the gentle, regular swaying of the carriage was causing the surface of the tea to erupt and swirl about in the cup. Little did he know that very soon he would be on board a steamship, which would carve its way through waters which were just as angry, as it carried him ever nearer to his quarry.

13

Edfu

The Nile, late morning – 21st July 1928

'In your own time – just keep going straight ahead,' Rupert called, holding out his arm like a road sign and pointing up the centre of the temple complex. 'Just keep going and you can't go wrong. Take your time and just meander through. Don't forget to keep looking up at the wealth of wall carvings...' He paused and then added, for the benefit of the few of his flock still within earshot, '...And don't forget to keep looking down – the floors are not very even and we don't want any accidents...'

Surrounded by the knot of tourists, Rupert had just finished his talk about the complex of buildings that comprised the extensive Temple of Horus. He had been standing at the main entrance to the temple, which was a narrow passageway between two towering pylons, ancient symbols of the valley through which the Nile flowed. Most of his flock had wandered off at different stages during the course of his talk, in search of shade and an elusive cooling breeze, rather than seeking the enlightenment of ancient knowledge that was inscribed all over the surface of the vast walls. Rupert had also wondered, whilst he had been talking, if any of the other small groups of visitors to the temple were any different from his own charges. By the end of his talk, he had lost most of them; only Kormann,

FATAL TEARS

Colonel Ponsworthy, Stephen Hopkins and the large bulk of Elias B. Grupfelder remained. Following Rupert's invitation, they, too, began to walk off through the temple courtyard.

'Remember, Richard, don't drift too far away from us – stay where we can see you, just in case you need help.' Richard Lampton smiled and thanked the doctor for his kindly concern, but Stephen had a far more serious reason for saying what he did.

'Rather topical, don't you think?' said Stephen quietly, as he and Rupert walked some distance behind the stragglers and on into the courtyard.

'How so?' replied Rupert, again thrilled at the sight of the warm smile that had come to mean so much to him over the last few days.

'Well, Seth, Osiris and Isis – ancient murderers and avengers ... You know all about them. Therein is the stuff of novels and good stories, don't you think? Possibly, in our own times, even a similar story, starting with someone *falling* into the river?' He gave the word a slight emphasis.

'You mean on *Khufu*? With our party?' Winfield looked at Stephen earnestly. 'Do you really think so? But why?'

'Well, your company has an impeccable safety record and they also promise the "Holiday Experiences of Your Lifetime", to quote what it says on your own brochure. So why does it begin to look as if that unblemished record could well be about to be sullied and *Khufu* is at the centre of it?'

He looked sideways at Rupert.

'Think about it. The twisted ankle – probably an accident; the plunge in the river – probably not so; the mysterious late arrival of Mr Printon and his *abscess*,' he stressed the word, 'or whatever it was supposed to be. A definite oddity, I would say, which seems to have been healed by divine powers...'

He made an expansive gesture as if to take in the temple ruins and the ancient gods who had once been worshipped there. They walked on in silence and left the cloying heat of the open court, entering the welcome shade of the First Hypostyle Hall. Rupert paused to mop his brow with his handkerchief. As he gazed up at the carvings and hieroglyphics on one of the massive stone pillars, he said, 'Yes, you've got something there ... Even Mohammed seemed to find that abscess story a bit fishy. He was with the army in the war, you know, and saw more than his share of horses and camels with gum and teeth abscesses. He also commented on the miracle of Mr Printon's so-called *recovery*.' It was Rupert's turn to lay emphasis.

'Well, there you have it. Why the performance about catching the boat late and missing the start of the cruise? What was so special about *this* trip that he couldn't have done the next one? And what about the rest of your *flock*, as you call them?' He turned and smiled at Rupert, who flushed slightly.

'I suppose that is a little silly, isn't it?' said Rupert softly.

'Not in the least, old chap. What I meant was that they really are an oddly assorted bunch. None of them seem to have anything in common and, from what I can make out, hardly any of them seem to have any interest in ancient Egypt.'

'Oh, I don't know, Stephen', replied Rupert, as they moved slowly through the pillars and entered the second, smaller hypostyle hall. 'The Arlings seem quite interested – well, at least Mr Arling does ... I think.'

'But not a half as interested as his "Missus" is in anything with a bulge in the pants. But then, again, my dear chap, you might not have noticed that.'

They both chuckled.

'And Eric Kormann, he's asked some good questions. Then there's that American chap, Grupfelder. He's shown an interest, too...' His voice trailed off. '... But then he usually manages to think of something bigger and better back home!'

They both chuckled again.

'If I were to hazard a guess,' continued Stephen, 'I'd say the lady from Kenya is worthy of scrutiny, as is Saint Sebastian of the Miracle Jaw ... And as for our little Miss from Malaya ... well, she's almost too pathetic to be true ... but not quite as bad as the Manningtons. They've got to be the strangest by a head!'

They walked on in silence for a while.

'I say, you really do seem to be very interested in all of this – the cloak-and-dagger business, I mean – not the temple complex and the ancients,' said Rupert.

'Oh, not at all, old chap,' said the doctor, smiling. 'I have always had an interest in history generally and I find your talks very interesting – you have a very good manner about you.'

Rupert beamed back. 'Really?'

'Yes, most certainly. But you are quite right about the cloak-and-dagger stuff, too. You could say that Holmes is my middle name.'

'Oh, why would that be? Do you like reading the books?'

'There's a bit more to it than that,' said Stephen, turning to smile at Rupert again. 'All in good time, old chap, all in good time.'

Ahead of them they could see that the tourists had formed a scraggly little group just inside the entrance to the Offering Hall, close to the Sacrarium, or Holy of Holies. The complex was all the more remarkable because the massive stone roofs still sat heavily on the lotus capitals of the huge stone pillars that supported them. The roofs offered shade from the scorching sun, but made the interior of the temple oppressively hot and very dark. What light there was came from occasional, brilliant shafts of sunlight, which angled down to the floor from long, narrow rectangular slits, cut into the massive roof. The excavation work going on in the area to the rear of the temple, beyond the Central Hall, contributed to the oppressiveness of the atmosphere by filling the air with a fine dust of cloying sand. Several of the party were fanning themselves with their hats. Mrs Grassmere, her gossamer confection now ruined by the heat and sweat, had already emptied her own water canteen and was currently engaged in emptying her husband's in frequent, noisy gulps.

'Do we really have to catch up with *them*?' asked Stephen, 'Can we not simply wait here? You could show me some of the wonders of the pillars ... In fact, we could wander off over there – you can give me a personal discourse on the meaning of the more spicier of the carvings – I did notice them on the way in, by the way. You could explain all about the passions that fuelled the Ancients' beliefs...'

They both laughed, as Stephen put a hand on Rupert's shoulder.

'Come on,' he said, 'the floor is not that even and you might have to give an injured soldier a hand.'

By the appointed time, most of the party had assembled at the spot designated by Rupert. The heat was now becoming oven-like in its intensity and several of the group were showing very visible signs of wilting. Rupert told them about the more important features of the Chamber of the Liquid Offerings, through which they then passed to enter the narrow passageway between the complex proper and the outer perimeter wall of the temple.

'This is, perhaps, the most fascinating part of the complex,' said Rupert, indicating the walls of both the temple building and the outer retaining wall with a single, all-encompassing gesture. 'The surfaces of both walls are entirely covered with carvings. They depict the creation myth and other stories associated with the gods of ancient Egypt.'

He was warming to his pet subject and was finding his stride.

'I find it hard to believe that they actually believed in all of this for so long,' said Ruth Kirby, as she lit a cigarette. 'It's just so far-fetched.'

'I think some of these carvings are disgusting,' chipped in Sylvia Baxter, in her little voice. 'There was one a little way back there which had a man's thing...'

'Come along, my dear,' said Marjory Cuttle, in a motherly way, 'there is no need to distress yourself by dwelling on such things. There must be a place somewhere around here where we can sit down for a little while.'

Ruth Kirby gave Baxter a look of incredulous, intolerant disdain and took another drag of her cigarette. Lost in his dedication to his favourite subject, Rupert had walked ahead, to the front of the little procession.

'Well, I think it's absolutely marvellous that all of this has survived for as long as it has. That's all I have to say about it.' Mr Rotherham, who was standing up to the heat remarkably well, had, nevertheless, removed his hat and was fanning himself with it. 'And here we are, all those many hundreds of years later, standing here looking at it – just like they must have done in the old days.'

Stephen was bringing up the rear of the procession, with Colonel Ponsworthy and Grupfelder. The latter seemed largely unaffected by the heat; Ponsworthy was rambling on about his exploration of the architecture of Hindu temples during his time in India. For her part, Lydia Porter, carefully dressed in what she called 'sensible' attire, to protect her skin from the sun, was being careful to move within as much shadow as possible. She was part of, but nonetheless detached from, this rearguard and she found herself wishing the picnic would miraculously appear and shut Ponsworthy up! In front of them strolled the Arlings. They were accompanied by Sebastian Printon, who seemed to have become very friendly with Esther Arling. Of the Grassmeres there was no sign – it was as if they had simply faded into the heat haze of the desert.

'Must be nearly time for luncheon,' said Stephen, more to himself than to the others. The sun was sailing towards its daily zenith, which not only illuminated the walls on both sides of the passageway, but heated the stone to the point where those same inscription-covered walls became heating panels, warming the air between them alarmingly. *I could do with a sit-down*, he thought. His stump was beginning to throb slightly and he felt the need to take the weight off it. Although he had long since grown used to the artificial limb he wore below his left knee, the heat and fine sand tended to aggravate the stump of his leg and rub it raw in the socket.

'Come along, everybody, catch up please,' called Rupert, as he reached the opening, which led them back into the Central Court. 'Everything is ready for your picnic. Mohammed's chaps have done a first-class job in setting things up for us. Over in the far corner, everyone, next to the base of the far pylon.'

There was a noticeable picking up of speed, as, like a herd of thirsty beasts, the tourists sensed imminent relief from the heat with the promise of something cool and refreshing to drink. Unexpectedly, the Grassmeres emerged from the wrong side of the complex.

'I cannot even trust you to do a simple thing like that!' snapped Mrs Grassmere. Her husband cringed as if she had struck him with a whip.

'But, dear, perhaps we should have asked Mr Winfield where you could have go...'

'Don't be ridiculous! Why should I have to ask for his permission to attend to a call of nature?'

'No, dear, what I mean is that Mr Winfield might have

told us where the ... where ... where the facilities are ... He is very helpful, you must adm...'

'That is quite enough from you!' she snapped, before raising a podgy arm as if to swat her unfortunate husband. Although still just out of earshot, the Grassmeres were in everyone's plain view as they advanced across the Court. Mrs Grassmere, through her haze of temper and embarrassment, suddenly realized this fact. In an effort to disguise her action, she made a vague gesture to adjust her hat. 'And don't you dare tell me that those ghastly little urchins were only after a few coins. I have never been so humiliated in my entire life.'

She had stamped to a halt and glared down at her unfortunate spouse.

'The splashes are hardly noticeable and they will dry very quickly in this heat,' he mumbled.

Mrs Grassmere lashed out and deflected his hand away from where he was pointing to a rather large wet patch at her crotch.

For what seemed several minutes, Mrs Grassmere attempted to turn her husband into stone with a withering stare. Then she remembered her hat. She turned away from Mr Grassmere and, with a single smooth gesture, removed her hat and held it over the embarrassing stain. Some of the group idly watched the Grassmeres' progress, the others displayed an affected indifference.

'Too many confusing passageways,' wheezed Mrs Grassmere as she drew level with the rest of the party. Her diaphanous flounces were now definitely very much the worse for wear, with large sweat stains reaching out from under both of her armpits. She flopped down into a camp chair and firmly placed her hat on her lap. Mr Grassmere disappeared into the background to lick his verbal wounds.

'There is a basket for each of you,' called out Rupert.

'Just help yourself – you'll find your name written on a label and there is extra water packed in the ice chest. Don't forget to drink water regularly in this heat.' Baskets were searched for and, once found, taken away to the waiting shade. 'Just sit wherever you fancy – feel free to move the chairs if you wish.'

The chastened Mr Grassmere approached his still-fuming wife. He held out her picnic basket like some long-dead priest would have held out an offering in the confines of the temple. She grabbed it and, before anyone could notice, had deftly exchanged it for her hat, which she rammed angrily back on her head.

Within a few seconds, or so it seemed, the party had dispersed to the shade of the umbrellas or the massive mud-brick pylon which towered over them all.

'Noticed our "Man with the Miracle Jaw"?' asked Stephen, as Rupert settled himself down next to him, on the fallen capital of one of the lotus-topped columns.

Stephen glanced in Printon's direction.

'I was right,' he whispered. 'Look ... he seems to be able to manage an apple without too much trouble ... And where is our friendly recluse, Miss Kirby, do you think? She was here a few minutes ago – do you remember her pronouncement on the credibility of belief?'

'Yes ... that's a point ... Where is she, I wonder?' replied Rupert, searching around his dispersed flock. 'I'd better go and see if I can find her.'

'Not to bother, old chap,' said Stephen, gently putting out a restraining hand. 'If I'm right, she'll be along in a minute or two.'

Rupert was more than a little confused.

'You know, sometimes I really don't understand...' he said. 'How do you know that?'

For a moment, Stephen did not answer, but looked straight across the Court in the direction of the two massive entrance pylons, where most of the party had settled themselves under the umbrellas and the single, large awning the crewmen from *Khufu* had erected. A smile tugged at the corners of his mouth.

'Have you ever noticed her eyes?' he asked, without looking at Rupert, 'or, more specifically, her pupils? Did you also notice her standing in the far corner of the outer passageway whilst the rest of them were making their way towards the Central Hall? She was talking to a rather overdressed Egyptian chap – the one in a Western-style suit?'

Rupert thought for a moment and then replied, 'No, I can't say I did, really. And what do her pupils have to do with things, anyway? I wish you'd stop talking in riddles, Stephen.'

'Not riddles, old chap, just observational detail. Her pupils are, more often than not, dilated. So, I'd guess that she's either smoking a nasty substance or introducing it into her unfriendly, frigid body by some other means...'

'You mean ... she takes drugs?'

'And I'd go so far to say that she is ensuring her supply through contacts with these Egyptian chappies she keeps finding en route. Esna, Edfu, and, if I'm right, there'll be another one at Aswan. So – she's either buying regularly in small amounts, or, if her addiction is a serious one, in bigger amounts. The bush telegraph is totally reliable where there's money to be made, and selling that muck is one of the fastest ways there is to get rich quickly – provided you don't get caught, naturally,' he added, turning to smile at Rupert.

At that moment, something moved on the periphery of the doctor's vision, and he turned his head to look in response. Ruth Kirby had strolled around the corner of the outer passageway and into the Central Court. As she did so, she wiped her nose casually with the back of her hand.

'That's interesting,' said Stephen softly, as he watched her.

As she crossed the Court past them, Stephen raise his hat slightly, but she glared at him with unsteady eyes and strode off towards the rest of the party.

'That's *very* interesting,' repeated Stephen.

'Come and sit over here, my dear ... in the shade,' said Marjory Cuttle, as she drew two chairs further into the shadow of the massive pylon. 'I've got our baskets already. This one is yours.'

Sylvia Baxter let out a girlish giggle, as she took the basket and sat down.

'Isn't this such fun?' she bubbled. 'All of these ancient buildings to marvel at and a picnic lunch packed in my very own hamper. '"Miss Sylvia Baxter",' she read, holding the manila label in her hand. 'I wonder what I have to eat? Do you know, I'm not going to look – I'll just open the lid the tiniest bit and take something out – first out, first eaten.'

She giggled again, as she undid the securing leather strap and slid her hand into the basket, through the chink of the open lid. Across the Court, a silence had descended as the tourists' tired, overheated and sand-bedraggled minds turned from the engraved wonders of ancient Egypt to the contents of the picnic hampers. Everyone that is, except Mrs Grassmere, who was holding forth on some further aspect of the trip which had exasperated her patience. The rest of the party had made the effort to move as far away from the Grassmeres as possible.

Mr Rotherham crossed to the ice chest and had just started to fill his water canteen, when a high-pitched scream caused him to spray the precious cold liquid down his front. He turned and saw Sylvia Baxter flailing the air with her right hand; Marjory Cuttle was vainly trying to calm the agitated girl.

'She's been bitten by something,' shouted the older woman. 'Quick, someone do something ... please,' she cried desperately.

Seemingly within seconds, the party had formed a protective laager around the girl, who had taken on a startled look and had slumped down in her chair. Cuttle was holding the girl's right hand aloft. Tiny trickles of blood were running down the girl's lower forearm from two angry-looking puncture marks.

'Can everyone please just move back – give me some room ... please!'

Stephen had grabbed his black bag and, despite his artificial limb, had covered the distance across the Court very quickly.

'Did you see what it was?' asked Rupert.

'No ... I was just ... I don't know. She was ... I mean she had just put her hand into her basket to take out something to eat ... I don't know what ... it all happened so quickly. Is she going to be all right?' asked Cuttle, in a voice quavering with anxiety. It had lost the high-pitched whiney which had become her trademark.

'Looks like a rattler bite, only smaller,' said Grupfelder.

'Yes, it certainly looks like a snake bite,' said Stephen. 'Double puncture mark, so it's not a scorpion. Without knowing what snake it was, it's difficult to administer the correct anti-venom, which I do not have, anyway. We'd need to get her to a hospital and by that time...'

He left the sentence unfinished.

Daoud and the crew from *Khufu*, who had erected the umbrellas and awning, were stung from their lethargy in the shade by the girl's screams and had gathered in a tight little knot, close to the party.

'We could try sucking the poison out, if we're quick,' said Stephen.

'Yessiree,' said the big American quietly, his usually

boisterous and loud personality now subdued by the seriousness of the situation, 'that's just about all the choices in one, I'd say.'

'That's what we had to do in India,' muttered the Colonel, in an ineffectual way, '... sometimes it worked.'

Stephen ignored the remark. There was no alternative to the suggested treatment.

'Rupert, you hold her arm steady. No, not you, Miss Cuttle – this needs a firm hand. Mrs Porter, can you please take Miss Cuttle out of the way...'

Sylvia Baxter had slumped even lower in her chair. She had lost the colour in her face and had become quite still. Stephen took a scalpel from his bag, made a cross incision over the bite marks and sucked out some blood, which he spat onto the sand. He repeated the manoeuvre several times. Colonel Ponsworthy had, in the meantime, been mopping Miss Baxter's brow with his handkerchief, moistened with some cold water from the ice-chest.

'I say, Doctor, she's not moving,' he said, '... and her eyes are closed.'

Stephen felt her neck for a pulse. There was none.

'I'm afraid that she's dead,' he said, in the matter-of-fact way that working amongst the fatalities on the Western Front had taught him.

'I had best send for Mohammed,' said Rupert.

He gently let go of the dead girl's arm and crossed to where Daoud was standing, being careful not to tread on the spilled contents of the unfortunate girl's picnic hamper, which were spread in a wide arc around her chair.

'Daoud, off you go back to the ship and ask Mohammed to come here as quickly as he can. And I think you had better ask him to tell the police to come here, too – just to be safe.'

14

The Portuguese Coast

Beira, Portuguese East Africa – Sunday, 1st July 1928

'Major Ashdown?' asked a voice, shouting above the hustle and bustle of Beira's railway station in perfect, almost accent-free English.

It was mid-afternoon and in all directions people were on the move. The train had no sooner stopped moving than the hawkers had crowded around the carriages, offering fruit and cups of dubious-looking water for sale. The train disgorged a seemingly endless flow of people in a variety of rainbow colours, some with the determined look of those confident of their business, and others, like Major Ashdown, not at all sure of what their next move might be. Above all these sounds of activity was the noise of escaping steam, competing with the incessant babble of myriad African languages. As if to add to the cacophony, unintelligible station announcements in Portuguese attempted unsuccessfully to relay arrival and departure information.

'Er … yes, I am Major Ashdown.'

'Lieutenant da Sousa, Sir, at your service,' replied the young soldier, giving Ashdown a smart salute and flashing a disarming, Latin smile.

'Pleased to meet you,' replied Ashdown, extending his hand for the Lieutenant to shake. As he was out of uniform, he did not return the military greeting. Since he had started following the trail of this 'Griffin', he had avoided military dress and had kept to civvies. He judged this the most appropriate dress, for the sake of anonymity, given the nature of his task. Da Sousa's handshake was firm and confident and he looked Ashdown in the eye.

'Do you have your luggage,' he enquired, 'or is it still on the train...?'

'Indeed I do,' replied the Major, 'just this one suitcase.'

'Excellent. Allow me to carry it for you.'

He motioned to a uniformed African sergeant, who was standing a couple of respectful paces behind him, to take the Major's suitcase from him.

'I have a car waiting outside and I think I have managed to uncover some information you might find useful. This way, Major.'

And with that, the little procession set forth through the mass of people that thronged the platform, the African sergeant in the lead, da Sousa and Ashdown bringing up the rear.

Outside the main building of the railway station, the broad boulevard was lined with shops and small cafés, several of which had tables and umbrellas set out on the pavements. Trees, mostly mature, were planted every few yards and the branches of these offered additional shade to those who were enjoying a cup of coffee or something stronger. Caught up in the unexpected bustle of activity on the streets of Beira, it seemed to Ashdown that everywhere he looked people were trying to sell things – informally, from trays they carried suspended from a sling around the neck, to more serious vendors, who had improvised a counter from empty wooden boxes on which to display the mountains of multi-coloured fruits they had for sale.

'We are a very busy port, Major, a centre of commerce in the region,' commented da Sousa, as the military car crawled its way through the throng and down the street.

'We are the gateway to southern Mozambique and are also the biggest town for hundreds of miles. You could say that everyone is imbued with the commercial spirit and is either importing or trying to sell something.' He laughed at his own observation. 'We have the usual shops, of course, as you will see, but we also have a large local population who are really very good at selling, without needing the confines of four walls to do so.'

'That certainly seems to be the case from what I've seen so far, Lieutenant,' replied Ashdown.

'You might also be wondering why it is so busy, Portugal being a Catholic country and today being Sunday...' He left the sentence unfinished and smiled at the Major, raising one eyebrow, as if to indicate that the answer was forthcoming, whatever Ashdown's reply might have been.

'Although we are a province of Portugal, we are six thousand miles from Lisbon. So, although we naturally follow the norms of Portuguese life, we have modified things a little to suit the circumstances. You could say that on a Sunday, the Church has control of people's souls until lunchtime; after that, well...' – he gestured out of the car window – 'see for yourself. The escudo could be thought of as more powerful than the confessional!' And he chuckled again.

They drove slowly onwards for a short time in silence.

'Is this your first time in Beira?' asked da Sousa.

'Yes, it is. My family are from Kenya originally, but I left there just after the war and moved further south. So I've been around our part of Southern Africa quite a bit, but this is my first trip over the border into foreign territory, as it were.'

'Then I hope your experience is a pleasant one,' said the Lieutenant, smiling.

The car continued its progress along the broad streets of the city, past buildings that would have looked just as cosy in a Lisbon suburb, as they did in the humid heat of Southern Africa.

'So, what do you think of our city, so far?' smiled the Lieutenant eventually.

'I am impressed with what I've seen. People seem to have a definite purpose about them and your architectural style is quite different from ours.'

They drove on for a while, both men making companionable conversation.

Eventually, after what he considered a suitable length of time, Ashdown said, 'You mentioned back in the railway station that you had some news that might interest me…'

'Ah yes, I have been busy on your behalf, Major. I received a telegram from my superiors in Lourenço Marques and am quite fully briefed on your reason for being here.'

'Indeed,' replied Ashdown, at once impressed by the cross-border cooperation, but, in equal measure, concerned at the free flow of information.

'Once we had received instructions, we placed some of our men to watch the arrivals at the railway station. Regrettably, by then, much time had passed since you, presumably, had requested our assistance from Salisbury.'

The car suddenly bounced violently, as it hit a pothole in the road. The Lieutenant let fly a stream of Portuguese at the unfortunate Sergeant, who gripped the steering wheel even more tightly than before.

'I am sorry about that, Major, the nature of our weather here can sometimes cause such things to appear unexpectedly in the road – the municipality will, no doubt, soon have the matter repaired.'

He smiled his disarming smile again, all trace of the anger gone from his face, but it did little to hide the iron determination in his eyes.

Definitely a thoroughly focused, career soldier with ambition, determined Ashdown.

'I am afraid that we have had no success in identifying anyone arriving by train who comes close to matching your description, as sketchy as it is,' said the Lieutenant. 'In any case, if, as you suspect, this person arrived here from Salisbury on the train prior to yours, we would not have had the time to prepare our men to watch the station.'

Ashdown gave an involuntary grimace of disappointment.

'I see that you are disappointed at the news, Major,' said da Sousa, 'but fear not. That is not the news I have to give you. I have also had my people looking at other forms of transport – both in and out of the city.'

Thorough and imaginative as well, added Ashdown to his previous opinion.

'One of my men located something very interesting. It seems a tall, aristocratic European gentleman, more or less as per the details you supplied us, purchased a ticket for Dar es Salaam, further up the coast, in what used to be German East Africa...' – there was a slight pause again – 'but which now belongs to you, Major.'

The Lieutenant paused to let his words sink in. Ashdown gave no indication that he had fully understood the implication behind the remark.

'Are you sure that he was going there?' asked Ashdown.

'As sure as we can possibly be, given the circumstances,' replied da Sousa. 'It is the only thing we have been able to discover that might help us.'

'When was this, then? I hope your trains to Dar es Salaam are more frequent than ours are from Salisbury to Beira.'

The Lieutenant laughed.

'There *are* no trains to Dar-es-Salaam, Major. You have to go by sea – up the coast.'

'By sea?' echoed Ashdown, his voice showing signs of bewilderment.

'Indeed,' replied da Sousa. 'It is only a matter of some three days at most, if the voyage is a good one. The gentleman

I referred to purchased a single ticket to Dar es Salaam on the *Principe Antonio,* one of our own passenger ships. She sailed on Friday, on the afternoon tide – almost immediately after he had purchased the ticket. In fact, I am reliably told, he was lucky to catch the sailing at all.'

Ashdown was beginning to sense the feeling of hopelessness he had experienced so often before, since becoming involved in this case. He would have felt a lot happier if the trail was warmer and not two days old. When could he get closer to his goal?

'We will shortly be arriving at the harbourmaster's office in the docks. He will be able to give you further information. If you wish to pursue this gentleman, then I am afraid you will have to do so by ship, Major.'

Standing in the harbourmaster's office, Major Ashdown was impressed by the sight of the busy docks, which spread out before him as he looked through a large, panoramic window. Da Sousa had introduced him to the harbourmaster, who was an elderly man, burned brown by a combination of the African sun and many years before the mast.

'You are in luck,' said the Lieutenant. 'The next sailing to Dar es Salaam is tomorrow afternoon,' he continued, translating the Harbourmaster's response to his question. 'The steamship *Zambesi* – one of yours,' he added, 'is part of the Southern Trading Steamship Navigation Company. They are based in Durban, but they have an office here in Beira.'

Da Sousa then asked for details of the tides and expected departure time.

'... And she sails at 4.30 tomorrow afternoon,' he translated. 'I suggest we make haste to their offices and reserve you a berth, to use the correct nautical language.' He flashed his Latin smile again. 'If we are fortunate, they will still be open – even on a Sunday!'

'Thank you, my thoughts exactly,' replied Ashdown. He was beginning to warm to this young man.

Back once again in the car, as the vehicle moved through the last hours of the Sunday traffic, they made slow progress towards the steamship offices.

'Do you have a more reliable description of the man you are following, Major?' asked the Lieutenant, after a spell of silence.

'Not really, no. There have been a couple of incidents which possibly contain a common thread: a tall European of aristocratic bearing. He seems to be possessed of a fiery temper and we have a vague description of his physical appearance, but that's about it. We have no indication of his facial appearance as yet. We have nothing else to go on. The only other fact is that this chap carries a heavy black cane, which would appear to serve more as a weapon than a support.'

The Lieutenant smiled.

'Here in Mozambique we have many tall Europeans of aristocratic bearing who possibly possess fiery tempers. That does not narrow the field much, I am afraid. Black canes are also easily come by. I would venture to suggest that you are looking for the proverbial needle in the haystack, as you would say...'

Again, Ashdown was reminded of the seeming hopelessness of his task. He chose to ignore the Lieutenant's simile.

'Possibly, but this cane is different; it keeps appearing. From what reports we have, it has a highly ornate handle in silver – a bird – possibly a griffin – with red rubies for eyes. One of the porters was set about the head with it at Salisbury railway station. When the poor chap had calmed down, the one thing he remembered clearly was the flashing red eyes of the handle as it came down on his head.'

They continued for a few minutes in silence, enfolded by the noises of the street.

'As a matter of interest, have you had any reports of unusual crimes over the last few days?' asked the Major, eventually.

For a few moments, da Sousa thought, whilst staring out of the window. Then he turned to Ashdown.

'No more than the usual for this time of the year,' he said. 'In Mozambique, the army works very closely with the police, so we keep each other mutually informed of events. We find the system works well – a lot of uniforms are good for order – *pour encourager les autres.*' He looked at Ashdown with a raised eyebrow, as if to emphasize his last point. 'Why do you ask?'

'I was just wondering if there had been any out-of-the-ordinary crimes, particularly murders, if you can regard murder as anything *but* out of the ordinary…'

Realizing that this was a fruitless avenue of enquiry, Ashdown decided to keep the rest of his information about the murders at Beit Bridge and Salisbury to himself.

The car bumped to a halt outside a double-storey office block, along the ground floor of which ran a cool, spacious, arcaded veranda in what Ashdown took to be the Portuguese colonial style. Like most of the buildings he had seen, this one was painted brilliant white.

'Here we are, Major,' said da Sousa, as he opened the door to get out.

The Major had shown his letter of authority to da Sousa almost as soon as they had left the railway station and da Sousa had assured him that, in the interests of Southern African cooperation between empires, Portugal would offer him full assistance. And so it proved to be. Within a very short time the ticket, a single passage to Dar es Salaam, had been purchased on the written authority of the Lieutenant. In fact, it had occurred to Ashdown that the desk clerk who wrote out the ticket seemed to be uneasy, faced as he was by an army lieutenant. He had not hesitated for a second when da Sousa had informed him that he would authorize the ticket and that the payment would follow through the normal channels.

'As you wish, Sir,' said the clerk, 'we are only too pleased to be of service.' But the faint look of nervousness and unease, which had lingered around the man's mouth and eyes, told another story. Ashdown had understood nothing of the conversation.

'Do not worry yourself about anything, Major,' said da Sousa, as they left the cool shelter of the offices and emerged once again into the lengthening shadows of early evening. 'My superiors in Lourenço Marques will sort things out with your superiors in Salisbury ... or wherever they are,' he added, after a short pause.

Back in the car again, the shadows deepened into the first fingers of twilight, which began to caress the sparkling white buildings. Ashdown, for the first time since his arrival in the city, suddenly turned his thoughts to where he was going to stay for the night.

'I forgot to ask the clerk in the shipping office if I could perhaps board the ship tonight. Otherwise, I have nowhere to stay.'

'Not practicable, I'm afraid, Major. The *Zambezi* does not dock until nearly midnight tonight – she is still on her way up from Durban. I did not bother translating that part for you.'

'I see,' replied Ashdown. 'Could you then recommend a good hotel for tonight?'

'That will not be necessary Major – you are to be the guest of myself and my wife for the night. It is not that often that I have the chance to brush up on my English and my wife will welcome the company. Whilst Beira is a commercial hub, the social opportunities are somewhat limited and even a career soldier and his wife occasionally get bored with the same, predictable social calendar.'

He smiled again, as the car turned off the main avenue and slowly headed out of the commercial district of the city.

Later that evening, after a chance to bathe and change, Ashdown had enjoyed a very pleasant meal, during which da Sousa had helped his wife with the occasional translation. She was an attractive woman in her early thirties, her black hair drawn back into a bun on the back of her head. Her shapely form was encased to advantage in a tight-fitting summer dress and her full, rounded breasts were still filled with the last of the milk with which she had suckled their recently born baby. Although she spoke passable, if somewhat halting, English, her vocabulary was not extensive and she often lost the thread of the conversation. After the meal, the two men sat on the balcony of the Lieutenant's married quarters and enjoyed the sight and sounds of the city by night, which sprawled out in a compact cluster a little below them. The conversation was companionable and interlaced with the smoke of cigars and the flavour of a good port.

'If you don't mind me asking, Juan,' – the two men were now on first-name terms, the formality of military rank totally dispensed with – 'where did you pick up such a good command of English?'

Da Sousa laughed.

'Would you believe, Jeremy, at public school in England? My mother is English. She met my father whilst he was military attaché at the Embassy in London. After they were married, she returned with him to Lisbon and then I came along. My whole family is bilingual and my parents thought it a very good idea that I absorb a little of your famous British education, so I spent four years at Richborough College. Do you know it at all ... in Berkshire...?'

'No, I can't say that I do,' replied Ashdown.

'That accounts for my broader view of things, I expect,' continued da Sousa, 'which does tend to raise me a little above my colleagues, at times,' he said, with a smile. 'Some of them can be dreadfully parochial. I have to confess that I also find the benefit of having been in a Protestant environment for those few years to be mind-broadening, although I dare say my superiors might take a different view, if they knew my thinking,' he continued. 'They can see no further than the end of their rosaries, as far as belief and rational thought are concerned. Bless them all,' he added after a short pause. 'And you, Jeremy, what is your background?'

'I'm Kenyan – born, bred and educated. I never had the chance to go to school back in the Old Country. Didn't really need to, I suppose – it was more useful growing up and being educated in Kenya. It taught me about the land and the people. My family were coffee farmers in the Highlands – have been almost since the white settlers arrived there. My sister and her husband carry on the family traditions now, as best they can. He was married before – nice chap, but he was wounded in the war, so it's quite difficult. The farm is ten thousand acres – pretty big.'

Da Sousa noticed that the reference to Ashdown's family was in the past tense, but said nothing. For some time, the two men continued in similar vein, each telling the other about their careers, family backgrounds and career hopes for the future. It was approaching midnight when they moved to turn in for the night. They rose from the comfortable chairs in which they had been sitting for the last few hours. As they stood on the balcony, looking down on the lights of the city, da Sousa took hold of the Major's arm.

'Look, out there,' he said, pointing into the inky blackness where the night sky met the endless ocean. 'Lights – green, red and white. See them? That's probably your *Zambezi*.'

Ashdown made a mental note not to become overly concerned with the fact that the lights of the approaching ship were the size of so many pinpricks in a vast sheet of black paper. He had never been to sea before.

'She is a good ship. You will have an enjoyable voyage,' continued da Sousa, as he leaned on the balcony railings. 'The ship is nearly twelve thousand tons and carries cargo and passengers between Cape Town and Port Said, stopping off at several ports along the East Coast. The *Zambezi* has been on this route for years and was one of your surface raiders during the war. She narrowly missed a scuffle with the *Königsberg* – the German cruiser that was eventually trapped in the Rufiji river delta. The story was that a junior navigating officer on your ship made a miscalculation and that was enough to keep the two ships apart. That was lucky for the *Zambezi* – and your country, of course. If they had met, the superior firepower of *Königsberg* would have made short work of *Zambezi*.' He laughed, 'So there you are – she is a charmed ship.'

The next afternoon, her loading complete, *Zambezi* was carefully inched away from the quayside, stern first, and hauled out into the current by two nervously fussy tugs, black coal smoke belching from their funnels. Suddenly, somewhere high up on the bridge of the steamship, a bell rang shrilly and, almost immediately, the water astern of *Zambezi* erupted into a heaving mass of bubbling foam, as her double screws slowly began to beat the Indian Ocean into submission. The bows, untethered from the massive iron bollards on the quayside, slowly swung around away from the quay and the vessel steamed majestically out into the roadstead. On the quay, the smartly turned-out figure of Lieutenant Juan da Sousa stood rigidly to attention, saluting. Major Ashdown waved his hand over his head at the steadily receding figure in a gesture of gratitude and farewell. He had rapidly grown to like the genuine warmth of the young soldier and wondered if their paths would ever cross again in the future.

15
Edfu

The Nile, the Temple of Horus – 21st July 1928

The expedition to the Temple of Horus at Edfu had come to a very unpleasant and abrupt end with the death of Sylvia Baxter. Marjory Cuttle, usually a bastion of reliable respectability and decorum, had dissolved into a gibbering heap that not even the considerable contents of Colonel Ponsworthy's hip flask could steady. Mr Rotherham, too, had unsuccessfully attempted to console her.

'I know what you are feeling,' he said, 'I felt exactly the same way when Edith went. Of course, it was not at all like this...'

The sentence trailed off, unfinished. He realized that he had said the wrong thing, even before he had finished saying it. Any calming effect he thought his words might have had evaporated as immediately as water in the Egyptian heat and Miss Cuttle once again became hysterical, dissolving into a river of seemingly unstoppable tears.

'Do you think you should give her something to calm her down?' asked Rupert. 'She really does seem to be in a bad way.'

'Not half as bad a way as Miss Baxter,' muttered Stephen, turning his head to look at the sobbing woman. 'It's probably delayed shock more than anything else. We used to see a lot of it in the war. Good hard slap across the face usually does the trick and calms them down,' – he looked around at the little knot of concerned faces – 'but let's hope it doesn't come to that – not with the rest of them staring...'

He was saved the trouble.

'Miss Cuttle, please – this is for your own good!'

Simon Arling lashed out with a well-aimed hand, which struck the gibbering woman across the cheek. The results were almost instantaneous. Marjory Cuttle stopped her wailing and stood stock still, staring ahead of her with eyes as blank as those of the massive statue of the hawk-god Horus, which stood at the entrance to the First Hypostyle Hall.

'I am sorry I had to do that,' continued Simon Arling, 'but it seemed the only thing *to* do.'

Miss Cuttle slowly turned her blank eyes on him, with a look somewhere between bewilderment and understanding.

'Yes ... of course ... how weak of me...' she mumbled.

'Take my hankie, dear – it will be quite all right, you'll see,' chirruped Rebecca Eggerton who, up until now, had maintained her usual inconsequential presence and had passed largely unnoticed by the majority of the party. 'Mr Winfield will sort everything out and make all the arrangements.'

At the mention of 'the arrangements', it looked for a split second as if Marjory Cuttle would once again burst into a flood of tears. But she seemed suddenly calmed by the sight of the recumbent form of Sylvia Baxter; her hands drooping to the sandy floor from under the discreet anonymity of the spare tarpaulin placed reverently over the corpse by Khatose.

'Yes ... of course ... the arrangements will have to be made...' she mumbled.

'Come with me, my dear,' twittered Miss Eggerton. 'Look, here's Mrs Porter to help as well. Let's just go for a little walk over here – away from this spot – off we go – into the shade of those columns. Come along, now, mind the food on the floor...' Rebecca Eggerton had taken Cuttle by the arm and was turning her away from the sight of the covered corpse. As Lydia Porter took her other arm, she nearly tripped.

'Oh! Get out of the way, you stupid dog! Go on – shooo!' she snapped, angrily.

Marjory Cuttle, her mind in turmoil, allowed herself to be led away through the spilled contents of Sylvia Baxter's picnic hamper. In the near distance, to where it had scuttled away, resentfully, the stray dog barked its displeasure at having been chased away from an unexpected windfall meal.

'Ladies and gentlemen,' said Rupert, taking charge of the situation, 'I have sent one of the crew back to the ship for help. Mohammed should be with us soon and then we will all have to return to the boat, I'm afraid. Under the circumstances, I'm sure you'll understand that we have to cut short our visit.'

There was a general murmur of consent. Eric Kormann made to pick up the scattered picnic lunch and return it to Sylvia Baxter's picnic hamper.

'I really think that you should leave things exactly as they are, Mr Kormann,' said Stephen, his hand held out in a restraining gesture. 'You never know, the police might want to have a look over things just as they are.'

'The police?' echoed the Swiss. 'Will they be here?'

For a split second a look of near-panic swept across the little man's face, before being dismissed by the flash of the sun in his spectacle lenses.

Rupert, Stephen, Simon Arling and Grupfelder all fancied they had detected this, but none of them said anything.

'Is it really necessary to involve the police in this?' asked Sebastian Printon, who had made his way to the front of the group. 'Surely this is just an unfortunate accident and could have happened to anyone?'

Stephen eyed him curiously for a second before replying. 'We don't know one way or the other. So, yes – for the moment, of course the police must become involved. There has been an unexpected death and they will have to be told about it and to investigate, even if it is just purely routine.'

There was a momentary hiatus in the proceedings before Kormann continued. He seemed to have regained his usual composure.

'But naturally,' he said, as he removed his spectacles and proceeded to clean them with a large white handkerchief, 'it must be so and purely routine, as you say. There can surely be no question of a crime ... I am sorry for asking such a stupid question,' he continued, in his slightly accented English. 'My family have bad memories of the police – that is all,' and with that he replaced his spectacles, resumed his usual innocuous appearance and literally melted away into the background.

Colonel Ponsworthy stared after him, as did Mr Rotherham. It was Grupfelder who ambled off to follow him.

'There really is no point in us all just standing around here, waiting for Mohammed and his chaps to arrive,' said Rupert. 'I know it's a bad show, but please feel free to have a look at the carvings around the Court. Just don't wander too far...'

In the far corner of the Court, Grupfelder and the little Swiss were sitting on a chunk of fallen granite that had once been half of an enormous statue of a pharaoh that had not stood the test of time.

'You OK, buddy?' asked the big American, in his friendly manner.

'Yes, thank you, I am fine,' replied his diminutive companion, looking down at the sandy floor.

'Don't fret yourself about things,' continued Grupfelder. 'These are British police and play the game according to British rules. It'll all be smooth as a ride in a well-sprung buggy.'

'Yes ... I am sorry for my reaction.' He turned to the American. 'Even the Swiss police make mistakes when people lie to them,' he said enigmatically, and then, pushing his spectacles further up the bridge of his nose, he turned and stared blankly at the sandy floor again.

A short while later, accompanied by two armed Egyptian policemen, a British police inspector arrived in the Court. After a reasonably thorough look around and a cursory investigation of the body, the inspector announced himself satisfied that the unfortunate incident had been the most regrettable accident.

'You and your party may return to your ship,' he said to Rupert, just as Mohammed and some of *Khufu*'s crew appeared at the entrance to the complex. 'For my part, I would ask that you accompany me to the station and give me a written statement. I'll file a report about this incident and pass the information on to Aswan. They may require you to give them a statement once you arrive there. There are also certain procedures regarding the body of the deceased, which Aswan will be far better equipped to deal with than we are. Do you have provision to store the body on your vessel until the formalities have been completed?'

'Of course,' replied Rupert, 'we will make provision. Miss Baxter is still one of our party until Aswan authorizes release of the body for burial.' *I hope Mohammed can find a space that is large enough and cold enough*, he thought, surreptitiously glancing back towards the corpse.

The muted conversation between Rupert and the police inspector had not gone unnoticed by the rest of the group.

'They're all the same,' muttered Simon Arling, 'they are all joined to *the station* by an invisible thread...'

As the policemen and Rupert left the Court, Mohammed and the additional crewmen he had brought with him advanced.

'It's just an accident, Mohammed, a bad accident,' said Rupert, who was attempting to calm down the little Egyptian, who had begun to display the familiar, tell-tale signs of agitation. 'Just stay calm – perhaps you should have a word with our guests...' he added, gesturing towards the huddled groups of deflated travellers.

Mohammed set about this task with sincere, if annoying dedication. After making many appropriate expressions of consolation, in some instances twice to the same person, he retrieved the canvas sheet that had covered the picnic hampers. With subdued words of command he set his men about the task of preparing to lay the body on top of one of the carts. Once he had respectfully covered Sylvia Baxter with the canvas, his men would have to quickly pack away the picnic equipment and load it onto the other carts, which he had already summoned from the shade where they had dispersed on arrival at the temple a few brief hours before. The tourists, too, started to wander out of the Court and back towards their waiting transport.

'Darling, did you notice dear Mrs Grassmere saying anything?' asked Esther Arling, slipping her arm through her husband's as they walked back to where the carts were drawn up.

'No, I can't say that I did. Why do you ask?' he replied.

'Oh, it's just an idle observation, that's all. She's moaned and groaned about almost everything since we started this trip and yet – faced with this, the golden opportunity to hold court – neither of us can remember her saying anything.'

'Perhaps she was just overcome by events,' replied her husband.

'Well, if she was, it would surely have to be the first time ever! She has a mouth on her the size of Tower Bridge!'

'Dar-ling!' reproved her husband. 'Tolerance ... one of the strongest assets of our race. But you're quite right. In fact, the shadow-like and otherwise totally ineffectual Mr Kormann left more of a mark on things than she did. Now *that* must surely be a first!'

They allowed themselves a private laugh, despite the solemnity of the occasion and walked slowly on. They were joined by Sebastian Printon.

'And what do you think?' asked Esther, as she put her other arm through Printon's and drew him closer.

'I'd say it was an accident. No doubt about it. When you consider the ferocious nature of most of the smaller animal and insect life in Egypt, I suppose we could all count ourselves lucky to have progressed this far without having been bitten by something.'

They laughed again.

'Oh, Sebastian,' cooed Esther, 'you are amusing. What are your plans for this evening?'

She seemed to be rather unmoved by the sad events of barely an hour before and incurred a withering glance from Mrs Porter, who had formed a low opinion of her at first sight and now thought even less of her. Lydia Porter certainly did not appreciate her unseemly frivolity in such unfortunate circumstances.

'Well, there's no need to drag ourselves along as if we're following the hearse!' Esther replied in response to the frosty glare, thrusting out her chest in a provocative gesture. 'After all – it's not as if we are part of a cortège now, is it?'

Esther's strength lay in her obsession with beauty and her own body. The fact that they had, indeed, suddenly all become members of a slow funeral procession back to *Khufu* went completely over her head.

FATAL TEARS

The sad little convoy of carriages and carts had returned to *Khufu* in almost total silence, save for the whinnying of the horses and the noise of the wheels sucking their way through the fine sand covering the quay. Even the hawkers and omnipresent urchins seemed to have been forewarned of the sobriety of the occasion and had either fallen silent or disappeared altogether. The recumbent form of Miss Sylvia Baxter, respectfully arranged on a trestle table top and still covered with the canvas sheet, was ceremoniously unloaded, then gently manhandled up the narrow gangplank and onto the strangely silent steamship. Mohammed, who had managed to regain some of his former composure, now stood awaiting the body in the reception foyer. He had been supervising the sad little procession with something approaching his usual aplomb. Bringing up the rear were the Lamptons.

'Excuse me a moment,' said Richard Lampton to the little Egyptian, who was replacing his fez, which he had reverently doffed as the table top had been borne past him and away into the depths of the boat.

'Indeed, Sir?' he replied.

'I know this might not be the right time or place, but I really need to talk to you about my luncheon basket.'

Mohammed flashed a subdued version of his gold-toothed smile and motioned Lampton to continue.

'Well, I just couldn't eat it. When I opened...' and his voice faded as Mohammed waved Lampton and his wife into the ship, towards the door to his office.

Despite the blazing sunshine outside, a chilled pall of gloom descended rapidly over the little steamer. By late afternoon, when *reis* Tarek decided that the time was right to cast off and press on to Aswan, the sombre mood of the earlier afternoon had not been dispelled. So, as the crew went quietly about their allotted tasks, the mooring ropes were slipped in silence and *Khufu* glided gracefully out into the river. Even the slowly revolving paddle wheel seemed to hardly disturb the mirror-like face of the water, each languid revolution smacking the surface like the sound of a muffled funeral drum. By early evening, with the first warming glow of sunset embracing the eastern hills, a gentle breeze had sprung up, banishing the last rearguard of the day's stifling heat. Even such a welcome relief did little to lift the gloom.

After consultation with Rupert, Mohammed had decided that the daily routine was to be followed, by way of hastening a return to something resembling normality. And so, at the appointed hour, the guests had been summoned to the dining room for their evening meal, as usual, by the three bongs of 'Three Blind Mice'. The kitchens had done themselves proud and had produced a spectacular display of cooked meats, salads, vegetables, cheeses and fruit. Nestling amongst lumps of ice were bowls containing a large selection of assorted dairy-based desserts. To the acute embarrassment of her husband, Mrs Grassmere seemed to be the only one in the dining room who had managed to find her appetite since the unfortunate event in the temple. She said nothing, but managed to do justice to the splendid fare. Grupfelder, too, had not lost his appetite and asked if there were any steaks on the menu.

'I can't be dealing with all this fancy food stuff,' he said to Kormann, who was beginning to become his regular companion. 'I'm a cattleman, damn it!'

The little Swiss had found that he could draw a feeling of security and confidence from the American's gregarious, outgoing nature. He sat next to Grupfelder, picking idly at a modest plate of lamb, chickpeas and rice.

'Yessiree! Give me a good slab of steak any day,' continued the American.

Kormann smiled back wanly. His own appetite had largely deserted him.

FATAL TEARS

Of the assembled tourists, sitting in their by now familiar groupings in the dining room, it was only Mrs Grassmere and Grupfelder who, quite literally, made a meal of the food on offer. Apart from their efforts to do it justice, most of the rest of the display of food went untouched.

'Come on, old chap, eat something – we're not the dead ones and you have to keep the old engine fuelled, y' know,' said Stephen, as he finished his modest meal.

'Yes, Stephen, I suppose you're right. I just wonder what's going to be said about this at Head Office.'

'What *is* there to say, old chap? As far as the police are concerned, it was an accident. Open-and-shut case. Eat your salad.'

Eventually, after nearly forty minutes of subdued, whispered conversations, Rupert tapped his glass and rose to speak.

'Ladies and gentlemen,' he began, 'I have no wish to remind you unnecessarily of today's sad events. However, the police are happy enough that it was an unfortunate accident and have advised us to continue with our cruise to Aswan.'

There was hardly any response from the room. For one brief moment, it looked as if Esther Arling was about to say something, but she did not. Mrs Grassmere continued spooning a yoghurt and pastry-based dessert into her mouth. Marjory Cuttle had taken to her bed and Miss Eggerton had volunteered to sit in her cabin with her to keep her company. Lydia Porter found herself on a table with the Manningtons, who had said practically nothing the whole day and said even less now. The Lamptons were sitting with Mr Rotherham, who, at least, had had the decency to avoid his favourite topic of conversation and had steered clear of the condiments. Mrs Kirby, as usual, was sitting by herself.

As he spoke, Rupert glanced around, thinking that Stephen was not far off the mark with his earlier assessment of the characteristics of this particular group of tourists.

'Given the circumstances, once we have clearance from the police in Aswan, I feel it would be for the best if we carry on with our itinerary,' he continued. 'The inspector at Edfu assured me that obtaining such clearance will be a formality.'

The silence was broken by the sound of a flint striking against a friction wheel. Esther Arling threw back her head and blew out a long plume of cigarette smoke. Her bright-red fingernails at the ends of the slim fingers that held the cigarette were, despite the events of the day, as immaculate as they had been at breakfast that morning.

'Thank you, Sebastian,' she said, smiling at Printon, 'how *gallant* ...'

Her last remark was loaded with meaning, which was not lost on Printon.

'You're welcome,' answered Printon, who returned the lighter to his inside jacket pocket.

She had sat forward for him to light her cigarette. Under the discreet cover of the table top, unseen by anyone else, her other hand was inching its way up the inside of his thigh. Rupert gave her a slight look of annoyance – why was it that this woman always seemed to take things so frivolously? As she sat even further forward, getting her wide lips even closer to Printon's ear, Rupert cleared his throat and continued, before she could say anything further.

'I am, therefore, going to suggest that, whilst we must remember our late companion, we should look to the future and carry on ... As she would, no doubt, have wanted us to...',

Rupert was interrupted by Ruth Kirby.

'May she rest in peace.'

Several others in the room turned to look at her.

'Well ... what are you all staring at?' she asked testily. 'Isn't that what usually gets said? So why should this time be any different?'

Remembering what Stephen had said about her pupils, Rupert tried to look at them, but she was too distant and had turned her head away from him.

'Perhaps Miss Kirby has a point,' said Rupert, turning to once again address the whole gathering. 'May she rest in peace. She did certainly seem to be enjoying herself. Who is to say that she would not want *us* to continue doing so?'

There were a few muttered responses from around the room.

'We should be in Aswan by mid-morning tomorrow. As a mark of respect, I propose that we spend the day reflecting. There could well be loose ends we need to secure with the paperwork and the police, once we arrive. The following day we should continue with our programme and start with a visit to the Unfinished Obelisk. I'll give you more information about the site later. In the meantime, please feel free to help yourselves. Mohammed and Faisal will be only too pleased to provide you with whatever you wish. Thank you.'

Casting a furtive glance at the almost untouched mountains of food, Rupert sat down again. Standing in the entrance doors to the dining room, Mohammed was looking far from pleased and Faisal, the affable maître d'hôtel, was looking positively suicidal. Culinary matters were always taken very much to heart and any loss of appetite on the part of the guests, for whatever reason, was always taken as a personal insult to the chef and kitchen staff. The general feeling of gloom and the whispered drone of muttered conversation continued to fill the dining room.

'I've had enough of this,' whispered Stephen, as he rose and placed his napkin on the table. 'Fancy a cigarette? I'll wait for you on the upper deck,' he said.

He nodded a good night salutation to the rest of the room as he left the dining room.

Shortly afterwards, having taken Stephen's departure as

their cue, the other members of the group started to leave the dining room. Within a few minutes the dining room emptied, save for Rupert, Mohammed and Faisal.

'Well done, you two – a really terrific spread,' said Rupert, but his words seemed to be of little consultation to Faisal.

'They have hardly touched a morsel, *Effendi*,' he said. 'Hardly a morsel.'

'I know,' said Rupert, given his shoulder a reassuring pat. 'You ought to pack things away now. Mohammed, I think it only fair to please tell your chaps to help themselves to whatever they want – and thank you, Faisal.'

The maître-d'hôtel managed a wan smile of gratitude, but was not really convinced by the explanation. He turned and made his way back towards the kitchen.

'Don't take it personally,' Rupert called after him. 'They are upset, that's all.'

'And I, for myself, am also most distressingly upset, Mr Rupert,' said Mohammed, 'and I have considerable fear that Head Office is also being for themselves very upset,' he continued, gesturing at the mountains of untouched food.

'Calm down, Mohammed, you did what was the right and only thing to have done, given the circumstances. Poor Miss Baxter had to go somewhere, so all of that had to come out of the cold room,' he said, gesturing to the food, 'and Faisal had very little option other than to prepare it all. You know as well as I do that nothing would keep in this heat. Head Office will understand that, and I will speak for you with them. You and Faisal did absolutely the correct thing.'

Mohammed looked appreciatively at Rupert and smiled. He had great respect for this young Englishman.

'Let Daoud and his chaps have a feast with it. Faisal will calm down in a few minutes and then we can all try and get back to normal. What do you say?'

He gave Mohammed an affectionate pat on the shoulder, but underneath the smile, Mohammed looked less than convinced. In Egypt, ruffled feathers took some considerable time to smooth themselves out again.

16

Dar es Salaam

The East African coast – Wednesday, 4th July 1928

The sea was as flat as a highly polished mirror. Out in the roadstead, the white hull of the *Principe Antonio* gleamed in the bright, post-dawn sunshine as she cut a clean swathe through the unresisting waters. Dense black smoke tumbled from her single, aquamarine stack. She was still coal-fired and would have to spend at least twenty-four hours in port when she reached Mombasa to refuel, but this was Dar es Salaam and here she would stop for only a few hours.

Arab dhows sailed majestically alongside her, as they, too, brought their cargoes to port and sought the shelter of the 'Haven of Peace'. Spices, herbs and incense – cargoes unchanged since ancient times – together with rice, carpets and other luxury commodities from the Arabian Peninsula and far-away India, would soon be offloaded and replaced with grain, ivory and any other cargo that would fetch a fair price on the return to home waters. Despite their picturesque appearance, there were occasional rumours of slaves being used to crew the dhows. There had been a recent report of a dhow master being questioned by the authorities over a crew member who had been seen tied to the mainmast all day in the blistering African heat. 'Punishment for transgressing the will of Allah' was the usual, universal reply.

FATAL TEARS

A sturdy tug suddenly appeared on the port beam and a heavy cable was secured between the *Principe Antonio* and the energetic little workhorse. With two blasts of her whistle, the little tug belched forth clouds of smoke to rival that of the bigger ship, churned the water astern of her small hull into a steaming frenzy, and slowly started to turn the bows of the much larger ship around to line her up with the waiting quay. In turn, the liner gave a deep-throated blast on her own hooter, as a warning to the other smaller ships hovering around her to clear out of the way.

The quay itself was a bustling hive of activity in anticipation of the impending docking. African stevedores, their muscular, ebony bodies already cooled with the first beads of the day's sweat, would soon manhandle the unloaded cargo into waiting carts or railway trucks. Dressed in Western suits and sheltered from the glare of the sun by their solar topees, port officials mingled with passengers' relatives and the occasional curious onlooker. Amongst this mêlée of people there were also many uniformed policemen. The frenzied activity on the quay was reflected on the decks of the towering, gleaming steel giant. Her crew scuttled backwards and forwards preparing thick mooring hawsers, uncovering hatches and swinging derricks up and out of their cradles, in preparation for the unloading and loading that would commence almost as soon as the hawsers had taken the strain of holding the starboard side of the ship against the quayside. Passengers lined the rails watching this well-rehearsed spectacle with interest. Some recognized friends or relations on the quayside and waved to them excitedly. Others busied themselves with their cameras, attempting to capture the scene for the eternal posterity of their memories and souvenir albums.

All of this energetic movement was countered by a bubble of calm, almost cold serenity, up on the promenade deck. A tall, thin man of aristocratic bearing stood silently, alone.

He had remained standing on the port side of the ship and was staring not at the hustle and bustle of the activity on the quayside, but out, across the broad, blue expanse of the roadstead, to where the Governor's residence gleamed, dazzling white on the side of a hill. From the tall flagstaff fluttered a large Union Flag, the morning breeze enough to stretch the banner out to its full length and proudly display the colours and device of the new masters of Tanganyika. As he watched through narrowed, hawk-like eyes, the tall man's hand gripped the ship's rail in a vice-like fury, which drained the blood from it, leaving it white and claw-like. In his mind's eye, he saw the red, white and black of the Imperial Eagle fluttering from that same flagstaff, as it had done in the past. If he had anything to do with it – if, in any way, he could help bring about such an event – then the Imperial Ensign would, once again, soon flutter over this kidnapped territory of the Fatherland. As he stared and remembered times lost, his other hand tightened around the handle of the heavy cane he carried. The highly ornate silver handle was almost obscured by the splayed fingers, yet the bird's ruby-red eyes still managed to reflect the bright, early-morning African sunlight with a sparkling intensity, which was only matched by that of the hatred which flared in the eyes of the cane's holder.

'Once again, we will have what is rightfully ours,' he muttered to himself through clenched teeth.

Further down the coast, almost a full two days' sailing behind the Portuguese vessel, *Zambezi* was making good progress on her voyage north. As soon as they had cleared Beira's busy harbour, Major Ashdown had introduced himself to the Captain, shown him his letter of authority and asked if a radio message could be sent ahead to Dar es Salaam.

'I don't see why not, Sir,' replied Captain Calvers, returning the letter to the Major. 'We might have to wait a while, though, until we get nearer. Our wireless range is a little limited as we do not have the transmitting power of an ocean liner. Neither do we have a large ship's speed, although we usually make up a little time on this leg of our voyage,' he continued. 'Things have speeded up a little since they replaced our coal with oil. We can refuel very quickly with no mess and we make far less smoke en route.' By force of habit, Calvers had lapsed into his prepared description of his ship, which he usually reserved for the guests at his table in the evenings. 'That means it's much more difficult for anyone to see us coming,' he continued, chuckling and thinking back to his war years, when a sizeable smudge of smoke could get a small ship like his sunk by the massive guns of a much bigger capital ship, still hidden from view over the horizon.

'Indeed, replied Ashdown,' a little irritated by the Captain's deviation from the matter in hand, 'but the message ... When we are within range ... can one be sent ahead of us, please ...?'

'Of course, and to whom should the message be sent?' asked the Captain.

'The Governor himself,' replied Ashdown and then added, 'Naturally, this has to be of the utmost secrecy, Captain. I need hardly remind you that there are issues of national importance attached to the letter you have just read.'

'Of course ... if you say so, Sir.'

After a lifetime at sea and service in the Royal Navy Volunteer Reserve, Captain Calvers was used to not asking questions when the situation obviously did not involve him. Whatever this man was up to did not concern him. He would carry this man on his ship just like any other passenger and then he would watch him disembark and that would be that.

'If we receive a reply, shall I have it sent to your cabin, Sir, or would you rather go up to the radio room and read it there?'

Despite his natural tendency to follow orders, the Captain had allowed himself a little leeway with his remark, managing to make it sound less facetious than it actually was. Calvers put it down to his approaching retirement and the happily anticipated return to his sailing boat and family on the Cornish coast. Although he would miss the fine weather and heat of Africa, like many others in positions of authority in the Colonies, he had grown tired and secretly yearned for escape from the responsibility he had shouldered for so long. He also anticipated the time when he would no longer have to pander to the occasional requests of his more eccentric passengers. He was still not certain if this man fell into this category.

'Thank you, Captain, an excellent suggestion. Given the security aspect, a visit to the radio room would, perhaps, be the more satisfactory course to take.'

Twenty-four hours later, still with three-quarters of a day's steaming ahead of them before reaching their destination, Major Ashdown found himself standing in *Zambezi*'s radio room. Captain Calvers, who had summoned him and then escorted him there, stood respectfully in the background.

'There you are, Sir,' said the radio operator, in an accent which Ashdown recognized as South African. 'It's quite a long one. It came through about fifteen minutes ago.'

Ashdown took the rectangular message form and silently started to read the neat, pencil writing which covered it:

From Police Commissioner Bowgood, Dar es Salaam

To Major Ashdown, SS Zambezi

SECRET

Your message to His Excellency refers. Have monitored activity of Principe Antonio, *as requested. No disembarking*

passenger resembling your description recognized. Principe Antonio *sailed for Mombasa today 3.30pm. His Excellency approves further assistance, if required. Please advise if you wish your message forwarded to Commissioner in Kenya.*
Yours, Bowgood.
Commissioner, Tanganyika Police.

'You might send a further message for me, Captain,' said Ashdown, as he reached across the radio operator and tore the top few blank sheets off the message pad.

'I shall need to reply to Dar es Salaam … a message for Commissioner Bowgood.'

As he spoke, he looked at the impression of the radio operator's handwriting that had been etched into the blank sheets of paper, and, in a seamless movement, tore them into several small fragments, finally stuffing the pieces into his pocket. He had long ago learned the value of taking care not to leave a trail.

'And there is another thing,' he continued, smiling at the Captain, 'I require an extension to my passage – I shall need to continue my voyage to Mombasa.'

17

The Portuguese Coast

Military Headquarters, Beira, Portuguese East Africa – Tuesday, 3rd July 1928

Lieutenant Juan da Sousa took a careful sip from the cup he was holding. Without taking his eyes off the distant view of the sea, he felt the wakening comfort of the strong, hot liquid course down through his body as he swallowed.

Another day at the centre of civilization, he thought and smiled.

Things were very good for him and his small family – the baby was doing well and Maria, his wife, was the happiest she had been in years. Since the arrival of their firstborn she had become a new person. The burden they had both carried for so long – of being childless in a community of large families – had become a serious problem and had caused each of them to silently blame the other's presumed infertility. But all of that had miraculously fallen away with the birth.

And what will this day bring, I wonder, he thought, crossing to his desk and putting down the now-empty cup and its saucer.

He started to wade through the pile of official papers and other documents which appeared on his desk first thing every morning. They related mostly to the security of the province and to the movements of certain of the more suspicious citizens within it. As he worked, he started to hum to himself – for some reason, Parry's tune 'Jerusalem'.

How strange that I should think of that, he thought, as he looked up from the page he was reading. *It is years since I sang that at school in England. It must be Jeremy's influence,* he mused, thinking of the enjoyment he had experienced during the Major's visit.

He returned to his reading. Suddenly the humming stopped. In his hand he held a routine police report, of the kind that was regularly passed to the military as a matter of courtesy. He read the content with growing interest:

... was found in an alley within the perimeter of the docks. The victim is one Antonio Jao Pirez, a petty criminal who has served a sentence for theft. He is also known to us as a handler of stolen goods, a pimp and a dealer in drugs. The motive for this death, which is suspicious, is not clear, other than to suppose criminal dealings of some sort are involved. The victim was killed by a single wound to the heart, delivered by a fine, stiletto-type blade several inches long. The motive cannot have been theft, as the body had over a hundred escudos in the trouser pocket and, strangely, another forty stuffed into the mouth. The possibility of a ritualistic killing, somehow involving the figure of 140 cannot be ignored, although, given the lack of an obvious motive and the absence of further evidence, this notion cannot be taken further at this stage. Following on the initial...

Da Sousa remembered the conversation he and Ashdown had had in the military vehicle, the day the Major had arrived in Beira.

Jeremy asked if there had been anything out of the ordinary recently. I wonder if he'd be interested in this? he thought, staring at the typed sheet. *A stiletto-like blade – now that is a little out of the ordinary. The likes of this Perez individual and his sort would be more used to the broader blade of a hunting or switch-knife, I would have thought.*

There was a knock on the door and a sergeant entered with another tray of papers and a request for the Lieutenant to go and see the Colonel immediately. It was only much later, when da Sousa was once again in the comfort of his home that evening, after he and Maria had played with their baby, eaten their meal and enjoyed each other's bodies under the cooling breeze of the ceiling fan, that he awoke from his contented slumber and suddenly remembered the report of the stiletto murder in the docks.

He slipped quietly out from under the single cotton sheet and, silently taking his cigarettes and lighter from his bedside table, crossed the bedroom and walked out onto the balcony. As he stood in the moonlight, his naked, finely proportioned body still warm from the security of his bed despite the cooler air of the African night, he once again thought through the report he had read at his desk that morning. His day had been a busy one and he had let the possible connection between the strange murder in the docks and the English Major's hunt for a mysterious diamond smuggler slip to the back of his mind.

Perhaps I should have sent it on to Jeremy in Dar es Salaam? he thought, as he smoked his cigarette. *He wanted to know...*

Behind him, in the darkness of the room, Maria turned in her sleep and made a low moaning sound. She would probably miss the warmth of his body near hers and that would wake her with alarm. He did not want that.

Perhaps I will *send it on to him,* thought da Sousa, as he stubbed out the end of the cigarette in an ashtray that stood on the balcony table. *Or perhaps to Salisbury – or whereever his superiors are. I'll read it again and see...*

He slipped gently under the sheet again and felt the comforting sensation of his wife's breasts against his muscular chest, as he placed a protective arm around her sleeping shoulders. By instinct, her hand went down his chest to the bushy mound below. He smiled the smile of grateful happiness.

'We'll see...' he said out loud, as he drifted off to sleep again.

18

The Nile

On Board Khufu – Late Evening, 21st July 1928

'Thanks,' said Stephen, as the flaming glare of the match diminished into the luminous dark of the Egyptian night. He exhaled a cloud of smoke, which wafted over the side and hung suspended in the air, to be left behind as the vessel steamed steadily on its way. 'It certainly has been quite a day, hasn't it!' he said. It was a statement rather than a question.

'It certainly was. What a mess!' replied Rupert, trying to stifle a cough. He was still not used to Stephen's hand-rolled Turkish cigarettes.

The two men were leaning on the railings on the top deck. The moon shone brightly and cast a shadow of silver on the waters. Occasionally, on the far-distant bank of the river, tiny pinpricks of feeble light identified the simple dwellings of the local farmers. On the steamer, little oases of brighter light formed puddles on the deck cast by lamps which were sparsely dotted around the vessel's upper superstructure.

After a little while, the urge to cough having receded, Rupert chuckled.

'I'm pleased to note that you can at least see the funny side of things, then, old chap,' said his companion, turning to look at him with a quizzical smile on his face, 'whatever that might be...'

'Well, I suppose you *do* always have to try and see the funny side of things,' said Rupert, still chuckling. 'You should have seen the look on poor Mohammed's face.'

'You did the right thing – and so did he. The late Miss Baxter had to go somewhere in this heat. The cold room seemed to be the logical – if not the *only* place.'

Even the cool-headed doctor saw the funny side of what was far from being an amusing situation, and allowed himself a chuckle before continuing.

'I don't think I've ever seen him look so tired and frayed,' continued Rupert. 'He wanted to talk to me once the dining room had emptied.'

'And...?' said Stephen expectantly. 'Something routine, or anything interesting? Company matters or issues of a more profound nature?' he continued, in a mock-serious tone.

'Company matters, actually. He said very early this morning he nearly physically bumped into Printon, who was going into his cabin carrying something – a small rush mat with a dirty piece of cotton sticking out of the end of it. He said his shoes were dusty, too, which made him think Printon had been ashore.'

'Nothing odd about that – your guests are free to come and go as they please, aren't they?'

'Of course they are, but this was at crack of dawn this morning, when Mohammed was doing his round of wake-up calls. He thought it a bit unusual. Apparently, Printon said that the continual motion of the ship made him feel ill, so he simply *had* to go for a walk on shore – at *that* ungodly early hour of the morning? He was quite rude and closed the cabin door in Mohammed's face.' The sounds of a ship under way at night filled the air for a few seconds before Rupert continued. 'Then there was something inconsequential about the Grassmeres, but it was so unimportant that I can't remember what. Also something about Grupfelder complaining that the plates are too small to hold his food – well, Mohammed rolled his eyes at that one. Then he was going on again about what Head Office might say about the gangway railing opening and...'

'Has he had any luck trying to get to the bottom of that one?' asked the doctor, cutting across Rupert.

'Well, he says that Daoud has that responsibility and that Daoud swears by the Prophet – so that's very serious – that he dropped the securing pin down through the loops when he closed the railings – exactly the same way he always does. Mohammed believes him and so do I. But that doesn't answer how it swung open and Lampton fell through.'

'No,' said Stephen slowly, 'it really doesn't.'

'Speaking of Lampton, Mohammed also had a complaint from him, when we returned from the temple. Apparently his basket contained chicken and salad ... but he's a vegetarian – doesn't touch meat or fish at all. Something about being upset when he was a kid – all a bit muddled. You know what Mohammed is like – when he gets going it's really quite difficult to follow him at times.'

Rupert told him how, upon their return from the temple that afternoon, in Mohammed's office the Lamptons had been obliged to register a complaint.

'I'm a vegetarian and have been for years,' said Richard Lampton, 'ever since I was a little boy and they used to slaughter pigs ... Oh, I beg your pardon ... no offence meant,' he said, suddenly realizing that Mohammed was a Muslim, but the little Egyptian simply smiled his all-purpose smile and motioned to Lampton to continue. 'Yes ... years ago when I was a lad, on my father's farm. I'd have to hide under my bed – I couldn't stand it – the noise and the blood. Do you understand?'

Mohammed had nodded in agreement, but inwardly couldn't really see why anyone should have reacted to routine slaughtering of livestock in this way – even if the animals were unclean pigs.

'I haven't eaten any flesh since then, and, when I booked my ticket, I told them this. The food has been very good so far, for which I thank you,' he said, as the little Egyptian beamed, 'but today I had chicken in my basket and couldn't eat it.'

The beam froze on Mohammed's face, but Lampton carried on before he could reply.

'And we were very careful to make sure we had the correct baskets,' he said. 'Both my wife and I checked our names on the labels and they were correct.'

'And then what happened?' asked Stephen, on the upper deck in the cool of the night.

'Mohammed apologized in his best, most obsequious manner and the Lamptons went back to their cabin.'

Stephen frowned as he looked down at the phosphorescence of the waves breaking along *Khufu*'s hull.

'Consider your fellow travellers,' he said after a short pause, 'how would you sum them up?'

He waited for a response.

'How do you mean exactly?' asked Rupert.

'Well ... how do you think you would describe them – character wise and all that,' continued Stephen.

'Oh, I see. They are a little aloof; I suppose you could say – some of them. The American is pleasant enough, in small doses – and that Arling chap can hold a good conversation. Rotherham usually manages to steer any conversation around to his business interests and as for the Manningtons, well ...' He shrugged slightly, as if to emphasize the pointlessness of even attempting a conversation with them. 'Then there's Mrs Porter – she's quite talkative, provided you catch her well away from the American.'

Stephen chuckled at the thought. 'Rebecca Eggerton is friendly, if a little irritating, and Miss Cuttle is quite chatty. Then there is Miss Kirby from Kenya, who usually keeps herself to herself, except when she talks to Western-dressed Egyptians in dark corners.' There was a pause, which was filled with the noises of the night, then Rupert continued. 'Poor Sylvia Baxter was one of the few who seemed to be really interested in things, in a childish sort of way. That's about it, really.'

'Thank you for that,' said Stephen, 'but there are those in our little band of travellers whom you haven't mentioned at all. What about that Swiss chap, Kormann? He's hardly the life and soul of the party – in fact, he's so retiring as to be generally unnoticeable most of the time...'

'...And yet, almost always in the background,' said Rupert.

'Indeed,' continued Stephen, 'you could say "either shy or possibly a spy". He did seem a little agitated at the mention of the police.'

'You are quite right about him keeping a low profile,' added Rupert. 'I don't recall having seen much of him this morning... before the snake bite business. But he has asked some relevant questions, so I think he has a genuine interest in Egyptology. He's just a bit backwards in coming forwards, you might say.'

'Some people make it their business to be "a bit backwards in coming forwards",' said Stephen softly. 'They like to keep a very low profile, for whatever reason.'

'What exactly are you getting at?'

'You haven't mentioned Printon or the Lamptons – neither the husband nor the wife,' replied Stephen, without looking at his companion.

'Well ... the Lamptons seem decent enough and he's always ready to pass the time. Printon seems to keep himself to himself as well ... except for when it comes to Mrs Arling...' replied Rupert, smiling.

'That's as maybe,' replied Stephen, 'but none of them made an impression on you, otherwise you would have had them in your list without me having to prompt you.'

'I'm not sure I follow you,' replied Rupert, a puzzled look creeping across his face.

'I was simply wondering if there was some tenuous connection between our Messrs Printon and Lampton, considering the events of the last couple of days.'

'I really don't see how that can be,' said Rupert, at a loss to understand how his friend had arrived at such a conclusion.

Stephen Hopkins turned to look at Rupert, his voice now serious and devoid of amusement.

'Cast your mind back to the Central Court, in the temple this morning,' said Stephen. 'Did you notice what the late Miss Baxter had in her luncheon basket?'

There was no reply.

'Well, I did. In the excitement of things, the poor girl dropped her basket onto the earth and the contents spilled out, all over the place. For one moment, I thought that Miss Eggerton and Mrs Porter were going to trample over everything, when they helped the Cuttle woman away from the body. Luckily they didn't.'

'What's the significance of the contents of her hamper, then?' asked Rupert.

'It was what a vegetarian might eat – bread rolls, an apple, some cheese, a couple of boiled eggs and some salad,' added Stephen. 'It was spread all over the ground...'

He continued to stare at his companion, his eyebrows raised, as if waiting for Rupert to continue the sentence.

'Yes ... well ... I'm not sure I follow you,' said Rupert.

'Think, old chap. Why would Miss Baxter, a true carnivore, have a basket fit for a vegetarian?' asked Stephen encouragingly.

'But Miss Baxter wasn't vegetarian,' replied Rupert suddenly. 'Judging by the way she tucked into her bacon and eggs, lamb casserole, steamed fish and all the rest of it, I'd say she definitely had a taste for flesh.'

'Exactly,' replied Stephen, 'and vegetarians are not exactly a common breed, are they? So why did she end up with the hamper which was obviously meant for Richard Lampton?'

'Mohammed said that the Lamptons had made sure they had the correct hampers – they checked their names on the labels and all that,' said Rupert. 'I remember him saying that.'

'Yes, I'm sure that's exactly what Mohammed tried to ensure would happen. He's very conscientious.' Hopkins paused, as the water continued to swish along the hull, below them. 'Whichever way you look at it, you must agree that it seems as if there have been rather too many *incidents* of late, wouldn't you say...? I'm reminded of the old saying about accidents not just happening ... "One is unfortunate, two is just carelessness, three is" ... well,' he turned to look at Rupert, 'to misquote Mr Wilde.' Stephen raised his eyebrows again, as if to invite further opinion.

'So why do you think Printon and Lampton seem to feature so regularly...' asked Rupert, who was slowly working things out to the point the doctor had arrived at several minutes earlier. 'Perhaps she had picked up the wrong hamper,' he suggested.

'No she didn't. The basket she upset had her name on the label – I checked,' continued Stephen. 'Also, consider how the snake – viper, asp or whatever it was – got into that same hamper in the first place...' he paused, then continued slowly: 'It couldn't have just slithered in on a whim. Once the lid was closed and secured with the leather thong, you'd be lucky to slide a sheet of paper between it and the basket proper,' he added. 'Something the size of a small snake wouldn't have a chance in hell of squeezing through.'

There was a moment of silent understanding, as the implication of what Stephen had just said sank in.

'You mean that someone deliberately put it in the hamper before the lid was secured?' asked Rupert. He was starting to feel uneasy.

'It seems highly unlikely that it could have been done any other way. So, we have to face the unpleasant possibility that that nasty surprise in the hamper was probably not meant for her at all, but for someone else...'

'Lampton...?' asked Rupert, after a silence.

'He's the vegetarian, so yes – and we're back to him ... again...'

He turned and once again stared down into the phosphorescence of the water.

'Why are we tending to mention both of them, more often than not, in the same sentence?' he asked, more to himself than to Rupert. 'Why? Think back to Lampton going into the river – wasn't it Printon who was standing next to Marjory Cuttle? Wasn't he leaning on the gangway gate, just before they all shuffled around and he took the photo ... and Lampton fell through?' Stephen's voice had fallen to a barely audible whisper. 'And he wasn't too keen on us having to call the police this morning, either.'

'Isn't this all becoming a bit *Boy's Own*-ish? I'm starting to have an uneasy feeling about it all,' said Rupert, straightening up. They had been leaning on the rails for some time and his back was starting to stiffen.

'Perhaps,' replied Stephen, 'only possibly far more real and a lot more dangerous than anything you might read for amusement in a weekly paper.'

'What do you mean, "a lot more dangerous"? Do you think there's something going on?'

'Christ knows,' replied Stephen, 'but it always pays to be vigilant.' For a split second, he thought that, if he himself had been more vigilant, he might not have lost his leg. 'We live in difficult times and people have their own, secret motivation for doing all sorts of unexpected things.'

'Can I ask you a question?' asked Rupert, eyeing Hopkins intently. 'Are you just interested in all of this, or is there another reason for you to be so observant. I know you've mentioned Sherlock Holmes and all of that – well, I used to read Conan Doyle as well when I was younger – but you seem to see a lot of things that I don't. I was just wondering why...'

'Don't do yourself down, my dear chap; you take in just as much as I do.'

'Perhaps, but it doesn't seem as important to me as it does to you. Have you had any training for all of this?'

'Good lord, no,' replied Stephen Hopkins, laughing. 'I'm just observant, that's all. I'll tell you why a little later. The simple answer is that there's always more to everything than meets the eye, Horatio, as Shakespeare might have put it.'

Stephen stood up straight and, for a short while longer, both men lingered at the railings watching the dark river in affable silence, each lost in their own thoughts. Below them, the Nile continued its playfully rhythmic slapping against *Khufu*'s hull. Eventually, the doctor spoke.

'Come on, old chap, it's been one hell of a day and the old stump is playing up like a fiddler at a wedding. Do you feel like rubbing in some soothing ancient Egyptian balm to calm it down?'

In the semi-darkness, he smiled and winked at Rupert.

19

The Nile

On Board Khufu – 2.30 a.m., 22nd July 1928

'There's something quite hypnotic about the sound of the water, isn't there?' asked Stephen.

'Yes, I suppose there is. What I find even more interesting is how a boat with so many people on board, and with so much heavy machinery, can be as quiet as the tomb in the dead of night. Listen...' replied Rupert.

There was nothing, except the feeble sound of the river, clawing its way along the hull and, somewhere off in the very far distance, the repetitive, barely audible thud of the engines, driving the single paddle wheel at *Khufu*'s stern.

'Well, you weren't too quiet,' winked Stephen.

Rupert blushed.

'Made enough noise to mask an artillery barrage,' laughed the doctor, as he reached out to the bedside table and stubbed out the end of his cigarette in the ashtray.

'You weren't that quiet yourself,' replied Rupert. 'Pot calling the kettle black, I'd say.'

Rupert was sitting on the edge of the bed. He made pretence of wincing with mock pain as Stephen planted a friendly punch on his still-sweating shoulder. The heat of the night, together with the energy which they had recently expended on each other, had made Stephen's cabin close and airless. On his way to fetch a new packet of cigarettes from Stephen's wardrobe, Rupert had opened the single window slightly. He hoped by doing so, together with the ineffectual efforts of the small rotating fan above them in the centre of the cabin ceiling, a draught would be created. Now the two of them sat in companionable silence, their bodies naked in the glow of the single reading light which was fixed to the bulkhead behind the bed.

'How is it feeling now?' asked Rupert, gazing with contentment at the recumbent form of his friend.

'As you see, old chap, off duty at present, but ready and willing to answer the call … in a little while…'

'I meant your leg,' said Rupert, cutting across the doctor's answer with a laugh.

'Oh, it's not too bad, thanks. This heat doesn't do much for it, I'm afraid, and the sand out there can cause merry hell, if I'm not careful. But we manage to carry on – best foot forward and all that … even if it is artificial!'

He took a mouthful of boiled water from the glass on the bedside cabinet and lay back, staring up. There were still faint wisps of smoke from their last cigarettes floating next to the ceiling, above the air circulated by the little fan. He thought of how ideas were just like the wisps – once conceived, they lingered in the mind and either fermented into something far bigger, or simply withered and faded away.

'Do you feel any resentment?' asked Rupert.

'About what, old chap?' answered the doctor absently, still staring up at the ceiling.

'Your leg?'

'You wouldn't last five minutes in this wicked world if you did, that I can tell you.' He turned to look at Rupert, a look of seriousness clouding his face. 'Yes, I was unlucky enough to lose a bit of me, but the rest still works – including the important bits – and I can still say my tables, tell the date and time and I know who's on the throne.' He paused, as his eyes went off to a distant place in his memory. 'There are hundreds of thousands of poor bastards who are far worse off than I,' he said, with only the slightest hint of anger. 'They had bits blown off, their wiring all scrambled up, their existence totally wrecked and here's the really cruel thing' – he paused – 'they survived to get on with what was left of their lives – if you can call that living...'

His voice trailed off, as his gaze went further into the past, deeper into his private emotions. He put the cigarette, which Rupert had lit and passed to him, into his mouth, but did not draw the smoke into his lungs.

'I'm sorry,' said Rupert softly, 'I didn't mean to upset you.'

The doctor said nothing, but continued gazing off inwardly, into the closed distance of his mind. For what seemed an eternity neither spoke, the only sounds being the Nile and the swishing of the little fan. Then Stephen put his hands behind his head and spoke – very matter-of-factly and with no trace of any anger in his voice.

'There was this chap they brought in – during the Somme business. There were injured men all over the place, awaiting attention – we couldn't cope really. As quickly as we patched them up and sent them away, they were replaced with even more wounded. We just kept going – on and on and on. Then we started to run out of just about everything – demand simply far exceeded supply. Eventually, the Surgeon-Major decided that they would just leave the no-hopers and we'd concentrate on those who might have a chance, if we took a quick look at them first...'

He lapsed into a remembrance of a situation he would rather have forgotten – but it was forever seared into his consciousness, and he could not. Slowly, he rubbed his hand up and down his left leg, above where the lower part had been cut away. Rupert sat in silence, waiting for his friend to continue.

'This chap they brought in – I remember how daft it was. With bodies everywhere, blood everywhere, chaos everywhere, this chap was carried in by two bearers accompanied by a military policeman, immaculately turned out, when the rest of us looking like we'd been dragged through several muddy shell craters, a Turkish bath and an abattoir.' He chuckled at the thought; somewhere in his deepest, private memory the scene struck an illogical, humorous chord of recollection. 'This chap had gone to pieces and wandered off, out of his trench towards the enemy lines. Somehow they'd managed to get him back, but not before he'd been hit in the stomach. Poor bastard was rambling and flailing around like a dervish. "Don't waste your time on him, Sir; he's for the firing squad, anyway." That's what that Military Policeman said – *Don't waste your time on him...*'

The cabin was silent for a few seconds.

'Then what happened?' asked Rupert softly.

The doctor lay on the bed, his hands still clasped loosely behind his head, staring straight ahead into the nothingness of the cabin. In his mouth the cigarette continued to burn gently. After what seemed minutes, and without turning to look at Rupert, the doctor continued.

'They'd tied him down to the stretcher and tried to stop the bleeding with a couple of field dressings, but he was still twisting around all over the place. We were busy with a case on the table – trying to sew back most of what had been blown off, so they just put this chap's stretcher on the floor, next in line. Just before we got him on the table, the orderlies untied the rope. He suddenly went berserk and started waving a knife he'd had hidden in his pocket, or somewhere. Anyway, being on the floor, he managed to stick it into my calf – twice. With the threshing about he made a nice mess of it. I was patched up and just carried on – we had to – we had no choice...' A faint smile tugged at the corners of his mouth and his face was still covered with beads of sweat, caused by being back, at least in his mind, in the field hospital. 'It didn't seem to heal and ... well, eventually an infection set in and it started to turn gangrenous and that was that. God only knows where the knife had been before it ended up in my leg...'

His eyes slowly took in the surroundings of the cabin, as he returned from the private recesses of his mind.

'It wasn't his fault – the poor bastard didn't know what he was doing ... like so many of them.'

The ash had fallen from the end of the doctor's slowly smouldering, unsmoked cigarette and lay white amongst the dark hair which covered his chest.

'I'm one of the lucky ones, my dear chap,' he said almost inaudibly. 'At least everything still works...'

'Did they send you home ... afterwards, I mean?'

'They tried to, but I wouldn't have it. My family is quite influential, so I managed to get myself posted to the Middle East. Fell in love with the climate – except for the flies and the sand.' He looked at Rupert and smiled. 'And I've been here ever since.'

He pulled himself further up the bed, taking what was left of the cigarette out of his mouth as he did so.

'Do you have a practice out here?' asked Rupert.

'Not really. I do enough to keep the old hand in, but that's about it in the medico line these days. A little bit of clinic work or sometimes a bit in the hospitals around Cairo. They're always looking for help. My uncle has interests out here and he gets me to do a little work for him, from time to time' he added, mysteriously. '"Things are seldom what they seem, skimmed milk masquerades as cream", as Gilbert put it in *Pinafore*,' he said, breaking into the warm smile, once again.

The doctor sat looking at Rupert for several seconds before continuing.

'Tell you what, old chap, best close the window – would you mind? It'll take you far less time to get there than it would me. You know – restricted movement without the artificial bit to lean on, and all of that...' He grinned. '...And then come and cuddle up. Whispers only from now on,' he said.

Rupert did as he was asked and then settled down in the bed, next to his friend.

'How much do you know about the state of play in the modern Egypt of today?'

'How do you mean...?' replied Rupert. 'Politically?'

'Hmm.'

'Well, not that much, I suppose. Politics don't really interest me. Why?'

'Do you remember that I said my Uncle has interests out here? Well, what you don't know can't hurt you – and I wouldn't want *anything* to hurt you,' he squeezed Rupert's shoulder closer to him, 'so let me just say that my family have interests throughout the Empire, but prefer to keep a low profile.'

'Pardon?' asked Rupert, turning to look at the doctor, a look of genuine puzzlement on his face.

'Whitehall and all that, old chap. Your *Boy's Own* stuff, as you might say, in reality. My family has been there for generations – dull as dishwater, if you ask me. It was all far too boring for an energetic, sport-mad youth, with the world at his feet. So I chose to do the medical thing and became a doctor, instead of entering the hallowed portals of power. I've never forgotten King and Country and all that, you see, because that's the way I was brought up. So I keep an eye and ear open for the odd thing every now and again. It keeps my uncle happy...'

As he spoke, he rested his free hand on his chest, and had been idly twisting the signet ring on his right-hand little finger with his thumb. Rupert had noticed the ring on the first day, with the ornate crest deeply engraved into it. Suddenly, Stephen held up his hand, so they could both see the ring clearly.

'"If you ever need help, get this to the Embassy" – said my esteemed Uncle, although quite how that was to be accomplished was left as an unresolved mystery, presumably for me to solve...'

'Which embassy?' asked Rupert, drawing imaginary patterns on the doctor's chest, with his finger.

'The British one, of course!' replied Stephen, with a look of tolerance on his face.

'Oh, I see,' muttered Rupert, but he was not at all sure that he really did. There seemed much to this man which was either mysterious or downright confusing, but Rupert had never felt so happy or secure with anyone as he had over the preceding few days.

'Be a chum and give me a top-up, would you?' asked Stephen.

Rupert refilled Stephen's glass from the carafe of boiled water which stood on the bedside table, next to the ashtray.

'Thanks, I needed that,' he said. 'Now ... here *is* a plot straight from *Boy's Own*. Unlike our friend Arling, there are those who are convinced that this Hitler chap is going to be the next problem on the world stage. They are convinced his party is being funded in large part by diamonds, smuggled up from either old German South-West Africa or from the Belgian Congo. Of course, the government would think you mad to even suggest such a preposterous scenario, but there are several powerful people in high places who are convinced of it.'

Throughout the whole of the conversation, the doctor's voice had hardly risen above a barely audible whisper.

'They think that the Germans are using either the railway or the Nile as the easiest and least contentious means of transporting the stones up to the Mediterranean and then sending them over to Germany. Apart from anything that Whitehall might or might not have to say on the topic, the authorities in Egypt and the Middle East seem jumpy about the Zionists in general and the Arabs in particular. That is why the powers-that-be, here in Egypt, have been persuaded to put police and troops just about everywhere. No one is quite certain of where we go next. It could all be just a storm in the proverbial teacup, or it could be the prelude to something far more serious – an adventure on a grand scale which could well involve all of us.' He looked at Rupert with a quizzical smile on his face. 'So ... what would you say about that, then? That really is the stuff of *Boy's Own*, wouldn't you agree?' and he laughed softly.

At about the same time, on the main cabin deck one level above them, the door handle of Cabin 3 turned slowly and silently. Sebastian Printon, still dressed in his dinner jacket, but with his bow tie dangling loosely around the open collar of his shirt, checked to make sure that the passageway was empty and then stepped nimbly out of the cabin door. As he made to walk away and back to his own cabin, number 10, he turned and looked once again at the shapely and alluring form of Esther Arling. She was standing just inside the cabin, her silk dressing gown hanging limply down from her shoulders exposing the more desirable parts of her white body. Behind her, sprawled naked on the rumpled bed, lay the sleeping form of her husband. She put one hand on her hip, causing the gown to open even more. With the other she made little waving motions at Printon as he disappeared down the passageway, his shoes in his hand. The three of them had enjoyed each other's bodies and she felt satiated, at least for the moment. The thought of a repeat session excited her as she remembered Printon's muscular body, taller and more powerfully built than that of her husband. She felt a surge of gratification tingle through her body and she shivered; all three of them had driven each other to the heights of sensual pleasure from which there was only one possible way of descent and all three had relished the experience. Printon had been an unexpected bonus on this trip; more so than the tour guide, who, despite his handsome face and her seductive attentions, had not taken the bait. She remembered Printon's performance, how he had been more than able to satisfy them both, and she smiled at the thought that, by comparison, the conquest of the tour guide would not really have been worth the effort. Only after Printon had turned the corner of the passageway and disappeared, did she draw the gown tightly around herself with an exquisite shiver of satisfaction.

She closed the door again, as silently as it had opened.

20

Kenya

Approaching Nairobi – 9th July 1928

Major Ashdown smiled rather vaguely at the steward who, despite the heat of the African sun outside, was incongruously and smartly turned out in his heavily starched white tunic.

'You just let me know if there's anything else you need, Sir,' he said, steadying himself on the door frame against the rhythmic swaying of the railway carriage.

'Thank you,' mumbled the Major, as the starched jacket disappeared down the corridor. He found the over-eagerness to serve distasteful; he had been brought up to be self-sufficient to the point of being able to do everything himself. His father had taught him the value of only having African servants to do things for you provided that you could do those same tasks for yourself. The fact that the steward was a European did not sit too gently with him either. In the Colonies it was not usually the Europeans who tugged their forelocks at other Europeans whom they waited upon.

If you can't do it yourself, it's not worth doing at all!

God! How many times had he heard his father say *that*? He thought of his family; of his father and of his two younger brothers. Full of spirit and pride and now, before their time, all part of the earth of Africa – the same earth that in happier times had been good to them on the farm in the Highlands. Perhaps they should have been brought up in the familiar surroundings of the English countryside, where their forefathers had lived, rather than in the hard, unforgiving African bush. It was a hard life, farming the coffee bushes of the Kenya highlands, but it was 'a life of satisfaction and self-development, which is not easily won'. That was what his father had always said. But was it? Were they all out of place in the surroundings of Mother Africa? In happier times she could be a bountiful, caring mother; often, depending on her mood, she could be a very unforgiving and cruel one. With their roots lost in the comforting pleasantness of England's green fields, were they, as children of this Mother Africa, as out of place as the starched steward seemed to be, far from his native Scotland? As the Major stared at the scrub and bush, which seemed to blur past the carriage window, he forced himself not to dwell in the past. What had gone had gone for good. What mattered was the here and now – not what had once been. That was another legacy from his father and that was what had pulled him through. He smiled and caught his reflection briefly in the glass of the window. He remembered that his father's exhortation to live in the here and now had been one of his mother's favourite sayings as well.

The following morning Major Ashdown once again found himself seated in yet another commissioner's office, this time in front of the desk of the Chief of the Kenya Police in Nairobi. The man's left hand rested on a folder on his desk, from which he had extracted and read the report he had been sent from the police in Mombasa. Ashdown had already shown him his single-sheet letter of authority which, by now, had become rather creased. When he read it, the Commissioner had openly bristled at what he saw as a trespass into his own area of authority.

'Are you serious about this?' asked Alex Halkyard. The

Commissioner of the Kenya Police stared at his visitor over the top of his half-frame spectacles.

'Yes, Sir, perfectly,' replied the Major. 'For some time now we've had suspicions that something like this was going on, but we've been largely in the dark – until now. There could be a pattern emerging...'

Ashdown followed his well-trodden path and once again spoke in broad terms. Yet again, and partly because this man had displayed barely hidden signs of hostility, he wasn't going to give too much away. Secure behind his letter, he left the sentence hanging in the air. He judged Halkyard to be hardly older than himself and had quickly formed the opinion that he was fired with energetic ambition. In many respects this could be a useful asset, but in other ways it could also prove to be a liability – often a dangerous one, particularly when – as in the case of this commissioner – the uninvited appearance of an external force into his tightly controlled sphere of influence brought with it the potential of an implied threat. As was often the case with colonial officials, power, once granted, was very jealously guarded and any intrusion was deeply resented. The Major thought it best to err on the side of caution; he was getting rather good at saying a lot and giving away only a little.

'So you think that this '...tall, thin European with the aristocratic bearing and bird-handled cane...', as you describe him, is a diamond smuggler?'

'We've suspected that diamonds have been smuggled out of the Forbidden Zone in South-West Africa and on to, presumably, Europe,' replied the Major, 'probably Amsterdam, or possibly even London.' He purposely gave misleading destinations. Something in his head had already warned him to be careful and that this commissioner was not to be trusted.

'But who would mastermind such an operation? *If* there is any truth in your suspicions, then surely this is the work of organized crime. I hardly think an individual would have much chance of succeeding in such an undertaking, do you?'

The Major did not like the way the man had emphasized the *if* – in fact, Ashdown did not like the man at all. The Commissioner was asking a lot of questions, the answers to which Ashdown was not sure he either possessed or, if he did, wanted to divulge. Halkyard did not wait for a response, but continued directly, looking at the report.

'At least you have a name for this "Griffin" individual of yours...' – he paused, looking stone-faced – 'this Swiss chap. At least your description of him was fairly accurate. That's something to go on...'

The Major thought that the Commissioner had attempted to criticize him yet again.

'It's a pity your men lost sight of him, Sir,' Ashdown said, enjoying the opportunity to point out the failings in this man's chain of command. 'It would have been helpful to have known where he was going and whom he was seeing...'

The unfinished sentence hung in the air like a sudden storm cloud over the Plains of Thika. The Commissioner stiffened visibly and glared back at the Major.

'Yes,' he said slowly, 'that was unfortunate. My men did what they could, but they lost him in the crowd on the street outside the station. This cloak-and-dagger stuff is not really what they've been trained for.'

'With respect, Sir, would you not say that methods of policing are changing, given the present political climate and the tensions developing around the world? Policing is not just a matter of pounding a beat these days.' Ashdown was enjoying himself. 'Surely we must be seen to be one step ahead all of the time. The perspective is changing and we have to change with it.'

For a moment, Halkyard looked as if he was going to explode. The red blotches which had framed the top of his neck now slowly spread to cover his lower cheeks. Ashdown, enjoying every second, said nothing, but waited in planned, respectful silence for the other man to say something.

'Well then – how do you think this investigation of yours fits into the wider picture?' asked the Commissioner eventually, something of a sneer suggesting itself around his lips. 'Do you see us at the centre of an international cartel of professional thieves?' He raised his eyebrows in the manner of a parent admonishing a naughty child and sat back in his chair, almost in triumph. Ashdown found the gesture particularly irritating.

'I'm sorry, Sir, but the possible implications of this investigation are such that national security could well be at risk…'

Halkyard stared with even greater intensity at his visitor, studying his face intently. Ashdown continued.

'…With respect, Sir, I'm sure you appreciate that this investigation has to operate on a need-to-know basis…'

The Commissioner's blotches had risen further up his cheeks, but he persisted with his questions.

'So, what makes you think you are on the right track, then? Do you have any proof? Do you have any information? Where did you get your intelligence from? Is the source reliable?'

Given Halkyard's flood of questions and the manner in which they were asked, the Major was finding it difficult to distinguish between genuine interest and open derision. His first assessment of this man had been correct – he did not like him at all.

'Not everyone subscribes to the notion of King and Country, Sir,' said Ashdown wryly. 'All information has a value, either patriotic or monetary. The former is volunteered for the best possible of reasons; the latter is simply exchanged for gain. Either way, it all has to be assessed and, where appropriate, responded to.'

Halkyard felt that his string of questions had been side-stepped.

'And the information you have – what you know about this aristocratic chap – into which category does *your* information fall?'

The Commissioner looked at Ashdown, again with raised eyebrows, as if to add emphasis to his question. If this upstart Major was going to solve a riddle of national importance, then he was determined to get his share of the credit. He had ambition which extended well beyond the boundaries of his Nairobi office.

But Ashdown's mind had switched from listening to Halkyard's voice to the scene down on the coast of a few days before. *Zambezi* had reached Mombasa and docked in the new deep-water harbour of Kilindini. Secured two berths further up, the massive purple bulk of a Union Castle mail ship towered up out of the sea. The quay itself was alive with the comings and goings of a legion of passengers, relatives and stevedores. Wedged in between the massive cargo cranes and the low, grey bulk of the warehouses, which lined the docks, a military band resplendent in scarlet and gold was playing as the passengers and their luggage moved fussily about. From the ship's yardarm fluttered the Blue Peter – the signal flag announcing imminent departure. The Major had been leaning on *Zambezi*'s rails watching this activity, when he noticed a reception committee waiting for him on the quayside. A chief inspector, two inspectors and several African constables, all well turned out in their uniforms, boarded *Zambezi* almost as soon as the gangway had been secured to the dock. A short while later, in the privacy of the captain's cabin, Ashdown had been told by the Chief Inspector that a European, matching the description he had been given, had indeed disembarked from the *Principe Antonio*. His documents had all been in order and he was travelling on a Swiss passport, in the name of Benschedler.

'We were very careful not to arouse suspicion,' said the Chief Inspector, with a look of satisfaction. 'He went straight from the ship to board the train for Nairobi. As you can see, here at Kilindini, our new harbour allows many large ocean-liners to berth at once. The old harbour on the other side of Mombasa Island wasn't deep enough – it's all right for dhows, but not much else. Kilindini affords the facility to go straight from the ship to the train and then connect to the main line to Nairobi.'

'Indeed,' answered Ashdown, 'and is that what our man did, then?'

'Yes, Sir, he should be in Nairobi by now. I informed the Commissioner of this, so there should have been a watch placed on the railway station. I assume you will wish to follow on...?'

The Chief Inspector left the question open.

'Naturally,' replied Ashdown, 'but with as little fuss as possible. When is the next train?'

'Not until tomorrow, I'm afraid. The *Dunorland Castle* is due in, bound for Cape Town. There'll be the usual train load of passengers wanting to go further inland.'

The Major made a slight grimace at the news.

Bugger it! I also have to go further inland, he thought, angrily, *and now I have to contend with yet another delay.*

By lunchtime the following day, the huge steam engine had hauled the long line of carriages off Mombasa Island and onto the mainland. For the next hour, the train had puffed and wheezed through a pleasantly luxuriant belt of vegetation. Tall palms, mango and other exotic fruit trees swayed gently in sympathy with the gentle breezes that blew inland off the Indian Ocean. The sheer scale of the canvas of the African landscape tended to dwarf most things. The effect on the train, long as it was, had been to give the impression that they were hardly making any progress at all through the veldt. Soon, the lush vegetation would give way to a much more open expanse of country, populated by zebra, elephant, antelope and lion. Nearer Nairobi, after the train had climbed in altitude, there would be vast areas of fertile farmland sharing space with this wildlife. This, in part, was what many people came to Kenya to see. The Major had been born into it and had grown up respecting and loving it. It was *his* earth, *his* land. But now, he paid it little heed: his mind was focused on other things besides this natural, yet cruel beauty. He thought for a brief moment of his sister – Julia – and the farm up in the Highlands. Then he thought of his quarry – 'The Griffin', or Benschedler, as he now knew him to be. What was *he* feeling or thinking? Had any of this natural beauty caused *him* to deviate from his purpose for even the briefest second? Ashdown doubted it very much. As he watched the passing landscape, he stared at his reflection in the window and smiled. He might not know what his quarry was thinking or feeling, but at least he knew that 'The Griffin', or Benschedler, or whatever his real name was, though still elusive, was no longer a man totally cloaked in mystery.

'... So that's *not* the best idea,' continued Alex Halkyard, his voice bringing the Major back from his recollection of the events of the previous days. 'Your chap could be anywhere – we just don't have the manpower to search every street and building.'

Ashdown had not been listening and had no idea what the Commissioner was talking about. For a split second he was not sure what to say next, then he continued.

'Sir, we have the man's description from several sources, all of which seem to complement each other and which have led us to a confirmation and a name – Benschedler,' said Ashdown, smiling a faint, reassuring grin. 'There have been a couple of suspicious deaths, which do seem to have a common thread and could or could not be linked to my chap. It's the best of the information we have to work with. A couple of weeks ago we had nothing.'

The Commissioner stared at his visitor with open hostility. By the nature of his response, it appeared that the man had not been listening to him.

'I must thank you for your assistance in watching the harbour at Mombasa. At least your men were able to confirm that my chap got off the ship...'

The Major's implication that they had at least managed that much, even if they had subsequently managed to lose their quarry outside the railway station in Nairobi, struck a resentful nerve with the Commissioner.

'Well, your telegram could hardly have been ignored, coming as it did with the highest clearance. His Excellency has asked to be kept informed of developments...' Halkyard stared hard at Ashdown. 'I assume that you have no objection to this request...?'

'Of course not, Sir,' replied the Major disarmingly. *And you, no doubt, will be the one to tell him how you were a vital part of the solving of this case – if I ever do,* he thought to himself. He would find it impossible to work with this commissioner for any length of time. How much of whatever he might find out he would actually pass on to this ambitious, dangerous man also remained to be seen. He had started to feel, instinctively, that he should hold his cards even closer to his chest.

'Well, Major Ashdown, to sum up: we are watching the station and Mombasa are doing the same; we are also watching the docks – both harbours – to be on the safe side. Your chap might decide to retrace his steps. You have no idea of his next move.'

Ashdown glared back at the Commissioner. The man's

use of 'you' could be interpreted very personally, in which case it was an open insult and slur on the Major's professionalism, or it could be taken in its wider context to embrace the entire Kenya police. The Commissioner rose to his feet, signalling the end of the interview.

'I would suggest that it's safe to say your chap is still somewhere here in Nairobi. We'll just have to keep looking – not much else we can do...'

The voice trailed off, almost gloating at the frustration of Ashdown's fruitless enquiries and the coldness of the lost trail.

'Thank you,' said the Major curtly, as he, too, rose to leave. It was perfectly obvious that there was to be only the bare minimum of assistance coming from the Commissioner. *I will be very pleased to see the back of you*, thought Ashdown, who considered that he was being openly taunted by this man.

That irritated him severely.

As the Major crossed through the cool, spacious foyer of Police Headquarters a voice came softly from behind him.

"Scuse me a moment, Sir. Can I 'ave a word...?"

Ashdown turned and looked into a ruddy, full-moon face. Despite it only being mid-morning, the features were covered in little beads of sweat, the cool shade of the foyer seemingly having no effect in stemming the flow of perspiration.

'Was you investigating the Swiss gentl'man?' continued the man. He was short and dumpy, the ample dimensions of his cheeks dangling down over the struggling boundary of his shirt collar. Had they been in Germany, the man's features would have destined him to become the victim of the Nazis' hatred of his race and yet another statistic in the record of their 'Final Solution'.

'Why do you ask?' replied Ashdown cautiously.

'Could we walk on a little, Sir, out on the street...' asked the man, gesturing with a thick finger towards the sunlit door.

He spoke with an accent, which the Major thought was cockney. Despite his considerable size, the man walked with the silent precision of a big cat. He seemed to be nervous and occasionally turned, surreptitiously, to look over his shoulder.

'Ta for that, Sir,' he said, once they had turned the corner of the street and were out of sight of the Headquarters building. 'Was you askin' 'bout the Swiss gentl'man? I fink 'e's gorne – left Nairobi.'

'What makes you think that?' asked Ashdown, unused to following the accent.

''At's what I told 'im, but 'e never listens to no one, he don't.'

'Who is "him"?' – he used the correct form of the word – 'and, more to the point, who are *you?*'

'Inspec'tr Lyons, Sir, and 'im is 'is Lordship up there,' he said, stubbing a podgy thumb over his shoulder in the direction of the Headquarters building. 'We lost your gentl'man in the crowd, fair 'n' square, I'll say that. But then I got to thinkin' – 'is train was goin' on t' Kampala – it didn't end 'ere.' Ashdown slowed his walking pace and turned his head to look at the shorter man. 'So I finks to m'self, what if 'e – the Swiss gentl'man – got back into the station 'n' gets back on the train? We wasn't finkin' a' that – leastways, I wasn't till the train 'ad left already.'

Ashdown had stopped walking altogether.

'Did you report this idea of yours to the Commissioner?' he asked.

'Do me a favour, Gov. Wha'd'ya fink? Course I done – the very same time I fort 'baht it meself.'

'And nothing was done to follow it up?'

'Nout! But that's 'is Lordship for ya. Why d'ya fink I'm still only an inspector after goin' on ten years?'

Ashdown had no idea and so said nothing.

'It's 'cos I didn't go to no fancy school, like 'e did, that's why. I ain't got no smart tie with them stripes all down it – that's why. But I'll tell y' this much for nothin' Squire, I'm damn good at what I do – so I'm putting it to ya – your bloke's away – probably up in Kampala by now, I shouldn't wonder.'

He leant back against the top of a low brick wall, which ran along the perimeter of a nearby schoolyard, a look of triumph on his ruddy jowls.

Ashdown stared hard at him for a second, before he realized that, if this embittered man's theory was correct, then the Commissioner was wasting valuable time by simply sitting back and waiting to see what happened next.

'You could very well be right, Lyons,' he said.

'An' if I is, then your chap's going to go on to Sudan – Khartoum, I shouldn't wonder. Nout else for 'im to go after Kampala, 'cept Khartoum.'

Inspector Lyons had taken a crumpled packet of Woodbines out of his equally crumpled jacket pocket. He offered Ashdown one, but the Major refused. Lyons lit one himself and blew out a lungful of smoke.

'I says you should follow on to Kampala, that's me gut feelin'. 'E's not 'ere in Nairobi no more.' The Inspector smiled. 'I can 'elp ya make the arrangements at the station,' he said softly, 'if ya find 'im, just remember it was Inspector Samuel Lyons what helped ya – 'hat's all.'

21

Cairo

The British Embassy – 23rd July 1928

The Ambassador stood at the side of an ornate escritoire in the corner of his office. In his hand he held a half-empty cut crystal whiskey tumbler. He had downed the other half of the contents in a single gulp; recently, he found the pale brown liquid was the only thing that helped him get through each boring day of endless telegrams, official papers, luncheon and dinner parties, poor digestion and the difficult and uncooperative Egyptian administration. He had also had to contend with the endless burning in his stomach.

'Bloody ungrateful bastards!' he said to himself, as he looked down into the amber liquid.

He had never understood why it was that the Egyptians resented the security being under British protection offered them. At a recent State function some Court officials had politely cracked jokes, saying that having the British around was almost as bad as it had been in the old days, when they had had to pay lip-service to the Sultan in Constantinople. It had all been made in good taste and in the appropriate diplomatic language, but he had not been fooled by the implied menace that lurked just under the surface of the polite smiles and heavily embroidered Court uniforms.

One day we shall have to teach them a lesson, if we are to remain in control, thought the Ambassador, as he drained the glass and returned it to the secret compartment in the escritoire. He did not want anyone to know about his need. As he saw things, even the staff of the Embassy seemed to be playing the universal Egyptian game – up to their eyes in spying and watching, listening and checking. Nothing in Egypt could be relied upon or trusted. It was only his upbringing and obligation to do his duty that kept him from resigning and going home to the peaceful anonymity of his garden. It would not be the same without his wife, but he still had his son. He rubbed his eyes – then he remembered. No, his son had been killed on the Western Front – along with most of the unit he had led. Then he remembered that that was why he needed the alcohol – it confused the pain in his mind to the point where his losses became almost bearable.

He was halfway across the large, ornate room, when he heard the discreet knock. The sound made him stop, turn and stare blankly at the heavy door which connected him to the world outside.

'Enter,' he said, in a firm but tired voice, which betrayed not even the faintest sign of the alcohol he had just downed.

'Ambassador, I thought you should see this immediately,' said a young, smartly dressed private secretary, holding a telegram form in his outstretched hand.

'What is it, then? Urgent?' asked the Ambassador, as he took the sheet of paper and stared at it. He tried to focus on the writing and suddenly remembered that his spectacles were on his desk.

'Possibly, Sir,' replied the secretary, as the Ambassador crossed slowly to retrieve his glasses. 'It is marked for the attention of "Cecil"...' He left the sentence unfinished.

By the time his secretary had finished talking, the Ambassador had placed his spectacles on his nose. Both men looked at each other, expectantly. As rare as they were, both men knew the significance of communications marked for the attention of 'Cecil'.

For Cecil
Advise personal details of Sebastian Albert Printon, Engineer, born 12th February 1886, passport 132012. Further, advise personal details of Richard Edward Lampton, Engineer, born 9th September, 1884, passport 121408. Reply soonest to Aswan. Hopkins.'

'You had best telegraph this to Whitehall immediately,' said the Ambassador, removing his spectacles as he handed the paper back to his secretary, 'and ask the police at this end if they have any information; usual form – total discretion and hush-hush.'

He smiled lightly at that thought. In matters involving the Egyptian State there was no such thing as discretion.

'At once, Sir,' replied the secretary, putting the sheet of paper back into a folder he was carrying.

'I want to know if anything turns up,' added the Ambassador, as the other man reached the doors.

The private secretary turned and gave a curt nod of acknowledgement before making his exit.

The Ambassador remained seated behind his desk, his gaze fixed absently on the escritoire. It would not be long before he would surrender to the demons of his memory and once again cross the carpeted expanse of his office in search of comfort and support.

22

Aswan

The Nile, Early morning – 23rd July 1928

On the steamship's bridge, *reis* Tarek rang down that he was finished with the engines. The bridge telegraph jingled across the stillness of the broad expanse of the river, as the engine room acknowledged Tarek's order and the huge paddlewheel started to slow on its endless, circular journey. As if to announce that the little white ship had arrived safely and had survived the trials of the last few days, Tarek sounded off three long blasts on the ship's whistle.

'Look how spread out it is,' said Mr Rotherham, fanning himself with his hat.

From under the shade of the deck awnings, most of the group had gathered to watch their arrival in Aswan. Their mood had lightened somewhat and was almost back to what passed for 'normal'. They sat about in little groups or stood leaning on the rails, surveying the scene. Along the elegant Corniche, which ran in a broad sweep along the quayside, the life of Aswan heaved and flowed. Horse-drawn carriages and donkey-drawn carts filled the road and there was the occasional motorcar or truck. Everywhere, the flowing robes of the local men and women mingled with the Western dress of those of higher status, from further north. Colour filled the streets. The sound rose up like a fountain, as if to challenge the calm tranquillity of the deep blue river which basked languidly under the already hot sun.

'Not quite what you'd expect, is it?' said Lydia Porter, standing next to the rail and gazing down at the frenzied activity on the quay, 'For Africa, I mean,' she added.

'It ain't as big as New York, ma'am,' said Elias Grupfelder, 'but it sure ain't that small, neither.'

She gave him a disdainful leer and turned her back on him, staring fixedly at the buildings which towered above them on the bank.

Rupert, who had heard this exchange from where he had been standing towards the bows, took the opportunity to interrupt and diffuse the situation.

'Yes, it is quite big – Egypt's second city, actually. And look,' – he gestured out across the river, over the flat expanse of Elephantine Island, towards the small clusters of buildings which occupied parts of the left bank of the river – 'they've even started to spread over there – the western side of the river – the realm of the dead, remember – the same side as the Valley of the Kings. We'll be visiting that when we get back to Luxor.'

Mr Mannington turned his face away from the view and seemed about to say something, but did not. Instead he glanced at his wife and then returned his gaze to the shore.

'You'll find things quite different in Aswan,' continued Rupert, getting into his stride. 'We're almost on the ancient border between Egypt and Nubia – the name which means "Gold". And that's from where the pharaohs obtained most of theirs – together with spices, ivory, ostrich feathers and – importantly – Pharaoh's best fighting troops.' The separate groups had begun to gather around Rupert as he spoke.

'Is this Nubia?' asked Rebecca Eggerton.

'No, Miss Eggerton, this is Egypt. Nubia, or Sudan as it is now called, is many miles up the river to the south. We will be close to the border once we reach Abu Simbel,' answered Rupert.

'I find this "upriver to the south" and "downriver to the north" very confusing,' said Mr Mannington suddenly. It was more than he had said during the trip thus far. Heads turned in his direction in surprise.

Rupert pressed on with his narrative, not keen on becoming involved with Mannington's confusion. What was taxing the man's mind was really a very simple geographical fact.

'Aswan itself is famous for its granite, especially the pink kind. This is where the pharaohs quarried all the granite used in their temples and also for their statues. Any granite you see in Egypt – throughout the entire country – would have come from here. We'll be visiting the Unfinished Obelisk and the granite quarry.'

'Look at how tall and how black that man is,' said Rebecca Eggerton, in a mixture of disbelief and awe.

'He's a Nubian, from the south.' answered Rupert. 'They *are* much taller and blacker than the Egyptians – now you see why Pharaoh wanted them on his side,' he chuckled.

'Are there elephants on this island?' asked Eric Kormann. 'You said it was Elephant Island, yes?'

'Elephantine Island,' corrected Rupert. 'No, there aren't, but Aswan was the key to trade and communication between the African continent and the rest of ancient Egypt. They think that ivory was probably traded on the island, hence the name. In fact, the original Egyptian name for the island was *Yebu*, which does mean "elephant". Does anyone remember to which god the temple we visited in Esna was dedicated?'

Rupert had taken the opportunity to see if any of his flock had learned anything about ancient Egypt so far on their trip. He half expected a stony silence, but was pleasantly surprised when Susan Lampton answered.

'Koonumb, wasn't it?' she said. 'The pottery god who cast everyone's fate on his potter's wheel,'

'Indeed it was, the god Khnum,' repeated Rupert, correcting her pronunciation.

'So we have him to thank for our problems, do we?' asked a voice sourly, from the stern. Miss Kirby was sitting by herself, her feet resting in the seat of an empty chair, a cigarette in her hand. She was wearing sunglasses. 'He wasn't all that good a god then, was he?' she said mysteriously and with more than just a hint of bitterness in her voice.

Some of them had turned to look at Ruth Kirby, but the majority decided to simply ignore the remark. She was always offhand, or even rude, and most of them had learned not to even attempt social intercourse with her. Rupert ignored her remark and continued.

'There's a shrine to him on the island, as well as a small museum, which is quite interesting. We are also entering cataract country – the first one is just a very short distance from us – further up the river. Some of you might have heard of Aswan's famous Cataract Hotel…?'

'I think I remember Lady Renton mentioning it once,' announced Mrs Grassmere, who was more than amply filling her wicker chair, 'but I couldn't be sure…'

Apart from this one vacuous remark, said more for impression than anything else, Rupert was rewarded with blank faces. 'Well, it's one of Aswan's best and it's built on the bank overlooking the First Cataract. The views from it used to be quite spectacular during the flooding season, but the disruptive effect on the current, caused by the rocks in the river, has been muted quite a lot since the dam was built. We'll be taken over the dam when we go to catch the steamer down to Abu Simbel.' He turned to gesture upriver to where the dam blocked off and controlled the power of the Nile. As he did so, he noticed the neatly dressed form of Achmed, Mohammed's very able right-hand man, standing in the bright sunshine in the middle of the deck.

'Excuse me a moment, please,' said Rupert, smiling, as he walked quickly through the gathered group and up to Achmed. 'Do you need to see me, Achmed?' he asked.

'Indeed, *Effendi*, and please excuse the interruption.' He spoke better English than Mohammed, a result of being Coptic and having been partly educated by missionaries. 'You are wanted in the office, Sir,' continued Achmed. 'The police...' he added softly.

Rupert had become so involved in his talk on Aswan that he had not noticed the arrival of two policemen on the quayside. In fact, none of the party on the upper deck of *Khufu* had seen them.

By the time the formalities had been concluded and the questions answered to the satisfaction of the two policemen, the sun was well advanced towards its zenith. The groups had been forced to retreat even further under the cover of the shade awnings on the upper deck. Eventually, the police announced themselves satisfied that the regrettable death of Sylvia Baxter had been an unfortunate accident and they gave permission for the tour to continue. The travellers watched silently from the railings of the upper deck, as the stretcher carrying the covered form of Miss Baxter was carried reverently down the gangway to be borne away to the British High Commission, for return of the body to Malaya. Miss Cuttle had accompanied the little procession to the head of the gangplank and now stood impassively with her hands dangling loosely at her sides. With some considerable effort she set her face hard against her emotions, watching as the lifeless body, still rigid from its seclusion in the ice room, left *Khufu* for the last time. Behind her stood Miss Eggerton – as ever, ready to help if needed.

'It's terribly sad, isn't it?' whispered Rebecca, as she put her hand on Cuttle's arm. 'Such a sweet girl...'

'I shall have to write to her parents ... in Malaya. They should know how she had blossomed since she left home. They should know what they have lost...'

'Pardon?'

'If she had not been so restricted at home ... if she had been allowed to bloom the way we encouraged her to do ... then perhaps they would not have driven her to the point where they have lost her,' mumbled Marjory Cuttle, fighting back her tears.

'Oh ... I say,' responded Eggerton, 'we cannot really blame her parents for her death, can we?' She had not fully understood the implication behind what Cuttle had muttered and felt at a loss for something more meaningful to say. 'Do you know where they live ... in Malay, I mean?' she continued.

'Oh yes. She lent me this...' replied Cuttle, bringing out a small photo album from the folds of her skirt. 'There are a few snaps in here. She called them her treasured memories. I was going to just lift the blanket and put it in with her when they carried her past ... but I just couldn't bring myself to do so.'

She dissolved into a series of heart-rending sobs.

At one o'clock, as usual, the melodious chimes of 'Three Blind Mice' had summoned the travellers to the dining room for luncheon. Despite the sad departure of Miss Baxter, a little over an hour before, appetites had returned and the room was soon filled with the subdued babble of conversation. Sebastian Printon, who had avoided the upper deck that morning, was once again at a table with the Arlings. The three were in animated conversation, which was interspersed with frequent outbursts of laughter. It was nearly one thirty when Rupert cleared his throat and rose to speak.

'Ladies and gentlemen,' he began, 'I must apologize for yet another delay to our planned programme of events...' and he let any further mention of Sylvia Baxter rest there. 'Despite the cooler breezes of Aswan, which I hope you find agreeable after the heat of our previous stops, it is going to be far too hot to go and visit the Unfinished Obelisk this afternoon. Accordingly, I propose that we use this afternoon as time to pursue our own interests, whether they be a trip around the bazaar, a walk along the Corniche to the Cataract Hotel for tea, or just to rest on board *Khufu*.'

As he spoke, Printon quietly slipped out of the dining room, a fact that was not wasted on Stephen, but which attracted little interest from Rupert. People left the dining room after a meal, so there was nothing unusual in that, he thought.

'Tomorrow, we have an early start to the obelisk,' he continued, 'but this afternoon is your own. Please do not hesitate to ask me for directions or for any other information you might require. Also, please remember to let the reception desk know where you plan to go, if you go ashore – we all need to be careful...' he concluded and then sat down again.

'I need to go ashore, old chap, the sooner the better. Are you up for it? Care to show an old soldier the sights and sounds of Aswan?' said Stephen, smiling.

Later that afternoon, as the activity in the city began to resume its hectic pace after the siesta of the early afternoon; most of the travellers had gone ashore to either explore the exotic sights, the smells and sounds of the bazaar, or to relax over afternoon tea in the refined, genteel opulence of the Cataract Hotel. In one of the backstreets, set back from the river, an ornate carriage drew up outside a small office.

'Wait for me,' said Sebastian Printon, as he stepped down from it.

He stood for a moment facing the building in front of him. The brass plate next to the door proclaimed 'Kohler & Zehler, Importers of Fine Gourmet Consumables'.

At luncheon Esther Arling had suggested that they should all join up on a sojourn ashore, but he had managed to slip away whilst she and Simon had been involved in a whispered conversation with Grupfelder, Kormann and Colonel Ponsworthy, who were sitting at the dining table next to theirs.

The Jewish bitch has a useful purpose, he had thought to himself, as he made good his escape and hailed a passing carriage on the Corniche. *So does her arrogant husband* – for he had never been particularly concerned where he found his sexual gratification. *But that is all she is – a Jewish whore and no more.*

Inside the small office, which was a miniscule establishment, he introduced himself to the sole employee. Following an agreed sequence of questions and answers, both men lapsed into whispered German.

'I want to send a message to Cairo,' said Printon.

23

East Africa

Mpigi, near Kampala, Uganda – 10th July 1928

The tall, thin European sat straight-backed in his chair, hands resting on the ornate handle of his silver-topped walking stick.

'It has become more and more difficult,' he said softly to the thickset man who sat opposite him. 'My instructions are to move the shipment forward immediately. Such action, as dangerous as it is, might well outflank those who would prevent us. I have reported that it might not be possible to deliver any merchandise in the future, if the net continues to close in around us.'

His companion, a man with broad, muscular shoulders and a bullish, square shaped head, looked sternly at his visitor, but maintained a respectful silence. There was nothing he could add; he was only a small cog in the mechanics of a much larger operation, the workings of which were not his to understand. He raised a powerful arm, turned brown by the African sun, and, with the subtlest of gestures, moved his hand to indicate silence. An African servant, carrying a large tray, was approaching them along the broad expanse of veranda.

'A moment, Herr Graf, if you please,' he whispered in guttural German.

As both men watched, the servant, a not unattractive

native girl, probably in her late teens, silently placed cups, saucers and plates, a large pot of steaming black liquid and a cake stand, full of delicately made sandwiches and sweet pastries, on the wicker table between them. Then she retreated down the veranda, as silently as she had come.

'I can assure the Herr Graf that they are all totally trustworthy,' said the thickset man. 'Their families all started working for mine back in the '90s, when all of this was just waste bush land.'

He swept his arm around in a broad, graceful gesture, which belied the muscular heaviness of his build. Vast, cultivated fields reached out in all directions from the large, squat farmhouse buildings. Prosperity was obvious – as obvious as the marks on those powerful hands, which showed the hard work that had brought about that prosperity.

'...But in matters such as ours, it is best to trust no one – only ourselves. If you wish, Herr Graf, please help yourself...'

The Count reached out a bony hand and delicately took one of the small, chocolate-covered cakes.

'*Torte* from the Old Country?' he asked in surprise after he had eaten it. 'In the heart of Africa?'

'Indeed, the Herr Graf is correct, but it is not from the Old Country,' replied the other man. 'Our cook has been with us for years and has been very well taught, as have all of our servants here. We may live on the fringes of civilization, but we must make every effort to make our lives as comfortable as possible. Even if we are exiles in a foreign land, like His Imperial Majesty himself, we must still not forget our roots and that our duty lies with the Fatherland.'

'Your commitment to duty is commendable,' said The Phoenix softly.

He nodded his head, almost imperceptibly, as he delicately wiped a crumb from the corner of his mouth with a linen napkin. He had enjoyed his second cake and it had been some time since he had enjoyed the taste of home. Back in the days when he owned vast tracts of land and a large *Schloss* just outside Windhoek, he had found his own servants to be generally incompetent. His wife had imported a German housekeeper in an effort to improve things, but now his Elspeth, like the *Schloss* and most of his other possessions, were long dead and gone – prisoners of the irretrievable past. He had lost it all – everything, except the fortune in his Swiss bank accounts.

'If I could rely on more people like you, Lindhof, our task would be much easier to accomplish,' said the Count, as he replaced the napkin on the table. The other man stiffened at the compliment and gave the slightest nod of his head in acknowledgement. They were both Prussian: one from the aristocratic, militaristic level of that society, the other from the lower orders of good, reliable stock who could always be counted on to realize that obedience and duty to the Fatherland came before all else. The war had removed some of the long-established class barriers that separated these two men, but here, in the African bush, such social reform had not penetrated. They were still aware of the importance and significance of each other's status.

'Given the urgency of my instructions, it has been necessary to make use of contacts that are not of our race,' continued the visitor, as he stared out at the fields and the ant-like figures of the workers who were tending them. 'They value monetary gain far above any sense of patriotism or duty. Still, with so little notice and very few of our usual avenues still open to us, I suppose we should be grateful for their ... *help*,' he said, stressing the word mockingly.

The other man nodded. He understood the need for total success.

'I thought it best to close the route behind me,' continued the Count, without turning his gaze away from the fields. 'None of our former *friends* will be able to talk about the role they played in our glorious enterprise; neither will they be able to spend any of the money they thought their greed had earned them.' He smiled, but it was little more than an unpleasant grimace, his thin lips barely showing his white, even teeth. 'We cannot afford to be careless – too much depends on the shipment getting through successfully. The order came from the highest authority.'

'Naturally, Herr Graf,' replied the other man. Both of them were of the old school. Lindhof, like his father before him and his grandfather before that, believed unquestioningly that duty to the Fatherland always came first. Even if he were to allow himself the briefest moment's speculation as to whether the Herr Graf had the stones on his person, or whether his visitor had lodged them somewhere more secure in nearby Kampala until the time for departure drew near, he would have kept such thoughts to himself.

'The Herr Graf has to journey back to Kampala and time is of the essence. We will not reach the city until late this evening,' said the thickset man, 'so, with the Herr Graf's permission...?' He waited for a nod before continuing. 'I have the Herr Graf's travel documents, papers and some banknotes – Sudanese and Egyptian. They, at least, are genuine.' He said this in a very matter-of-fact way which contained not the faintest hint of humour. Reaching into a leather case, which stood on the veranda floor between his feet, he extracted a small bundle of papers.

'I will drive the Herr Graf back to Kampala shortly. Thereafter, there is the train to Namasagali. After that there is the motor ride and river journey to Nimule, which is on the Sudanese border. A motor transport will take the Herr Graf on to Juba and from there, both the river and the train lead directly on to Khartoum and Aswan. There is no time lost with the connections,' he said, 'but the terrain is unpleasant and sometimes dangerous and there is no safety zone if something should go amiss,' he added, as he unfolded the papers and carefully laid them out in the small space still left clear on the table. 'I hope these arrangements meet with the Herr Graf's approval?'

'Excellent as always, Lindhof,' replied the Count, as he expertly scanned the documents one at a time, holding them in his left hand, his right remaining firmly grasping the ornate silver handle of his cane. 'At Aswan I am to be met by one of our own. I myself will make all the other arrangements from there,' he added, but kept the details to himself. Experience had taught him not to trust anyone – no matter how loyal – with too much information. Not that The Phoenix could possibly have known it, but that single aspect was, perhaps, the only thing he and his opponent, Major Jeremy Ashdown, had in common.

He balanced the cane against his leg and, with one smooth movement, quickly placed the papers, which he had refolded, in his inside jacket pocket. For a few moments both men sat in silence, a silence which was broken only by the sound of a flock of birds in the nearby trees. Incongruous as it was in the heart of Africa, the trees formed the boundary of a passable re-creation of a baroque European formal garden.

'We have nobody between here and Cairo,' said the thickset man softly. 'It is the most dangerous part of the route.'

The Count turned his hawk-like head and smiled at his companion – a smile that was more threatening and ominous than warm or welcoming.

'There has been nobody between Kolmanskop and here,' he said wryly, 'but that has not stopped us. Swiss citizens, when they travel, rarely cause an eyebrow to be raised,' he said, in a matter-of-fact way. 'The chocolate and the clocks have made them far too respectable and soft. Besides which, the stupid British are still far too wedded to their notion of a gentleman and his "word". Whatever a gentleman says is always taken as his word – they think it is not in a gentleman's nature to lie. Fools! But now it is time for us to prepare for the return journey to Kampala,' said the visitor, as he pushed his chair back and stood up. 'Your duty and service to the Fatherland will not go unrewarded,' he said, looking at the thickset man, who had sprung to his feet almost before the Herr Graf had regained his.

'It is nothing more than should be expected,' replied Lindhof, clicking his heels and bobbing his head slightly.

'True,' replied the Herr Graf unemotionally. 'As I have a bumpy ride back to Kampala, I have a mind to wander around your garden before I leave. Another reminder of the Old Country, would you not agree...?' he continued, but neither waited for, nor expected an further comment. 'And then, perhaps, a final, small glass of schnapps...'

Later, at about the same time that the Herr Graf was being bumped along the dirt track towards Kampala, Major Jeremy Ashdown had opted for an early night. In his room at the Delamere Hotel in Nairobi, he lay naked on top of his sheets, entombed like a foetus within the depths of the mosquito net which hung down from the ceiling. Above this a small fan gently turned. Despite the resultant movement of air, the room remained stuffy. Outside in the street, the noises of the day had given way to those of the night and the hotel, which was one of the centres of Kenyan society, had gradually filled with the well-to-do who were seeking escape from the exertions of the day to eat, drink and dance. Ashdown had no interest in any of that – he never had had. He lay in the darkness of his room, running through in his mind what information he had collected. It did not amount to much. All he had was a name: Benschedler, a Swiss national. As he lay in the warmth of the Nairobi night, under the revolving, battling blades of the little fan, he once again began to feel that he was getting nowhere. Purely on the gut feeling of a totally disgruntled inspector of the Kenya police, who had an axe to grind with his commissioner, Ashdown was now about to continue looking for both the needle *and* the haystack. He had warmed to the Inspector; he felt empathy with the man and his situation. Like Inspector Samuel Lyons, he had not warmed to Commissioner Halkyard at all. Ashdown was glad he had taken the cockney's advice and that he would be leaving Nairobi the following morning.

He sighed once again and passed his hand over his chest, the hair of which was moist with sweat. In the darkness, he stared at the barely visible flashes of light reflected off the blades of the fan as it turned. The curtains were heavy, but they did not totally block out the light from outside, which crept into his room, uninvited, from around the extremities of the window opening.

If this Swiss chap was the diamond smuggler, as they suspected, did he have the stones with him still? Or was he smart enough to have passed them on to a second link in a much bigger chain? Was the Swiss anything to do with the stiletto murders? What if every one of his suppositions was wrong and the events were totally unconnected – where would that leave him as far as Pretoria was concerned?

Suddenly, his sister's face filled his mind – Julia – and her crippled husband, Roderic. The Major tried to remain focused on his quarry and the diamonds, but Julia's face kept pushing into his vision. Perhaps it was because he was on home territory; perhaps it was because, at the back of his mind, he was still troubled by past events. She had never even thought of blaming him for the fiasco in Tanganyika – the blunder of Military Intelligence which had needlessly taken the lives of the other men of the family. Why did he sometimes feel that maybe she did? He had no grounds to even think this. He fought to make his mind concentrate on the diamonds. Perhaps the Swiss was not a Swiss – what if ... but his mind drifted again to the family farm, up in the Highlands – but now the veranda, with its breath-taking views out over the rolling hills, had emptied – only Julia stood there, looking at him and, behind her in the background, Roderic, in his wheelchair.

Ashdown sighed and moved his position, yet again. The images of his sister and their past life had made him nervous and he was quite wet from the sweat. The near-invisible flashes of light, flicking off the fan's blades, seemed to grow more blurred through the heavy netting of the mosquito net. Julia had always been very supportive – he had no reason to think otherwise. No – the Swiss must be a Swiss: or were the documents the police had seen at Mombasa forged? Or had Julia never forgiven him for the debacle of his wedding – the highlight of the social season, which was supposed to have happened, but which never did? Despite the scandal that had followed in the tightly knit social vacuum inhabited by the white settlers, Julia had never condemned him for what he had not done. She understood him. Why should she not do so now, even if only in his imagination? The stiletto knife or blade – there must be some sort of link with the murders – same person, same weapon, same ... Julia was being called, from further down the veranda, by Roderic. As she turned and walked away, Ashdown shouted for her to stay, but the sound was only in his head. He shouted again – even louder than before – but she just kept walking away from him, towards the wheelchair in which Roderic spent most of his working day. Ashdown shouted her name once more, even louder than before, but still the lips did not move. Then there was another woman on the veranda. She looked a little younger than his sister, but he couldn't see who she was. Her back was towards him. He asked who she was, but, again, the words only echoed silently around his brain. The woman started to move and then, suddenly, she stopped and turned to face him. For a split second he thought that he recognized her, but then her face suddenly changed. In an instant she suddenly had a bird-like face of silver. Everything gradually faded into a muddled mess of recollection and fantasy, as Ashdown, his body now completely covered in sweat, lay still, his breathing shallow and in gasps. He moaned out loud and twisted on the wet sheets. Then, suddenly, his mind was completely blank – the image of his family, of his past and the thoughts of the present – of his quarry and the diamonds – all erased.

As he lay in the darkness, under the confines of the mosquito net, his chest relaxed into a more gentle rhythm of movement, as his breathing became easier and returned to normal. His movements also eased, until he lay peacefully on the still-wet sheets, his steady breathing being the measure of his now relaxed sleep.

Above him, the blades of the fan continued to rotate slowly. As they did so, they caught and reflected the nearly invisible light from outside. It was a continuous, steady pulse, much like that used to unlock the mind through hypnosis.

24

Aswan

On Board Khufu – 24th July 1928

It had been another pre-dawn call for the tourists. Mohammed had done his usual round of the cabins, knocking on each door and extolling the occupants to stir themselves and prepare for the activity of the day. He had especially enjoyed disturbing the occupants of Cabin 8, as he visualized the dreadful Grassmere woman sweating and complaining as she stumbled through the heat at the ancient granite quarry. In that place, the sun attacked twice – first from overhead and second by being radiated back up from the very heart of the stone itself. There would be no real shelter, once the visit got into its stride.

Oh yes, Missus Always Complaining, you are going to have a very hot time, he thought to himself with a smile, as he continued down the corridor.

When he reached Cabin 10 and rapped on the door, he was somewhat mystified by the acknowledging voice he heard in response. It was Printon's cabin, but the voice had sounded like a woman's. Mohammed had never ceased to be amazed at the seemingly endless reserves of energy for pursuits other than archaeology some of his guests harboured – particularly in the hours of darkness. He raised his eyebrows until they touched the rim of his fez and he smirked to himself as he continued on his round. When he returned to the entrance lobby, he found Rupert sorting through the sheets of his itinerary for the visit to the obelisk.

He has been a much changed person since this trip started, thought Mohammed. *Especially since the Mister Hopkins ...* And he smiled his gold-tooth smile. 'Good mornings to you, Mr Rupert. You have made an early start, yes?' he asked, as he joined Rupert behind the reception desk.

'Morning, Mohammed,' replied Rupert brightly. 'Yes ... I just needed to make sure I have all my papers and diagrams ready before the flock descend upon us.' He looked up from his sorting, which he had almost completed to his satisfaction. 'Did your door-knocking go all right?'

'As smooth as the silk is to the skins,' he replied, in his particular form of English.

Rupert smiled. Mohammed was a very genuine person and the affection and respect Rupert felt for him was returned, unreservedly, by the little Egyptian. 'I am noticing especially Cabin 10,' he continued idly as an aside, whilst he busied himself with that day's list, ready to tick the tourists all out and then all back again at the end of the excursion.

'Oh? I thought your special interest this trip was number 8,' said Rupert, chuckling, 'not our friend in number 10.'

'Indeed, the lady in number 8 is being worthy of the utmost unworthy attentions' came the reply. Mohammed cast a knowing sideways glance at his colleague. 'But the voice being of Mr Printon in number 10 was being of even more worthy attentions...' He lowered his own voice to an unnecessary whisper, as they were the only occupants of the foyer. '... It had become as a woman's, *insha'Allah!*' he concluded, rolling his eyeballs in mock, mystified wonderment.

'Nothing new there, then,' replied Rupert, smiling, as he gathered his papers and replaced them in his folder. 'I'm off to have something to eat before the rest of them descend.

I wouldn't be surprised if your friend in number 8 is like a bear with a sore head again this morning.'

Mohammed was totally mystified by this last remark, which was beyond the powers of his not inconsiderable English to comprehend. He could not remember any of his friends complaining of a sore head in the morning. Neither did he understand what a bear had to do with anything, although he had seen one in Cairo Zoo during the war.

I will never understand these Europeans, he decided, as he went into the inner office.

***

The convoy of carriages had carried the tourists along the Corniche and out to the fringes of the city to where the granite quarry, the only source of quality granite for the whole of ancient Egypt, was situated amongst a barren, desert landscape. The town of Aswan hugged the riverbank, in peril of being pushed into the water by the desert and the angry, dry hills which rose up dramatically on the near horizon. Their departure from *Khufu* had been almost as dramatic as the scenery which now surrounded them. Mohammed had had a heated argument with Fairuz bin-Salaah, the owner of the principal tour guide establishment in Aswan and, by virtue of this exalted position, the company's duly appointed local agent.

'That is not good enough!' ranted Mohammed, his hands waving in the air and the black tassel of his fez swaying about alarmingly. 'You promised me the new motor coach this time – and look what you have sent me!' He stabbed the air repeatedly, up in the direction of the Corniche, to where several ornate carriages waited in the early-morning light, their drivers swathed in their galabeas and outer cloaks against the nip of the desert night which still clung, lingeringly, to the air. Their horses flicked their tails angrily at the squadrons of flies, which had started their new day even before the tourists on board *Khufu* had started theirs.

'The new motor coach *is* here in Aswan,' replied bin-Salaah, who was several inches taller than Mohammed and, from the much darker colour of his skin, probably of Nubian descent. 'It has been safely driven from Cairo and is now here, *insha'Allah...*'

'So why do you send me the carriages again?' interrupted Mohammed, hands on his hips, glaring at the other man.

'The motor coach has an illness – it needs to have new pieces from Cairo. It is an English motor coach and does not understand the sands or the desert,' continued bin-Salaah, 'the trip down here from Cairo has broken it – and I am still waiting for the new bits to arrive – *insha'Allah!* So I have brought you my finest carriages as usual!' And he shrugged his shoulders, as if to signify both an end to the conversation and the hopelessness of Mohammed's situation.

The little Egyptian had been about to launch into a counter-argument, but thought better of it, as he caught sight of the tourists assembling in the foyer. They had had breakfast, it was approaching eight o'clock and they must make a start. He flung both arms up in the air in exasperation and turned on his heel to join them. Fairuz bin-Salaah went back down the gangplank to rejoin his waiting carriages, muttering to himself that Mohammed simply didn't understand how difficult it was, maintaining the high standards demanded from the best tour operator in Aswan.

'Gather around please, everyone,' said Rupert, as the foyer filled with his flock, one or two still showing the remaining signs of sleep. 'This morning we are going to visit the ancient granite quarry of Aswan. This is the only source of granite in Egypt and it was from here that the pharaohs extracted the granite used throughout the whole of ancient Egypt. We think the original quarry stretched along the river for over four miles, but today it is really just the area around the Unfinished Obelisk that remains of interest.'

'Say, fella, y' mean to say everything came from here and had to be shipped out elsewhere?' asked Grupfelder, 'I'm OK with cattle, but lumps of this stuff? Ain't it too heavy fur them Ancients?'

'A good question,' replied Rupert. 'Yes, it is very heavy and the blocks they removed from the quarry were often massive, weighing many tons, but they had worked out a way of getting the granite onto boats and then taking it by river to where it was needed. They used it for facing the pyramids and for monumental statuary. Statues were carved here in rough first and then finished when they reached their final destination. That avoided any possible superficial damage en route.'

Mohammed appeared at the exit doorway from the foyer, restored to his usual good nature after the fracas over the non-appearance of the motor coach. Rupert acknowledged him and continued. 'I see our transport is ready, so if you'd please make sure you have all of your possessions and your water, I'll hand over to Mohammed.'

As the vanguard of the group started to move out of the foyer, across the deck, onto the gangway and down to the quayside, Lydia Porter tapped Rupert's arm.

'What is the significance of the Unfinished Obelisk? Why didn't they finish it?' she asked.

'Don't worry about that now, Mrs Porter,' replied Rupert. 'I'll explain all about it when we reach the quarry – it'll make much more sense if you can see it as I do so.'

'Oh good, because I always like to...'

She was interrupted by hearty laughter from the back of the group.

'We obviously have the same outfitter!' laughed Richard Lampton, pointing to Porter's head.

'Excuse me?' she asked, turning to look at Lampton, surprised.

'It's a joke, Mrs Porter. We have the same headgear, so we must have been to the same outfitter.'

'Oh, I see,' answered Porter, somewhat displeased by the familiarity, 'but I do not think so.'

Lampton continued with his attempt to make friendly conversation. 'Actually, my brother sent this to me from Australia. It's the best protection against the sun there is – much cooler than a topee.'

They were both of the same height and were of very similar build.

'Really?' replied Porter, somewhat acidly. 'My husband was a geologist and we spent some little time there after we retired – he was interested in the Western part of Australia. I brought my hat back with me,' she declared. 'Excuse me, please,' she said, red blotches spreading over her cheeks, as she walked determinedly out of the foyer.

'Only trying to be friendly,' said Lampton as she did so, turning to his wife with a look of perplexity on his face.

At the quarry, the sun had started to make itself felt. Despite this, the traders and urchins of Aswan, as numerous as sand flies, seemed to have appeared as if from nowhere, as the carriages came to a halt at the entrance. It was just a little short of nine o'clock. Fairuz bin-Salaah, resplendent in his flowing gown and turban, had also appeared, and was busying trying to keep the traders away from his carriages.

'Get away, you sons of she goats!' he shouted. 'Do not dare infuriate the Infidels. Get out of the way.'

Because of his height and build, he cut an imposing figure, which seemed to intimidate the traders and produce the desired results. They retreated a few paces from the disgorging carriages and resentfully continued to shout the praises of the items they had for sale. To the visitors, and in his fractured English, Fairuz bin-Salaah was all smiles. Over the years, he had perfected the knack of ingratiating himself with the unworldly-wise by smarmy obsequiousness, which was delivered to a polished standard that many other Egyptians could only marvel at.

'You to be enjoy the sight,' he kept saying. 'We will be your return awaiting, have no problem.'

'This way, everyone, over here, please,' shouted Rupert, as he made his way towards the shade of a little building that guarded the entrance to the site.

The Manningtons were the first to follow him into the shade.

'It's quite sticky already, isn't it?' said Mr Mannington. 'Yes ... quite sticky, already,' added his wife, echo-like. 'And it's still quite early, isn't it?' she added. Her husband nodded in agreement. 'Yes ... quite early, too...' Apart from Mr Mannington's earlier statement of confusion as to what was up and what was down on the river, it was the most either of them had said as a duet since the start of the trip.

The Grassmeres were next to arrive. Having decided that her blouse with the flounces had served its purpose and was beyond saving, Mrs Grassmere had decided, instead, on a long cotton skirt and a long-sleeved, white cotton shirt. The perspiration was already creeping outwards from her armpits. As she peered out from under the topee she was wearing, sweat had also started dribbling down her ample cheeks. The large, hard hat was wedged firmly on her head and the combination of the flabby cheeks, crossed by the rivulets of sweat, and the pig-like eyes, which peered out from beneath the brim, gave her the appearance of a hippopotamus in woman's clothing.

Rupert watched as the rest of the group assembled in the shade: Printon, as usual, with the Arlings – Simon Arling with his tanned skin, a souvenir from time spent in Palestine perhaps? It was certainly not a product of the English climate. And Esther, with her red fingernails and sultry, pouting posturing – what was her background? Miss Cuttle, accompanied as usual since the incident in the temple by Miss Eggerton; Kormann and Grupfelder, the latter very talkative and outgoing; Colonel Ponsworthy and Mrs Porter; the unpleasant Ruth Kirby, as silent and offhand as ever from behind the anonymity of her sunglasses.

Rupert waited for the others to join the party before continuing.

'We will make our way up over the rocks to a viewing point above the Unfinished Obelisk,' he said. 'From there you will be able to see how it was quarried and also get some idea of the size.'

'So how *big* is it, then?' asked Esther Arling from where she, Simon and Printon had formed a tight little group of their own. Rupert had expected her question with the emphasis on the word – always the same implication. The *woman is obsessed with size*, he determined. He caught the look on Stephen's face, which revealed that he, too, had arrived at a similar conclusion – except that in his estimation the woman was simply a nymphomaniac.

'It's *huge*,' replied Rupert, taking delight in mockingly repeating the stress. 'If it had been finished and successfully *erected*' – again, he looked casually at Esther Arling – 'it would have been nearly three hundred feet tall and would have weighed in the region of twelve hundred tons – that's well over half of *Khufu*'s gross tonnage.'

There were comments and gasps from some of the group.

'Excuse me, please,' said the Swiss, 'why was it not finished – why is it still here?'

'Mrs Porter, this answers your earlier question, too,' said Rupert, turning to look in her direction. 'It is seriously flawed – a crack in the granite ruined it. Perhaps an earth tremor, perhaps a chunk of poor-quality stone, we don't know for sure, but work stopped and it was abandoned.'

'Thank you ... I see,' replied Kormann. 'How unfortunate.'

'For the Ancients, yes, but not for us,' said Rupert, warming to his pet subject once again. 'Because of the obelisk and the other marks around this quarry, we have a good idea of how the ancient Egyptians went about quarrying their granite. You'll be able to see the marks of their tools as we climb higher up.'

He made sure everyone was present and correct.

'Right, then, off we go. Remember to keep drinking your water and watch your footing – there are some nasty drops in the quarry and we don't want any accidents. We need to be careful at all times.'

And with that he led the party off towards the beginning of the steep climb up into the quarry proper. Stephen made sure that he was close to the Lamptons, just in case he might be needed. He had also brought the walking stick he had bought from one of the shops along the Corniche. The terrain in the quarry would be hard going and there was the question of his leg.

The group made tortuously slow progress up the smooth boulders and outcrops of granite, as they made their way to the high vantage point above the obelisk. They had been at the quarry for less than an hour and the rocks were not only already becoming too hot to touch, but they had also started to reflect the heat upwards. Eventually, the first of the travellers crested a ridge and there, to their right, lay the massive bulk of the obelisk.

'That's one mean critter,' said Grupfelder, as he wiped the inside of his Stetson with his handkerchief.

'Similar to the sort of scale you'd expect in Indian monumental architecture,' added Colonel Ponsworthy.

'Oh,' replied Grupfelder, 'would that be Sioux or Navajo?' and burst out laughing.

Ponsworthy looked bewildered for a moment, and then recovered his stride.

'On the Subcontinent, of course,' he said sternly, keeping his gaze firmly on the granite monolith, 'not your local chappies. They don't build with stone anyway, do they...'

He left the remark to linger in the already stifling heat of the quarry and Grupfelder's loud laugh died along with it.

'Look at this please, everyone,' called Rupert, as the last stragglers reached the ridge. 'From here you can see very clearly how the stone was removed,' he said, gesturing up to the large marks which covered the granite outcrops above and behind the trench in which the obelisk lay. 'They would have...' – he broke off in mid-sentence – 'Careful, Miss Eggerton! Don't go too near to the edge – look at the drop!'

From underneath her wide-brimmed sun hat, Rebecca Eggerton raised her hand to her mouth with surprise and whimpered her apologies, as she moved back from where she had been standing, the shock of her near-accident adding yet more moisture to her already sweat-stained blouse. Marjory Cuttle moved back with her.

'We cannot be too careful,' repeated Rupert. 'If you go over the edge from this height, the results could be very nasty indeed,' he continued, before returning to his explanation. 'Those grooves you can see were cut into the rock following the desired shape of the finished object. Then, wooden wedges, called quoins, were hammered into those grooves and water was poured onto them – they expanded and split the rock off in the desired direction. The nature of granite meant that the resulting surfaces were quite smooth and ready for polishing, before the hieroglyphics were added,' he concluded. 'Let's move on and reach the goal of our visit this morning, the viewing area above the obelisk – over there.'

They started to move on. Mrs Grassmere, gasping and wheezing, had decided she had had enough and had already turned back, to seek the shade of the building at the entrance. For once, her uncomplaining husband had agreed with her decision. Mr Rotherham had contemplated joining them, but had then decided that he would push on with everyone else. Ruth Kirby, as usual, was nowhere to be seen and the Arling-Printon group was continuing the conversation they had started at the entrance gate. Stephen, who was finding the terrain a little difficult, also began to have second thoughts about going on, but was brought back to the present by the sound of Richard Lampton's voice.

'Are you sure you wish to carry on?' he asked.

Stephen thought he had addressed the remark to him and was about to respond, when he turned slightly and saw that he was mistaken. Lampton was talking to Lydia Porter, who had propped herself on a narrow outcrop of rock, which was slightly sheltered by an overhanging crag. Stephen walked on, losing what they were saying as he did so.

'If you prefer, I can go back to the shade with you,' said Susan Lampton. 'I really wouldn't mind and it is extremely hot'

'More like being in an oven than a quarry,' said Lampton, in an attempt to lighten the situation. It was obvious that Mrs Porter was in some discomfort and her arms were already quite red and burnt.

'I regret the inconvenience,' she said. 'It is all of my own making. I cannot tolerate the heat – my skin burns far too easily. I was going to quickly return to my cabin and fetch my jacket, but I'm afraid I let our discussion in the foyer get the better of me and I simply forgot.' She took a swig of water from the canteen Susan Lampton offered her. 'It is very stupid of me,' she continued. 'My temper sometimes clouds my better judgement. My late husband used to remind me of it – constantly.' She tried a smile, but the skin around her mouth was already cracking and red. 'He was most upset when we had to cut our stay in Australia short and return to the English climate.' She took another swig. 'It was my fault – I burn too easily. Almost as intensely as my temper does...' She trailed off and sat looking at the ground.

'There is no damage done, Mrs Porter,' said Richard Lampton 'I am used to the sun – you are more than welcome to use my jacket to cover your arms. It is really no trouble,' he added, as he removed his jacket and offered it to Porter. 'Having come this far it would be a pity not to continue and see the obelisk from its best vantage point.'

'I agree,' added Susan Lampton, 'Richard is a tough old bird – please join us. We're almost there...'

Porter thanked them, contritely, and put on the jacket. The relief of removing the sun from her burnt, near-blistering skin was almost instantaneous. She smiled, embarrassedly, at the Lamptons, as the three moved off to catch up with the rest of the tourists, the leaders of whom had already reached the vantage point.

Lydia Porter, although having had a successful career, had led a comparatively hard life, devoid of any real friends and largely empty of real affection. She was not good at responding to kindness and had been taken aback by the Lamptons' genuine show of friendship.

'Thank you', she said, pulling herself up to her full height and looking Richard straight in the eye. 'Thank you for your concern and kindness.' The sentiment was sincerely meant, but the face remained set and unsmiling. She could not undo all the habits of a lifetime in one go.

Whilst he had waited for the Lamptons and Mrs Porter to catch up, Rupert had managed a quick word with Stephen.

'How are you doing?'

'I'm fine, thanks. The old stump's a bit of a niggle, but

this stick's a help and I dare say I'll survive. But there might be the need of a bit of a rub with those ancient...'

'I was hoping that you'd say something like that,' smiled Rupert, cutting Hopkins off in mid-sentence with a friendly punch to the shoulder.

Now, having positioned himself at the front of his group, he continued.

'Keep back from the edge,' he shouted, as the group gathered tentatively in a little huddle along the crest of the high ridge, which separated them from the mass of the Unfinished Obelisk, the base of which was still joined to the earth, some thirty rocky feet below.

'This gives you a very good idea of the scale of the thing,' he said. 'You can just imagine how it was done, in this heat and with very primitive tools. Once an obelisk had been quarried, the sides were rendered very smooth and the hieroglyphics would have been carved and then, very often, brightly painted. You'll see some original paint when we visit the Temple of Karnak back in Luxor.'

'Can I ask a question, please,' asked Mr Rotherham, who had ventured as near to the edge as he dared. 'There is still most of it intact; the crack is only in the top part. Why didn't they just cut it off at the good bit and reuse it. Seems a chronic waste to me,' he continued.

'Always the businessman,' said Simon Arling softly, 'counting every penny...'

'Another good question,' said Rupert, 'we have absolutely no idea. It could be that they thought it was a sign from the gods that they were displeased – they could have thought that the stone was cursed as a result – who knows? The answer is lost in the mists of time, I'm afraid.'

'It seems odd that they just abandoned it like this,' said Rebecca Eggerton.

'Would it have been difficult for them to remove it and cut it in two?' she continued.

FATAL TEARS

'Not really, they were past masters in the art of quarrying. If we look down at the base section there,' – Rupert pointed off to the right, all heads turning to follow his outstretched arm – 'you can see that most of the ba...'

Suddenly, there was a terrified scream. From where he was sanding, Rupert spun his head back and saw the body of Lydia Porter teetering on the edge of the drop, her jacketed arms flailing the air in panic-stricken circles. Everything seemed to suddenly lapse into slow motion. The woman was staring straight ahead of her, as she balanced on the fulcrum, between safety and oblivion. Her hat flew off and spun away into the air like a large discus, its broad brim keeping it spinning on the rising currents of hot air. There was a sudden glint of steel, as her spectacles flew off her nose and slowly sailed out over the abyss, spinning crazily, sending dazzling flashes of light as the lenses rotated and caught the glaring sun. Rupert's gaze followed them down, fascinated by the arabesque of their descent, until they shattered on the top of the granite obelisk. After what seemed an age, the still-screaming mouth seemed to drag the rest of its body out and down, beginning a trajectory that would follow that of the spectacles. There was hardly any other movement from the tightly packed group, other than the slow turning of heads in the direction of the scream. Then, suddenly, in actual time, two hands shot out of nowhere and grabbed the woman from behind by her jacket. Almost as quickly as it had started, it was over. The gibbering form of Lydia Porter was laid carefully on her back on the ground, a safe distance away from the edge. The rest of the group crowded around her to see if they could help.

'Stand back, everyone,' shouted Stephen, as he knelt down next to her and felt her racing pulse. 'Give her some fresh air – not that there is much of it in this heat,' he added softly.

'Is she all right?' asked several voices, in a concerned chorus.

'Shock – nothing seems broken.' He looked around at the sea of faces which crowded in on him. 'We need to get her out of here and back to the shade immediately. Keep her cool if you can, Mrs Lampton – here, use my handkerchief and keep it wet. Grupfelder,' he straightened up, 'can you and Arling carry her down to the carriages? Be careful, the rocks can be slippery if there is sand on them.'

'I will be able to assist,' said the Swiss.

'As, indeed, will I,' said Colonel Ponsworthy.

As they manoeuvred Porter into a comfortable carrying position, Rotherham spoke.

'I think it was a very brave thing to do, going that close to the edge to save Mrs Porter,' he said. 'I would like to be the first to shake your hand.' And with that he held out his hand, which was taken with some indifference by Sebastian Printon.

They made their slow progress back down the quarry.

'It was a very noble thing you did there, dear,' said Susan Lampton, as she walked on her husband's arm across the sandy, stifling yard to where the carriages had been drawn up, waiting. 'If it hadn't been for your jacket, and had she not buttoned it up, the poor thing would have gone over the edge. Her blouse wouldn't have held her when Mr Printon grabbed her.'

'Good for Printon,' answered her husband, 'I really must try and have a chat to him again – this evening, perhaps.'

Back on *Khufu*, the near-disastrous incident had been reported in detail to Mohammed, who had expressed his relief at the outcome and the fact, as he saw it, that it had been an unfortunate accident.

'*Insha'Allah!*' he had said, as he marched off to attend to his guests.

Events at the quarry were also being minutely analysed over a very late luncheon. The consensus was that luck had been on Porter's side and that Printon, through his prompt action, was the hero of the hour. In fact, Esther Arling seemed to be basking in the attention almost as much as the hero himself, although Printon seemed to be far less interested in the adulation than she was. As usual, Printon was sharing a table with the Arlings.

'Well done, there,' said Marjory Cuttle, pausing at the Arlings' table on her way out of the dining room. 'That was really a wonderful thing you did back there, saving Mrs Porter, I mean.'

Printon waved his hand dismissively, as if it had been nothing.

'Yes, he really is *too* wonderful,' purred Esther Arling, her red mouth seductively open as she entwined herself about Printon's arm. He did not seem to object. Neither did Simon Arling.

'Yes, indeed... it was truly marvellous,' chirruped Rebecca Eggerton, as she suddenly appeared from behind Cuttle. 'How brave.'

Printon looked at her for a moment, a look of intolerant disdain on his face.

'Please excuse me... but, if you don't mind... I wonder if I might ask a question? I do hope you won't think it impertinent of me...'

Marjory Cuttle made a tutting sound and looked at Eggerton, as if to dissuade her from proceeding further.

'I must just ask you...' continued Eggerton, ignoring her companion's attempt to deflect her curiosity. '... Well, I was wondering if I could detect just the faintest hint of an accent when you speak? I know you were not with us when we left Cairo and we had our introductory meeting with Mr Winfield...' Printon stiffened, like a jaguar preparing to pounce, but Rebecca Eggerton did not notice. '... So you might not know that some of our party are from foreign parts and I wondered if you might also be from somewhere overseas?'

'No, I am not,' replied Printon softly, his body still tensed, as if it was expecting some unforeseen trouble. 'What makes you think that I might be?'

'Oh, please forgive me, Mr Printon ... I did not wish to cause offence,' repeated Eggerton, becoming more sparrow-like with every passing word. 'It's just that I once had a good friend when I lived in Guildford – poor, dear Sarita. She was a South African, from Cape Town. She spoke a little like you do – sometimes.'

'Come along now, my dear,' said Cuttle, trying to take control of the rambling Eggerton and edge her towards the door. 'I'm sure Mr Printon doesn't want to be bothered with such questions, especially not after this morning's excitement,' she continued, attempting an apologetic smile in Printon's direction.

'South Africa? You are wrong. I have never been there,' said Printon softly, his voice carrying a warning, discouraging further conversation. 'I come from Melton Mowbray, actually.' That was what was recorded in the passport.

As Marjory Cuttle ushered Rebecca Eggerton out of the dining room, past the Lampton's table, Richard leant in close to his wife.

'Did you hear him say South Africa?' he asked, his voice even lower than Printon's had been, 'I could hardly hear, but I thought I heard him say South Africa...'

Mrs Lampton shrugged her shoulders. She had heard nothing of the conversation between Eggerton and Printon above the noise of the dining room.

'Excuse me, please,' said Kormann, as he slid into the vacant space at Rupert and Stephen's table. 'May I...'

'Of course,' replied Rupert, 'help yourself. Coffee?'

'No ... thank you.'

The little Swiss seemed to be on edge and nervous.

'What's up, Kormann?' asked Stephen, as he offered him a cigarette. 'Still got the jitters over this morning? Can't say I'd blame you if you had. It was a near thing.'

'This is what I have to say,' answered the Swiss. 'About this morning, I mean.' He looked around the room, nervously, his voice little more than a whisper. The other two found it difficult to hear him against the background conversation, which filled the dining room. 'But I do not know if I should say it. I have bad memories of the police – my family...' His voice trailed off to a previous time in Switzerland.

'Have some coffee, it'll do you good,' said Stephen, as he poured a cup. 'So, what about this morning?'

'Mr Printon, he saved the unfortunate Mrs Porter and is now a big hero, yes?' Once again, he turned and cast a furtive glance in Printon's direction, but the latter was too busy laughing with the Arlings to notice. 'But I was standing next to him and Mrs Porter and I saw...' He seemed to be fighting a Herculean internal battle with himself, willing himself to speak, and yet finding it almost impossible to do so. It was obvious that he was very much on edge, as he pushed his glasses further up his nose and cast yet another surreptitious glance over to where Printon was sitting with the Arlings. '...And I saw that the arms which saved her were also the arms which nearly killed her,' he mumbled in an almost inaudible whisper.

Stephen put down his coffee cup and leaned in close to the little man, not sure if he had heard correctly.

'What was that, old chap?'

Rupert threw Stephen a puzzled glance, then looked at Kormann.

'...I ... Printon was the...' – Kormann was starting to sweat – '...I cannot be sure, but I think I saw Printon push her ... and then he saved her.'

287

25

Sudan

Khartoum – 17th July 1928

Major Ashdown sat in the compartment of his carriage and stared out of the window. In the very near distance he could see the railway station buildings looming up out of the heat haze, which enveloped the city. Minutes later, as he stepped down from the carriage onto the broad platform, he was taken aback by the hot air he breathed in. He felt the dryness of the heat travel down the back of his throat to his lungs. Although the city had an altitude of twelve hundred feet above sea level, its inhabitants were never allowed to forget that they were the guests of the arid landscape that surrounded them. He was reminded of the threatening, nearby desert by the numerous tropical shrubs which grew in the sandy soil alongside the wide, uncovered expanse of the platform. For a moment he felt the familiar sinking feeling of not knowing where to look for the haystack, or even if the haystack, if he ever found it, would contain the elusive needle he was seeking. By the time he reached the ticket hall he was perspiring profusely, but that did not stop him recalling the events of recent days.

From Kampala he had sent a telegram marked for the attention of the Governor-General, in which he had requested assistance, and detailed his travel plans and expected time of arrival in the city. At Nimule he had crossed the border between Uganda and Sudan, before covering the hundred miles or so to Juba, using the motor transport operated by Sudan Railways. As he bumped and jolted his way along the dirt tracks, he found himself regretting that the vision of a double steel ribbon connecting the Cape to Cairo, so fondly espoused by Cecil John Rhodes, had met the spectre of financial realism and had simply never happened on this stretch of the proposed route. His only consolation for the discomfort he was enduring was that The Griffin – Benschedler, or whoever he was – had also had to endure the same bone-rattling experience – if, indeed, he had come this way at all. From the town of Juba the Major had sent a further telegram to Khartoum. For a few moments, given the seemingly chaotic state of the Post Office, he had entertained the dismal thought that his second request might not get through to its destination at all: only time would tell and he had plenty of that on his hands.

From Juba he boarded the government steamer and enjoyed a pleasant voyage on the White Nile, reaching the town of Kosti in the afternoon of the second day. From there, he boarded the railway once again for the two-hundred-mile journey northwards to Khartoum. As the train sped through the bush nearing the distant capital, Ashdown had been staring idly out of the window, his mind playing its usual game, going over and over again the tenuous evidence and possibly unconnected events which went to make up his case so far.

'I see you're impressed by the greenery,' said a voice opposite him, in a broad Scots accent.

Ashdown had been looking, but without seeing.

'Sorry?' he replied.

'Out there – the greenery,' repeated the jovial Scot. 'It's cotton – good-quality stuff, long-staple. It's a wee bit strange, do you no' think? All that greenery in this heat and with the wastelands just beyond, over there...' He pointed out of the carriage windows to either side of them.

'Yes, I suppose it is,' replied the Major absently.

He was not about to lose the thread of his thoughts for the sake of a pointless conversation with a fellow passenger.

'It's because of the dam. Down at Sennar – it's quite near here. I helped build it, y' ken.'

'Really?' replied Ashdown.

'Aye, we built it, the lads and me. And that's where they get the water from,' he continued, gesturing out of the window.

"Remarkable," replied the Major, but his mind had returned to the far more serious matter of his pursuit. He had absolutely no interest in irrigation dams.

Emerging from Khartoum station, Ashdown was met by a European official and was then driven straight to the Governor-General's Palace.

'I'm glad I arrived on time and didn't get you out to the station on a wild goose chase,' said Ashdown, as the car picked its way through the crowded streets.

'Not to worry,' replied his host. 'The rail service sometimes looks a bit of a shambles, but you'd be surprised at how reliable it really is, considering the different methods of transport involved.' They drove down broad, tree-lined avenues, which were bordered by well-kept grass verges. 'We have all the usual amenities here – racecourse, a fine golf course and, despite the heat, tennis courts...'

He continued listing the merits of the city, but Ashdown had stopped listening. The further away from his base he was forced to travel, the more he felt out on a limb. If only he had something more concrete to work with instead of just a name and a vague description: a tall, thin European with a Swiss name, who might or might not be his man. He sighed.

The vehicle finally entered the grounds of the Governor-General's Palace and came to a halt opposite an impressive flight of wide steps.

'Welcome to Khartoum,' said an elderly man who stood on the top step. 'Runnymede Gaythorne ... I haven't seen you since you were a youngster. How very good to see you ... again...' He extended his hand and Ashdown shook it. The Major had been momentarily taken aback at being recognized by someone he only vaguely remembered from his youth. 'No time to chat now. H.E. is waiting for you. We received your telegrams. This way,' he continued, indicating the passageway that led into the cool interior of the building.

They walked silently down a broad hall, which was hung with large paintings emphasizing the glory of Imperial might and conquest. Ashdown thought that one of them looked like George Joy's well-known painting 'General Gordon's Last Stand'. As a boy he had been given a book in which there had been a reproduction of the same painting. Although they did not stop walking, Gaythorne sensed his visitor's curiosity.

'That's not the original,' he said over his shoulder, 'but it's a fair copy. This palace is built on the site where Gordon met his end, y' know. Kitchener arrived too late, but he soon sorted out the Mad Mahdi and his lot and had the old buildings flattened. They build this new complex instead. A far more fitting symbol of the new Anglo-Egyptian Sudan than the buildings associated with a humiliating military defeat and the death of one of our heroes. I'll get someone to show you Gordon's statue, if you have the time...'

After the usual introductions, Ashdown presented the Governor-General with his letter of authority, which was, by now, somewhat the worse for wear. A pleasant conversation then ensued, at the end of which the Major had been assured of the cooperation of the Commissioner of Police and the other departments that made up the Government of Sudan under British Protection.

'The Commissioner is a good chap – part Egyptian, y' know; not that you'd know it to look at him. He'll have his chaps out and about – never fear, they'll find your man if he's here,' the Governor-General told him, as he was ushered out of the presence.

Ashdown wished he could share the Governor-General's confidence; instead, he found himself in the position of not being able to do anything other than to just sit and wait.

'Come and stay at the Golf Club,' said Gaythorne, as they retraced their route. 'We'll fix you up there. Anyone who is anyone in Khartoum society is a member. They do a very reasonable spread and they offer excellent accommodation – it's run by a Swiss hotelier, y' know, and much better than one of the hotels in the city.'

Once ensconced in the Khartoum Golf Club, Ashdown passed a quiet afternoon alone with his thoughts. He had enjoyed a swim in the club's large pool and had then managed to sleep a little, released from the muddled dreams of which he had lately become a prisoner.

Now it was early evening and he was sitting in the lounge bar of the club, waiting for the arrival of Gaythorne. For the first time in weeks, he felt able to relax – but only a little.

The elder man arrived punctually, as arranged. After exchanging the usual pleasantries the two men emerged onto the broad veranda that overlooked the first six holes of the course. They sat down and ordered drinks from a white-jacketed waiter.

'I knew your father well,' reflected Gaythorne, as he sat opposite the Major lighting a cigar, 'fine chap, actually. And I remember you, too. You've grown – only knee high to a grasshopper you were then. You have your father's eyes.' He chuckled softly to himself at the memories his younger visitor was stirring. 'So ... what about you, then,' he continued. 'Did you not want to carry on with the farm?'

Ashdown smiled at the older man's remembrances, but did not particularly wish to be reminded of that chapter in his life.

'Not really, Sir. After the Tanganyika business, I thought I could make myself more useful elsewhere. My sister and her husband have it now.'

The waiter returned with their drinks. Whilst they were being placed on the table the two men fell silent. The elder looked at Ashdown through a cloud of cigar smoke as he recalled the fine, sprawling homestead surrounded by the vast expanse of cultivated fields; the happy children, eager to see what he had brought them from Nairobi; the beaming parents, arm in arm on the veranda. Memories of happy days in Kenya, before everything was turned topsy-turvy when the war came – the Great War that engulfed everyone.

'And little Julia,' he said. 'I remember her long hair and the smile...'

Ashdown changed the subject abruptly. He had no wish to talk about his sister.

'And how do you find it here, in Khartoum, Sir?'

'Eh...? Here, in Khartoum? Well, it's quite acceptable, as far as it goes. When the Kenya posting was about to finish, I was concerned that I'd end up back home behind a desk in Whitehall. The usual thing: long career of good service, lifetime of foreign experience, but now time to make way for new, less-experienced younger blood and all that rot!' He had begun to flush in the cheeks, 'but I managed to call in a couple of favours and ended up with a posting to Cape Town and then here, to Sudan.' He took a draw on his cigar before continuing, 'This one should see me out, then I might take the knighthood and settle down in Fish Hoek in the Cape – do you know it? Just outside Cape Town?'

Ashdown nodded. Years before, he had made the train journey from Cape Town to Naval Headquarters in Simonstown, and had passed through the sleepy little community, which hugged the base of the mountains on one side and beat off the Indian Ocean on the other.

'Couldn't stand the weather back home!' added the elder man violently.

Ashdown held the fine brandy in his mouth for a few seconds, before swallowing it.

'I am, indeed, fortunate that you were posted here, then,' he said. 'It always helps to know someone in an unfamiliar town. *Particularly someone with useful contacts* he realized.

The older man was on the Governor-General's personal staff, as advisor on African and local affairs. He basked in the name of Runnymede Gaythorne, an inheritance from his father, who believed that all concepts of the rights of the common man stemmed from the sealing of a lengthy parchment in an English field in 1215.

'I'd say it was a stroke of pure luck, us finding that chap of yours,' continued Gaythorne, as he sat back contentedly in his chair.

'Pardon?' replied Ashdown, who was not sure if he had heard correctly.

'Our chaps have turned up some news on your Swiss. I only received the report from the Commissioner very late this afternoon, so I didn't see the point in bothering you with it until now.' The look on the Major's face showed that he did not share the same opinion. 'Seems there was someone matching your description who got on the train up to Atbara – it was an unusual name for these parts and they remembered the walking stick.'

He took a swig from his drink and then a draw of his cigar. Ashdown had to control himself; this man had not passed whatever it was on to him immediately and now he was taking far too long to do so.

Don't you realize that time is of the essence, thought the Major, but he kept quiet and sat forward a little. The veranda was quite crowded and he did not want to miss anything the other man had to say.

'Apparently it was something to do with his ticket – a bit of a misunderstanding, actually. Your man said that he was going to Aswan, but the ticket chap thought the ticket was incorrectly filled in. Apparently your Swiss got quite nasty about it and was rather rude. Anyway, the ticket chap remembered the cane with the silver bird handle. He remembered the red ruby eyes on the handle and said that it was held by "a hand that was like a white buzzard's claw". I suppose that it's all quite exaggerated – the locals are quite prone to that sort of thing. There was just enough time to check the records before everything shut down for the day and it seems that it *was* your Benschedler chap – at least, that was the name on the ticket...'

Runnymede Gaylord sat back in his chair. He returned his cigar, which he had been waving around in the air as if conducting an invisible orchestra, to his lips and took another draw. He was satisfied that the locals had done their bit to help the Major's investigation, as had been promised earlier in the day.

'Where's Atbara?' asked Ashdown, suddenly tense once again. He was also on new geographical territory.

'Next big town up the line from us,' replied the other man, through a haze of slowly ascending cigar smoke. 'He'd have gone there first and then on up the line to Wadi Haifa – that's about five hundred miles or so – God-awful terrain, too – hot as blazes.' He took a mouthful from his glass. Ashdown was beginning to find the cigar smoke irritating. He disliked cigars at the best of times and now was definitely not the best of times.

'Bandit country, too, on the way to Wadi Haifa, so one has to take extra care. Anyway, after that you'll be almost home and dry in Aswan. It's just a couple of days down river to Abu Simbel and then another couple onward to Aswan.'

'When was this, Sir?' asked Ashdown, now sitting very upright in his chair.

'Three days ago – the fourteenth,' replied Gaythorne, looking at the younger man, 'so you're going to have to try and enjoy the comforts of the Golf Club for the next couple of days, until we can organize your travel to coincide with the next steamer leaving for Aswan from Wadi Haifa. That's the last place in which you want to spend any time, I can assure you. It's Nubia,' he said, raising his eyebrows, as if to indicate that the Major should already know of the perils of that part of Sudan, 'the Writ of Law – anyone's law – does not extend much beyond the limits of the town. It's been like that since the Pharaohs' days – even *they* found it troublesome. You'll be all right on the river – they haven't taken up piracy yet!' He released a hearty burst of laughter, which did little to reassure Ashdown, but caused several of the other guests to turn and look in their direction.

'How long will that take, Sir,' he asked, sensing the gap between himself and his quarry widening again.

'Up to Wadi? No more than three days, assuming that there are no problems with the engine or the natives! The last two hundred miles are a real wasteland – just vast stretches of sand and rocks, the occasional Bedouin and bandit, but even they are usually few and far between. If everything goes according to the timetable, once you reach Wadi Haifa you'll be straight onto the Government Steamer. There are two of them. They follow each other up and down the river in a kind of circular motion, every five days.'

'So, Benschedler could be in Aswan a good five days before I can get there,' said Ashdown, more to himself than to his companion.

He was beginning to think that he would have to telegraph ahead and ask the police in either Aswan or Cairo to detain the Swiss on the most nebulous suspicion of diamond running. If he had calculated incorrectly and the man was, after all, innocent, he would have to face the repercussions of such drastic action. He imagined that the Swiss would not take too kindly to one of their own being wrongly detained.

His host was still talking.

'... So they stop off at the landing for the temples at Abu Simbel for a couple of hours. One of the steamers drops tourists off on its way up the river to Wadi and the other steamer collects them again a couple of days later going down the river to Aswan. The touring companies buy the tickets in advance, so the steamer people are happy.'

Ashdown was studying the toecap of his shoes, as he ran through yet again the timings his companion had just given him. He was five days behind his quarry – barring any unforeseen incidents, which, if they happened, could quite easily make it six or seven days behind. Once Benschedler had passed through Cairo and reached Port Said, he was as good as free. Out at sea, on the Mediterranean, he would be in open international waters and a free man.

'Cheer up,' said the older man, 'it could be far worse. At least you know you're heading in the right direction.'

'That is, indeed, a positive consideration,' replied Ashdown, although he did not feel that comforted by the thought. Suddenly, quite involuntarily, a smile crossed his mouth as he thought of the futile attempts Halkyard would have put his men to, back in Nairobi, in an attempt to find the bird that had already flown the nest. *And it's thanks to Samuel Lyons*, he mused to himself, *poor chap*. The Major had not shared the disgruntled Inspector Lyons' theory with the Kenya Commissioner.

'Something tickling you, old boy?' asked Gaythorne, as he watched the smile grow on the younger man's face.

Before anything else could be said, the chimes announcing the start of the evening meal rang out through the cool interior of the Khartoum Golf Club.

'About time, too,' said Gaythorne, as he started to get up, 'come along. I think you'll enjoy this – the chef is European trained, you know.'

'One thing before we go in, Sir,' said the Major. 'Do you by any chance have a reliable contact in the police at Aswan?'

26

Aswan

On Board Khufu – Very Late Evening, 25th July 1928

Following the near disaster at the quarry, which had been so narrowly avoided, apparently, by Sebastian Printon's timely intervention, the tourists seemed to have become fired with new enthusiasm. The mood of gloom, which, to varying degrees, had lingered over them following the death of Sylvia Baxter, had, despite the near fatality at the quarry, largely dissipated like an early-morning mist on the river. It was nearly midnight and *Khufu*, like Aswan itself, had fallen largely silent.

In his cabin, Stephen Hopkins' leg was starting to throb – only slightly, but just enough for him to be aware of it. He took off his dinner jacket and hung it on its coat hanger. From the inside pocket he removed an envelope, which had been delivered to the boat earlier in the afternoon, whilst most of the tourists were on an excursion to Elephantine Island and then to the smaller Kitchener Island. He had already torn open the top of the envelope and now, for the second time, he removed the contents and opened the folded paper. It was a telegram. He put it down on the bed, removed his black bow tie, undid his front collar stud and then, moving the chair closer to the bed, he sat down, swinging his left leg up and onto the mattress. Having made himself comfortable, he once again picked up the telegram form and looked at the message it contained:

> *Sebastian Albert Printon, Engineer, widower, formerly Royal Engineers. Degree in Mechanical Engineering. No known criminal record. Military Cross for gallantry 1917. Right hand damaged in construction accident, 4th and 5th fingers and upper arm badly disabled, but still partly useable. Left England 5th instant on holiday to Egypt and Levant.*
>
> *Richard Edward Lampton, Engineer, married with no dependants, formerly Royal Engineers. Degree in Engineering. Involved since 1920 in railway construction, West Africa. No known criminal record.*
> *Cecil.*

For several minutes, Stephen sat back in the chair, rubbing his leg, as he stared up at the ceiling. What did any of this mean? Was he imagining something, when there was absolutely nothing to imagine, save for pure coincidence? Or, more alarmingly, was he being drawn into something which could well prove to be hopelessly beyond him – and was he dragging his new friend into possible danger with him, albeit unwittingly? His head had started to ache, along with his leg. Perhaps he should just tell his Uncle that enough was enough, before it was too late to do so. But that was not a real option – such a thing was unheard of in his family, where duty always came first – but that raised another question in his mind: what duty? What was this all about – if it was anything other than a series of unrelated events?

Eventually, when the throbbing had eased, he got to his feet and crossed to the table under the cabin window. Normally the window looked out over the vast expanse of the river, but the view was now shrouded in starry darkness. He took his lighter from his pocket, triggered the flame and then held the flame to the corner of the telegram. As he watched the paper blacken, curl and disintegrate into the ashtray, he could not rid himself of the thought that something was amiss within this happy little band of tourists, and that someone was up to no good. He replaced the lighter in his pocket and took the ashtray into his bathroom, where he flushed the charred remains down the lavatory.

'The situation has suddenly taken on a very nasty aspect,' he said softly to the empty cabin. *The telegram confirms my suspicions about Printon, so we possibly have the 'who',* he thought to himself, *although I can't honestly say that I have ever taken a close look at the fingers of his right hand, but I strongly suspect that they are in perfect working order.* He had started to quietly pace his cabin. *The real problem in all of this is that I have absolutely no idea as to the 'why' and even less of an idea as to the 'what'.*

'Who, what and why?' he repeated to himself, under his breath, as he crossed the cabin to the door.

In light of the telegram, the only certainty was that the travellers on board *Khufu* could well find themselves in considerable danger. With his hand on the door handle, he suddenly stopped and stared blankly at the notice affixed to the back of the cabin door.

Printon, or whoever he is, is up to something. The question is what? And who else is involved in whatever his scheme might be? His head started to ache as he pondered on the situation. *We are all going to have to be very vigilant and ready for action.*

'God, but that sounds hopeless,' he said out loud, 'exactly who is going to be ready for a fight? A retired relic of Empire and a damaged survivor from the war! Ponsworthy and Hopkins! Hardly an inspiring line of defence, but it's the best we have if the balloon goes up.'

Stephen Hopkins found very little solace in his stark assessment of their situation. He had never been one to work with uncertainties or unknowns. It also occurred to him that, despite his uncle's confidence, a gold signet ring sent to the Embassy in time of trouble would be next to useless when it came to summoning immediate help.

Just as well I still have my Webley. It's been a good friend to me in the past. Let's just hope that I don't have to use it in the near future. Do I tell Rupert and Mohammed about the telegram, or do I keep things to myself for the time being?

He stood staring at the back of the door for a few moments, as if expecting an answer, but there was none. He sighed, his gaze fixed once again on the heading of the notice. 'Action in the Event of An Emergency' it read.

'Abandon ship! Not bloody likely. Not yet, anyway!' he muttered, as he turned the door handle.

Closing the door silently behind him, he walked off down the deserted passageway towards Rupert's cabin. His stump and head still ached, but he was smiling. He would soon be rid of his artificial leg and the dull throb it sometimes caused after a long day. His discomfort would very soon be lost in a great deal of anticipated pleasure that the appointment he was about to keep would generate.

27

Nubia

Abu Simbel – Afternoon, 29th July 1928

Escaping from the oncoming current, the government steamer glided slowly towards the shore, accompanied by the shouts of the deckhands and the excited buzz of the deck passengers, for whom the short stop in front of the massive temples was a welcome diversion from their cramped voyage. The ship rubbed itself against the stout wooden pier before the mooring ropes were secured and the engines stopped. Having leisurely covered the distance from Aswan in a little over two and a half days, they had arrived.

Even the fulsome grandeur of Mrs Grassmere stood no chance, when compared to the magnificent temple complex of Abu Simbel. This was one of Rupert's favourite sites in all of ancient Egypt and he looked forward to each visit with renewed enthusiasm. The visit also represented the halfway point in each tour, which he found encouraging; he was that much closer to saying goodbye to those of his tourists who had, in his opinion, not really been worth his efforts.

Now the fun starts! thought Rupert, as he began marshalling his flock.

The process of disembarking from the steamer was no

leisurely affair, as he had learned from previous trips. He would have to lead them as they jostled their way through the rest of the assembled humanity waiting on the pier and who were bound upriver into Sudan. They were as eager to board the steamer as Rupert was to get his party off.

'Over here everyone. Please check that you have all of your hand luggage. We will manage the heavier items,' he shouted above the noise of their arrival.

He hoped that this time bin-Salaah had brought enough of his men to carry the luggage. On the previous trip he had not and Rupert had been obliged to manhandle several of the suitcases himself. He had not been amused.

'Effendi! Here is me! We are most prepared for the luxury movement!' shouted a voice from amid the crowd on the pier.

'That's your chappie, isn't it?' asked Stephen Hopkins, nudging Rupert to attract his attention.

'Yes, that's him,' replied Rupert, as he waved at the imposing figure of Fairuz bin-Salaah.

Some ten minutes later, to the accompaniment of an endless commentary from bin-Salaah and an almost continual onslaught from the squadrons of flies that had suddenly materialized, Rupert had managed to assemble his tourists and most of their luggage at the head of the pier.

'The transport will be here directly,' he said, cheerfully, 'there are just one or two more cases to come and then we will be able to board the vehicle for the hotel.'

Whilst the luggage was being loaded, Grupfelder took the opportunity to stand and stare at the impressive structure which faced him.

'Well, wa'da y' know!' he exclaimed, fanning himself with his Stetson as he stood in front of the massive statues of Egypt's greatest pharaoh, 'that's a message ain't no one's gon'na miss. Wa'da y' say, General?' he asked, as he slapped Colonel Ponsworthy playfully on the shoulder with his hat.

FATAL TEARS

Over the previous few days, Ponsworthy had found the American's informal attitude more and more irritating. The fellow did not seem to have any idea of decorum or of how to conduct himself correctly in polite society. He had also developed the annoying habit of calling him 'General'. In fact, Colonel Ponsworthy, retired, was not the only member of the group to find the large American irritating. Lydia Porter, the Grassmere woman and her mouse-like and totally ineffectual husband found him equally so, but for considerably different reasons.

'You have to build on a large scale, if you are to impress the natives,' said Ponsworthy to the large American, somewhat offhandedly.

Just as he began speaking, the steamer gave two piercing shrieks of its whistle.

'Did y'a say something, there, General?' asked Grupfelder, replacing his hat on his head and smiling innocently. He knew perfectly well what Ponsworthy had said.

For his part, Ponsworthy was not about to miss the opportunity to hold forth on one of his favourite topics, neither was he about to rise to the American's taunting bait. For a few seconds he glared at the bigger man before continuing.

'I said that you have to build on a large scale to impress the natives, just as we are busy doing in India. I don't suppose you've ever been to New Delhi, have you – marvellous place. A new Rome, a symbol of the best of our Imperial might. I was...' But Grupfelder, whose smile had broadened, was no longer listening.

'Ladies and gentlemen ... your attention please ... everyone...' shouted Rupert, through the confusion at the head of the pier, where the motor transport of dubious origin and reliability had been parked and loaded with their luggage. 'I know you are all overawed by the scale of both of the temples, but can we please concentrate on getting ourselves sorted out and onto the vehicle. We have two full days ahead of us to explore the temples. At the moment our priority is to get you to the hotel and settled in.'

Some thirty minutes later, as the government steamer diminished to a smudge of smoke on the horizon on its way upriver to Wadi Haifa, the motor transport rattled its way up a steep incline and out into the desert above the temples. In theory it was a forty minute bump-and-jostle ride from the landing to the Abu Simbel Hotel, but the discomfort of bin-Salaah's *Luxury Transport* had an unpleasant knack of making the journey seem much longer than it actually was. The combination of a very poor road, which was little better than a dirt track, and the erratic driving of bin-Salaah's driver, who narrowly missed colliding with a small herd of camels and wasted minutes in a heated argument with the irate camel driver, added considerably to the travel weariness of Rupert's party. It was well over an hour later that the tired and travel-stained tourists staggered gratefully into the welcoming embrace of the cool foyer of the hotel, where the staff had already begun the process of allocating rooms and sorting out luggage.

Following a good night's sleep, the day dawned bright and clear. After an early breakfast, Rupert had assembled his flock outside in the cool air of early dawn to await the transport. Everyone was in high spirits in anticipation of the return to the temple complex. Despite the early hour, Mrs Grassmere was in good humour for a change; she was looking forward to the promised packed lunch the hotel kitchens had prepared for the expedition. A loud, vibrating engine noise and a cloud of fine sand announced the arrival of their vehicle.

'Here comes the rattle box,' called Simon Arling, jokingly. He had named it so on their journey from the pier to the hotel. 'It bounces around like the mesh box they use on an archaeological dig, when they sort out the rubbish from the artefacts,' he said, laughing. Most of the rest of the group were also laughing, despite the knowledge that very soon they, too, would be bouncing around in bin-Salaah's vehicle like so many objects in a large sieve. There were also one or two who approached this tour to the temples with a pang of misgiving; there had been unfortunate events on certain of the previous expeditions during the trip.

By the time bin-Salaah had deposited them all outside the façade of the main temple, the sun had already raised itself well above the eastern horizon, as it had done since long before the age of the Great Pharaoh.

The three massive faces of Rameses II stared blankly out over the river and onwards, across the eastern expanse of nothingness. This was the desert of Nubia – the troublesome source from whence had come so much of what Rameses had relied upon to keep his empire going. Then, as now, the message was clear: he was in control and anyone who journeyed on downriver beyond the massive statues was entering his domain, where he was Lord of All. The fourth massive face, toppled from its torso by an earthquake almost as soon as the temple had been finished, would have given the same stern warning, had its fractured segments not been buried in the loose sand. Despite this stern warning, his sacred space was once again to be defiled by curious onlookers – not from Nubia, as of old, but from lands which did not even exist when, for the first time, the dawn light flooded his temple with the sun god's life-giving warmth.

'Gather around, everyone ... over here, please,' called Rupert, as his flock ambled towards the entrance to the temple. He had clambered on top of the left-hand plinth, on which rested two of the massive statues. The base of the plinth was covered with hieroglyphics proclaiming the divinity of Rameses and his right to rule the known world. As Rupert stood there, like a diminutive pygmy in the shadow of the enormous statues, his flock assembled dutifully beneath him.

'Well ... here we are at the temple complex of Abu Simbel,' he made an expansive gesture taking in both temples. 'Just to remind you, these four statues are each over sixty feet tall, and were cut into the solid rock during the reign of Pharaoh Rameses II, that's around 1280 to 1210 BC, when Egypt's control over Nubia was at its height. As you will remember from my talk last evening, what you see before you is just the external aspect of the temple. Both this one and the smaller one over there' – he gestured away to his left – 'copy the exact plan of a typical Egyptian temple, but cut into the very rock itself. An amazing feat of ancient engineering, I think you'll agree.'

There was a murmur of agreement.

'Did he come here often?' asked Mrs Porter, who had been obliged to resort to her spare pair of spectacles. Being an older pair, the lenses were of an earlier prescription. The result was that her vision was not as sharp as it had been. She adjusted her hat, which had been retrieved from the abyss of the Unfinished Obelisk in Aswan, to shield her eyes from the glare that was already being reflected off the lightly coloured monument. She had also taken care to wear her protective clothing. 'If it was such a monumental undertaking, why on earth go to so much effort out here – in the middle of nowhere?'

There was a muttering of puzzled agreement.

'Good question, Mrs Porter. The very monumentality of the whole thing is the answer – it was a notice to the Nubians as to exactly who was in control. Like a giant poster advertising the fact, if you will...'

'Excuse me, please, but is it not unrealistic to build such

a place without thought of defending it?' asked Eric Kormann, from behind his round glasses. 'We have not seen any signs of a ruined fortress or other such settlement, and if the area down there was always troublesome' – he turned and pointed south, out across the broad expanse of the river – 'surely you would have to have an army here?'

'Yes and no, Mr Kormann – we live in far more secular and unbelieving times than did the Ancients. This complex, consisting of Rameses' temple and the smaller one of his favourite wife, Nefertari, which we will explore tomorrow,' continued Rupert, pointing once again to his left, 'were held to be mysterious, sacred places into which you went with trepidation. The temples are also dedicated to several gods, so upsetting any of them in a very superstitious age was not a good idea either. Even if the gods in question were not your gods, you certainly did not want to run the risk of bringing foreign divine retribution down on your head.' There was a ripple of laughter. 'There could well have been a fort of some sort around here, but we haven't found it yet. There probably was a garrison as well, but details of that are very vague and sketchy,' he continued. 'We do know how important this place was, though, because the earthquake which knocked the king's head off his shoulders, there...' he pointed down to the fallen fragments of the giant head, '...also caused severe damage to the interior of the temple. We have records of Pharaoh's viceroy in this region ordering restoration and repairs. Everything was attended to, except for this head. And we have no idea why it was left.'

'So y' reckon that this group of statues was supposed to put the heebie-jeebies up the restless natives, do ya?' asked the American, turning casually to Colonel Ponsworthy as he did so.

'In a word, yes,' replied Rupert, 'that and, of course, the mystery of the gods and the divine nature of Pharaoh himself. When we go into the temple proper, I'll show you something truly remarkable about the accuracy of the Ancients' mathematic calculations and building skills. Extraordinary, when you consider that everything was cut out of the living rock.'

He moved back into the main entrance to the temple, dutifully followed by his flock. Away in the distance, under the shade offered by a spindly group of stunted trees, Fairuz bin-Salaah's men lounged about, near to where they had parked the motor transport. They would not be needed for a couple of hours yet. Sitting a little way removed from them was a small detachment of Egyptian troops – yet another reminder of the lawlessness that was an ever-present threat so close to the border with Sudan.

'Let's move on and into the temple. Here, perhaps more so than in any of the other temples we have visited so far, it is essential that we all stay together. The floors are very uneven and the interior is very dark. Gentlemen, please check your torches before we go in. Follow me, please.'

And with that, the group set off towards the temple entrance, which was a high doorway cut into the cliff face, but which was dwarfed by the Pharaoh's massive statues that towered above it on either side.

'I think I am beginning to understand what Mr Winfield was meaning when he told us about the power of this place to intimidate,' said Miss Eggerton to both Miss Cuttle and the Manningtons. Marjory Cuttle agreed, pointing out a feature of interest that had caught her eye in the carvings on the walls of the entrance. The Manningtons, joined by their invisible thread, had simply mumbled something that could have signalled either agreement or disinterested confusion. Rupert's flock had largely written off the odd couple and now barely attempted more than the perfunctory politeness of the morning greeting or evening farewell.

The crocodile moved off, resembling as it did a school

outing in partial disarray. The three to whom Rupert had given the electric torches tested them, as they had been asked to do. Once inside the furthest reaches of Pharaoh's temple, the tourists would rely almost exclusively on the power of the batteries in each as the only reliable source of light. They entered the temple, leaving the Egyptian officials at the entrance. They had been reminded yet again, through a combination of broken English and hand gestures, not to touch the paintings or wall carvings once inside.

'Gather around, everyone,' called Rupert, shining his own torch up onto his face from waist level, making him look like one of the carved faces of the Pharaoh. 'We're in the *pronos*, or rectangular hall, which would be like the first court of an open-air temple.' The light from the dazzling day outside barely reached the back of the *pronos*. It lingered on the floor in a distorted rectangle, its intensity diminishing as the top of the rectangle pointed into the depths of the building. 'On the walls you can see carvings depicting Rameses' great victory over the Hittites at the Battle of Kadesh around 1270 BC. There are particularly fine ones on the north wall over there.' He flashed his torch slowly across the expanse of wall. His beam was joined by the other three, giving the effect of small searchlights. 'Please don't move when the light is not on the floor in front of you,' he continued.

He then proceeded to shepherd everyone around the vastness of the hall, between the eight massive statues of the Pharaoh which held up the ceiling and, above that, the mass of the mountain into which the temple had been carved.

'The pictures and the hieroglyphs are all one enormous propaganda statement for Rameses,' said Rupert. 'Look – he is shown beating the entire Hittite army all by himself, except for the help of the god Amun.'

The group continued to shuffle quietly around the hall,

seemingly overawed by the scale of the place. Eventually, they returned to the starting point, their progress having kicked up little motes of dust and fine sand from the floor, some of which trespassed occasionally into the strong white beams thrown by the torches.

'Now we enter the Hypostyle Hall,' said Rupert. 'Remember that this temple might be cut into a mountain, but the layout is exactly the same as for any other major temple complex in ancient Egypt. Once we've had a look around the walls and pillars, we'll move straight through to the really interesting part – as I promised you.'

'You've done all of this before, haven't you?' whispered Stephen, as he walked closely behind Rupert.

'Several times,' replied Rupert, smiling, 'but I can't say I've ever enjoyed the experience quite as much as I'm doing this time.'

Within a few minutes they found themselves at the entrance to the sanctuary of the temple.

'This is the interesting part of the complex,' said Rupert, gathering the flock and their torches around him. 'This is the Holy of Holies, to which extremely few people would have been allowed access.'

He flashed his beam into a narrow, rectangular room. The other beams followed suit.

'We are about two hundred feet from the entrance back there,' he said, flashing his beam back down through the passageway and the cloudlets of sand, which still floated majestically in the dark of the still, unmoving air. 'This is the level of skill the Ancients had perfected in their mathematics and building ability,' he said, drawing the beam slowly back up the passageway and turning it through 180 degrees, until it fell on a group of four seated statues, all more than life size. 'There's Rameses, the god, in the company of the other three principal gods of the temple. Twice a year, on the twenty-first of February and October, a beam of the rising sun travels down this passageway and briefly bathes the gods in sunlight.' He moved his torch across the figures, 'all except the chap on the extreme right. That's Ptah, god of darkness, and that's exactly where he stays.'

There was a round of approving comments, followed by a few questions, which Rupert was easily able to answer. He then continued.

'I suggest that we now keep ourselves in our four groups, one torch per group, and make our ways independently back to the entrance. Take your time and look at the carvings and murals, but be careful to watch your step as you go.'

They found moving back towards the entrance easier than the inward journey towards the sanctuary, possibly because their eyes had acclimatized to the feeble levels of light in the temple, or perhaps because it was a particularly bright day outside and the glare reflected quite brightly into the central passageway for perhaps half its length. Only in the further recesses of the innermost rooms did darkness prevail.

'Well, I have to repeat that I find all of this totally pointless – all of their gods didn't stop the earthquake or put his head back for him...' The voice was that of Miss Kirby, who had been obliged to remove the ubiquitous sunglasses in the gloom. 'It's all just so pointless – and all for one man!'

'Absolutely – I agree,' said Simon Arling, holding his torch under his chin, so that his face was illuminated from below, 'and the human race has not really moved on from that point in nearly three thousand years,' he continued. 'Equality is not for the masses – it never has been – and this just about proves it.'

'But the pharaoh was the kingpin of their society,' added Mr Rotherham, 'as Mr Winfield has told us. Without him, ancient Egypt would have been nothing. If he made a success of things, perhaps he was entitled to some form of aggrandizement – as a kind of seal of approval from the people, as it were.'

'Real democracy – the true voice of the people – only worked in ancient Athens,' said Kormann. 'There, the people had a voice. But today…'

Before he could finish his point, the stuffy air of the temple was rent by two short, stifled screams. As the echo faded away into the darkness, there was the sound of a heavy object falling and the clatter of metal bouncing off stone.

'Oh … no, please … I'm fine … I just…'

It was the voice of Marjory Cuttle.

'Let me help you up. Are you certain nothing has been broken?' asked Susan Lampton, as she bent to help Cuttle back to her feet.

'Thank you … I'm really quite all right … just winded, that's all,' puffed the shocked woman, as she tried to stand up.

'You've torn the sleeve of your blouse, I'm afraid,' said Richard Lampton, as he played his torch over the sand-covered form. 'It looks as if you've scraped the skin on your arm.'

There were little spots of blood welling up, where the skin had been broken or scraped off. The ragged edges of the tears in the fabric of the blouse were already soaking up the droplets.

'Everything is fine,' called out Richard Lampton, 'we've had a little accident, that's all, but it's all right now.'

The party re-assembled just inside the entrance to the temple. After ascertaining that all were present and accounted for, Rupert suggested that they adjourn for refreshments, which the hotel had provided. Bin-Salaah's men had set up several large umbrellas near the jetty a short distance away

FATAL TEARS

from the cooling water's edge. In the shade collapsible tables and camp chairs awaited the tourists.

'D'ya think this trip is jinxed?' asked Grupfelder, as he walked next to the Colonel.

'Don't be ridiculous and I think that such thoughts are best kept to yourself! It does not do to scare-monger,' snapped Ponsworthy.

He knew how disruptive panic could be in a tight corner.

'Let me have a look at that for you, Miss Cuttle,' said Stephen, flashing his smile. 'You can never be too careful in Africa...'

Marjory Cuttle had been settled in one of the camp chairs before the rest of the group took theirs. They relaxed into muted chatter as the refreshments were served.

'It was very stupid of me, I'm afraid. I was looking up at the inscription right at the top of the wall – behind the furthest most statue in the first hall. Mr Lampton was standing right next to me, pointing the light up, so we could see things better – and then...' She winced as Stephen daubed iodine into the scratches. '...And then I just fell over. I must have tripped, I suppose, but I don't remember even moving about at the time – I was looking...'

Stephen caught sight of Sebastian Printon, standing behind Cuttle's chair.

'Are you all right?' Printon enquired. 'I have your camera,' he continued, without waiting for her reply. 'It must have bounced off the pillar as you fell.'

'Oh, yes ... I really don't know why I brought it today. There isn't any light to take photos inside. Is it still working?'

'Oh, I would think so,' he replied, standing next to her. 'It is a Leica and they are very good German cameras – possibly one of the best on the market. I have one myself and have never had any trouble with it.' He held the camera in his hands and sighted through the viewfinder, then he adjusted the aperture ring with his right hand, whilst holding the camera up to his ear, listening. 'Everything seems to be satisfactory and in working order – I cannot hear any grinding or see any misalignment, but that will only be confirmed once you have taken some more shots and had the film developed. I would continue using your camera as normal.'

Everything is *in working order, isn't it?* thought Hopkins, as he watched Printon manipulate the small ring with dexterity. Whilst dabbing Miss Cuttle's scratches with the iodine-soaked cotton wool swab, Stephen suddenly froze as he realized the significance of this fact.

Despite his act of thoughtfulness in retrieving Cuttle's camera from the sandy darkness, Printon's face betrayed not the slightest trace of any emotion. It was as impassive as that of the long-dead Pharaoh. He held out the camera for her to take.

'I hope I can,' she said. 'My arm is already becoming rather stiff and sore...'

'Here, let me take your camera for you.'

Miss Eggerton had appeared, to add moral support.

'And look at that... your poor blouse... it's ruined, I'm afraid... the tears... and the iodine stains...'

'Never mind, Miss Eggerton, dear, it's only a blouse after all,' said Cuttle, regaining her usual composure, 'is there perhaps a cup of tea...?'

On the second day of their stay, Miss Cuttle had decided to remain at the hotel whilst the rest of the group returned to the complex to explore the smaller of the two temples. The day had passed without further mishap and Miss Eggerton had spent some considerable time on their return, telling Marjory Cuttle all about the marvellous things she had missed. In fact, so detailed had been the report, that Cuttle had found herself wondering which of the two was the most painful: the throb in her grazed arm or Eggerton's endless wittering on. Then she felt ashamed of herself. The woman was only trying to be friendly.

The next day...

'Please make sure that you have all your belongings before we leave,' announced Rupert. 'It's quite a job to have anything sent on if you forget it!' he added.

After breakfast the tourists had assembled in the hotel foyer and were about to board the transport for the last time and return to the pier. Whilst lacking any of the exoticism of the site after which it had unimaginatively been named, the Abu Simbel Hotel at least offered acceptable accommodation, reasonable meals and welcome respite from the heat of the day. It consisted of a series of single-storey buildings grouped around a large central atrium, in the middle of which a large fountain splashed soothingly into its three tiers. Beyond the hotel, a modest cluster of motley buildings passed for the town of Abu Simbel, which had slowly developed since the discovery of the temple complex in the time of Napoleon. Indeed, it was true to say that, if it were not for the four enormous statues of Rameses II and the trickle of hardy tourists they attracted, the town would probably not exist at all.

'If you would please just put your hand luggage next to the door, the boys will load it onto the motor coach for you,' announced Rupert, as the ancient and sand-worn vehicle clattered to a noisy halt in the rudimentary street outside.

'Not that thing again!' said Ruth Kirby, from behind her sunglasses, 'I'd rather ride a donkey!'

'It is a little uncomfortable,' chipped in Miss Eggerton. 'Not that I would wish to complain, but it is a little bumpy.'

'Like ridin' a bucking bronco, y' mean...' said Grupfelder, laughing. 'Hell, ma'am, going to rodeos makes ya kinda used to 'em...'

'At least you can ride in the shade,' said Rupert, as he began marshalling his group out of the hotel entrance. 'Before the motor coach, you'd have ridden in open donkey- or camel-drawn carts. The journey would have taken twice as long.'

In reality the battered vehicle was a large truck, which had been sold off cheaply when an oil prospecting company had given up and gone home. With typical Egyptian ingenuity it had been converted so that it could assume a passenger-carrying role. This had been accomplished through the installation of two rows of benches, which ran along the outside edge of the truck's flatbed, so that passengers faced each other and could attempt to indulge in a conversation, as they bounced and swayed along on the sandy track leading down to the temple complex and the pier. Any concept of comfort was restricted to a very thin cushion on each of the long benches. Along the sides of the truck in letters which had, over the years, been severely attacked and worn by the fine sand of the desert, ran a sign which proudly proclaimed *Luxury bin-Salaah Tour Co.* The luggage was stacked in a neat row down the centre of the truck, leaving just enough room for the legs of the passengers. With her usual lack of aplomb, Mrs Grassmere had insisted on occupying the last seat in the row, nearest the tailgate.

'I can't be squashed in the middle or up the front,' she bleated, 'and I can't have that awning banging on my head.'

And so it had been. The necessity of clambering up the makeshift wooden steps and onto the truck had also offered the opportunity for further complaint. Several of the bags were knocked off the end of the line and onto the sand as Mrs Grassmere, who had gone up the steps never ceasing in her condemnation of the arrangements, tried to turn her considerable bulk around in the confined space underneath the awning.

'Well, what a ridiculous arrangement,' she wheezed in answer to the murmurs of protest from the owners of the bags, as she spread herself out onto the bench.

'I'm really most awfully sorry about that,' whimpered Mr Grassmere, who was uncomfortably wedged between his wife and Kormann.

'No harm done,' said Rupert brightly. 'Here you are,' he said, as two of the hotel porters handed up the errant bags. Stephen was sitting next to the Lamptons and Rupert caught his eyes, which rolled heavenwards.

'Isn't this nice,' said Esther Arling in her vampish manner, 'sitting this close?'

Her husband had his arm around her shoulders and she had hers resting on Printon's knee. By now, her behaviour had started to attract attention and there were some looks of ill-disguised disdain.

'Well, Mr Winfield, you were right about one thing – at least we are out of the sun,' said Susan Lampton, pointing to the fabric awning, which was suspended from a large rectangle of tubular steel, supported by four upright steel poles, one in each corner of the flatbed. Originally, it had been very colourful, brightly striped yellow and red, like an oriental beach hut on Brighton beach, but now, thanks to the merciless onslaught of the sun, sand and wind, it had faded to a colourless, neutral nothingness. From the sides, a short, pelmet-like extension hung down, edged all the way along with threadbare tassels. This part had always been a neutral colour. Painted all the way along it in faded black, in the spiral arabesque of the calligraphy of Islamic art, ran lines of Arabic script.

'Well, I think it's all been very exciting – the last couple of days, I mean,' continued Susan Lampton, as the truck roared into surprisingly regular life. Marjory Cuttle winced at the turn of phrase Susan Lampton had used. That was what Sylvia Baxter had been wont to say, in her enjoyment of life.

'And I also like the way they have imaginatively decorated the sides of the awning – better than just leaving the fabric plain white.'

'They are verses from the Qur'an,' said Rupert, who had watched the tailgate safely secured and had then jumped over it, to take his place at the end of the row, opposite the Grassmeres. 'You often find that sort of thing in Muslim countries. They ask for the blessing of Allah on the travellers...'

'Having already had several trips in this thing, I shouldn't wonder but that they'd need all the help God can give them!' muttered Ruth Kirby to herself.

She was overheard by Miss Eggerton, who found the remark amusing and chuckled, as she held on to the side of the truck.

'How is your arm today, Miss Cuttle?' asked Rotherham, across the row of luggage which separated them. 'And the camera?'

'A little sore, thank you, Mr Rotherham,' she replied, 'and I think the camera is still in working order.'

The reminder of the events of two days before caused her to gingerly rub the upper part of her right arm, which had suddenly started to throb.

Fairuz bin-Salaah's *Luxury Tourist Transport* finally drew to a clattering, vibrating halt close to the jetty. Marjory Cuttle was still gently massaging her aching arm. It had been feeling much better until Rotherham's well-meant enquiry had caused it to start aching and throbbing again. Seventy minutes of jolting along the dirt track from the Hotel had not helped the situation either.

'Not long now and we will be able to enjoy the cooling breeze on the river,' called Rupert, as bin-Salaah's men began to stack the luggage on the pier.

Stephen Hopkins smiled at him, then took a cigarette out of his silver case and lit it.

'Fancy one?' he asked, raising an eyebrow at his friend.

Out in the middle of the river, *Sudan,* sister ship to the government steamer *Nubia* that had deposited them at Abu Simbel three short days before, was making speedy progress towards them, belching a cloud of black smoke and egged on by the swiftly flowing current.

'Another couple of days and we'll be back aboard *Khufu,*' said Rupert, as he and Stephen stood watching the docking procedure and the animated gaggle of locals who would also board the steamer for Aswan. 'I hope Mohammed will be pleased to see us.'

28

Sudan

Wadi Haifa – Mid-afternoon, 31st July 1928

Major Jeremy Ashdown sat in the cool of the first-class lounge of the government steamer *Nubia*, drinking a beer. As the ice-cold liquid flooded his mouth, he thought back to the last stage of his journey through the burning wastes of northern Sudan.

True to his word, Runnymede Gaythorne had organized Ashdown's journey to perfection. Punctually, the train had pulled out of Khartoum station and headed north, passing through pleasant villages and large tracts of cultivated land. It had spent only a couple of hours in the large town of Atbara, with its important junction to Port Sudan and link to the Red Sea. Then it had continued on its way, moving ever northwards towards the much smaller settlement of Abu Hamed on the banks of the Nile. As the train pulled out of the town on the final stretch of its journey to Wadi Haifa, the Major had not been prepared for the sudden change in the climate and the vegetation – or, more accurately, the almost total lack of any of the latter. Nor had he been prepared for a travelling companion. As he sipped his beer he thought back to that last stretch of his railway journey through Sudan.

'There's nothing for nearly three hundred miles,' said a broad Scots accent from the seat opposite him, 'just desert.' It was a very matter-of-fact statement of the truth. 'Once we reach Wadi Haifa, it'll be better – the river will cool things down.'

For this last stretch of the journey they had changed trains and boarded specially built carriages, designed to protect travellers from the extreme temperatures encountered in this torrid region. The sun blinds had been screwed down permanently against the heat, which was intense. Hardly surprising, as it was an area where the total annual rainfall – in a good year – took hardly more than a couple of hours to first fall and then rapidly disappear into the parched, gasping earth.

'Have we no' met before?' asked the Scot, the look of recognition spreading across his face.

Ashdown disliked travelling companions; he found his patience stretched when trying to sustain a conversation which, in his estimation, served no purpose in the larger scheme of his endeavours. Despite the comfort of the carriages, the well-furnished dining saloon and the well-equipped sleeping-cars, the Major was not enjoying his journey, due to the oppressive heat. As a result he was more intolerant than usual when it came to conversing with his fellow travellers.

'Aye, going up to Khartoum,' added the other man, answering his own question.

'Oh yes, I remember now,' replied the Major, seeing that there was no way of avoiding the situation. 'You built the dam down at Sennar, didn't you?'

'Aye. Me and the lads, but it was old man Sherlock who designed it.'

If Ashdown had known that for the next few hours he would grudgingly be drawn into a conversation which was largely one-sided, he would have been more inventive in his manufacture of an excuse to avoid the situation in the first place. As it was, his mind was on other things – the diamonds, the Swiss, Julia – things far more important than the idle chit-chat that this man had to share. It was also extremely hot and close.

'... So they've asked us to look at the possibility of raising it again. They feel the present water supply is nay going to sustain the projected growth in agriculture and they will need a lot more water for the irrigation, y' ken.'

'Really?' answered Ashdown, but his mind was on other things in other places, 'Is that at Sennar?'

'Och, man, nay at Sennar – I told you, it's Aswan. The dam's already been raised once – back before the war. Now they want to see if it can be done again.'

'And you build dams,' said Ashdown, as his companion continued with a seemingly endless discourse on the pros and cons of dam building. The Major had been momentarily relieved when they had been summoned to the dining car, but was once again frustrated when he and the Scot had been allocated the same table.

The Major was grateful to discover that the Scot would not be joining him on the government steamer for Aswan, as he was due to survey and then report back on the condition of a small dam some forty miles from Wadi Haifa.

'It was built in Kitchener's day,' the Scot had continued, 'and it's no youngster, y' ken? It's starting to show its age.'

Ashdown had no idea if the man was referring to the dam outside Wadi Haifa or the much large one in Aswan; he could not have cared less.

Now, sitting in the cool of the first-class lounge aboard *Nubia*, far removed from the heat of the desert and the incessant conversation of dam-building engineers, he felt relieved that, within five days, he would be over the border and into Egypt. As he placed his tall, frosted glass back on the low table next to him, he looked into it and saw the little concentric circles that vibrated up through the liquid and what was left of the frothy head of the beer. *Nubia* was moving.

29

Cairo

The British Embassy – 2nd August 1928

The discreet knocking on the door sounded like a 21-gun salute in his alcohol-soaked brain. His Britannic Majesty's representative in Egypt did not take too kindly to being woken early in the morning. In fact, given the predictable regime into which his life had slipped over the last few years, the Ambassador seemed to resent waking up at all.

His secretary stood next to his bed.

'What is it now?' the Ambassador asked, in a poor temper. 'Couldn't it have waited?'

He looked at his private secretary through eyes that refused to either focus or shake off the last vestiges of the whisky-induced sleep in which he had fought so hard to remain. He became aware of something his underling held out in his hand. The Ambassador concentrated his fuzzy vision on the object.

'Excuse me, Sir, but I think you should see this,' said the secretary, placing the small silver salver on the bed and then stepping respectfully back. 'It is an urgent message ... to be forwarded to Cecil.'

The Ambassador flinched, his heartbeat suddenly increasing. Was it news of his son? Was it a telegram? The one everyone had come to dread? For a second, he did not know what to do next – he felt suddenly trapped by the bedclothes. Then his mind cleared a little. The telegram about his son had arrived years ago. This message *must* be about something completely different ... hadn't the man mentioned something about Cecil?

He struggled to raise himself up onto his pillows. The private secretary had silently crossed the room and was opening the heavy brocade curtains, which had so far kept out the dazzling morning sunshine. He could do nothing to rid the room of the smell of stale alcohol other than to discreetly open the window. The Ambassador fumbled on his bedside table for his spectacles as the private secretary retraced his steps and once again stood a respectful distance back from his master's bed. The Ambassador's brain was now a little more in focus. He turned his attention to the message sheet: the last thing he wanted was to become involved in something big – something that would involve the arrival of officials from Whitehall. They might discover things about him he would prefer to keep hidden. He started reading with a sinking feeling.

> *For Cecil*
> *Yours regarding Printon and Lampton received. Printon has perfectly normal hands, all fingers working. Advise further action and when assistance available. Situation possibly quite desperate. Reply to Aswan immediately.*
> *Hopkins.*

The Ambassador took off his glasses. What was all this about normally functioning hands? He slumped down further into his bed and rubbed his eyes with the backs of his hands – the telegram crumpled in one, his glasses dangling from the fingers of the other.

30

The Nile

On board Sudan, between Abu Simbel and Aswan – Mid-afternoon, 1st August 1928

The day following Major Ashdown's departure from Wadi Haifa aboard *Nubia*, Rupert and his flock of tourists were also on the water aboard *Sudan*. They were now over halfway between the temples of Rameses II at Abu Simbel and Aswan, where their Nile steamer *Khufu* was patiently waiting. The breezes that blew across the cooling waters of the river had a calming effect and seemed to have done much to make the tourists gloss over the discomfort they had experienced at the hands of bin-Salaah's *Luxury Tourist Transport*. Now, in the early part of the afternoon when the sun was safely past its zenith, but no less merciless in its blistering heat, the little steamer chugged her way down river pushed along by the current.

   The European passengers, most of whom had embarked at Abu Simbel and comprised mainly Rupert's tour group, had retired to their cabins for an afternoon nap to sleep off the quite acceptable luncheon they had been served in the first-class dining room. This was the reality of travel for the wealthy privileged few. On the main deck surrounding the raised superstructure that was the bastion of the European travellers on the river, the local humanity – the almost black skins of Nubia and the much paler, bronzed skins of

Upper Egypt – squatted in whatever shade they could find. Their meal had been one they had brought with them, or one that they had prepared over the brick-encased fires which were located fore and aft. Two of *Sudan*'s crew, each provided with a large bucket of water on the deck at their feet, stood watching the activity. The esteem that went with the level of responsibility they had been given had not escaped them. They leered disdainfully at their fellow travellers, never losing the opportunity to bolster their own status by reminding them of how important their exalted fire-watching station made them within the confined society of the little ship. They also never missed the opportunity to correct what they perceived as improper behaviour, whenever they spotted it amongst the huddled groups of travellers on the decks. Such was the way of things in African society; a little power and responsibility came with a lot of social arrogance.

Sudan was one of a pair of steamers operated jointly by Sudanese and Egyptian Railways, which closed yet another missing link in Cecil John Rhodes' envisioned line of British steel joining Cape Town to Cairo. Like her sister ship, *Nubia*, she was reliable and comfortable, at least in first class. Indeed, there was no option for European travellers on the river, because there was no other class open to them other than first. At the foot of the companionways, where they met the main deck, cordons across the steps held signs warning first-class passengers not to proceed any further; they were effectively prisoners of their own luxury, safely preserved in the central superstructure.

Although it was nearly time for tea, there were hardly any passengers to be seen in the forward observation lounge. Miss Cuttle and Miss Rebecca Eggerton had arrived early and sat at one of the tables, waiting for the steward to bring their order.

'How is your poor arm?' asked Eggerton, trying her best

not to look too concerned, as she had read in a book somewhere that by doing so one could upset the person to whom the enquiry was directed and make them feel worse.

'As right as rain ... or it will be by the time we reach Aswan,' replied Marjory Cuttle, 'at least we won't be shaken to pieces on that truck again. That did not help in the least, I can tell you!' she continued, laughing.

At the other end of the rectangular room sat a husband and wife with their small child – a boy of perhaps six or seven, who was contentedly looking at the pictures in his storybook. The boy's parents had exchanged a few words of greeting with Eggerton the previous afternoon, when tea had been served under the awnings on the upper deck.

'There's that nice family from Berkshire,' said Eggerton, softly, 'I had a lovely chat with them yesterday. He works for the Sudanese Administration. They are going back home on leave.'

Miss Eggerton had been especially taken with the little boy, and now waved a greeting at him across the room. He returned it to her with the broadest of warm, childish smiles.

'Oh, what a dear, dear little boy,' she whispered to Miss Cuttle, 'just look at that smile.'

Marjory Cuttle, who was still feeling the fading effects of her recent fall in the temple, despite what she had told Eggerton, also nodded a greeting, which was somewhat more reserved. She was not as enamoured of children as was Rebecca Eggerton.

A white-jacketed steward suddenly appeared carrying a tray of tea and placed it on the low, round table between the two women. On the tray was also a tall glass containing a mixture of fresh lemon juice, crushed mint, sugar and crushed ice.

'Really, my dear, what a strange combination,' said Cuttle, as she watched her companion take a good mouthful of the yellowish-green liquid. Since Luxor, she had been very careful to avoid any drink containing even a hint of mint leaves. She would never allow the embarrassment she had suffered at the Winter Palace Hotel to repeat itself ever again! In her mind she returned to that day, when she and Sylvia Baxter were about to leave the hotel. She had excused herself and had stood transfixed in front of the large mirror in the ladies' room, her lipstick unopened in her hand. She had looked, aghast, at the reflection of her teeth, still spattered with the last, tenacious remnants of the mint she had had in her drink there. Sylvia – poor, dead Sylvia – had obviously been far too polite to say anything, but that consideration for her feelings had done nothing to settle Marjory Cuttle's mortification. Now, she glared at the yellow-green liquid with disdain and distrust.

'How many glasses of that have you had today?' she asked.

Rebecca Eggerton seemed to resent the question.

'Two, I think – but it is really quite the most refreshing thing. Why don't you try a glass? It's the speciality of the bar, apparently. Colonel Ponsworthy said they had something like it back in India...'

'He was probably referring to a *chota-peg*, my dear, which was totally alcoholic – two of those and nothing would matter anymore – *pukka sahib* or not ... so I'm told,' she added, as if by afterthought.

'Shall I be mother?' chirruped Miss Eggerton, reaching for the milk jug. 'I'll pour for you, if you like, and then I'll pour for me once I've finished my lemon and mint – the glass is nearly empty...'

Cuttle tried very hard to see her companion's teeth, but Miss Eggerton was not in the habit of displaying them when she smiled.

The two women settled down with their drinks, Cuttle still occasionally eyeing her companion's mouth with curiosity. For the most part, they stared idly out of the large picture windows, across the water to the endless dessert, which glided silently past them on the banks. As they did so, they talked of their return to Aswan and the next event on their itinerary, which was a trip to the Temple of Isis on Philae Island in the middle of the river, just to the south of Aswan.

As they chatted, the family group collected their belongings and prepared to leave. Before they did so, the mother crossed the lounge to their table, holding her young son by the hand.

'Excuse me,' she said, 'please don't think him presumptive, but William has done a drawing that he would like to give you,' she said. 'Go on, then, William, what do you say?'

The young lad held out a sheet of paper, on which he had rendered his version of *Sudan*, complete with the yellow desert in the background and the blue of the river in the foreground.

'Mummy said that I can ask you to please have this,' he said, confidently.

'For me?' chirped Miss Eggerton. 'Why, how kind of you,' she continued, scratching around in her handbag for her glasses. 'Is this our boat?' she asked, pointing to the drawing.

'Yes,' replied the boy, grinning.

'And who is this?' she asked, pointing to a birdlike stick figure, which seemed to be attempting to escape from the side of the steamer's single funnel, arms waving in the air, fingers splayed like the feathers on a giant bird's wings.

'You,' was the simple reply.

Marjory Cuttle had difficulty in suppressing an amused chortle. She was reminded of the old adage about what came out of the mouths of babes and sucklings.

'Why ... er ... thank you very much,' Eggerton said. 'How very kind of you. Thank you for allowing William to bring the drawing over to me,' she said to the boy's mother.

As they watched the family group leave the lounge by its single set of double doors, Cuttle leaned in close and looked at her companion's face. There were tiny tears lining the bottom eyelid.

'I'm for another cup, my dear,' she said, holding out her empty teacup. 'What's the matter?' she asked, wondering if the shock of the accuracy of young William's assessment of her character had upset her.

'I just find it so wonderful that they can be so genuine at that age – and then, when they grow up – they become total *bastards*!' said Eggerton angrily, almost under her breath. 'Oh, I'm sorry...' she said, wiping her eyes with a little lace kerchief, 'what appalling language. Do forgive me...'

'Not at all, my dear,' commiserated her friend, 'we all have our reasons. What about a second cup, then?'

'Excuse me for just a moment,' said Eggerton, as she got up from her chair. 'I must just go and spend a penny.'

That'll be all of those lemon drinks, decided Cuttle as she watched her friend go, *either that or the innocence of youth has struck a very deep chord. How very interesting. I wonder what that deep chord could possibly be?*

Marjory Cuttle had poured herself some more tea and was contemplating the conundrum of her companion's sudden outburst, when the sound of the door opening caused her to look up. Sebastian Printon ignored her as he entered the lounge and causally made his way towards the left-hand cubicle near the door.

Immediately adjacent to the entrance doors were two glass screens. These were incorporated into woodwork on either side of the entrance and were built out into the room from the walls, forming two semi-private cubicles. These tastefully decorated glass panels, covered with deep-etched scenes of ancient Egypt and Nubia, effectively cut off the top quarter of the room from the rest. The original concept had been to protect the sensibilities of the ladies by affording gentlemen smokers a discreet area in which to indulge their habit. Although not totally masked off from the rest of the lounge, the screens did offer a degree of anonymity. Tucked snugly within the space behind each screen were a large table and four leather chairs.

The door opened a second time and Eggerton returned. By the time she reached the table her face was flushed with excitement.

'I say,' she whispered, as she lowered herself into her chair once more, 'don't look now, but that gentleman sitting at the table – he's the one I saw standing on the deck yesterday when we were getting on at Abu Simbel. I think he looks terribly scary – he looked so angry standing on the top deck, staring at us all with a face like granite – like the face of the Pharaoh on those three statues – only a lot thinner.'

Marjory Cuttle stared blankly at her companion.

'What are you talking about, my dear? That's Mr Printon – I've just seen him enter and sit at that table over there ... behind that etched glass screen.'

'No, not Mr Printon. Well, yes, he was sitting at the table, too, but the other one is in the corner. You can't see him from here.'

Cuttle managed to change her position slightly, under cover of which she tried to manage a surreptitious glance at the subject of Miss Eggerton's observation. From where she sat she could not see into the cubicle, where a tall, thin man was sitting, the ornate silver handle of a heavy walking stick clasped in his bony hand.

'All I can see is the shape of someone behind the glass and I wouldn't know who it was if I had not seen him enter,' replied Cuttle, a little impatiently.

'I told you who it is,' whispered Eggerton, as she poured herself some tea. She had one eye on her cup and one on the cubicle. As a result, she spilled some tea in her saucer.

'Careful, dear ... you're spilling...' snorted Cuttle.

'The other man – the one you can't see – he's the one I saw. He has the face of a bird – a hawk or some such bird of prey. He doesn't look at all friendly. He was standing as straight as a column. He must be a military man – or was, judging from his age. Mind you, he could still teach Colonel Ponsworthy a thing or two about posture...'

Eggerton sniggered at the bluster such a suggestion would provoke from Ponsworthy, who regarded himself as the perfect model of a military man.

The two women continued whispering like a pair of schoolgirls, suggesting and postulating as to the identity of their mysterious fellow traveller. Oddly, it never entered their heads to ponder why it was that Printon had seemed to ingratiate himself so easily and quickly with this man, whom he had met only the day before.

Into this atmosphere of relaxed speculation walked Mr Rotherham. He nodded to Printon as he passed the table, but the other man was far too deeply engrossed in his conversation with his mysterious companion to acknowledge him. Noticing the two women at the far end of the lounge, Rotherham made his way towards them, crossing between the empty tables.

'Ladies...' he said, 'may I join you?'

'Please do,' replied Cuttle, gesturing to an empty chair. 'Won't you have something? Tea ... or perhaps a glass of Miss Eggerton's favourite lemon and ... what was it, dear?'

'Mint,' replied the other, 'and it is very refreshing. It is the speciality of the boat, you know,' she added authoritatively.

'And what did you ladies think of the famous Abu Simbel?' he asked, as the steward went off to fetch his order.

'It lived up to everything Mr Winfield had told us to expect about it, didn't it, dear?' said Cuttle, consciously refusing to rub her arm, which had twinged slightly in remembrance. 'More to the point,' she continued, lowering her voice to a barely audible whisper, 'what do you make of our Mr Printon and his conversation companion?'

Rotherham made to turn around and look in the direction of the cubicle, but thought better of it and looked down at his shoes instead.

'Mr Printon seems to have hit it off with him, wouldn't you say?' chirruped Miss Eggerton, 'and you know how offhand he usually is.'

'Except when it comes to Mrs Arling,' added Miss Cuttle, with a knowing grin.

Across the lounge, at the table in the glassed-in cubicle, Printon was talking in earnest, low tones. And he was speaking in German.

'The Phoenix has done well to have made such progress on his own, but now that I am here, your journey will become much easier.'

The tall, aristocratic form of the Herr Graf von Hohenstadt und Waldstein-Turingheim – known as The Phoenix to his masters in Germany and firstly as The Griffin and then as Benschedler to Major Jeremy Ashdown – seemed to bristle at what this man had just said.

'What do you mean, "easier"?' he hissed, his claw-like hands clasped even tighter on the handle of his black cane.

'I am at The Phoenix's disposal to ensure the safe passage of the stones through the enemy's territory and...'

'What are you implying?' snapped the elder man. Though barely raised above a whisper, his voice was tinged with menace. 'Do you think that I am incapable of doing so on my own?' he added. He was a Count, a Prussian and a distant relation to the now-deposed Kaiser. He resented the type of remarks this upstart in his cheap suit was making.

'Certainly not,' replied Printon, conscious of the tension that suddenly hung in the air between them and wary of attracting the attention of the other three at the far end of the lounge. 'These are dangerous times and we have to be very cautious. I have had experience under such circumstances and...'

He was cut off in mid-sentence.

'Are you implying that I have not?' snapped the Count, his hawk-like face resembling the fierce falcon-headed god Ra Horakhete over the entrance to Rameses' temple. His hands, drained white, were now both clenched tightly around the handle of the cane. Things had not gone well, almost from their first meeting the day before, when Printon had recognized the ornate handle of the cane, the symbol of the Count's ancient family, and had initiated the prearranged recognition procedure. Now, within a few short hours, any notion of their cooperating seemed to be heading for rocky and very dangerous waters.

'Of course not, The Phoenix has a reputation which precedes him,' replied Printon, who was finding the Count's attitude hard to understand. 'Perhaps it would be best if I were to safeguard the stones – may I see them?'

The Count stared at Printon for what seemed an eternity. There was no sense of a common purpose in his glare – only the ice-cold realization that this was possibly the last run he would make with any stones and that this fool who had been sent to help him was turning out to be a liability. He had not requested any assistance; he was used to working on his own.

'I do not have them on me,' he lied, 'and I do not see any reason why I should not continue with the task which was assigned to *me.*' He emphasized the last word.

'I am not for a moment suggesting that The Phoenix should not,' replied Printon, realizing that the reputation for steely determination that the Count possessed was probably somewhat under-exaggerated. 'I am simply suggesting that it might be bet...'

'It is better that you remember the purpose of our common goal,' hissed the Count, his teeth clenched tightly together, 'and do what you were sent here to do, although I have to say that I did not request them to send anyone!' His eyes burned with a red-blackness that echoed the ruby eyes of the cane's handle. 'Perhaps it is best if we keep our contact to a minimum. Once we reach Aswan and are on the train to Cairo, there will be no real need for a *twin*,' he said, his voice edged with meaning. 'Perhaps a *shadow* would be more appropriate.'

Printon stared at the Count. He had not expected to encounter such a fixed sense of unwavering purpose. This man had a reputation for achievement and his loyalty was beyond reproach, even if his attitude towards his fellow man was more than a little tinged with the aristocratic arrogance of a bygone age.

'I have tickets for the train to Cairo,' responded Printon, retreating from any further mention of the stones. 'Our agent in Cairo told me of your progress and I purchased the tickets ... in anticipation of you being on time and on this steamer.'

Printon's thinly veiled insinuation that the Count might not have been on time with his own predictions did not pass unnoticed.

'Your telegram from Khartoum was received just in time,' continued Printon. 'I was able to acquaint myself with its contents through the message Cairo sent on to the Aswan office. I purchased the rail tickets several days ago – only shortly before we left for Abu Simbel.'

The doors of the lounge opened once again and Grupfelder strolled in, accompanied by the diminutive Kormann. It was now time for tea and the European passengers aboard *Sudan* were slowly returning to life after their afternoon siesta. Kormann pointed to a table next to one of the large picture windows and the two men walked over to it, beckoning the steward as they did so. They ignored the two behind the glass screen, as they appeared to be locked in deep conversation. Kormann commented on the fact that Printon had a reputation for not encouraging conversation at the best of times.

'Unless it's with a certain little lady,' Grupfelder responded, laughing.

Behind the engraved screen, Printon began to realize that, possibly, he had gone a little too far with the Count. He was going to have to be careful with this man.

'For the moment, then, we will wait until we reach Aswan tomorrow', he said. 'Perhaps then, I might be permitted to see the stones?'

'You do not need to see them,' hissed the Count, 'I have them safely hidden and they shall remain so until our masters see them in Germany. And I think it best that I do not speak to you until we are on the train,' he continued, standing up abruptly as he did so. 'We do not wish to create the grounds for suspicion.'

Printon rose to his feet as the tall figure swept past him and out of the lounge. For a split second, he harboured the thought that, possibly, there *were* no stones and that this man had simply used the pretence of couriering them as an excuse to escape the net he reported was closing around him.

The sudden movement of the door, as the Count left the room, caused the other five occupants to look up. Printon, who was now the object of their interest, stood looking back at them for a few seconds and then, turning on his heel without a word, he left the lounge.

'That didn't seem to go very well...' said Marjory Cuttle.

In Cabin 5, on the deck below the forward observation lounge, Susan Lampton was sitting in a chair reading.

'Oh ... you're awake,' she said, as her husband stretched and yawned on the bed.

'Hello, darling,' he said, sleepily. 'Yes ... just about. Is it time for tea yet?'

'Almost, dear,' she replied, returning her attention to her book.

'What is it this time?' asked Richard Lampton, as he swung his legs over the edge of the bed and sat up, his hair tussled.

'My book of poems,' she replied, turning the volume over to show him the cover. She was an avid reader and always carried her book of poems with her. Indeed, she had read the book so many times that, long ago, she had been able to recite nearly all of them by heart. Despite this, she still delighted in reading the lines of words, as they marched across each page.

'And which poem is it today?' he asked, yawning away the last vestiges of his afternoon nap.

'*The Rubáiyát of Omar Khayyam*,' she replied, 'it's just so beautiful. This is one of my favourite passages in all poetry,' she said, starting to read from the book:

> '*Here with a Loaf of Bread beneath the Bough,*
> *A Flask of Wine, a Book of Verse – and Thou*
> *Beside me singing in the Wilderness –*
> *And Wilderness is Paradise ere now.*'

'And then this one,' she continued, turning a page.

> '*The Moving Finger writes: and, having writ,*
> *Moves on: nor all thy Piety nor Wit*
> *Shall lure it back to cancel half a Line,*
> *Nor all thy Tears wash out a word of it.*'

'How true that is ... and to think that we nev...'

'That's it!' exclaimed her husband suddenly, in the middle of smoothing down his hair, 'that's what I remember about Printon. His fingers...'

The anaesthesia of sleep had focused his brain on the thing he had been trying to remember about Printon, ever since the first rebuff he had received, when trying to make contact with him. His wife's reading of one of her favourite poetry passages had finally triggered off the memory.

'What about his fingers?' asked his wife, resting the book in her lap.

'There was some sort of accident on a large construction project somewhere – just after the war – Printon was the supervising engineer and saved some chaps, but was injured himself in the process. He lost the use of some fingers on one of his hands – can't remember which. Spent some time in hospital and was given an award for his gallantry. He was a plucky chap – he'd already won the Military Cross in the war, if I remember correctly.' He was staring out of the cabin window, out across the blue water to a place where he recalled the memory. 'It was in the papers – and there were photographs of him receiving his bravery award.'

'But Mr Printon doesn't have any damaged fingers – on either hand. Does he?' she asked, somewhat mystified.

31

Cairo

The Offices of Kohler & Zehler – Early Morning, 1st August 1928

Siegfried Holtzecker opened the French windows and walked out onto the balcony. Below him the congested streets of the city were already full of the arterial flow of humanity that would carry the financial lifeblood of Cairo to all parts of the Egyptian economy.

As he blew out the smoke from his first cigarette of the day, he thought of how the unexpected problem of getting the stones to Cairo and beyond could best be resolved. Behind him on his wide desk lay that morning's copy of the *Egyptian Mail*. At first with alarm and then with curiosity, he had read the report contained on page two; then he had begun to speculate as to how Sebastian Printon, to use his assumed name, would have to adjust his plans to suit the unexpected turn of events. After all, had they not discussed the possibility of such an eventuality occurring?

Out in the street the strident hoot of a truck's horn blared disapprovingly at a donkey-drawn cart, the driver of which, unwisely, had tried to reverse direction and cross the road against the flow of traffic. The resulting fracas had led to general confusion and to the cart losing most of its overloaded cargo of watermelons, which bounced along the road in all directions. From the safety of his balcony,

Holtzecker watched the chaos find its expression through a crescendo of angry voices, blaring horns, hee-hawing donkeys, braying camels, horns, flies and dust. Then, almost as suddenly as it had begun, it reached its climax and was over. The noise level returned to its usual rumble and the flow of traffic resumed.

'Could this be a sign?' he asked himself softly, as he looked up across the skyline of the city, 'order restored from chaos? Just like the Ancients and their belief in *maat*?'

He thought of how his masters in Germany would disapprove of anything even remotely suggesting the existence of a state of chaos. The Party stood for ordered progress at all times and nothing less was acceptable. From the ashes of the humiliation of the war and Versailles, a new Germany was fast emerging; a new Reich that would be infinitely more powerful than the Kaiser's old empire. Germania would take her rightful position of world dominance – that was her due, and that was the end goal to which they were all working, each one doing his infinitesimal bit in the greater scheme of things. But empire-building took money – a great deal of it – and anything that could possibly delay the fortune in uncut stones from reaching their final destination was not only unacceptable, but also totally unthinkable.

He looked down again at the street scene below him. The donkey-cart was pulled up next to the kerb. The driver, between waving his arms in the air and talking loudly to no one in particular and the entire street in general, was trying to repack those of his watermelons that were still saleable back into their positions on his overloaded cart. Totally focused on this single task, he seemed oblivious to the assorted traffic that swirled about him.

That is as we must be, observed Holtzecker, looking down from his balcony at the irate carter below, *of single purpose and committed to following a master plan.*

As he watched, taking a last draw on his cigarette, the restored pyramid of watermelons suddenly moved, cascading several layers onto the pavement against which the cart had been parked.

But, my friend, we will not achieve anything if we let the likes of you survive. You have no idea of the value of order and careful planning. In our new Reich you would serve no purpose and would be eliminated ... for the greater good.

Holtzecker flicked the stub-end of his cigarette out and down into the street before walking back into his office and resuming his place behind the desk.

Tomorrow was an important day in the capital's busy social calendar and Kohler & Zehler would once again provide the best gourmand consumables money could buy. On the desk to his left lay a folder, which contained the details of the items required to feed the nearly four hundred guests who would be attending the function at the Abdeen Palace. The King was to play host to the Diplomatic Corps and it was anyone's guess as to what useful snippets of information might be gleaned from the careless talk associated with such Court functions. Kohler & Zehler had built their reputation on being able to faultlessly cater for such important events and now, as he sat behind his desk with the folder held aloft in his left hand, he thought it amusing that such reliability had been created in the names of two people who, to the best of his considerable knowledge, had never even existed. He moved the copy of the folded newspaper that lay in front of him out of the way and replaced it with the folder. As he did so, his eye caught the article's headline on page two and he remembered once again the report he had read.

Luxor, Monday 30th July 1928
Egyptian Railways have announced that the rail service between Aswan and Luxor has been suspended. This is due to the

temporary closure of the line at El Kilh, approximately halfway between Aswan and Luxor.

'*It is most regrettable, but such things are often beyond our control,*' *said Mr Tarek Mohammed, Regional Director of the Southern Area.* '*The repair force will have to wait for a heavy lifting crane to be sent up from Cairo, before repairs can commence,*' *he added.*

When pressed for more details, Mr Mohammed was able to report that an incident had occurred as a night goods train was travelling towards the recently completed branch line, which has been specifically built to serve the mineral mine at Geb Nezzi, a short distance before Luxor. Whilst still on the main line, having passed through El Ridisiya, the train was passing over a bridge, when the rear axle of one of the goods trucks seems to have suffered metal fatigue and was shorn clean through, causing the truck to leave the rails. It is reported that several trucks were dragged off the line, to end up in a heap of mangled wreckage around the base of the central stone pillar supporting the bridge as it crosses the wadi. This vital support was severely damaged and has rendered the bridge unsafe. The engine itself was dragged back along the tracks and was only saved from disaster by the driver applying the brakes and the fact that the damaged trucks had piled up to the raised level of the track itself, thus removing the drag effect on the front part of the train.

'*We must be grateful that there were no injuries,*' *said Mr Mohammed,* '*but the line will be unusable for perhaps seven or eight days.*'

When he had first read the report Holtzecker had thought of sending a telegram to the Aswan office for Printon to collect when the group returned from Abu Simbel, but then thought better of it. According to the timetable, they would not return to Aswan until tomorrow, by which time the news would be common knowledge and the arguments of frustrated commuters would be well under way at Aswan's railway station. It was not his concern – he had completed his part of the operation successfully, perhaps, even far more efficiently than usual, thanks to the unfortunate, but timely demise of the real Printon still lying, unidentified, in the police mortuary. *His* Printon would have to use his own initiative. Besides which, there was always the eternal river. After all, had they not discussed the possibility of such unexpected complications to their plans a few brief days before, in the very same office in which he now sat?

32

On the Nile

The Steamer Nubia, Abu Simbel – 2nd August 1928

Nubia had made good time from Wadi Haifa. Now, against the backdrop of the massive double-temple complex of Abu Simbel, the little vessel was slowly freeing herself from the current and drifting in towards the jetty, the throb of her engine still vibrating through both the decking and the air.

On the upper deck, safely entombed within the area reserved for the exclusive use of first-class passengers, Major Jeremy Ashdown stood looking at the monumental carvings as they slowly began to emerge from the shimmering haze of the Nubian heat. From below him rose the noise and excitement of the lower orders, who were forbidden the luxury of the upper superstructure, but who seemed happy enough to make the best they could of the open deck space their ticket bought them. He was pleased to be so close to Aswan – another couple of days and he would be there, having chased his quarry three-quarters across the African continent.

As the steamer drew ever nearer to the riverbank, in his mind's eye he recalled that conversation he and Runnymede Gaythorne had had a few days before, in the refined luxury of the Khartoum Golf Club.

* * *

'You can leave all of that to me, old boy,' Runnymede Gaythorne had said. 'I know some people in Cairo and I'll tell them to expect you. I'm sure they will make certain the Chief of Police in Aswan knows that you are on your way. And, yes, I will request that they follow your Swiss chap without making it too obvious.'

'Thank you,' replied the Major, smiling at the thought of the Commissioner in Nairobi, his full force presumably still turned out looking for the man who had given them the slip almost before they had even identified him at Nairobi railway station. 'Did I mention the Commissioner of Police in Nairobi?' he continued.

As he related his experiences at the hands of Commissioner Halkyard, Ashdown took considerable delight in recounting the tale of that man's ambitious incompetence. 'If it had not been for the canny insight of a frustrated Jewish inspector from the East End of London, I would have lost our quarry by now.'

'When do you anticipate moving in on your man, once you actually have him in your sights?' the elder man asked.

'As soon as I can,' Ashdown had replied. 'We're running out of territory, so we'll have to move quickly, preferably before anyone reaches Cairo, otherwise things will become a bit too close for comfort. Once out on the Mediterranean they'll be in international waters and I'd hate to lose him over some imaginary borderline drawn on the ocean.'

They laughed at the picture Ashdown created, but both men realised that there was a very real possibility that that could well be the end result of all Ashdown's efforts.

'That is also assuming that the Egyptians do not become high-handed and decide to interfere,' added Gaythorne. 'Involving the Aswan police does have its risks. Since we gave up the Mandate back in '22 the Egyptians have proven quite difficult at times when it comes to internal matters.'

Not that either man even suspected it, but the partial

relinquishing of control over Egypt was part of the beginning of the process of retreat from Empire.

The conversation in far-off Khartoum had left a nagging doubt in Ashdown's mind. Once he reached Aswan he would be dealing with the unknown factor of the local police. That could well be very helpful, or it could be a millstone around his neck. Only time would tell.

The Major's mind returned to the present as he stood on the deck of the little steamer and stared out at the temples. Lost in his own thoughts, he had remained unaware of the quiet voice, heavy with the experience of understanding and kindness that was talking to him, drawing him into the mystery that was Abu Simbel. As the voice continued, Ashdown stared at the two temples that filled the panorama opening up before him; the larger one, built by a pharaoh who was a god, and the smaller one, built by him for his favourite wife. They stood as a symbol of the love that bound the god-king to his earthly wife – a symbol that had endured for thousands of years, long after their bones had turned back to the clay of the earth. And yet, here they still were, joined together in stone, as much as they had been joined together in life. The voice, which had so subtly attracted and then held his interest whilst *Nubia* fought to free herself from the river's grasp, belonged to an elderly, bearded priest.

'There are many facets to life in Egypt,' the priest continued, his eyes sparkling like the sun dancing on the surface of the river, 'and all of them tell a different story whilst, at the same time, linking the fabric of society together.'

'Thank you for the information,' replied Ashdown dryly.

He was not about to be drawn into a conversation with the stranger and yet something about this priest arrested his attention. Ashdown thought he could detect the faintest hint of what he presumed was an American drawl in the man's accent.

'You are remarkably well informed,' he said, not taking his gaze off the temples.

The priest turned his smiling face towards the Major.

'For a priest, y' mean,' he said, humour in his voice. 'Well, yes, I suppose y' could say that, as I do, indeed, find it all fascinating. There are several orders that practise religion with the heart, whilst also practising archaeology with the mind,' he continued, stroking his long, grey-flecked beard as he spoke, 'but that's more in Jerusalem and the Holy Land than here in Egypt.'

'Are you from Jerusalem, then?' enquired the Major, being drawn deeper into the conversation, but still unable to place the man's accent.

'Good Lord, no,' laughed the little priest. 'I'm originally from Canada, but I joined the Royal Army Medical Corps when the Boers were being a problem down south. I was a whippersnapper then, a pharmacist fresh from university and looking for adventure and excitement – I thought a war was much better than staying behind some dreary counter dispensing pills for the rest of my days back in Ontario,' he said, the smile deepening on his tanned, lined face at the memory of times long past. 'So I signed up for Queen and Country and that was that.'

'We are a long way from South Africa,' replied Ashdown, breaking his own rule for a change and indulging in conversation with this stranger.

'Well, after the fighting I decided to go and explore, so I kinda ended up here – well, in Luxor, actually. Then I got to thinking, being surrounded with all this ancient monumental statuary and ancient beliefs and such…' He paused and gestured towards the temples which now spread out across the whole of their view, above and behind the jostling group of humanity who were busy preparing to board the now securely moored *Nubia*.

'Ever heard of the Gnostic Gospels?' he asked quietly, after a short pause.

Ashdown shook his head.

'It's a Greek word. It means "knowledge" in the sense of our English word "enlightenment". It's a philosophy which teaches us to look inside ourselves for answers. To put it simply,' he continued, 'it teaches us not to rely too much on external things for the spiritual solution, if y' get my drift...'

'You mean like big temples and huge statues?' replied Ashdown, smiling.

'Sure, y' could put it like that,' replied the little priest, 'and things like churches, too,' he continued, raising his eyebrows. 'Anyway, it got me thinking and I reckoned that line of thought might be worth pursuing. And I'm still here nearly thirty years later. Y' know what ... apart from the scale of things,' – he waved in the direction of the temples – 'is there any real difference between what they were looking for and what drives us?'

'What do you mean, exactly,' asked the Major, whose strong point had never been belief or theology.

'Look inside yourself or look inside a temple; look through what a priest tells y', or work it out for yourself – it's all the same. Y' just gotta keep looking till y' find something that suits you – then cling on to it. That's what I mean. It's the *humanity* that counts and that ya gotta find for yourself.'

Ashdown was a bit taken aback by what he had just heard. He had not expected such talk from someone who, presumably, was an adherent to one of the organized religions.

'As far as the ancient Egyptians saw things, the whole of your life ended up with your heart being weighed against the purity of the feather of truth and righteousness. Tip the scales in the wrong direction and you were done for – for all eternity. No way back from that one – not even pharaoh was exempt...'

He chuckled softly and stroked his beard.

'Are you with a monastery?' asked Ashdown.

'Sure was – or used to be, but that was a little too cosy. Y'know, they reckon that the Coptic Christians are the nearest to what Christ was about. I tried that for a bit and they might be right. But it still didn't really plug the gap. I'll skip the details, but I'll just say that I found what I was looking for in a little settlement down there called Wadi Haifa,' he said, gesturing over his shoulder and up river with his thumb. 'Been there ever since. We run a little hospital an' they call me "Pill Man *Pasha*" He smiled once again – a smile that radiated a serene calm of contentment. 'I'm off to Aswan for fresh supplies. We have a deal with the hospital there.'

They continued to stand next to the rails watching the activity on the shore, the elderly priest talking in his quiet, comforting accent with the open vowels, but the Major had ceased listening. Instead, he was thinking about what this kindly man had said – the part about looking inside for the answer. Perhaps that was what he needed to do – to look inside himself for a solution to his sleepless nights and the visions of his sister, Julia.

Their conversation had lasted for some time, during which final preparations were being made on the jetty to free the little steamer, allowing her to be embraced once again by the current and to sail on the final leg of her journey downriver to Aswan.

Despite the activity, which seemed to be all around him, Ashdown had retreated to the troubled calm of his own mind, pondering what the priest had said in such a casual fashion. He remembered what this little man had said about the purpose of the two temples – the tangible celebration of the invisible, inward love between two beings. He suddenly began to think of his own union – the union that had so nearly happened and yet, at the very last moment, had not. The memory was something he usually tried desperately to avoid, but the remembrance had suddenly flooded into his mind, uninvited, prompted by the kindly priest's remarks.

As he stared at the three faces of the Pharaoh on the shoulders of the colossal statues, which were still massive in the growing distance, he imagined that the identical images of Rameses had changed into three images of his father's face. All three were shouting at him, asking him what the hell he thought he was doing. On the shoulders of the statue with the fallen head he saw his mother's image. Tears were pouring down her cheeks, not from the same anger that his father made no bones about displaying, but out of compassion for her son. As he turned away from the vision, towards the smaller temple of Nefertari, the heads on the Rameses statues there, although slightly smaller than those of the main temple, also turned into faces he could recognize: the three male statues became his father and brothers. As they berated him for letting the family down and creating a scandal which had rocked White Kenyan society to its very core, the three female statues also changed faces – again, his mother, the tears still streaming down her cheeks, then his sister, Julia, trying to pacify his father and brothers and telling him that it was all right. Finally there was Ruth's face. She was the one he was to have married; she it was who had been rejected by him – humiliated by him in front of everyone. Oblivious to the activity and noise that surrounded him, in his mind's eye Jeremy Ashdown relived the angry scene from all those years ago, as if it were a memory of yesterday.

He saw again the dreadful scene in the sitting room of their homestead in the highlands of Kenya. He had never thought that the endless talk of the union would come to anything. Neither had he realized that his family was in such perilous financial trouble and that they desperately needed the injection of capital the liaison with Ruth would bring.

Don't you see, I couldn't marry her? he remembered saying. *I am a loner and always will be. I can't let myself be tied down – not for the family or anything. I just can't! You have no right to make me...*

He recalled his father's words vividly ... *We need the money. You're the eldest and you have to – the family expect it of you! It's your duty!* He had thundered, the sound of his voice booming out into the darkness and down amongst the coffee bushes, filling the valley beyond with the echoes.

Jeremy had nothing personal against his intended bride – indeed, they had grown up together. He had enjoyed her charms, and she his, as they reached puberty and young adulthood. She had shown him how to smoke, having taken two cigarettes from her father's gold case. The thought of having a body next to him at any time of the night caused his groin to glow with the excitement of the anticipated erection and release, but then the cold reality of the millstone around his neck that a binding union such as marriage would create had got the better of his fantasies and he had refused to continue with any discussion of a wedding. He was first and foremost a loner and was not about to give up his freedom – not for his father, his family, his sexual desire – not even if his intended was a member of one of the richest and most well-connected families in Kenya. He had been forced into the decision he had taken. It had been a desperate attempt to save his most sacred possession as he saw it – his individuality and freedom. His decision had given rise to the awful row he was now reliving in his mind's eye and on the faces of the statues.

* * *

The slow movement of an arm suddenly swept across the bottom quarter of his vision. It was the little Canadian, who was gesturing towards the rapidly receding temples on the distant shore.

'... So y' see, what they did over there was simply a labour of love, which has endured for thousands of years and still stands as a testament to the devotion we humans are very capable of showing to each other when we really want to.'

The elderly priest was still talking, but Ashdown had heard very little of what he had been saying. He was taken aback and turned to look at the priest. He thought of how calm and at peace he looked, in his simple cassock and with his long, flowing beard. For a moment he panicked, as he remembered the faces on the statues. He turned again towards the temples and screwed up his eyes tightly. When he opened them again the faces of his family had gone, to be replaced with the stone ones – all, except for the statue with the fallen head. There, instead of his mother, Ashdown now saw in the distance his sister's face, smiling, comforting and peaceful.

'Don't worry, Jeremy,' she seemed to be saying. 'I understand, everything will be all right, you'll see. It's not true, what they're saying.'

What *they* – the idle, malicious, wagging tongues of the scandalmongers of Kenyan society – had said was that, if it hadn't been for the unexpected war and the sudden need for guides to join the Imperial army fighting the Germans in their East African Tanganyika colony, Jeremy, through his refusal to go through with the marriage, could well have been the cause of his father's death. As it was, his father and brothers would not return to the highlands from their war, but he could hardly be blamed for that. *He* had returned, but everything had changed, almost beyond recognition. That was why he had left again.

'It's not true what they are saying,' repeated his sister's voice, from the shoulders of the headless statue. 'Everything will be all right, you'll see.'

'And so everything came full circle you see. They thought everything would be all right...' continued the elderly priest, pointing back up river to the now distant monuments, '... because they had ensured their place in the heavens by building these temples to their love and the worship of their gods. That's what they believed.'

The little priest, still with the twinkles in his eyes, turned to Ashdown.

'And who's to say there isn't a message in that? Perhaps they did find what they were looking for – perhaps everything did turn out all right for them...'

33

The Corniche

**The Banks of the Nile, Aswan – Afternoon,
2nd August 1928**

Stephen looked out over the Nile. Rupert and he were sitting on the slats of one of the ornate cast-iron benches that lined the elegant expanse of Aswan's Corniche. It was late afternoon, but, behind them, Aswan showed no signs of winding down towards evening. Quite the contrary, as the populace were coming to life again, having taken refuge from the heat during the afternoon.

'This business is rapidly getting out of hand,' he said softly to Rupert, who was feeding pigeons with some peanuts he had bought in a cone of newspaper from a pavement vendor. The lad had been a mere child, staggering along the Corniche carrying, it seemed, more than his own weight in sweets and other delicacies. 'We are going to have to ask for help before something really awful happens,' added Stephen mysteriously. 'The more I try and think things through, the fewer our options become ... the more I think of it, the current situation seems to resemble a pantomime.'

Rupert was laughing at the antics of the pigeons and the noise they were making; squawking and flapping their wings over the unexpected bounty of nuts.

'You mean send the ring to the Embassy and wait for the

relief column to arrive?' he said over the sound of his own laughter.

'I say, old chap, can you take this seriously for a minute, please!' There was a slight hint of annoyance in Stephen's voice, which was now ominously low. 'No! What I mean is that the situation we are now aware of is full of danger and yet we just carry on as normal. We could be in the middle of something really nasty here – something that has nothing to do with us, but could well turn out to be our nemesis!'

'How do you mean?' replied Rupert, heeding the tone of his friend's voice and screwing up the open end of the newspaper cone. The pigeons continued their squawking in disapproval of the sudden termination of the supply of nuts.

'What I mean is, that, at the moment two and two do not equal four. Remember I told you about being asked to look and listen?' Rupert turned to look at the doctor and nodded his head in recollection. 'Well, I've – no, *we've* looked and listened, and since we started on this trip from Cairo, things have taken devious twists and turns. What seemed to start out as a couple of genuine *accidents* now has a very different undercurrent attached.'

'I remember you telling *me* about being asked to look and listen, but you never did tell me who it was who asked *you* to.'

'Some things are best left untold,' replied Stephen, 'because sometimes even a little knowledge can be a very dangerous thing.'

'So you're still not going to tell me, then,' said Rupert staring down at his feet, which extended out in front of him onto the cobblestones.

'Don't feel hurt about it – it doesn't matter. What does matter is that nothing happens to you. I'd hate that and would never stop blaming myself if it was because of something I had told you, when you didn't really need to know it in the first place.'

'Oh, I see,' replied Rupert, but he was not sure that he really did.

Below them, a flotilla of heavily loaded feluccas glided silently by, the placid water of the river almost level with their brightly painted sides.

'Cast your mind back to our conversation about Messrs Printon and Lampton. Do you remember how we were of the opinion that their names have a tendency to often crop up in the same situation – sometimes even in the same sentence? Well, there is something very wrong with one of them.'

'I don't quite understand what you mean, Stephen. Which one? And in any case, how do you know?'

'Have you noticed how Lampton has tried to have a friendly chat with Printon on a couple of occasions and has been quite rudely rebuffed? It's almost as if Printon doesn't want to talk to him?'

'I have,' replied Rupert. 'In fact, shortly after Printon joined us, Lampton told me that he once knew of a Printon in the Royal Engineers during the war. It's not a common name, he said, but when he asked our Mr Printon if it was he, the man was quite rude to him and just walked off.'

'Odd that, when a simple "No, it's not me" would have sufficed, don't you think? Also, who was standing next to the Misses Cuttle and Eggerton when Lampton fell through the gangway gate and disappeared into the river? And who "saved" Mrs Porter from a sizzling end on the granite griddle of the Unfinished Obelisk?'

Stephen looked at Rupert with raised eyebrows.

'Printon?' replied Rupert, more by way of a question than a firm answer.

'Printon!' echoed the doctor, who, ramming his hands into his trouser pockets, slumped further down onto the bench whilst extending his legs out in front of him. 'And what was remarkable about the miraculous rescue of Mrs

Porter that day of her merciful salvation in the granite quarry?'

He asked the question without turning his gaze from the river or its traffic of small pleasure boats and large feluccas. Rupert didn't answer.

'What was she wearing that she shouldn't have been?' continued the doctor slowly, prompting his companion's memory.

There was another pause, as Rupert tried to think back to that day in the blast furnace of the granite quarry.

'Well, she was wearing Lampton's jacket and that's how Printon was able to save her by grabbing hold of it from the back ... Luckily, she'd done up two of the buttons and...'

'No, my dear boy, she was not lucky,' replied the doctor, cutting him off in mid-sentence. 'Quite apart from saving her, it bloody well nearly did for her. That jacket of Lampton's she was wearing to protect her badly burning skin from the sun, was very nearly her funeral shroud. What was it our friend Kormann said to us when we got back to *Khufu*?'

Rupert turned to look as his friend.

'Well?' prompted Stephen.

'Something about "the hand that saved was the hand that pushed", wasn't it?'

'Yes it was, and that's what...'

'*Effendi* – you buy lucky beads? From pharaoh day. Very cheap...'

It took some persuading to ward off the vendor of ancient good luck charms, most of which, Rupert believed, had probably been made a few days earlier in a workshop in the backstreets of Aswan. Eventually, realizing that a sale wasn't forthcoming, the disgruntled salesman fixed his attention on another group of tourists and rushed off, as suddenly as he had appeared, to assail them with his wares.

'Persistent little chap, isn't he?' Rupert commented, as

the little figure moved off along the Corniche. 'He could probably sell snow to an Eskimo, given half a chance.'

'They're all like that – it's the Arab way of things. Now listen carefully, Rupert,' said the doctor, returning to the thread of their interrupted conversation. 'That's what I remember Kormann saying – and he looked very nervous when he was saying it, so he must have been scared. Why? Perhaps by spilling the beans, he feared the possible retribution from the owner of the hand that pushed. More to the point, we have the Printon-Lampton link; Lampton and Printon again, in the same sentence and in the same scenario.'

'Mohammed doesn't think too much of our Mr Printon,' added Rupert, sitting upright on the bench. 'Ever since Printon upset his timetable by arriving late at Luxor, I mean. And then there was that early-morning cabin round, when Printon was going *into* his cabin, when Mohammed was busy going around trying to get everyone else *out* of theirs for an early-start excursion. Mohammed took him by surprise. Printon acted rather sheepishly and tried to hide something – Mohammed said it looked like a piece of dirty cloth wrapped in a square of rush matting...'

Stephen was listening intently.

'And here's an odd thing,' continued Rupert, 'Mohammed told me when we got back on board this morning, one of the chaps in the kitchen has gone missing. Took his stuff and vanished while we were all up at Abu Simbel. Says he even lifted the bedding from his bunk – company property – but left the apron he was always wearing. His storage box was empty, except for a square of rush matting. Mohammed remembered the pattern woven into it – he thought that it was the same one Printon was carrying that morning.'

'What did the absconder do on *Khufu*?' asked the doctor.

'He worked in the kitchen – a cook or something. Apart from being angry over the stolen bedding, Mohammed wasn't sad to see the back of him. Apparently he was a bad penny. Mohammed said he could be bought as easily as a pomegranate. Some of the other crew had already complained about him.'

'I wonder if he had anything to do with the unfortunate Miss Sylvia Baxter and her picnic basket, then?' said Stephen softly, more to himself than to his companion.

'You mean with the snake that bit her?'

'Well, think of this – how else could the thing have slithered into a basket with a tightly secured lid – other than by being *put in*...?'

'Really? So what do you think he might have had against Miss Baxter, then?'

'Oh really ... of course not *him*,' said Stephen, sitting upright on the bench, 'Come on now, concentrate. Think of the picnic baskets – think of who had which basket – think of Lampton's complaint about not getting the right food in his...'

Rupert turned and looked earnestly at his friend.

'You mean to say that she had the wrong basket?'

'Yes, in a word I believe that she did,' replied the doctor, 'and the one she did get was full of the kind of food Lampton complained that he didn't get in his ... so...'

'So ... someone wanted Lampton to be bitten, not Sylvia Baxter,' replied Rupert, sitting forward.

'Exactly! So, to answer your last question, I'd say that our dodgy kitchen hand had nothing against anyone. If he could be "bought as easily as a pomegranate", I'd say that's exactly what happened – he was paid to put the snake in the basket. Simple, my dear Watson.' There was a pause, and then Stephen added: 'Question is, by whom? And why did the basket have Baxter's name on the label? That doesn't make sense. Lampton would hardly pay to have himself assassinated! What about Printon ... but what could his motive be ... other than we know he doesn't seem too keen to talk to Lampton?'

Stephen continued to churn his unanswered questions over in his mind, searching for a link or solution.

'It's all a bit of a mystery, isn't it? Shouldn't we be getting back?' asked Rupert, glancing at his wristwatch. 'It's nearly time for tea.'

'Too dangerous to talk like this anywhere near the boat, old chap,' said Stephen earnestly. 'That's why I suggested a nice long stroll along the Corniche. I don't think we were followed.'

'Followed?' echoed Rupert. 'But who would want to do that?'

Stephen raised his eyebrow and curled his lip into a mock leer.

'Guess!' he said.

'Surely not Lampton ... or Printon,' he replied.

'Do you remember we went off into the town the first day we were here? And do you remember that we went to the post office? Well, I sent a telegram to Cecil...'

'Who's Cecil?' asked Rupert.

'Someone so high up that you get dizzy just thinking of him,' replied Stephen vaguely. 'Anyway, I asked for details of our friends – the first telegram confirmed more or less what Lampton had told us – about being engineers and the connection with the Royal Engineers. I burned that one before coming to your cabin to ravage you...'

'Stephen!' whispered Rupert, who started to redden. He still found such talk embarrassing, even in the open air.

'What very pleasant memories are prompted by that visit,' said Stephen, touching his friends arm for a fleeting moment in a gesture of sublime tenderness. Then his mood changed and he was once again concentrating on the unsolved riddle of their situation. 'The telegram said that friend Printon had been decorated for gallantry, but had damaged his hand and arm in an accident – two fingers mangled, but useable.' He held up the fourth and fifth fingers of his right hand. 'These two, to be precise.'

'But Printon doesn't…'

'…have any mangled fingers – on either hand,' finished Stephen. 'Odd, wouldn't you think? And Cecil is not known for inaccuracies – anything he is involved in usually carries extremely high risks and any mistakes invariably cost lives.'

Rupert looked alarmed at this revelation.

'Then who is this Ce…'

'Not now, old chap. Time and place for everything,' muttered Stephen, interrupting his friend. 'More to the point consider our clumsy Miss Cuttle and her bouncing camera down at Abu Simbel. Who checked the aperture ring, with all fingers working perfectly?'

Stephen turned to look at Rupert, waiting for the answer that he knew would come.

'Printon,' whispered Rupert.

'Exactly, Printon,' echoed Stephen.

'But shouldn't we tell the police?' asked Rupert, suddenly fidgeting with the paper cone of nuts he still held in his hands.

'Already ahead of you on that one, old chap,' replied the doctor calmly. 'I sent another telegram asking for instructions and telling Cecil that, seeing as he got me – or should I say *us* – into this mess, could he please get us out of it. This was waiting for me when we got back from Abu Simbel this morning.'

'I wondered where you had disappeared to,' said Rupert, as Stephen reached into his pocket and drew out a crumpled telegram slip and his lighter.

'Have a read of this – and then I'll burn it. I wanted you to see it, so that you have no illusions as to how real and – do I dare say, perilous – things could well become. If anything happens to me, you must contact Cecil – just send a telegram to the British Embassy in Cairo, addressed to

Cecil. They'll know what to do. Here, read this,' and he handed the crumpled paper to Rupert:

From Cecil
Advise extreme caution. Your man Printon possibly connected with current investigation by Military Intelligence. Make no attempt to apprehend him. Expect assistance from Khartoum.

'That doesn't tell us much, does it?' said Rupert. 'From Khartoum?' he said, re-reading the telegram, 'that's not going to be much help if we need it!'
'Keep your voice down, old chap; sometimes even the street has ears. Read on...'
Rupert returned to the telegram:

... Major Ashdown joining you. Expected government steamer ex-Khartoum 5th instant. Utmost secrecy essential. Aswan Police notified of Ashdown's expected arrival. Authorities in Cairo notified. Appropriate steps instigated. Advise latest position.
Cecil.

'What are these "appropriate steps" do you think? And who is this Major Ashdown? This really is *Boy's Own* stuff,' said Rupert, as Stephen took the paper and set fire to the corner.
'Not quite, old chap,' he said, as the flames licked hungrily at the dry paper. 'Nobody actually gets killed in *Boy's Own*, now do they?'
He stamped on the carbonized remnants of the telegram, grinding the powdery remains into the gaps between the cobblestones. They had been so engrossed in their conversation that neither of them had noticed the first early hint of the evening breeze, which had wafted in from the cooling river. It caught the fine grains of charred paper

that still lay on the cobbles and wafted them up into the air and away, to disappear into the fine sand of the riverbank below them.

'Time to get back,' said Stephen, as he stood up stiffly, rubbing the lower part of his leg. He had not brought his walking stick with him.

As he got up, Rupert unscrewed the top of the paper cone and unwound it, scattering the remains of the nuts onto the pavement. The pigeons, almost by magic, suddenly returned and resumed their squawking. He was about to crumple up the square of newsprint and put it in a nearby bin, when his eye caught the headline of one of the reports on the page.

'Oh dear,' he said, 'another train derailment – outside Luxor this time. It says the track's closed for the next week or more. That would normally please Mohammed,' he added.

'Why is that, then? What do a closed railway line and friend Mohammed have in common?' asked the doctor, playfully, as they started to walk down the busy street and along the Corniche, back towards the little white steamer.

'It's usually good for business – if they can't get through on the train we sometimes carry a passenger who's in a hurry to get to Cairo or Luxor. Even *Khufu* is faster than sitting in a hotel waiting for the track to be repaired.'

They both laughed as they continued strolling, the threat of impending danger not alleviated, but, just for the moment, pushed a little further back into the distance.

'Anyway, he won't be able to do anything this trip – we're fully booked back to Cairo.'

But Rupert had forgotten that Sylvia Baxter was no longer with them.

34

Aswan

Afternoon, 2nd August 1928

'He is late!' muttered Printon, as he stood outside Aswan's railway station looking at his wristwatch.

   During the short trip downriver from Abu Simbel, communication between himself and the Count had become increasingly difficult with every conversation, no matter how short. Printon had quickly become suspicious at the other man's reluctance to show him the stones – or even to tell him where they were hidden. Suspicion had led to doubt and doubt had caused him to question if there was a shipment at all. This Count – The Phoenix – had a reputation for dedication to the Fatherland, but, in Printon's experience, even the most unquestionable loyalty could go sour. During the short time it took them to return from Abu Simbel, it had occurred to him that perhaps he would have to take control of the stones himself – even if it meant discovering their whereabouts by force. Printon was an ambitious man and this Phoenix, upon whom so much praise had been heaped by the Party, was an anachronistic upstart with an attitude arrogantly anchored in a much earlier, different time. Printon could avenge himself on this aristocrat by taking the stones back to Germany himself. The waiting Party hierarchy would then cover him with the praise and glory that would normally have been heaped on The Phoenix.

Whilst basking in this attention he would, of course, express the deepest remorse at The Phoenix's demise and the resultant loss to the Party. These were the thoughts that filled his head as he paced the pavement outside the station. The more he thought about it, the more the idea appealed to him. Once he had the stones in his possession and had rid himself of this man, he would have the trip back to Cairo to formulate a reasonable explanation as to what had led to the regrettable demise of The Phoenix and why he, Printon, had brought the stones to their destination on his own.

At least continuing the journey by train will rid me of these annoying people, including that inquisitive Lampton fool! he thought, as he looked yet again at his watch. *What is the old fool doing? The instructions were clear enough.*

It crossed his mind that he could not go anywhere without the stones. He could not do anything to assume control of the operation until he had them in his possession; until The Phoenix let him see them, he had no hope of succeeding with anything. He was at the elder man's beck and call and he resented him all the more because of this stark fact. He took out a cigarette and lit it. At one stage during their return from Abu Simbel, he had even contemplated luring Lampton somewhere discrete and dark before making sure that the stupid fool never bothered him again with his nonsense about being in the British army. Lampton's disappearance could be excused as a case of man overboard.

Yes, that would have been good, he reasoned, as he dragged his valise, which stood on the pavement between his legs, into a pool of cooling shade.

He had not had blood on his hands for some time now and he missed the heightened rush of adrenalin that went with it. Not even the thought of Esther Arling, the overeager, cheap Jewish whore lying naked on the crumpled sheets, sandwiched between his own sweating form and that of her husband, produced the same sense of excitement as did someone's blood on his hands.

The man is late! Does the arrogant old fool not think it advisable to follow arrangements when we are surrounded by the enemy? fumed Printon, as he angrily tossed the butt end into the gutter and looked at his watch yet again. The Phoenix was only just under ten minutes late, even so Printon's anger had risen with each passing minute and it continued to do so.

'There will be no place for such incompetence or arrogance in the new Reich,' he muttered, turning to look up the road.

Printon knew a little of the rumours that had circulated about this man's money and how it had been mysteriously moved to the safety of a Swiss bank during the war, when others of his rank were giving a substantial part of what they owned to the war effort. It was rumoured that this single action, this error of judgement on the part of The Phoenix was not appreciated in the rarefied levels of the Party hierarchy. There had even been talk of treason, but such talk had been suppressed for the moment in the interests of what was deemed to be far more important than simply a question of a past misjudgement. As far as the Party was concerned The Phoenix, as archaic as he might seem, was very useful to the cause. Until the Reich was an established and irrefutable fact, the Party needed as many useful people as it could get. For the time being that was what mattered: past transgressions could be reviewed at a later, more convenient time.

Perhaps you are not as good as you would have Berlin believe. The English do say that there is no fool like an old fool! thought Printon, who had just about reached the end of his tether.

What he did not realize was that the Count was far from being an old fool. In fact, the Count was playing a personality game in which Printon was the unwitting subject and the

Count – The Phoenix – was the master. All the time he had been fuming outside the railway station, Printon had been watched by the object of his sudden hatred. In the shadows of an anonymous narrow alleyway, a little way further up on the opposite side of the street, a bony hand gripped the silver handle of a heavy black cane. From the protection of those same shadows two eyes smouldered with distrusting detestation, like the ruby eyes that studded the bird-shaped handle.

This arrogant young upstart is going to have to be taught respect, he decided, as he watched Printon glance yet again at his wristwatch. *Those with so much naked ambition are a danger.*

He stepped out of the alleyway and across the road, taking Printon completely by surprise. The younger man was considerably annoyed.

'You are late,' hissed Printon, as he watched the other put his slim suitcase on the pavement.

'It does not pay to be careless,' replied the taller man calmly, refusing to be drawn by Printon's subdued outburst. 'The safest route is not always the shortest. Are you certain you were not followed … or observed?' *You have made such a display of your impatience, my young friend, that it is a wonder the whole of Aswan does not know of our movements*, he thought, but he said nothing.

He would keep that barbed observation for later, should the circumstance in which to use it present itself.

Printon opened his mouth and was about to make a suitably antagonistic reply, when he stopped short. No, he was not at all certain he had not been followed. And he had let this older man suddenly appear at his elbow, without any warning. He resented the implication The Phoenix was making. He also detested the snakelike grimace, which passed for the man's smile.

'In these times, everyone is nervous and is watching everyone else. You should remember that and be more aware of the person you have standing next to you,' added the elder man, as if admonishing an errant schoolchild.

He was relishing putting this younger man, who had now effectively become his opponent, in what he saw as his proper place. Why had they sent this man to meet him, anyway? He was used to working on his own and found such support as this man had to offer a hindrance rather than a help.

'Is that all the luggage you have?' he asked, nodding towards the valise, which Printon had picked up.

'I travel light,' he replied, glaring at the elder man with an incense-igniting hatred, before turning on his heel and walking off quickly into the railway station.

'Come! There is little time left,' he barked over his shoulder as he did so.

Things were to get even worse for Printon before the day was out. At the enquiry desk a tall, dark-skinned man of Nubian ancestry politely informed him that there were no trains for Cairo because they had stopped running. At that moment, he would not even be able to get to Luxor.

'What are you talking about?' Printon railed, trying somewhat unsuccessfully to control his temper. 'There must be trains to Cairo. I have purchased a ticket already. I have it here.'

Secure behind the protection of the stout, wooden counter, the Nubian smiled his best smile, revealing two rows of dazzling white teeth, and simply repeated the fact that there were no trains.

'*Effendi* does not understand – there are no trains to Luxor – there is a problem. From Luxor to Cairo it is possible, but that is all. To Luxor – no – *insha'Allah.*'

The Phoenix had removed himself from this spectacle and was standing a short distance off, pretending to read the displayed timetables and notices.

'There has been a derailment,' said the Count softly, as

Printon crossed the foyer and stood next to him in front of the notice boards. The two men spoke without looking at each other, as the Count read from one of the notices.

'Just south of Luxor,' continued the taller man. 'It could take up to ten days to repair and, in the interim, all rail services between Aswan and Luxor are suspended.'

Printon gave no outward sign of his annoyance. Beneath his usual ice-cold, detached exterior he knew full-well that the tone of The Phoenix' voice was mocking him. He determined to guard against the irritation this man evoked. Any loss of his temper, as involuntary as it might be, would lead to carelessness that could lead to mistakes that usually proved fatal. For the moment, faced with this new obstacle to overcome, he would tolerate the taller man's superciliousness and superior attitude. But only until they had reached Cairo and the way back to Germany lay before them. Then, he would take steps to redress the arrogance of this man. He had been told that the Party needed heroes – figureheads that could be used to win over the hearts and minds of those who might still harbour doubts.

And dead heroes are far more useful as figureheads than live ones, reasoned Printon.

'So, Mr Printon, what is to be our next step?'

There was taunting mockery in the question.

'The river,' replied Printon. 'At least there is no chance of a derailment. I suggest that you proceed to the Corniche and wait for me near a white paddle wheel steamer called *Khufu*.'

'Why?'

Printon stared hard at the taller man before answering. He was not used to having his instructions questioned.

'If we are to get to Cairo, we will first have to get to Luxor by the river,' replied Printon, barely managing to control his anger, 'unless you fancy it might be quicker over the desert on a camel?'

'*Khufu* you said?' repeated The Phoenix, refusing to rise to the bait.

'In about an hour's time,' said Printon.

'Why an hour's time?' asked The Phoenix.

The man's questioning of everything Printon was saying had raised his anger to a dangerous, unstable level.

'I have a task to do before then' came the curt reply.

'Where are you going?' asked The Phoenix, but Printon had already turned his back on him and was striding purposefully off towards the exit. He would have to instruct Kohler & Zehler's local agent to send a telegram to Cairo informing them of the change of plan. Still fuming with suppressed rage, he charged impatiently through the few people still gathered in the concourse, where they milled about in the vain hope of finding that the line had been re-opened.

At about the same time that Rupert and Stephen were sitting on the bench reviewing the increasingly alarming situation Stephen felt they were in, Mohammed was beginning to think that the evil eye, which he was convinced was dogging the footsteps of the tour, had, at last, wandered off to exert its malevolent gaze elsewhere.

'You are welcoming aboard *Khufu*,' he beamed, his gold tooth sparkling in the electric light of the palatial splendour of the highly ornate entrance foyer. 'Your ticket for returning to Cairo, Sir. Your passport I will return to you directly within the next immediate minutes, thanks you,' he continued, holding out the travel document. 'It is of fortunateness that there is also another gentleman from *Switcherland* in our tour,' he added, mispronouncing the name.

'Really?' replied the tall man of aristocratic bearing, who stood in front of him. And that was all he said.

373

This will make a pleasant change at Head Office, the little Egyptian thought to himself, beaming his most ingratiating smile. *After the trouble we have had, an additional fare will be smiled upon with the utmost appreciation.*

Mohammed observed that Printon, who had boarded *Khufu* in the company of this tall, birdlike man, was now standing next to him and was looking at the new addition to the passenger list with what seemed to be a mixture of resentment and open hostility. Indeed, once the formalities had been completed, Printon turned and stalked away without a word. Mohammed watched him go with some curiosity and made a mental note to have another quiet chat with Mr Rupert, who knew far more about the thinking and manners of these Europeans than he did. He would sound out Mr Rupert once more about this Mr Printon.

In response to Mohammed's bell, one of the cabin crew appeared and, picking up the solitary slim, leather suitcase, escorted the new traveller to his cabin. The sound of the heavy black, silver-topped cane engaging regularly with the deck echoed steadily around the foyer.

Another odd European, reasoned Mohammed, as he watched the men disappear down the corridor. *He carries such a heavy cane and does not seem to have the need of it.* He turned, went through the door behind the reception desk and entered the inner office.

It is regrettable that the poor Miss Baxter is not longer amongst us, Mohammed mused, *but at least the cabin will not be empty on our return – insha'Allah.* He smiled to himself, as he locked the metal strongbox and put it back in the small safe that stood on a low plinth behind the desk. Returning to his desk he opened the heavy ledger in which he was obliged to record all passenger details. He had just finished entering Benschedler's particulars when Achmed appeared at the office door.

'*Effendi* ... pardon, but there is trouble,' he said.

FATAL TEARS

'What trouble?' replied Mohammed, looking up from the page.

'Mrs Lady 8 is complaining again and I cannot stop her,' he replied, shrugging his shoulders in that peculiar Egyptian attitude of irresolvable helplessness.

Mohammed let out a sigh of resigned annoyance.

'A thousand curses be her gift,' he muttered, putting down the pen and standing up. 'The Mrs Lady 8 is too much trouble.' He crossed to the office door. 'Here,' he said, holding out the passport, 'you give this back to the *Swich* man.'

Eric Kormann was sitting with Grupfelder, listening intently to what he was saying. He still found some of the big American's language hard to follow at times, but, on the whole, he was reasonably confident with the progress he felt he had made in trying to understand it.

'... So it wasn't a real one at all!' thundered the American, roaring with laughter. Kormann, too, laughed and was in mid-sentence response when Achmed appeared at his elbow.

'Excuse, please, *Effendi*. I have been instructed to give the Swiss gentleman this,' he said, pronouncing the nationality correctly.

With his mind still half on the conversation, Kormann took the passport without thinking, only pausing to do so the split second after Achmed had turned and left. Quickly he opened the document, glanced at the holder's details then looked quizzically at Grupfelder. 'But I have my passport already...' he said, turning to the empty space where Achmed had been standing a brief moment before, '...so why this?' he said, turning back to the American and holding up the passport as the signs of laughter faded from his face. Concurrent with the momentary confusion that had suddenly arisen in Kormann's mind, Mohammed strolled purposefully into *Khufu's* lounge, a smug look of satisfaction on his face.

As usual, 'Mrs Lady 8', as he now called Mrs Grassmere, had whinged and whined about what, to a sane, un-self-centred person, would have been absolutely nothing at all. With his gold-tooth smile pinned firmly to his face, he had listened to her for a couple of minutes, during which time she had prompted her reluctant and defeated husband to agree with her several times. Mohammed had seized the opportunity to cut across her as she paused for a much needed breath, her reddened jowls quivering.

'Madam may rest insuring,' he cooed, 'all shall be resolving. Also, I myself, will order afternoon refreshment to be sent here to Madam's cabin, in the ordering that Madam may resting be herself. It is no troublings, thanks you,' he crooned, as he closed the cabin door behind him. *A large plate of food and the she-hippo will not even remember what she thinks her troubles are*, he reasoned, as he strode off down the passageway, smiling to himself as he did so.

'At tea time send a tray of cakes and some tea to Cabin 8,' he said to one of the stewards behind the table. He was about to add a humorous by-line, when he heard a soft cough behind him.

'Excuse me, please,' said Eric Kormann, looking apologetic and somewhat puzzled. 'I think there has been a mistake. I already have my passport, but now I have been given this one. It is not mine,' he said, holding it out.

Later still, towards the end of that same day, Mohammed was making his customary evening circuit of the decks before the chimes of 'Three Blind Mice' sounded to summon the passengers to their evening meal. He saw Eric Kormann leaning on the rails of the upper deck, watching the activity on the Corniche above him through the fading light. Next to him towered the substantial frame of Elias P. Grupfelder, as solid and muscular as one of the hundreds of thousands of cattle he owned. In fact, Mohammed had come to equate him with one of the monumental statues of Pharaoh.

He has the shape of a pharaoh, but, sadly, he does not possess the dignity and decorum of kingship, thought the little Egyptian as he approached them. *I will never understand these Europeans. What strange companions they make for each other.*

'Ah! ... gentlemens!' he called, brightly, as he reached them, 'is it not being a pleasant evening beginning? Most cooling after the heat of the day.'

The two Europeans turned and made suitable replies in response to the friendly greeting.

'Mr Kormann, Sir, a thousand pardons for the giving for you the passport of Mr Benschedler,' he continued, smiling, the gold tooth glinting in the lights reflected from the Corniche. 'A most regrettable misunderstandings, but I hope it is of interesting to you that we now have another man from your country in our esteemed grouping – yes?' he said, raising both hands in a gesture of all-embracing vagueness. 'From your own land – *Switcherland*. A gentleman who goes with us to Cairo, yes Sir.'

'Oh ... yes ... one of my countrymen,' said the Swiss, finally comprehending Mohammed's tortuous English. 'I know ... but that is unusual, as we are only a very small country and I do not know if it is that popular to venture this far south into the heat. For me, I have an interest in ancient Egypt, but for my countryman, I cannot say...' The look of an un-retrieved memory, lost in the labyrinth of puzzlement, flickered across Kormann's face once again as it had done earlier, when he had read Benschedler's name in the passport.

He fell silent, as Grupfelder and the little Egyptian exchanged another few sentences, before Mohammed excused himself and sauntered off to complete his rounds.

'That guy's OK,' said Grupfelder, as he returned his gaze to the Corniche.

The lights of Aswan had begun to glow more robustly, as the sunlight continued to decay and the nightlife of the town slowly awoke.

'He ain't so much as to stop an old doggie in its tracks, but an OK guy, all the same,' boomed the big American, as he replaced his cheroot in this mouth.

'I find his manner of expression somewhat confusing,' said the diminutive Swiss. 'Do you not find that?' he asked, without taking his gaze from the scene before him.

'Hell no!' thundered Grupfelder. 'Back home when we dunno what's been said it's because the liquor takes over and then it don't really matter, anyways,' and with that, he slapped Kormann on the back and roared with laughter.

The little Swiss nearly went sailing over the rails with the force of the affection expressed. He steadied himself and smiled back. He had gotten used to the brashness of his American companion and had warmed to his sense of humour, the nature of which he had found confusing at first.

'Sometimes I am unable to deduce exactly what it is he is trying to say,' continued Kormann, 'like just now.'

'Who gives a damn?' replied the American. 'The fella's nice enough with it and he gets ya anything y' ask for – an' that's what counts. Who cares if ya' don't understand what he's on about sometimes?'

'That is possibly true, but it is sometimes quite important in a conversation to be able to get the point,' replied the Swiss, 'and I must say that I always like to. And that is what I am not doing with Benschedler at the moment. Why do I have the feeling that I have heard of him before, and that I know this name, yet cannot think why?' Several times that afternoon he had retreated into the furthest recesses of his memory, but could find no clue. 'I was only a little boy,' he said, almost to himself, 'I remember my games and books ... and my mother, crying ... all the time.'

There was a lengthy pause, during which the sounds of Aswan flooded over the top deck of the little steamer, enfolding the two men.

'And my mother ... why did she sometimes mutter this name ... Benschedler?' said the little Swiss eventually.

35

London

Whitehall, Early Afternoon – 3rd August 1928

Smoke rose from the Uncle's cigar as it rested in the large glass ashtray on the desk. The wisps of smoke intertwined and danced, making fantastic sculptures in the air, as the elderly man sat intently reading a typed sheet that he had removed from a red-stamped folder in front of him.

'This puts rather a bad gloss on things,' he said quietly to his private secretary, who stood at his side a little way back from the desk. The secretary had already read the communication, as it had been delivered to his desk from the cipher room, which was hidden away high up in the attic of the building.

'Indeed, so it would seem, Sir,' he replied quietly.

'He's done us proud – even if he has compromised his own position somewhat,' said the Uncle, looking up at the other man's face. 'Quite by chance, he seems to have found a wasps' nest and then unwittingly made his bed in it, so to speak, eh?' But there was no trace of humour in the voice, only a deadly concern. He returned his gaze to the sheet of paper and read it for a second time.

From Ambassador, Cairo.
For Cecil.
URGENT.

FATAL TEARS

Recent deceased found in Cairo street refers. European male of middle age, height approximately six foot. According to local witnesses a victim of motor vehicle accident. Body badly mangled; facial features unidentifiable. Held in police mortuary, Cairo, pending routine post-mortem. This now complete, revealing death due to large sub-cranial haemorrhage, consistent with accident. Damage to right arm also identified, radius and ulna out of alignment at elbow, showing signs of earlier trauma, now healed. Third, fourth and fifth phalanges of right hand have severe bone misalignment, consistent with being crushed. This not caused by recent accident, as the bone had grown around fracture and break points.

Recent communications to you from Hopkins have referred to person Printon, who has damage to fingers consistent with that noted above. Regarded information as being important, given this previous interest.

Please advise if any further action required.

Looking up at his private secretary, the Uncle placed the sheet of paper face down on the desk and picked up a second, smaller piece of paper. It was a telegram which had been transmitted late the day before.

'And then we have the final piece of this particular puzzle, wouldn't you say, Collingwood?' he said, without looking at the other man, his features as fixed as those of the small marble bust of Wellington that stood on the desk in front of him.

For Cecil.
Your last communication refers. Printon in full control of all digits, both hands. Planned departure from Aswan late tomorrow, 4th instant. Please advise next step and when assistance can be expected. Situation now deteriorating and becoming desperate.
Hopkins.

He replaced both sheets of paper in the folder, closed it and then handed it to Collingwood.

'Remind me if you would, Collingwood, do we have any further information on this chap in the police mortuary in Cairo?' he asked, reaching out to retrieve his cigar from the ashtray, now that the blotter in front of him was clear.

'I took the liberty of asking Cairo to confirm if they had any other means of identifying the body, but they replied in the negative, Sir. It would seem the gentleman was found in the gutter of the street on which he was killed. There were no identifying documents.' He paused, and then added discreetly, 'Not even a wallet, Sir.'

The Uncle looked up at him and, with a knowing smile, replied, 'That is hardly surprising – vultures usually do a good job cleaning the bones of carcases they come across and vultures come in many different forms – human and animal.'

Collingwood said nothing, but continued tying the folder closed with the red tape that circled it. Then he tucked it under his arm and waited for instructions.

'We must act – and swiftly,' the Uncle said. 'Miracles do happen, but only a hopeless optimist relies on them. Our Mr Sebastian Printon would seem to be very dead, given the evidence. So who is it that now carries his name and passport in Aswan – and why?'

He took a draw of his cigar before continuing, his brow knitted in deep thought. His nephew had done what was expected of him, but was now in a dangerous situation which seemed to be getting more and more serious by the hour. As his brow became even more heavily furrowed, the worst possible outcome flashed through his mind and he suddenly shuddered at the thought of having to tell his brother that his son, the Uncle's own, beloved nephew, was dead – a survivor of the war, now dead in peacetime, caught up in something that he didn't understand and in a far-off country. The fact that he, the boy's own uncle, could be directly responsible for that death and that he would have to keep the knowledge of that responsibility from his brother, for the sake of their own relationship, appalled him. He had got the boy into the situation; he would have to get him out of it.

His brow relaxed and he placed the cigar in the ashtray. Once again the dense wisps of smoke started to trace their patterns in the air as he spoke.

'Where is Major Ashdown?' he asked, his gaze once again firmly focused on the bust of his hero, Wellington.

'I believe on the government steamer between Wadi Haifa and Aswan, Sir,' replied Collingwood.

'How near is he to Aswan?'

'He should arrive the day after tomorrow, Sir, on the fifth.'

'Damn!' said the Uncle, 'and they leave Aswan for Cairo tomorrow. He'll miss them.'

'So it would seem, Sir,' replied Collingwood softly. 'Perhaps the police in Aswan should be informed...'

The elder man sat behind his large mahogany desk, like a large bird of prey squatting in the branches of a tree, waiting to strike. Without taking his eyes off Wellington, he spoke.

'Send a telegram to Aswan for Ashdown when he arrives – tell him he is to contact my nephew immediately and is to move in on his suspect without delay – we'll just have to hope that he has the right man and chance the unfortunate consequences if he does not! And copy it to the Embassy in Cairo, with instructions to forward it to Police Headquarters there, too. They had better tell their chap in Aswan to meet Ashdown and then give him all the assistance he might need – Ashdown will know what to do. Mark it top priority, with the usual security. And keep it discreet, Collingwood – the last thing we want is an all-out death or glory cavalry charge by the local bobbies, with what evidence there may be getting trampled underfoot in the process.'

'At once, Sir,' replied the private secretary, who then backed off a step and, with a slight nod of the head, crossed the room to the door.

'Oh, and Collingwood,' called the Uncle, as he did so, 'you'd better send something to my nephew – just tell him that help is on the way and to stay calm and not upset the applecart.' Despite his position of power and absolute authority, the Uncle felt alone and very isolated, being little more than a distant observer of the events which threatened to engulf his nephew. 'Tell him about Ashdown ... but not too many details.' He paused, as he stared off into the far distance for a few seconds. 'Perhaps the Aswan police can come up with a convincing delaying tactic to give Ashdown time to get there.'

In far-off Aswan, Rupert was shepherding the last of his subdued flock back aboard *Khufu* after what had proved to be an unpleasant visit to the Temple of Isis on Philae Island. Events that afternoon at the temple had ensured that the little paddle steamer would, indeed, be waiting another day in Aswan.

36

Philae Island

Aswan, Early Afternoon – 3rd August 1928

'Nothing like a boat trip on the river is there?' quipped Rupert, as he guided his straggling flock towards the water's edge. The omnipresent Fairuz bin-Salaah, whose transport would be parked in whatever shade could be found to await the tourists' return, also offered encouragement.

'Your experience will be of the utmost pleasure,' he crooned, as they neared the water, 'the temple is being the place of love and your luxury transport is to be waiting for you with love,' he beamed, drawing out the vowel of the last word, but careful not to get too close to the river and get his feet wet.

Rupert smiled at Stephen, who rolled his eyes at the banality of bin-Salaah's pronouncement.

Once at the water's edge and with varying degrees of ease, the tourists set about clambering over the high gunwales of the two launches that would ferry them the short distance out into the Nile and onwards to Philae Island. That afternoon the river was glasslike; the surface of the water was only disturbed by a slight swell, mirroring the movement of the cooling breeze and the occasional tell-tale stream of bubbles from a passing fish. The incidents of the past few days seemed to have receded into the subconscious and had almost become lost to the past. The overall tone of the group, with the exception of the predictable few, was both buoyant and expectant.

'Careful how you go, ma'am,' said Elias P. Grupfelder, as he lifted the lightweight form of Miss Rebecca Eggerton up and over the gunwale into the nearest launch. 'Ya gotta take care of that purty little ankle, now…"

'Oh … thank you so much … How kind … It's really quite better now,' she twittered breathlessly, as she arranged herself on the flattened and worn cushion of the narrow bench that ran along the length of the inside of the hull.

'Calm down, my dear,' muttered Marjory Cuttle, out of the corner of her mouth. She smiled at her friend from under the broad brim of her sunhat, which she had kept on her head despite the launch being covered with a high, brightly coloured awning. 'Was the experience *that* exciting?' she asked, behind a questioning smirk.

'Really, Miss Cuttle!' Eggerton replied, feigning an affront, before dissolving into giggles.

The Manningtons had clambered into the boat unaided. They sat on the cross-bench near the bows, staring straight ahead, their backs to the rest of the company, a statement as to their general attitude. This had not been lost on the rest, who, by now, had become indifferent to them anyway.

A second launch had been drawn up next to the first and both were a hive of activity, as the tourists clambered in under the experienced supervision of Abdullah, the boats' owner. Like the more corpulent Fairuz bin-Salaah, he was a long-time associate of the company in Aswan. Both of Abdullah's launches had been grounded at the foot of a gently sloping concrete ramp, the bottom of which disappeared into the lapping waters of the Nile. In the first launch, which was now almost full, Grupfelder had vaulted effortlessly over the gunwale and had seated himself next to Kormann.

'Handling a steer's one thing,' he muttered, pointing

through himself with his thumb, 'but that's a bum deal!' he said, indicating the substantial bulk of Mrs Grassmere, whom he had seen – or rather, heard – approaching down the ramp.

'Oh that *is* good,' she had wheezed, in a voice that was far too loud to be simply casual. 'The American gentleman is helping to get us into the boat.'

But Grupfelder had been far too quick for her. By the time she wobbled down to the water's edge, she was met with the backs of several people's heads, all of whom were safely seated in the launch. She stood there, on the sloping ramp, waiting for something to happen and looking more than a little ridiculous.

'This way, Mrs Grassmere,' called out Rupert, indicating the second launch, 'there's plenty of room here. Next to the Lamptons – there's a seat for both you and Mr Grassmere.'

Her diminutive husband, who had quite literally been standing in her considerable shadow, suddenly appeared from behind her and attempted to guide her towards the second launch. In the general atmosphere of excitement and expectation, Stephen, who had decided to sail with the first launch, had not failed to notice Benschedler, who was sitting impassively in front of the Manningtons on the single bow seat, facing into the launch. The resultant effect was of a pair of well-matched bookends; the Manningtons staring ahead, saying nothing – not even to each other – and this new member of the group with pale, claw like hands resting on the ornate silver handle of his heavy cane – staring impassively in the opposite direction. Stephen also wondered why this man always carried such a heavy cane. He did not seem to have need of it, as, despite his years, he moved with considerable ease. Of more immediate concern to him, however, was the fact that he had noticed Printon sitting in the second launch – the same one that held the Lamptons. Not that anyone knew it, but under his usual cold, detached exterior, Printon was seething. He had been incensed by the near-acrimonious exchanges of the previous day, when he had been belittled in all but deed by the arrogant, overbearing aristocrat he had been sent to escort to safety. During the small hours of last night, as he had listened to the snores of Simon Arling and the steady breathing of Esther, he had been driven by the boiling, pent-up resentment he felt towards this birdlike man, a resentment which resembled the restrained fury of the waters held back by the dam. In the early hours of the morning he had decided to take total control and remove the irritation from the equation completely. He had reasoned to himself that he would best serve his Fatherland and Party by assuming responsibility for the custody of the stones himself – by whatever means were necessary – and by making himself solely accountable for their safe delivery. In one stroke, he would dispense with this out-of-date aristocrat, who had provoked him so dangerously, and cover himself with glory and rewards in the process. All Printon had to do was to discover the whereabouts of the stones and then decide on the time, place and the method of The Phoenix's demise. He would make his choice carefully – and soon, very soon.

The first launch had been pushed out into the river and slowly started to swing its bows around, pointing towards the low smudge of land that was their destination.

In the second launch progress was a little slower. Mr Grassmere, as ineffectual as ever, was trying to help his wife over the barrier of the high gunwale. In the process, he stepped sideways and into the river, filling his shoes with water. At almost the same time, his wife, as if not to be outdone by her husband, managed to teeter off-balance and catch her ludicrously small parasol, which she insisted on carrying everywhere, in the launch's awning. Abdullah, a tall, dark Nubian whose muscular, well-honed physique stood in sharp contrast to her flabby, uncontrolled proportions, rushed forward to catch her before she fell backwards and down onto the hard concrete ramp. In truth, he was more concerned with saving his awning from damage, but Mrs Grassmere did not perceive events that way. As Abdullah pulled her back into a vertical position, the possibility of serious bodily damage was alleviated and her pig-like eyes flashed for a split second behind the blood-drained jowls. For once she had experienced the excitement of close contact with real masculinity. But, as quickly as the spark of physicality attempted to ignite itself deep within her, it was extinguished. Once manhandled into the launch – the process of which caused the vessel to lurch alarmingly, forcing several of the other occupants to make a grab for anything at hand to steady themselves – she began her litany of complaints, which had become the expected penalty of her attendance anywhere.

'Never mind, my dear,' whimpered her husband. 'At least the man caught you in time ... but look at my feet – they're saturated.'

Mrs Grassmere paid no heed to her husband's remarks, so he wilted silently into his seat and stared down at his wet feet. Abdullah and a couple of the young boat boys, all of whom were totally ignorant of her odious reputation, had fussed over her, making her feel important and valued. She beamed around at the other occupants of the boat to relish this moment of being the centre of attention, only to find that they had been ignoring this embarrassing spectacle.

The usually attentive Rupert also paid little attention to this incident as, following Stephen's instruction, he was more intent on observing Richard Lampton and Sebastian Printon, both of whom were sitting at opposite ends of the launch. As the second launch was finally pushed clear of the ramp and out into the Nile, Rupert thought back to earlier that day when the travellers had been assembling on the Corniche above *Khufu*, waiting for Fairuz bin-Salaah's transport. Lampton had approached Rupert and had quietly told him of his wife's love of the *Rubáiyát* – of how she had jogged his memory about the Printon he remembered by reading aloud from the poem. Stephen, armed with his walking stick and ever-present medical bag, had been within earshot and had taken Lampton into his confidence, telling him just sufficient to leave him in no doubt that vigilance and caution were essential for the next couple of days. He warned him of the situation which seemed to have developed around them, and of how it could well enfold them in considerable danger, the consequences of which could only be guessed at. They would all have to be on their guard until... And there he had stopped, for it was at that moment the transport appeared.

Now, as they made the short crossing to Philae Island, he thought further of what Stephen had told Lampton. Be on guard for what? And until when? That there was a real danger of something, he was convinced; but of what, precisely, he was uncertain. Perhaps Cecil would provide the solution. For his part, Lampton, the practical military man, had grasped the potential seriousness of what he had been told and had understood the situation at once. Despite the unanswered questions, and without hesitation, he had undertaken to act accordingly.

As the second launch started to swing round and face the direction in which it would be travelling, the first launch, which had already been pushed back off the concrete slipway and had been waiting offshore, now cruised past. Rupert caught a glimpse of the tall man sitting in the bows. Why this strange, remote man had decided to come on the excursion at all was a mystery to him. During the pre-excursion talk Rupert had given the previous evening, this man had sat ramrod straight staring rigidly ahead, just as he did now. He seemed totally absorbed in his own thoughts, ignoring everyone and everything around him – not in the disconnected manner of the Manningtons, but with a silent, steely, hidden purpose. Afterwards, as this enigma had sat sipping strong black coffee, all efforts on Rupert's part to involve him in conversation or discussion had proved fruitless. The man's only responses had been no more than was necessary to retain the social nicety of good manners.

Move over the Manningtons, Rupert had thought from behind his fixed, customer-friendly smile. *This one should keep you good company!*

He was brought back to the present by a sudden movement of the launch, which took him by surprise, and which caused him to grab one of the awning's supporting uprights to steady himself.

Sailing in a loose convoy, both launches made steady progress through the broad expanse of water that was, in reality, more a lake than a river. It had been created when the British had built a dam across the Nile at the First Cataract, just above Aswan. That had been thirty years ago, in the time of Lord Kitchener. Since then, the dam wall had been raised, as the demand for more and more water grew. The enormous energy that had driven the mighty river thousands of miles across Africa from its birthplace in Lake Victoria had been defeated by a thin, man-made barrier laid across its path. The mighty river was set free for only two months of the year, from late July to early October, when the mighty sluice gates were opened, freeing the waters to continue their ancient way down towards the Delta and the Mediterranean.

The benefits of a reliable supply of water to agricultural development had, however, come at a price. Behind the controlled obstruction created by the dam, the rise in the water level had flooded much low-lying ground, including

Philae Island and its magnificent temple complex. During his talk, the previous evening, Rupert had quipped that, if they had visited Aswan at any time other than when the sluices were open, they would have had to visit the temple by boat, drifting in and out of those parts of the complex which refused to be beaten by the river and which still protruded above the water level.

'The advances to agriculture made possible by the dam do have a penalty,' he had said earnestly. 'Over the decades since the dam was built, the continual flooding of the temple has washed away any vestige of the original, vibrant paintwork that would have covered the walls of the complex. However, we are lucky that the fabric of the buildings seems to have remained intact. It is checked every year when the level drops and the island dries out and, so far, there are no obvious signs of damage caused by the prolonged submersion. I think you will agree that this is a true testament to the building skills of the ancient architects and stonemasons. Let's hope *our* dam lasts as long,' he had said, to a round of chuckles and agreement.

In a little under twenty minutes, they reached the landing stage on Philae Island. The pantomime of boarding the launches, which had been acted out on the mainland a short time before, now had to be re-enacted in reverse, but this time without the benefit of the sloping concrete ramp. Instead, as the launches rocked gently on the slight swell, the passengers had to judge their timing and footing, so as to exit the launch and land safely on the bottom level of the broad flight of stone steps that led up from the river to a raised, paved area above. Towering over everything loomed the bulk of the temple complex itself, though they would not see it in its true grandeur until they breasted the rise and walked across the paved, column-lined forecourt.

Yet again, Ruth Kirby resisted any attempt to help her. She made the transition from launch to land with hardly a moment's hesitation and had then strode purposefully, if somewhat unsteadily, up the broad expanse of wide stone steps. Rupert watched her as she went before turning his attention to Susan Lampton. Despite the encouragement of her husband, she was having trouble judging the most opportune moment to attempt the transition from launch to step. As the launch suddenly rode up on the swell, making the gunwale almost level with the bottom step, she jumped. Rupert, who had been watching from the bottom step, saw her land safely and then walked her up to the top of the steps, where the others were grouped.

'Just think of it, ladies, as you climbed these steps, you were treading where Cleopatra herself would have walked over two thousand years ago. Do you feel as if you're walking along the Pathway of History?' he asked.

Ruth Kirby ignored him completely. Mrs Porter mumbled something about the enduring nature of the monument and Mrs Grassmere, who had attached herself to the muscular and able Abdullah, continued complaining, oblivious to the historical significance of the time warp they were all about to enter under the watchful and benevolent gaze of the goddess Isis.

Once everyone had ascended the steps and assembled on the extensive paved area, Rupert began to deliver his on-site encomium about the complex.

'Everyone turn that way and behold...' he said, dramatically indicating a right-hand turn. They were met by the full grandeur of the temple with its vast, open-air, paved courtyard. This area was lined on both sides by ranks of columns and at the far end stood the twin sloping pylons of the entrance gate to the complex. They soared up into the blue sky and were decorated with huge incised reliefs of Isis and her son Horus.

'This complex was in constant use for nearly a thousand years,' said Rupert, as they slowly crossed the vast court, 'from the fourth century BC, up until around 500 AD. It is actually a complex of several temples, but the main deity worshiped here was Isis. Remember that it was she who, by the force of her love, raised her husband, Osiris, from the dead after he had been murdered by his jealous brother, Seth. She breathed life into Osiris just long enough for her to impregnate herself with their son, the god Horus – the falcon-headed one, up there,' he continued, pointing up at one of the wall carvings. 'The concept of divine motherhood is very strongly represented here at Philae.'

They moved on a little further before Rupert continued.

'That pharaoh up there is one of the Ptolemies – he's from the Graeco-Roman period. Anyone remember when that was?'

There was a slight pause, before Kormann ventured an answer.

'Would that be first century BC?' he asked.

'Well done, Mr Kormann,' replied Rupert, encouraged. 'There is a strong Ptolemaic connection between Philae and the complexes at Edfu and Dendera,' he continued, as they moved further across the open court.

They had reached the shade of the imposing twin pylons that flanked the entrance to the inner court. As in all ancient Egyptian temples, the slope of the pylon walls symbolized the Nile Valley. They represented the mountains, which led down into the valley through which the mystical, life-bringing Nile meandered majestically across the Kingdom to the sea. The elegant lines of these massive structures, gradually sloping from the narrow top to the much broader base, belied the considerable expertise required to build them.

'Look at those two huge grooves,' continued Rupert, indicating the two deep, smooth grooves cut into the walls of the pylons, one on each side of the entrance. 'They would each have held a huge flagpole,' he said. 'The priests would have climbed up the narrow stairways that are built into the pylon walls to reach the roof.'

'Did the guys need the exercise, then?' asked Grupfelder, in his usual, forthright way.

'No, not at all,' replied Rupert, with a chuckle. 'They would have needed to get up there to change the coloured banners that would have streamed from the flagpoles in front of the temple. Different festivals had their own special associated colours, depending on the time of year. Everything was highly regulated.'

Grupfelder's question had provoked a general chuckle, which turned into low chatter as they moved further on.

'The Ancients believed that the source of the Nile was here in the vicinity of the First Cataract. This whole area was a very important, sacred place to them. Every year, when the Sotis star marked the beginning of the Nile's flood cycle, pharaoh himself would come to participate in the rituals and rites. We must not underestimate the importance of the annual Nile flood to the well-being of ancient Egypt.'

They paused to admire the sheer scale of the buildings before continuing on, through the massive pylons and into the inner courtyard. Once inside they again paused, gathering around Rupert.

'You might be interested to know that there are crosses cut into the stone. You should easily be able to find them, even allowing for the restrictions placed on our access to the complex, but I'm not going to show you where. I'll leave you to discover them for yourselves.'

'Excuse me, please,' said Eric Kormann, 'but why would there be crosses in an Egyptian temple dedicated to the goddess Isis?' he asked.

'A good question, Mr Kormann,' replied Rupert. 'This site was held so sacred that even the early Christians – the Copts – used parts of it as a church in the sixth century.'

Kormann nodded his thanks for the explanation.

Although they were bone dry in the hot Egyptian sun, the buildings had the faintest whiff of stagnation, of decaying algae and other extinct life, now removed from its natural habitat under the water.

'Remember, a couple of weeks ago all of this would have been submerged because of the dam,' continued Rupert. 'Most of the silt and algae have been cleared from the court in front of us and from the chapels and rooms that line it.' They moved further on into the centre of the courtyard. 'There is an archaeological team working in the rear part of the complex, through that second set of pylons over there, so we cannot go that far. Apart from that one area, we can go wherever we like. Beyond those pylons they're still working, so the rest of the complex is still closed off. Before we go any further have a look at this,' he said, pointing towards the temple to his left, which was completely contained within the courtyard. 'This is the Birth House – it's called a *mammisi* – it celebrates the birth of Horus.'

'That was the fella who was the son of Iris,' boomed Grupfelder looking quite pleased with himself.

Kormann pushed his glasses further up his nose and leaned in close to the American.

'Excuse me, but the name is Isis,' he whispered.

'I suggest you wander around on your own for the next hour or so,' continued Rupert, ignoring Grupfelder's gaff. 'Remember that there is quite a lot to see outside this court complex, too. Don't forget to go and look at the Pavilion of Trajan – that's off to the right, as you stand outside and face the entrance pylons. I'll be circulating and will be more than happy to answer your questions. Everyone clear...?' There were no dissenting voices, not even from Mrs Grassmere, who was still the worse for wear, having negotiated the steep walk up to the raised, paved area outside the approach court. 'Good, then off you go and enjoy your exploration. We will meet back at the top of the steps in about an hour,' he concluded, looking at his wristwatch.

The group disbanded slowly and drifted away in several directions, most of them chatting as they did so. As they gradually disappeared amongst the complex of columns and passageways, Rupert mused that, despite his earlier reservations, this particular flock might even have an interest in what he was sharing with them after all. His deeply rooted passion for the ancient civilization of the Nile, and his fascination with the tangible remains of that civilization – such as the temple on Philae Island – refused to remain submerged for very long. And then there was Stephen. It would seem that this trip was proving to be memorable in more ways than one.

37

Philae Island

Aswan, Mid-afternoon – 3rd August 1928

In the central courtyard of the Temple of Isis, between the two massive pylons that thrust up with ancient energy towards the life-giving sun, Rupert's flock had dispersed in all directions. They had spent the last hour slowly wending their way around the recently surfaced complex, submerging themselves in the abundance of ancient Egyptian art and religion that filled the complex.

Rupert had been quite busy answering a question here, demonstrating a point there. For the first time since arriving on the island that afternoon, he found he had some time to himself. He settled against one of the stone slabs, which formed a low wall along one side of the courtyard, and lit a cigarette.

'Well?' he asked through the smoke, as Stephen joined him.

'So far, so good,' replied the doctor, as he took one of the cigarettes Rupert offered him, 'although, I'll be a lot happier when this Major arrives.' He lit the cigarette from the lighter Rupert held out and exhaled a cloud of smoke. 'I don't know about you, old chap, but I can't say that I'm feeling any more confident than before. He picked a fragment of tobacco off his tongue. 'And you?' he asked, looking straight ahead, 'How are you doing?'

'Happy as a sand boy,' beamed Rupert, 'even if there is danger about.' He chuckled.

'You don't take anything seriously, do you?' replied Stephen. 'We could be in very hot water before we know it. What about...?'

'Mr Winfield ... a moment of your time, if you please?'

Eric Kormann called across to Rupert from the far corner of the courtyard, where he and the American were gazing up at a wall full of carved figures and hieroglyphics.

'Back in a jiffy,' whispered Rupert, as he stubbed out his cigarette underfoot. 'Curiosity calls and all of that!'

Stephen watched his friend stroll off across the courtyard. As he did so, the doctor became aware that during the time they had spent on the island his nostrils had become more and more aware of the smell of dried algae and the occasional dead fish. Exposed to the merciless sun since the water had receded, what had not yet been cleared away was all but scorched to putrefaction, the evidence of which lingered faintly about his nostrils. For an all-too-long instant, his mind recoiled back to the complex of large tents, close to the front line, and to the never-ending lines of damaged humanity waiting in hope and expectation of a miracle or a cure – or both. And he remembered the stench of decay and rotten flesh. His mind lurched back to the tranquillity of the Temple of Isis; his leg had started to throb.

Looking around the court, he took another draw of his cigarette. It occurred to him that the smell of the cigarette smoke was a useful mask against the malodorous memory that hung on the afternoon air. Still vigilant, his mind closed to the unpleasant memories of the war, he sat swatting flies and listening to Rupert's voice as it echoed around the large, colonnaded courtyard. He noticed Miss Cuttle and Rebecca Eggerton emerge from the shadows that surrounded the roped-off entrance to the Hypostyle Hall. Both were clutching small white kerchiefs, which they held to their noses from time to time.

The undoubted benefits of lavender water and old lace, he mused, as he rubbed his lower leg. A movement off to his left directed his attention to Mrs Porter, who was absently fanning herself with her Australian bush hat, as she and Mr Rotherham stood in the shade of the columns. Colonel Ponsworthy, who had privately enjoyed the curvaceous lines of the goddess's plump, exposed breasts, stood in the entrance to the centre court. He was contemplating the enormous, incised images of Isis, with their plate-sized, erect nipples – the source of nourishment for her son Horus and, through him, for all of ancient Egypt. Colonel Ponsworthy (retired) fingered his moustache in silent, suppressed eroticism.

Rupert had finished his explanation to Kormann and was crossing the courtyard to rejoin Stephen. As he did so, he noticed the scattered members of his flock returning as instructed, after their own private exploration of as much of the complex as they were permitted to safely view.

'This smell is getting a bit much, don't you think, old chap?' asked Stephen, as Rupert reached him.

'It'll pass, once they manage to clear away what's left of the silt...'

'...And dead fish,' added the other, screwing up his nose to emphasize the point.

'And then it will all be flooded again in a couple of months...' said Rupert, wistfully looking at the carvings that covered the walls.

'Everyone back yet?' asked Stephen, 'Can we go?'

'Looks like it, but I haven't counted them. Perhaps I should – I'd hate to leave anyone behind.'

'Especially in this fragrant corner of paradise,' added the doctor, with a laugh. 'Not that our friend Mrs Kirby would notice anything,' he said, thrusting his chin out in her direction.

FATAL TEARS

She was leaning against a column and she had a look of confusion about her.

'Did you see the way she walked up the steps at the landing? A bit unsteady, I thought,' said Rupert.

'Yes I did,' replied the doctor. 'Quite how she managed to get out of the launch in the first place, without falling into the water, is a bit of a mystery as well.'

'You mean...'

'... I would say so, with considerable certainty,' concluded Stephen. 'She has been at the powder again. I did read somewhere that they call it "happy dust" in the Southern United States... Would you say she looks particularly happy?' He looked around the court. 'I see Mrs Grassmere has subsided over there with her hen-pecked better half.' He stared at the mismatched pair for a few seconds. 'What on earth has she got the poor man doing now, for God's sake? Look at him sta...'

But the sentence was to remain unfinished.

The dull thud that had so abruptly terminated Stephen's sentence caused all of the tourists nearest to the entrance pylons to turn and look. Even the two members of the archaeological team who were in the courtyard accurately recording the wall carvings turned to see what the noise was. In the process, one of them ruined two days' work by accidentally dragging his ink-charged pen across his drawing with the surprise.

A crumpled form, hunched in the unnatural posture of broken, disconnected death, lay at the foot of the left-hand pylon. The fine dry sand that had been displaced into wispy clouds by the arrested motion of the inert, falling form gradually settled. As they looked, they were horrified to discover that the ruin of a man's body had hit the hard floor.

'Bloody hell!' shouted Rupert, as he ran across to the crumpled form, closely followed by everyone else. Stephen,

401

despite his leg, got there first. He leaned down to look at the blood-covered, battered shape. The clothing was torn and ripped in many places, as if dragged repeatedly across an abrasive surface.

'What's happened?' asked Rebecca Eggerton, as she and Cuttle craned over everyone else, to get a better view.

'Help me turn him over,' said Stephen, as Grupfelder squatted down opposite him.

Their hands were already covered with the still-warm blood that had drenched the damaged clothing and mangled body.

'Surface abrasions everywhere,' muttered the doctor, 'and a broken neck, by the look of it,' he added, more to himself than to those around him.

As the tortured face lolled over, to stare up at the blue sky with lifeless, unseeing eyes, a wave of shocked surprise ran through the tightly packed group. When he saw the bruised, bleeding features, Stephen's immediate thought was to find where Richard Lampton was. But he was saved the trouble.

'It's Printon!' said Lampton, grasping Stephen's shoulder from behind as he said so.

'Yes, it is...' replied the doctor, opening the torn remnants of the shirt to feel for a heartbeat, but in no need of confirmation that Sebastian Printon – or whoever he was – was very dead.

'How awful,' said Mrs Porter, by way of a chronic understatement.

Esther Arling let out a protracted shriek, which dislodged several birds perched atop the pylons. She fell backwards onto her husband, who put his arms around her and, with a look of regret on his own face, led her away across the courtyard to sit down in the shade.

'What do you think happened?' asked Mr Rotherham, in an unsteady voice.

'Perhaps he came down from up there,' said Colonel Ponsworthy, in a very dispassionate manner, his private erotic fantasies of a few short moments before now rudely interrupted and totally forgotten. 'Off the top of the pylon...'

'That might explain the tearing and all the surface bleeding,' added Rupert, as he looked up, shielding his eyes from the deep intensity of the blue sky. '... If he kept bouncing off the sloping walls, I mean. The stone is quite rough and if you're falling...' he let his voice trail off; the sentence did not need to be finished.

'But, surely, that cannot be,' said Kormann, pushing his spectacles up his nose. 'From such a height you fall in total silence?' he asked.

'Look – up there,' said one of the archaeologists, in heavily accented English, pointing up at the towering pylon. A sea of faces turned upwards, following the direction of his finger.

'It is blood, yes? ... There, over the pharaoh ... how you say it ... his crown, yes?'

'There's another one ... there, in the loincloth ... lower down,' added Kormann, pointing to a second, longer red smear on the stone.

'Hell, yeah, I reckon he did fall,' said the American, returning his gaze to the corpse.

'But from way up there?' asked Richard Lampton. 'It must be all of sixty feet, for Christ's sake,' he said, as he cradled his wife in his arms to shield her from the view of the bloody, broken body. 'How the hell do you get up there? *Can* you get up there?' he asked, forgetting that Rupert had already told them all that it was, indeed, very possible.

'Oh yes, there are stairs ... very small ... in the walls of the pylons...' replied one of the archaeologists, using mime to demonstrate the existence of the narrow staircases in the walls. His colleague, the ruined work of two days now forgotten in the drama of the moment, had already gone off to summon the rest of the archaeological team from where they were working at the back of the complex.

'That's true,' added Rupert, feeling suddenly uneasy. He wondered if his earlier, enthusiastic description of priests climbing to the top of the pylons to change the banners on the flagpoles had anything to do with the accident. Had it given someone an idea? As he quickly glanced around the assembled group, he realized that he had no cause for concern. Most of his flock seemed to be either verging on the brink of hysteria, shock or both, or were simply fascinated by the sight of the real, bloodied corpse that lay in front of them. Any connection in their minds between Rupert, his description of the staircases within the pylons and the broken body was purely a figment of his own imagination. For Printon himself – the cold, unsociable man – the tourists, with the possible exception of Esther and Simon Arling, felt nothing; it was more the shock of the close proximity of sudden death that had numbed them.

'Get everyone back to the boats,' said Stephen, as he stood up, his black bag in his hand, unopened. 'I'll stay here with Printon and wait. The police are going to have to be called again, just to be safe.'

The group slowly started to process towards the entrance, some looking back at the bloody shape at the foot of the pylon, others looking straight ahead, as if to blot out the unpleasant image. Stephen, who had thought it best to refuse Lampton's immediate offer to wait with him, caught Rupert's attention.

'While you're at it see if you can find out if that pylon is accessible or not – it might be silted up, not being on the tourist itinerary. You know about these things so you'll know where to look. Quickly and quietly – and be discreet, I'll organize getting this lot back to the boats. You join us as soon as you can.'

Sending Rupert off on his mission seemed a rather silly

thing to do. It was beyond doubt that Printon had started his descent from the top of the pylon – the blood blotches on the walls confirmed that. It was hardly as if someone had just carried him into the courtyard through the entrance gate and unceremoniously dumped him on the ground at the foot of the pylon. Stephen shook his head – he was being stupid. Of course the body had come down off the top of the pylon. There *was* no other possible explanation. He had to keep a grip on the reality of the situation. The question that needed an answer – and a very quick one, at that – was simply how he had started his final descent. Had he fallen – or had he been pushed?

The group once again assumed the familiar, but unwelcome, role of a cortège and slowly made its way back to the launches, following the instructions Stephen had issued. They straggled across the wide, open space leading up to the entrance pylons, which they had traversed in the opposite direction barely an hour before. Now, the pylons were behind them. Onward they walked, between the rows of columns that lined each of the long sides of the rectangle. Some of the columns had unfinished capitals, giving the eerie feeling that the ancient stonemasons were expected to imminently return and complete their otherwise perfect, if unfinished, work.

'Say, ain't that the new fella – your Benschedler guy from back home?' asked Grupfelder, turning to Kormann as he spoke.

He crossed to where the man was sitting, ramrod straight, looking out impassively over the water.

'Say there, fella, you OK?' he asked, his shadow falling across the seated man.

'Am I what?' replied the other man, in a low voice, without altering his gaze.

'You OK? You fine?'

'Perfectly,' he replied, in a tone that did not encourage further communication.

'We're going back now ... there's been an accident ... it's that Printon guy – he's dead. Fell from the top of that, up there,' he said, turning to point up at the pylon.

'How unfortunate,' said the other man, 'he should have been more careful.' But he still did not alter his gaze.

Eric Kormann, who had lingered to look at a carving that had caught his interest, now caught up with Grupfelder.

'Say ... you two guys met yet?' boomed the affable American. 'You both being from Switzerland an' all, I mean. D'ya know each other – it bein' a small place?'

It was the first time that an opportunity had arisen for the two Swiss to introduce themselves to each other. Kormann spoke in his native Swiss-German and extended his hand. The other man turned his gaze to look at him and, with a curt almost imperceptible nod of the head, replied.

'Benschedler,' he said in German. 'No, we have not met and I do not know you.' He got up abruptly, turned his disdainful gaze from the diminutive Swiss to the hulking American, and walked away towards the landing and the waiting launches.

'Well, what was that he said?' asked the American, as Kormann stood staring after the rapidly receding figure, but he received no reply. His face was etched with deep lines of heavy concentration. There was something about that name that had not yet resolved itself in his struggling memory.

Some thirty minutes later, after everyone had once again negotiated the bobbing gunwales, the two launches pushed away from the landing and started their journey back to the mainland. As they did so, Stephen and the chief archaeologist stood on the wall, above the landing, and watched them go.

'You get them back to *Khufu*,' Stephen had whispered, as Rupert was about to clamber into the second launch. 'I'll wait here for the police and then there's something I have to do ... Tell me what you found out when I see you later. All right?'

38

Aswan

On Board Khufu – Late Evening, Friday 3rd August 1928

It was shortly before midnight when Rupert heard a soft, repeated rapping on his cabin door.

'Where have you been?' he asked, as he looked through the open door and saw Stephen standing in the passageway. Silhouetted against the subdued glow of the night-lights beyond the cabin door, the doctor gave the appearance of a carved statue. 'Come in ... come in,' said Rupert, taking his friend by the shoulder and guiding him into the cabin. 'Are you all right? I've been worried...'

Stephen looked tired, his drawn features set into a seriousness that foretold of important news to come.

'I'm fine, thanks, old chap,' he said, smiling wearily, 'just absolutely exhausted!'

He was still dressed in the clothes he had been wearing when Rupert had last seen him that afternoon, standing on the wall above the landing steps on Philae Island.

'Things really are out of control, I'm afraid,' continued Stephen, as he sank wearily down into the cabin's single chair. 'I've been to the hospital.'

Rupert had caught the waft of a clean, antiseptic smell as he opened the cabin door. Now he was even more aware of it, as the cabin filled with the comforting, not unpleasant odour.

'The hospital?' echoed Rupert, suddenly alarmed, 'Why? Are you hurt?'

'Don't carry on so, old chap,' said Stephen, smiling in appreciation of his friend's genuine concern. 'It wasn't me who needed the medical attention...'

At his friend's stark and sudden revelation, Rupert's face had clouded with the suddenness of a tropical storm; now, with the relief of his friend's last remark, it cleared as quickly as it had formed.

'I'm fine,' confirmed Stephen, holding up his left hand in a kind of benediction, 'which is considerably more than can be said for friend Printon – whom I can now definitely confirm was *not* our man Printon of the passport!'

'Oh?' said Rupert, settling himself on the bed, opposite the doctor. 'Well ... tell me ... what happened then? We suspected that, but how do you know for sure?'

'I say, old man, you haven't by any chance got a snifter, have you? I could do with something a little more powerful than a glass of boiled water...'

'Er ... yes ... I've got some brandy. It's in the desk drawer over there. Just a couple of shots in a hip flask, I'm afraid. I'll get it for you,' he added, as he crossed to the small writing desk that stood against the cabin wall. 'Have you eaten anything?' he asked, as he did so.

'No time,' replied Stephen.

'I've got a packet of Bath Olivers and an apple – oh ... and an orange from dinner. Any good?'

Fortified by half the contents of the hip flask and munching on the apple, Stephen looked earnestly at his friend.

'We are in very deep water, I'm afraid,' he said softly, as Rupert resumed his position sitting at the foot of the bed, opposite Stephen's chair. 'After you left, the police finally arrived in a motor launch. Quite late it was – must have been well past five. Anyway, they had a look around, took some notes and asked a lot of questions. Then they decided that it had been a bad accident and the Inspector in charge mentioned how foolish it had been to have climbed up to the top of the pylon in the first place – "not a place for tourists to go – far too dangerous", I think were his exact words.' Stephen's worn face relaxed into a smug smile. 'He nearly swallowed his swagger stick when I told him that the man had been murdered!' He chuckled. 'It took the wind right out of his pompous sails.'

'What on earth do you mean?' asked Rupert, totally mystified by what his friend had just told him.

'Friend Printon was dead long before he bounced his way back down to Mother Earth,' said Stephen, in a level voice that had now lost any trace of humour. 'He was killed by a single stab wound to the heart – neatly administered upwards, from underneath the rib cage – a very thin blade, too. A stiletto, I'd say – very neatly done. The wound was administered by someone who knew exactly what they were doing...'

'Killed? ... Stabbed?' asked Rupert incredulously.

'Keep your voice down, old chap,' motioned the doctor, through a mouthful of Bath Oliver biscuit. 'Without a doubt he was murdered,' continued the doctor. 'When I felt for a heartbeat, after he'd crashed to earth, I noticed what looked like a small, circular tear in the skin. It was the entry wound, but it was disguised by the surface bleeding caused by the body bouncing off the rough stone surfaces on the way down.'

'Did he meet someone at the top of the pylon and have an argument or a fight with them? We didn't hear any struggle ... or scream or anything like that?' whispered Rupert, sitting forward.

'Well, to answer your second point first, I would say that there was no noise, for the simple reason that death was instantaneous and quite unexpectedly sudden – the heart just stopped. That was why there was hardly any blood loss through the wound – the pump had been switched off. As for your first question – well, that's the easy one – yes he did and the fall to earth was to make a murder look like an accident.'

Rupert's puzzlement deepened.

'But how did you find out all of this?' he asked.

'That's why I'm back so late,' replied the doctor, turning his attention to the orange, which he had just started to peel. 'When they took the body to the mortuary in the hospital, I asked if I could assist at the post-mortem – just to make sure that I had things correct. I told them I was the official doctor from the tour and that my superiors in Cairo would need to know what had happened – I hope you don't mind, old chap, but I had to do some thinking on my feet. Anyway, I then showed them my little black bag, sprouted a lot of medical lingo and I was in. I'd have used the Cecil card, if I'd had to.'

'I see,' said Rupert, filled with growing admiration.

'Whilst I was at it and our man was on the slab, I also took the opportunity to look at the fingers,' continued Stephen, 'and – surprise, surprise – there was no evidence of any trauma whatsoever – the fingers were as complete as the day he was born ... and so were his teeth – no sign of any abscess or inflamed gums – nothing!'

'... Which definitely means that Printon wasn't Printon ...' added Rupert.

'... Which means that we almost certainly have a murderer amongst our number on *Khufu*,' corrected Stephen ominously. 'The worrying question is who? And, God help us, *why?*'

'Well, it certainly wasn't Lampton – he was in the court all the time – and he was right behind you when we all rushed over to the body...'

'Hmm...' muttered Stephen, as he tried to think clearly through his weariness, 'God, but I'm tired!' he said, stifling a yawn.

'So ... what do we do next?' asked Rupert, but the doctor had already moved the conversation forward.

'What did you find at Philae? Anything?'

'Oh ... yes, I did,' replied Rupert, his eyes shining with an excitement that reflected the doctor's tiredness in inverse measure. 'The staircase was there all right ... and the steps were covered in silt for most of the way up – odd bits of algae, too. It was very narrow and quite dark. The ceiling was very low, so low in fact that I could only just manage to stand up straight and I'm not that tall.'

It was Stephen's turn to sit forward, his fingers spattered with the sweet juice of the orange that he had almost finished eating. He kept his gaze firmly fixed on his friend's face.

'Go on,' he muttered.

'Oh ... and there was something I thought a bit odd,' continued Rupert. 'There were marks – parallel with each other – like tramlines' – he made a gesture to demonstrate what he had described – 'they went up the steps in the silt as far as I could see,' he continued. 'It looked as if something had been dragged up them...' Now it was Rupert's turn to sit and focus more intently as he spoke, envisioning the scene he had discovered on the island. 'And there were footprints, too,' he continued, 'two sets – they looked the same size and they were both facing down.'

'How do you mean, old chap, "both facing down"?'

'All four pointed to the edge of the step – as if someone was coming down the steps ... twice...'

'So, how did they get *up*, then?'

'I don't know – I said it was odd ... and the two sets of footprints were *inside* each other,' continued Rupert. 'One set right out against the walls – almost – and the other set placed normally – between them ... and walking over the tramline marks, too!'

Stephen's face had lit up considerably.

'Why do you think one of the pairs was so far apart?' he asked, but answered his own question before his friend could even attempt a response. 'Elementary, my dear Watson, it's because whomever the footprints belong to was dragging something heavy in front of them up the steps – backwards! Something heavy like a dead body perhaps?'

'So, you think that caused the tramline effect?' asked Rupert, for once at the same point in the hypothesis as his friend.

'What else could have left such marks?' replied the doctor. 'And the person who did the dragging *up* had to then come *down* – so that explains the second set of footprints, of the same size, and also the fact that they are walking over the earlier tramline marks.'

The doctor was suddenly fired by a charge of renewed energy.

'Printon's shoes were quite badly scuffed – on both heels – consistent, you might say, with being dragged up a flight of stairs. The leather had been badly scratched on the heels – and there was our all-to-familiar faint whiff of decay. The plot thickens, my dear fellow, as Sherlock would say!' He got up, wiping his fingers on his handkerchief as he did so. 'There's also something out there in the passageway which could be of considerable interest. I think you should take a look at it. Come on,' he said, crossing lithely to the cabin door.

They made their way carefully down the softly lit, deserted passageway. Lining it on both sides were several pairs of shoes, which had been placed outside their respective owners' cabin doors for cleaning.

'Look ... what would you say that is?' whispered Stephen softly, as he held one of the pairs of shoes up to the light and pointed to several blotches.

'Silt?' mouthed Rupert, after having studied the marks for a few seconds.

'Indeed, I would suggest it is silt. And, judging from the smell, I'd say these rather expensive shoes have very recently been in very close proximity to a touch of decaying algae,' Stephen whispered back.

He replaced the shoes, as carefully as he had picked them up, and they returned to Rupert's cabin.

'And who is the owner of those shoes in the second cabin on the port side?' asked Stephen, once he had silently closed the cabin door behind them. He stood in the middle of the floor, his eyebrows raised in patient expectation.

'Benschedler,' replied Rupert.

In his small cabin, behind the safety of the closed door, the realization that help was now desperately needed finally also dawned on Rupert. In the shadow of the room's lighting he suddenly looked older than his years.

'What are we going to do?'

'Nothing – just carry on as normal with our deadly pantomime and hope bloody fervently that the lid stays on the pot until that Major gets here first thing on Monday morning. What else can we do, for Christ's sake?'

Stephen sat down once again in the chair, but this time he was sitting forward, almost whispering to himself.

'Why do we now have the names of Printon and Benschedler, rather than those of Printon and Lampton in the same context, if not yet quite in the same sentence? Printon was definitely not who his passport said he was – we now know that for certain; Benschedler we can now place firmly at the scene of the crime and he's only been with us for five minutes! If we try anything – God knows what – we could start a panic and then...' he looked up at Rupert, 'and then, you tell me!... Anything can happen...'

He got up once again, rather stiffly, and crossed to the bed removing his jacket, tie and shirt as he did so. Sitting on the edge of the mattress, he removed his boots and then stood up, dropping his trousers to the floor. He removed his underwear and then sat down once again to remove his artificial limb.

'I'm going to have to go and see the police in the morning – I'll leave before first light, so as not to be seen. Tell Mohammed the bare minimum to keep him in the picture. He's a good sort and has the right to be as ready as we are for ... whatever.' Hopkins shrugged. 'You stay put safely here on *Khufu* until I get back. Then...' he stopped in mid-sentence, '...then ... well, to be honest, old chap, I haven't a bloody clue!'

His clothes were in a heap on the floor and he had already stretched out on the bed, lying on top of the covers.

'I think the time has come to play the Cecil card for all it's worth...' he said, but the rest of the sentence melted into the air, as his voice trailed off into the oblivion of sleep.

39

Aswan

Saturday, 4th August 1928

'What is it that is so urgent that you summon me from my house at such an early hour?' demanded the Chief of Police angrily down the line. He had not even had time for breakfast before the telephone rang.

'There is a gentleman to see you, Sir,' replied the Chief Inspector, in response to his superior's brusque enquiry. 'He has been here since before dawn … the duty sergeant at first suspected that he was a drunken European who had lost his way in the dark.'

There was a pause as the Chief Inspector waited for a response and the Chief of Police tried to concentrate his still sleepy mind.

'You phone me to tell me about a drunk?' he muttered.

'No, Sir. You misunderstand. The European was not drunk. He says he must speak to you urgently.'

'Really? You say that he has been at the station since before dawn?' repeated the senior officer, looking at his watch. It was just 5.47 a.m. In the heat, early starts were the routine, but dawn was a little *too* early. 'A European, you say,' he repeated, trying to make sense of what he was hearing.

'Indeed, Sir. He is most insistent that he speak to the most senior officer in charge. I asked him what the nature of his business is, but he refused to tell me.'

Perhaps this is something to do with the Chief Commissioner, thought the Chief of Police, his head suddenly clearing as he remembered the telephone conversation he had received the previous day from the Chief Commissioner in Cairo, in which he had been advised to meet a certain Major Ashdown off the government steamer from Wadi Haifa in three days time on the 6th of August. He was to be offered every assistance as it was a matter of national security.

'Very well, Ishmail, send the car for me.'

Half an hour later the Chief of Police was seated behind the desk in his office when his Chief Inspector ushered in the European.

'It is a Mr Hopkins, Sir,' he announced, 'from London,' he added as an after-thought, wondering if the mention of London would give added gravitas to his introduction.

'I am the Chief of Police. You wish to see me? Please ... do take a seat.'

His visitor, although smartly dressed, looked somewhat the worse for lack of sleep. There were lines etched into his face.

Such deep lines on the face of one so young, observed the Chief of Police as he resumed his seat. 'What can I do for you Mr...'

'Hopkins,' said the visitor.

Stephen rapidly recounted the series of events that had so recently befallen *Khufu* and continued by voicing his serious concerns for their safety.

'The most recent incident was just yesterday afternoon, on Philae Island. A member of our party was murdered. I am a medical doctor and I can confirm that this death was disguised to look like an accident. I accompanied the body to the hospital and assisted at the post-mortem and it was very definitely a case of murder,' he concluded, a look of relief spreading across his face at having finally involved the forces of law and order.

The Chief of Police raised his eyebrows as he looked at his visitor with some surprise. A thought had suddenly flashed into his head. Was this man connected with the mysterious Major Ashdown in some way?

'There has not been time to write up a report, but I will do so and have it on your desk as soon as possible,' continued Stephen. 'This series of what I have called "suspicious events" might possibly be linked to this disguised murder. Of course, I could just be imagining the whole thing – except for yesterday's murder ... that was real enough.'

'This is all very interesting, Mr Hopkins, but from what you have told me everything could be a simple chain of coincidences. Do you have any real proof, or do you have only conjecture and theories?'

'The murder victim was an impostor and he was travelling on someone else's passport ... someone who, the medical evidence has confirmed, he most definitely was not ... I am absolutely certain about this.' Stephen Hopkins suddenly looked very drawn and tired. '... But, as I have said, I have no concrete proof as to how the theories I have concerning yesterday's murder on Philae Island interconnect with any of the other events of the past few days. All I have is suspicion...'

Despite his obvious tiredness, Hopkins kept talking rapidly. The Chief of Police had no chance of making any comment.

'I have a persistent nagging in my stomach that everyone aboard *Khufu* is in increasing danger. I feel totally out of my depth and am thoroughly confused. I'm a doctor, not a trained policeman!'

At first, the Chief of Police had wondered if this man was attempting some sort of a prank – a practical joke or hoax. Such things had been known to happen in the past, particularly when a visiting European thought he was far more intelligent than the local Egyptian Police. Perhaps what this man was telling him was the over-imaginative rambling of a hyper-active European mind – an imagination sent into an out-of-control spin by prolonged exposure to the sun – just like the hazy, shimmering images of a mirage. But this particular European, although quite tanned, was in no way badly sunburned, nor was he rambling. He was quite the opposite in fact. It was abundantly clear to the Chief of Police that this fully coherent young visitor was in deadly earnest.

'I need you to send a message to the Embassy in Cairo. Address it to Cecil. Tell them who I am and what I've just told you. Then ask them for instructions,' said his visitor in a voice of considerable gravity. 'I say, please forgive my bluntness, but do you think I could have of a cup of tea while we are waiting?'

'Of course,' concurred the Chief of Police, 'I will arrange for some refreshments to be sent through, while I send the telegram.'

Unbeknown to his visitor, the Chief also telegraphed his superiors to ask if he should take his visitor seriously or not. Despite the conversation with the Chief Commissioner the previous day, he thought it best to double check before acting. In the political atmosphere of Egypt, since the British had partially relinquished internal control, he could not be too careful when it came to matters at the highest level.

No sooner had the telegrams been despatched, than the replies were received. The prompt, somewhat curt answers left the Chief of Police in no doubt whatsoever that this Mr Hopkins must be taken seriously – very seriously, indeed.

'There is a Major Ashdown due to arrive here in Aswan from Wadi Haifa – the day after tomorrow,' said Stephen.

'So Cairo has informed me,' came the reply.

The policeman was now looking at his visitor with new-found respect.

Who are you and how high up does your influence go, thought the Chief, who suddenly realized that his visitor had not produced any identification.

The earnestness with which the young man had presented his case had knocked the thought of asking him to prove who he was right out of the policeman's head.

And how do you know about this Major Ashdown? His is a name which I heard for the first time barely twenty-four hours ago. 'I am to meet the Major and offer him every assistance. I assume that he will wish to be taken straight to you on board *Khufu* as soon as he arrives in Aswan?'

'Yes, as soon as possible, but with the bare minimum of fuss,' replied Stephen, looking at him in deadly earnest. 'I do not need to remind you of the seriousness of what we could be facing. At the very least we have a murderer in our midst. I had my suspicions about Printon, but it seems that I was mistaken. Was Printon a victim of the real murderer? Why? Is there a second killer amongst us…' He broke off and stared at the Chief of Police. He had also started to perspire. 'This whole business is just not cricket and is now out of control and I have no idea what to do next! The killing on Philae took everyone by surprise. The killer might not hesitate to strike again, if provoked … but provoked by what? There must be other factors in all of this about which I have no idea, nor would I even know where to start looking for answers … not that I have any wish to involve us further than we already seem to be.'

The Chief of Police nodded in agreement.

'Please calm yourself, Mr Hopkins,' he said, 'you are in the safest of places here in Aswan and you have the police to assist you. We will do all we can, but we must proceed with the utmost caution.'

Stephen Hopkins did not find the other man's remarks particularly reassuring. He felt totally helpless when faced with the unresolved riddle of their predicament and he felt powerless to do anything when he thought of Rupert back on board *Khufu*.

I think it best that I keep what muddled suspicions I still have to myself until this Major arrives, thought Stephen, as the Chief of Police smiled at him.

For a split second, and for reasons he could not fathom, behind his smile the Chief of Police wondered if there could possibly be a connection to diamond smuggling. It had been an on-going problem over the previous couple of years. For centuries Aswan had been regarded as the gateway to Upper Egypt for both honest traders and those of less legitimate pursuits. The river was a very convenient and often anonymous highway to the distant Mediterranean. On reflection, however, the Chief thought it unlikely, as this tour group had been going in the wrong direction when these alleged incidents had occurred. Neither did this young man, his face a picture of sincere earnestness, present any of the tell-tale characteristics of a person who was less than totally honest. No, the Chief thought to himself, there were no diamonds involved in this one. It was more likely to be a theft, or possibly some sort of love-triangle. In his experience, the Europeans had a knack of getting themselves involved in amorous affairs on the river, sometimes with dire consequences.

'The last thing we want is panic. Too much can disappear or go unpunished under the cover of panic,' said his visitor, 'and God knows we've come a little too close for comfort to that in the past few days.'

The Chief of Police sat and stared at his visitor for a few seconds, before he continued.

'As you can see, the orders I have received in reply to my enquiry about you are very clear. You are to keep everyone together on the boat – including your murderer – until this Major arrives. Then he will take charge of the situation...' – he looked again at his young visitor – '... That is what your Cecil has said.'

Stephen smiled, feeling a little easier at the thought that the police would now be on hand. But it was not quite a smile of relief – not yet.

'Is there any way we could use the murder as a smokescreen? There are only two others besides yourself who know that the Philae Island incident was murder and not an accident. Is it possible to announce that it *was* an accident and that you have to carry out police enquiries? It would be an excuse to keep *Khufu* here in Aswan for a couple of days – just until this Major arrives?' he asked.

The Chief of Police studied the tired features opposite him. *Despite the restrained signs of helplessness that I have twice seen flash across his face, this young man is far cleverer than I first assumed.*

'It might be possible,' replied the policeman slowly, formulating a plan as he spoke. The responses from Cairo left him in very little doubt that what this man said had to be taken at face value and very seriously. 'We can draw out the bureaucratic side of things – you know, paperwork and the like,' he said, 'but I'm not sure even that will buy you the time you need. Anything beyond, say, midday tomorrow is going to be difficult, without arousing suspicion.'

Stephen looked concerned, his brow furrowed. He had been about to ask if the legendary Egyptian incompetence could be used as a tool to buy more time, but stopped the thought in its tracks when he remembered that the Governor-General in Khartoum had told him that this man was part-Egyptian, although he didn't look like it.

'Do you have any other suggestions – to keep things together until this Major arrives?' asked Stephen, 'I hope to God he knows what he's doing,' he added in a muttered undertone.

'You could always use the river,' said the Chief enigmatically.

FATAL TEARS

'How do you mean, "use the river"?' asked Stephen, looking nonplussed at the policeman.

'When whatever excuse I can come up with to keep you here starts to wear thin, just cast off and use the river as a natural boundary ... to keep everyone together on board. Take them up the river and show them the dam – they won't be able to get that close to it and they won't be able to see all that much, but your *reis* will know how far he can safely take your ship. It is one way of filling in a couple of hours ... What is your next port of call?'

'Kom Ombo – early morning – or whenever we get there,' replied Stephen, his voice once again tinged with the gloom of frustrated insecurity. He reminded himself, yet again, that he was neither a policeman nor a secret agent. For a split second, and not for the first time over the past few days, he mentally and a little unfairly harangued his Uncle for getting him into this predicament in the first place.

'So ... I can keep you here until midday tomorrow – that is feasible, I think. Then, set off and visit the dam as an extra excursion. Afterwards, sail off down the river to Kom Ombo, as planned, but then order your *reis* to backtrack during the early hours – well before dawn. Retrace your route when everyone is asleep – almost back here, to Aswan – they'll be none the wiser.'

Stephen's mood brightened somewhat, as the Chief continued to outline his suggestion.

'I see,' said Stephen, the light of understanding beginning to race across his face, like a hungry bushfire. 'And Major Ashdown ... when and how will he reach us?'

'The government steamer docks first thing on Monday morning – you should remember the earliness of the hour from your recent return from Abu Simbel.'

Stephen nodded.

'I'll have a special train drawn up and waiting, with some

of my men and horses. Major Ashdown can go up the line to Kom Ombo with them. Let me show you.'

The policeman got up and crossed his office to where a large scale map of Upper Egypt hung on the wall. 'Here is the railway line,' he said, following the black line as it snaked alongside the Nile. Stephen turned in his chair and followed the man's finger. 'The line is very close to the river here, before it reaches Kom Ombo station, here. If my men and the Major get off there, they can cross the desert and meet up with you here,' he concluded, tapping the dot where Kom Ombo lay. 'At least that part of it is still open and, with the service suspended at the moment, the driver can break all the speed limits.' He paused, looking straight at his visitor, the faintest curl of a smile around the corner of his mouth. 'We just have to hope that there isn't another accident en route.'

He returned to his desk, the curl of his mouth broadening into a full smile, as if to indicate that his plan was a good one and that nothing could be easier.

'And you are really convinced that this plan will work?' asked Stephen.

'Let me say that I think it is your only option,' replied the Chief of Police, his smile now replaced with a sternness that left no doubt in Stephen's mind that he had understood the seriousness of the situation perfectly.

'If your *reis* can double-back up the river to just below Aswan by dawn on Monday, the same day Major Ashdown arrives, you will have a morning's sailing in front of you before you reach Kom Ombo. That should give the Major enough time to reach you with my men, who are all first-class shots.'

That was the plan they both agreed upon. To a large extent, they were both feeling their way. The policeman, in spite of not really being a part of the events which had now enfolded him, had years of service that instinctively told him to simply follow his orders; orders which, in this instance and at face value, were somewhat mystifying. His visitor, although obviously connected to the highest levels, was hopelessly out of his depth and was now solely reliant, both for survival and for the next step forward, on help from an unknown major travelling down the Nile on a steamer.

40

Aswan

Dawn, Monday, 6th August 1928

The tall shape of the little steamer loomed up out of the pre-dawn river mist, like a white-clothed priestess at the Temple of Isis. This surreal picture, so skilfully yet so naturally created, was suddenly shattered by the sharp repeated clang of the engine-room telegraph. The noise sliced through the chilled air like the sound of a number of sistra, jingling the praises of the goddess. The ship gradually swung around, through the diaphanous clouds rising from the flat surface of the water, until the steel hull was parallel with the little jetty. *Nubia* announced the end of her journey by gently bumping against it.

No sooner had the steamer docked than Major Jeremy Ashdown, his single suitcase in his hand, disembarked down the narrow gangplank. He was met by uniformed officers, who had been sent by the Chief of Police to await his arrival.

'Major Ashdown?' asked the senior officer.

'Yes,' replied the Major, as his suitcase was carried for him towards the waiting police vehicle.

'We have a short ride to Headquarters, Sir,' continued the officer, 'after which, the Chief of Police wishes to speak to you. He is waiting.'

Ashdown had not failed to notice that the little party of policemen had succeeded in clearing a wide thoroughfare through the locals who had gathered on the quayside. They had not done so by show of force, but rather simply by their very presence. Very few people in Egypt relished dealings with the police and so preferred to keep their distance. As the mist on the river began to dissipate before the growing warmth of the rising sun, so it seemed that most of the locals who had filled the decks of *Nubia* a short while before had also disembarked and evaporated into the morning air.

Despite the early hour, the noisy ride through the early-morning Aswan traffic at times resembled more a drive across a dodgem track than a progress along well-made main roads. Ashdown had been promptly deposited outside Police Headquarters and was now seated opposite the Chief of Police's desk.

'... So it was thought best to keep everyone together and on the water,' said the Chief. 'Mr Hopkins and I discussed this plan in some detail. I presume that you know about the paddle steamer *Khufu* and the group of tourists she carries? They seem to be unintentional participants in this affair, but I do not think they are aware of either your quarry – this Benschedler – or the danger they could well be facing, except for Mr Hopkins, of course. We thought it best to keep things that way, until you arrived and could take charge of the situation.'

Ashdown nodded. The Chief of Police sounded capable and seemed to have things under control – at least for the moment.

'Yes, I am aware of all of this, thank you. I have been kept informed of Mr Hopkins, too. What is the background to this murder you mentioned – on Philae Island? And this Sebastian Printon ... what do you know about him?'

Probably far less than you do, I would think, thought the Chief of Police, but he did his best to pass on what Stephen had told him about the man. 'If Mr Hopkins has succeeded in implementing the delaying tactics we discussed, they should now be only just beyond the bend in the river, out of sight of Aswan and just starting their journey to Kom Ombo. They will go slowly and even allowing for the current they should not reach there much before midday.'

The Chief of Police had quickly formed the opinion that this young major was very efficient and would not tolerate fools lightly. For Ashdown's part, he was pleased that for a change he had not had to rely on the by now very crumpled letter of authority which had been his passport across Africa. Unbeknown to Ashdown, the mysterious Cecil had taken care of any official sanctioning of the task long before he had even arrived in Aswan.

The Major listened carefully as the Chief of Police outlined his plan for using the clear railway line to Kom Ombo. As he spoke he glanced down at his watch. Time was moving quickly on.

'The train is prepared and I have several of my men ready to leave with you immediately – they have horses, which you will need if you are to get from the railway line to the riverbank and the temple ruins. Can you ride, Major?'

'Yes. I am also armed. A necessity, I am afraid, as I really cannot foresee any other likely outcome, given the nature of things.'

'My men are also armed and are all excellent shots – they have been very well trained. I have instructed them to follow your orders, without question. The officer in charge is very reliable and speaks good English. His name is Hussein. Direct your orders to him and he will make sure they are instantly obeyed.'

Outside the building the new day was now well under way, all traces of hidden mystery offered by the ghostlike mists now gone from the river.

'I will inform Cairo that you have arrived and have

departed again,' said the policeman, smiling, as he rose to escort Ashdown to the railway station. 'I myself will escort you to the train. We have had to close the line between Aswan and Luxor – an unfortunate derailment – so you will have a completely clear track to Kom Ombo and speed limits will not apply,' he continued. 'You should reach the rail-head within a couple of hours. Your ride from there to the river at Kom Ombo should be a relatively easy one.' There was a pause, as he straightened his uniform cap on his head, '*insha'Allah*,' he added.

Within thirty minutes Ashdown's special train had cleared the metropolis of Aswan and had accelerated to an almost dizzying velocity, the staccato clicking of the points sounding like a machine gun that drowned out the neighing of the horses. They were securely lashed to the walls of the single goods truck by their halters. The single truck, together with the speeding engine, made up the train.

At about the same time that the engine was belching a thick black line of smoke across the tracks, *Khufu* had resumed her interrupted voyage to Kom Ombo. The little ship was some twenty miles downstream from Aswan. During the night, following Mohammed's instructions, *reis* Tarek had turned the paddle steamer around and doubled-back up the river almost to Aswan. It was a manoeuvre that passed totally unnoticed by everyone except those who were expecting it: Stephen, Rupert and Mohammed. Now, with the sun having risen over the hills that framed the banks of the Nile, Tarek had resumed their course for Kom Ombo as if nothing had happened.

Had the religion of ancient Egypt still been alive the god Khnum would have been busy that night, casting the fates of the passengers on his potter's wheel. Indeed, *reis* Tarek, the passengers on the little white ship and the occupants of the hurtling, violently swaying railway carriage, were all following a preordained course that would, within the next few hours, bring them all close to the *fatal tears*.

41

Kom Ombo

Temple of Sobek-Haroeris – Monday, 6th August 1928

Khufu reached the narrow wooden jetty that jutted out into the river at Kom Ombo just before noon. Mohammed had been asked to tell Daoud to prolong the docking procedure for as long as he possibly could, without making it look obvious in any way that he was playing for time.

On the upper deck the tourists had gathered under the shade of the canvas awnings to watch the ruins of the double-temple complex materialize out of the yellow desert sand that surrounded and, in some places, still buried parts of it.

'It certainly is hot today,' said Richard Lampton, his shirt already marked with traces of perspiration, 'but there doesn't seem to be any heat haze.'

'It is a little different from what we have become used to, isn't it?' said Rupert, who was trying not to let the nervousness he had started to feel show through his voice. Stephen had told him to act normally and not to let anyone know that they were sitting on a potential powder keg. That was something Rupert was finding easier said than done. 'That's because of the river – even though we may be feeling the heat, it would be far worse up there in the ruins, if they were not so close to the water.'

He tried to present his usual tourist guide façade, which

was what his flock had become accustomed to. In reality, his mind was full of other far more important and desperate things than a pile of ancient ruins. He stared out over the railings at the row of massive pillars that held up the carved lintels over the double entrance to the ruin. Each bore the protecting symbol of the sun disc.

'You'll find that there is usually a slight breeze here,' he continued, 'so it should be much cooler for us to move around when we get on the shore. However, that will not remove the threat of dehydration. I want you all to remember that you must still drink plenty of water, just to be safe.' *God that sounded pompous! And you're rambling*, he admonished himself. *Don't let things get to you ... just stay calm!*

'It certainly is a majestic ruin,' said Kormann, who had just finished cleaning his spectacles with his handkerchief and was now busy replacing them on his nose. 'You mentioned earlier, something about it being unique because it is a double temple...' He left the sentence unfinished, inviting Rupert's explanation.

'Yes, indeed. It is very unusual actually. It's unique because it *is* two separate temples joined down the middle. It is also dedicated to two separate gods. It's not the usual thing, where you sometimes get one temple dedicated to several gods.'

'Ah ... thank you,' replied the little Swiss.

'I think we should start to gather in the lounge, everyone, so that I can tell you more about the complex before we go ashore.'

'Do we have to?' whined Mrs Kirby, who was sitting on her own towards the stern, her sunglasses over her eyes and her sandaled feet resting on the middle bar of *Khufu*'s railings. 'There can't really be anything that different from any of the other "treasures" we've already seen, can there?' She did not turn to look at Rupert, but continued staring with unfocused eyes out over the desert, her vision blurred at a point somewhere above the top of the columns.

'As always, Mrs Kirby, you are entirely free to suit yourself,' replied Rupert, dryly.

'Oh good! Yes – I've always been free to suit myself...' she said, with an obvious touch of sarcasm in her voice.

'Would you excuse me for a moment, please, Mr Winfield,' twittered Miss Eggerton. 'I'll join you in the lounge. You won't start without me, will you?' she added, as she shuffled past him and down the steps to the lower decks.

Marjory Cuttle smiled after her. *That'll be all that orange juice at breakfast,* she thought to herself smugly. *I keep telling her not to drink too much.*

'Right then, everyone,' continued Rupert, who felt that he had postponed his pre-excursion talk for as long as he possibly could. 'Let's move off and gather in the lounge in, say...' – he glanced at his watch – '...fifteen minutes? That should allow enough time for anyone else who might need to attend to other things to...' But his voice trailed off. He had begun to ramble and stopped himself in mid-sentence. 'I'll meet you there, then,' he said, attempting a smile.

Simon Arling and his wife, both of whom had been standing at the rails watching the docking procedure, turned to walk off. Simon gave Rupert a smile, of sorts, but Esther said nothing, keeping her gaze lowered. Neither of them had been quite the same since the death at the Temple of Isis.

'In a quarter of an hour then, Rupert,' Simon said, as they walked off.

Within a few minutes Rupert found himself almost alone on the top deck. As far as he was concerned, Ruth Kirby could stay right where she was. In his mind's eye he would like to put her, the Manningtons, the ghastly Mrs Grassmere, and the icily aloof Benschedler into a sack and throw it over the side into the river. Whilst he allowed himself this brief moment of imagined enjoyment, he shielded his eyes with his hand as he scanned the sandy horizon for … rescue? He wasn't actually sure what he was hoping to see up there, above them, where the blue sky met the yellow sand.

'Ya lookin' for something there, Mr Winfield?'

The American's booming voice took Rupert by surprise.

'Er … no, not really,' he replied, trying to focus on a plausible answer, 'just looking at the savage grandeur of the setting. Deserted splendour, wouldn't you agree, Mr Grupfelder?'

'Like them deserted, wide open spaces back home,' he replied. ''Cept, a' course, we ain't got no ruined temples…' he laughed as he turned and walked off, following Kormann towards the nearby stairway.

As Rupert watched the big American's back disappear down through the opening in the deck he was suddenly aware of Stephen, who had climbed up to the deck by the forward stairway and was now standing next to him. He shot the doctor an anxious, slightly worried glance.

'Nothing up there yet,' he said, nodding his head in the direction of the horizon. 'Now what?' he continued, raising his eyebrows.

He suddenly remembered that Ruth Kirby was still sitting in her chair and motioned her presence to Stephen. Casually, following Stephen's indication, they moved further towards the bows to lean on the railings behind a tall, steel storage locker, where they were hidden from her view.

'Christ knows – I bloody well don't,' whispered the doctor, as he cast his anxious gaze along the deserted shore. 'This Major Ashdown is going to meet us here – today – now. And, hopefully, with some idea of what we are supposed to do next!' His voice was little more than a whisper. It was heavily laden with hope, but also tinged with something approaching desperation. 'That's what the Chief of Police in Aswan said – this Major and some of the Chief's men were going to rush up the line and then gallop across the desert to reach us here and then sort things out – and look, there's nothing except sand and a pile of ruins.'

Given the urgency of their predicament, neither of them had had the time to stop and think that they were standing in almost the exact same spot where, in less trying times and at the end of a day, they had enjoyed each other's company over a final cigarette before going down to either one of their cabins and...

'And what the hell are we supposed to expect, anyway?' continued Stephen. 'A squadron of Arabs mounted on camels being led to our rescue by Lawrence of Arabia with the good Major at his side...?'

For a moment there was nothing, save for the sound of the almost completed docking and the single, shrill jangles of the engine telegraph. The vibration of *Khufu*'s engines abruptly stopped.

Then the doctor suddenly chuckled at his own foolishness.

'Highly unlikely, I'd say. I doubt that the able and mysterious Major Ashdown can even *ride* a camel!'

Rupert also chuckled at this friend's remark, but never took his gaze from the still-empty horizon.

'Right. Let us be positive. Ashdown will be here ... eventually. In the meantime, there's nothing else for it, but to carry on,' said Stephen, standing upright from his leaning position. 'You keep them busy, old chap,' he said, 'the de luxe version with all the stops pulled out – descriptions of everything ... and you might also like to reveal the hidden significance of all the hieroglyphics ... Lay it on thick, even if you've got to make it up. None of them will be any the wiser.'

'Well, there are some very interesting hieroglyphics here, actually,' started Rupert, warming to his favourite subject, 'and some very interesting wall carvings...'

'That's the spirit – lay it on thick,' said the doctor, cutting across his friend's sentence. 'I've had a word with Mohammed – he's been a good stick, since we had to let him in on things.' He turned to Rupert and smiled briefly. For a change it was not a smile that was restricted by the urgency of the moment. 'He's going to get Daoud and some of his lads to go with us, up to the ruins. They'll make it look all quite normal – carry water and that sort of thing. At least we'll have some extra chaps around if we need them.'

'Do you think something might happen, then?' asked Rupert, turning to look at his friend with an expression of alarm.

'Oh, come on, dear boy! How the hell should I know, any more than you do?' replied Stephen, looking at his watch. 'Just gone twelve,' he said, 'time for you to start your lecture. Then, time for lunch, and then ... "Hey ho, says Rowley", as that old song goes,' he concluded, raising his eyebrows and shrugging his shoulders. 'Off you go, old chap. Remember, we're playing for time...'

'This is a ground plan of the Temple of Sobek-Haroeris, which we will shortly be visiting,' said Rupert, pointing to a large diagram which he had pinned to a wooden easel in the forward observation lounge. 'Actually, the Arabic word *kom* means a small mountain,' he continued, 'so that could explain the temple's position above the river. I'd like to point out a couple of things to you on this diagram.' He picked up a wooden pointer and half turned to the easel. 'As I said to Mr Kormann a little earlier, this site is really unique because it is two distinct temples combined into a single building complex. This right-hand side of the complex was dedicated to Sobek, the crocodile-headed divinity, who was the god of fertility and creator of the world. The left-hand side' – he made a sweeping gesture with his pointer – 'was dedicated to Haroeris, a manifestation of the falcon-headed Horus, son of Isis and Osiris and the solar war god.' He turned back to face his flock. 'Is there anyone here who isn't sure who Horus is...?'

Not a single hand was raised.

Oh yes. A likely story! thought Rupert, but he carried on.

'You have already seen his winged disc many times before, over all the entrance portals to most of the temples we have visited. He was believed to protect everything from all evil. If you look here, an imaginary line divides the building exactly in half – right down the centre. What we are going to look at was built by the Ptolemies, on the ruins of a much older temple. So in this temple Greece and Rome come face to face with the ancient beliefs of Egypt, as it were.'

Rupert continued giving his flock facts and figures and even showed them an engraving of what the site had looked like in the early part of the nineteenth century, when David Roberts had spent years travelling around the Egypt of the Ottoman Empire, sketching and painting the half-buried monuments he saw.

'The interesting thing is that you will be able to clearly see the remains of the bright colours with which the reliefs on the walls and columns would have been painted. We will also make a study of the wall carvings here ... and here,' he pointed again to specific points on his large diagram. 'There is a very interesting depiction of the medical instruments the ancients used – very similar to those we use today, actually.' He smiled out at his audience then turned back to the easel. 'And here, we'll see the system they had evolved to count things and how they applied it.'

Shortly before twelve thirty, Rupert had begun to fill in the time with totally unnecessary information, some of which repeated what had already been said. He was not very good at waffling, but he was learning very quickly how to do it convincingly.

'I hope that has prepared you for what is coming this afternoon,' he said, suddenly blanching at the hidden implication behind the words he had just used. 'I suggest we now have our light luncheon – Faisal tells me it is a finger buffet, so as not to sit too heavily whilst we are walking around the temple. Shall we gather in the entrance foyer at, say, one?'

As he had said this, he looked up to see Mohammed standing on the other side of the double doors that led into the lounge. The little Egyptian, his hands clasped behind his back, had shaken his head at Rupert and then, once again, disappeared down the corridor.

'Right you are,' repeated Rupert. 'One o'clock in the entrance foyer it is, then...'

At precisely the same time that Ruth Kirby had asked Rupert, rather belligerently, if she really did have to attend his talk, Ashdown's special train had slowed and then finally screeched to a halt, more or less parallel to the site of the temple. Ashdown had been impressed with the precision, speed and efficiency with which the side of the single railway truck had been opened, the ramp removed from inside and then attached and the horses carefully unloaded.

'We are ready, Sir,' said Hussein, a pleasant-mannered, light-skinned Egyptian from further up north in the Delta. 'We should set off in that direction,' he continued, studying his compass, 'and cross the sands in a line like this...' He drew his finger across the folded map, from where they thought they were, to the point marked 'Temple', next to the river.

'Good,' replied the Major. 'How long do you think it will take us?'

'With camels, perhaps two hours. With horses, it will be longer – possibly three. The sand is quite fine on the surface, but underneath it should be firmer,' he continued. 'It is fortunate that there is no sandstorm, *insha'Allah*,' he added, gazing up into the clear sky, searching for the tell-tale signs of the wind's activity, 'otherwise it would take longer.' He turned in his saddle to look at the Major.

Ashdown realized that Hussein had done this sort of thing before.

'Very well,' he replied, 'are your men clear about their instructions?'

'Yes Sir. I have told them that they are to wait for your orders. They do not need to be told more – they will obey.'

They had then set off at a fast gallop, their mounts coping easily with the sandy terrain, which was dotted here and there with rocky outcrops. They carried water and some desert rations – biscuits, dates and a little dried meat. Each was armed, bandoliers full of cartridges slung across their left shoulders. Slung across the other shoulder, each carried a Lee-Enfield. Left over from the war, the rifle by western standards was nearly obsolete, but here in Egypt it retained its position as a symbol of authority that only the very foolhardy dared argue with.

'We will follow the wadi,' called Hussein. 'It will lead us almost to the river … and the surface is better for the horses.'

As the wind rushed passed his face, Ashdown, dressed in a police uniform provided by the Chief of Police in Aswan began to remember the thrill and exhilaration of having a pulsating, muscular horse between his knees. He had been an outstanding rider in his youth, becoming almost part of the horse his mother had given him for his tenth birthday. He had not been interested in the social round of horse riding, having eschewed what he saw as the formalized artificiality of the gymkhana for long gallops across the family's land. He had practically become a modern-day centaur; rugged riding for a rugged people in a rugged landscape. He had almost forgotten the experience – until now.

By the time Rupert had brought his drawn-out pre-excursion lecture to a close and the tourists had assembled in the dining room for Faisal's finger luncheon, Major Jeremy Ashdown, Hussein and the police troopers had crossed almost a third of the distance from the railway line to the banks of the river.

42

Nuremberg

Hotel Deutscher Kaiser, Königstrasse – Mid-morning, Monday, 6th August 1928

The heat of far-off Kom Ombo, where the strands of several people's fate were being drawn ever closer together, was not shared in the miserably wet early autumn that had descended, unexpectedly, on a still-demoralized and largely unsettled Germany. Despite having been allowed to join the League of Nations and the noticeable improvements in the economy generally, there were still far too many citizens who were disgruntled with the government of the Weimar Republic. There were also many who resented the unavenged humiliation of the surrender in 1918 and the harsh terms of the Versailles Treaty that followed. They harboured bitter resentment over the huge war reparations levied by the victorious Allies on the ruins of the Kaiser's Empire. There were many who applauded Stresemann's strenuous efforts to revive Germany, but a great many more blamed the severity of the draconian measures imposed on the ruined country from Versailles for the near collapse of their entire economy a brief five years before. Resentment had mixed dangerously with humiliation and an increasing desire for revenge, creating a volatile environment.

In a well-decorated room of the Hotel Deutscher Kaiser, a small group of men sat around a highly polished wooden table. They saw themselves as a force for change within this tired and battered Germany. The surface of the large table was almost entirely covered by files and piles of neatly stacked papers.

'I can report that we have made excellent progress in putting your vision for a new Reich before the *Volk*,' said a slim, diminutive man with a rather high-pitched voice. 'We now have well over one hundred thousand members in the Party,' he announced, his eyes gleaming, 'an increase of nearly ninety thousand over the last three years. We can expect revenue from membership to increase proportionately, as we continue to expand and build our support.'

'But it is still not really enough. That is the problem, is it not?' asked a dapper, well-built man of average height, who sat opposite the first speaker. He dipped into a bowl of sugared almonds that stood tucked between the papers he had in front of him. 'It is all very well to sit here and plan this membership increase of yours, Joseph, but is it going to be enough? We are not in a position to dictate to the *Volk* yet, and our methods of *gentle* persuasion cost money – a great deal of it. And where do you envisage this money coming from in sufficient quantities to enable us to buy our way into respectable power?'

You would know all about spending money, Hermann, thought the first speaker. *Just how much did you spend on that suit, for a start?* he mused, but said nothing. His own style of dress was far more modest.

'What news of The Phoenix?' demanded a voice from the head of the table. 'Heinrich, where are the stones? When can we expect them?' he asked, turning to face the man with round spectacles and receding hairline who was sitting on his left. As he spoke, he slouched down lower in his chair, his head resting on his hand, his index finger moving nervously along the bottom of his little moustache.

He was fidgety and on edge, which was a bad sign. He waited expectantly for the reply.

'Our latest communication from Cairo informs us that they have left Aswan and should be in Cairo within the week,' said the balding man, in a stilted, almost intimidated way, as if he was reading a report on the radio. 'The Phoenix has been met by our agent and things progress satisfactorily. Perhaps another fortnight after they reach Cairo...'

The man at the head of the table grunted.

'Then we must tell our people in Rotterdam to prepare to receive them,' he said.

A silence descended over the table, as the man at the head sat thinking whilst stroking his little moustache. Suddenly, he turned to the man who had first spoken.

'The Party Day Rally you mentioned, Joseph – for this time next year...' He moved a small pile of papers and opened a folder. On the front cover it bore an eagle, clutching a swastika in its claws.

'As you are aware, *mein Führer*, the moving picture we produced at last year's rally, the "Day of Awakening", has proved to be very successful in drawing new members to our cause. It was very well worth the expense...'

'... Which was quite considerable, as I recall,' said Hermann, popping two more sugared almonds into his mouth.

'Yes, it *was* very expensive, but well worth the effort, as I have said. We need to plan for next year's rally and moving picture,' Joseph continued, a little testily. 'What The Phoenix brings us will be put to very good use – as always,' he added, throwing a frosty glare across the table at Hermann. *Why did this man always have to make a comment? Interruptions like that were always irritating!*

Another silence descended over the little group, the fermenting spark of antagonism between some of them almost palpable in the stillness, which was broken only by the rustling of the occasional sheet of paper.

'We have the backing of many in the army, too,' said the man with the moustache, slamming shut the file in front of him. 'But we are going to have to extend our support to the barons of what is left of German industry,' he said, 'they are the ones with the money we need. Until we can simply take it off them, we have to be seen to be acting correctly, for the greater good of the Fatherland. When we control the Reichstag, we will be able to do as we please, but, until then, we need to move swiftly, firmly and carefully.'

He had become quite animated during his speaking, and a silence had descended over the table, as the others listened in rapt attention. Even Hermann had stopped rattling the sugared almonds around his teeth.

'When the time is right we will deal with the dissenters – those who stupidly did not support us – and the Jews. You, Ernst, you will deal with the dissenters. You and Heinrich – you will work together to deal with the dissenters – and then the Jews. There will be no room for dissenters and Jews in the Reich – in any of the lands of the Reich...'

He had started to ramble, which was not a good sign. Heinrich turned a frosty gaze on Ernst, who ignored him completely, keeping his gaze on the man at the head of the table.

Work together? thought Heinrich, sourly, *I think not. You are already too big for your boots and any quality boot can only have a single foot in it at any one time. My time will come and yours will go – and sooner rather than later.*

'Joseph, what are your further ideas for convincing the *Volk* that we are the only power they should trust...' Adolf stared long and hard at the little man, plainly dressed, who sat behind several piles of folders and papers. The others, too, turned and looked, waiting expectantly for what he had to say.

'*Mein Führer,*' began Joseph, a smile creasing his face, his somewhat overlarge mouth opening and closing in clipped, precise movements, 'the essence and meaning of propaganda must always be carefully considered. The purpose is to convince people – to win people over to an idea or a concept that is so vital – a living, expanding entity – which, they believe, they cannot exist without.'

Seated at the head of the table, Adolf stared hard at the shorter man, who had just addressed him in reverential terms as his *Führer*. Yes, it *was* his destiny to become *Führer* and save the *Volk*, and surely so demoralized a *Volk* would not take *that* much convincing. As he sat, thinking, his index finger again moved along the bottom of his little moustache, in the familiar gesture of deep contemplation. In the silence which suddenly enveloped them all, Heinrich removed his spectacles and set about cleaning them. Hermann popped another handful of almonds into his mouth, all the time focusing on the short, plainly dressed man. Joseph ignored him completely, waited for a few seconds, and then continued.

'In the end, when we have captured their very souls, they will have been won over completely to the ideology of the Party – *your* ideology and *your* Party, *mein Führer*. They will succumb totally, and never want to free themselves from an ideology they will have found so comforting and essential to their very existence. It must become as if we own and manipulate their very minds. That is what we must aim for...' he added, smirking at Hermann's much larger form, as if inviting some further comment.

'And for that, my dear Joseph, we need money...' replied Hermann, '...as you are always telling us.'

'Yes – and for that, we need a *great deal* of money...' repeated Joseph.

43

Kom Ombo

Temple of Sobek-Haroeris – Early Afternoon, Monday, 6th August 1928

There was still no sign of any rescue appearing over the crest of the nearby sand dunes. The tourists had disembarked and had been assembled on the jetty. After yet another time-wasting reminder to ensure that they all had sufficient water, adequate protection against the sun and, in a moment of genius, or so Rupert thought, their cameras, they were formed into the by-now-familiar straggling crocodile. Then they were guided up the incline to the ruins of the temple.

'Do you not call a line of children at kindergarten, a "crocodile"?' asked Kormann, as the loosely bunched flock meandered its way up the slope, like a small line of coloured ants.

'We do,' answered Rupert.

'Then it is, perhaps, most appropriate that we should be walking in a "crocodile" to the Temple of Sobek – the crocodile-headed god,' said the little Swiss in perfect seriousness.

Grupfelder burst into a hearty peal of laughter and clapped him on the back, but the reason for either of these actions was not at all clear to the little Swiss – after all, had he not simply stated a fact? Where was the humour in that?

'Crocodiles were a manifestation of the darker side of things,' said Rupert. 'Remember, the ancients always tried to keep things in balance, so, even if they were afraid of something – like a crocodile, for instance – they would still allocate it a place in their religious hierarchy. In Eastern philosophies, I believe they call that sort of thing *yin* and *yang*.'

They had almost reached the top of the incline and had drawn level with the first outlying remains of the complex.

'In fact, Mr Kormann, this building over here, which is quite well preserved, as you can see...' – he indicated a small, square, squat building – '...is called the Hathor Chapel. She was goddess of joy, love, fertility and music and, as if that wasn't enough, she was also thought of as the mother of the reigning pharaoh. Naturally, that was in a heavenly context.'

Rupert noticed that his mention of *love* and *fertility* had not produced the anticipated response from Esther Arling, who simply stood next to her husband, hidden behind her sunglasses.

'Hathor's Chapel, this is where the sacred crocodiles were kept, after they had been mummified,' continued Rupert, 'because she was also thought of as the mother of Horus – together with Isis.'

'How extraordinarily confusing,' said Susan Lampton, 'one god, two mothers? And why did they go to so much trouble over something as ugly and dangerous as a crocodile?'

'To the ancient Egyptians it was the *spirit* of the god that was important, not so much what they looked like. That's why the same deity crops up in all sorts of different manifestations, depending on where you are along the course of the Nile.'

Rupert was warming to his subject, but still cast the occasional glance both to Stephen, who was bringing up the rear of the column, and up over the temple walls, towards the nearby sandy ridge. The ridge still stood devoid of any human presence.

In front of Stephen, Marjory Cuttle leaned in close to Rebecca Eggerton.

'Have you noticed that we seem to have been joined by several of the crew?' she asked out of the corner of her mouth. 'Why do you suppose that could be? I don't remember it ever happening before – do you?'

Eggerton turned to look at Daoud and the rest of the crewmen, who had been instructed by Mohammed to walk with the Europeans, but not to get in the way.

'Perhaps it's to carry something – or maybe to bring us water?' she replied.

'Carry what? Look at them – they're not actually carrying anything, as far as I can see. And *water*? Well, we're only a hop and a skip away from the ship here – not like Esna or the Philae place we visited.'

Whilst Rebecca Eggerton had been looking at the crewmen and pondering what Cuttle had said, she had not been looking where she was going. Suddenly she collided with the back of Colonel Ponsworthy, who was walking immediately in front of her. She lost her balance in the process.

'Oh ... I say ... I'm most dreadfully sorry about that ...' she spluttered, more out of sudden surprise than good manners, as she involuntarily reached out with both hands to steady herself.

'Don't mention it, dear lady,' replied Colonel Ponsworthy, half-turning and clutching her, as she almost fell past him. 'No harm done, I assure you,' he said, steadying her back to the vertical position and releasing her arms.

'Oh, thank you ... how kind ... I am most sorry ... How clumsy of me ...' twittered Miss Eggerton, as she flushed profusely. She was not used to being the centre of attention – even if it was only for a few brief seconds.

Ponsworthy smiled, raised the Panama hat he had decided

to wear that afternoon rather than his usual heavier topee, replaced it on his head and strode on up the incline. He passed the Hathor Chapel and joined the front of the column, which had reached the dual-entrance portals of the complex.

'I say ... oh, how embarrassing ... the poor man...' mumbled Miss Eggerton, putting her hand to her flushed cheek.

'What on earth are you mumbling about, dear?' asked Marjory Cuttle, who had not had time to play any part in Eggerton's rescue.

'Colonel Ponsworthy,' she whispered. 'He must have some sort of medical device, poor man,' she whispered, her hand nearly covering her mouth.

'What?' snapped Cuttle, turning to look at her friend.

'When I thought that I was going to fall ... after I bumped into him ... under his jacket ... I felt straps going across his back and there was a big bulge of something under his arm. I hope I haven't damaged anything ... in reaching out like that, I mean,' she continued, almost mumbling to herself.

'Stuff and nonsense, my dear,' snorted Marjory Cuttle. 'There's nothing wrong with him that a couple of stiff *chota pegs* wouldn't fix!'

'But I felt...'

'Probably a pair of braces and his shirt ruffled up under the jacket, and nothing else. Perhaps we should get you out of this Egyptian sun, my dear, before something *really* serious goes wrong with you!'

Cuttle chortled in her whinnying way and smiled at her companion, giving her a reassuring pat on the shoulder. Eggerton was not at all sure what to make of things; she was not really convinced that what she had felt had been simply the gathered folds of the Colonel's shirt fabric.

Over the following half-hour, under Rupert's guidance,

the tourists made their way through the temple complex. By now they were reasonably familiar with the layout and purpose of an Egyptian temple, but Rupert, in the interests of playing for time, had reminded them all once again. Daoud, following a whispered conversation with Stephen, had told his men to spread themselves out around the perimeter of the group of explorers. That part had been very clear. What he was confused about, however, was exactly why they were there in the first place and precisely what it was they were supposed to be doing. Stephen had simply smiled and replied, '*insha'Allah.*'

By twenty minutes past two they had made their way through as much of the complex as had been excavated, with Rupert spending a few minutes in conversation with the leader of the French archaeological team that was busy working on the site. Their tents were pitched nearby and glared white against the sand – apart from *Khufu* and her passengers the campsite was the only visible sign of life for miles around. Everyone was now assembled at the back wall of the temple, where Rupert had started a protracted and very over-detailed description of the wall carvings.

'... So, even though these images are two thousand years old, anyone who has been through medical school would instantly recognize many of the depictions as the same instruments that are in use today in modern medicine. Perhaps Dr Hopkins would like to comment on that for us...?'

Stephen had been looking over the remains of the low wall, which separated the back end of the complex from the sand and desert beyond. He glanced at his watch and then up at the nearby ridge of sand. There was nothing. Rupert's voice caught him by surprise and dragged him unexpectedly back to reality.

'Oh ... absolutely ... I'd say so,' he said, not really certain of what it was that Rupert had said in the first place, his concentration having been on the horizon rather than on the wall carvings immediately in front of him. 'Without a doubt, old chap,' he continued, hoping that what he had said would answer the question and sound convincing.

'They were really quite advanced, weren't they?' asked Lydia Porter, who had been standing up close to the wall right in front of the group, gazing up at the carvings. 'Very modern, as Dr Hopkins has confirmed. I helped a little with the war and even I can recognize some of them,' she added.

'Absolutely,' repeated Rupert. 'Let's move off to the right-hand side of the complex. I want to show you how they applied mathematics to their everyday lives. There is a very interesting wall panel showing the months of their year connected to the seasons and all codified through mathematics – they had quite a good system for counting and – here's the interesting thing – they also knew about geometry. This way, everyone and watch the uneven ground.'

As they moved off, Stephen threw a quick glance in Lampton's direction. He had told Lampton what he knew about the events that had led up to the death of Printon, and also of the instructions he had received from Cecil, although he had stopped short of telling him anything about his uncle.

'We have to keep everyone together – until the promised help arrives and this Major Ashdown can tell us what to do next,' he had said.

'You can count on me,' Lampton had replied, without hesitation, 'just tell me what you want me to do,' which was exactly what Stephen had proceeded to do, making it clear to Lampton that it could well be a case of the blind leading the blind.

Lampton looked back at Stephen, over the head of his wife, who was bending down to study an inscription in more detail. Almost imperceptibly, he raised his eyebrows as if to signify that the unexpected was still to be expected. Then he continued waiting for his wife to finish her inspection.

The tour continued on its way and, shortly before a quarter to three, they were retracing their steps through the first hypostyle hall, in anticipation of their return to the ship and afternoon tea. As they approached the entrance portal, Kormann's eye was caught by a larger-than-life-size depiction of a pharaoh about to smash in a prisoner's skull with a large mace.

'Excuse, please, Mr Winfield,' he called, as Rupert was about to leave the main building through the right-hand portal. 'What is the significance of this?' he asked, pointing up at the wall. 'That must be Pharaoh, because he is wearing the double crown, but who is the prisoner? He is dressed in very fine robes and has an Egyptian headdress ... Why is this, please?'

Rupert crossed back to where the little Swiss, Grupfelder, Colonel Ponsworthy and Lydia Porter were standing. All of them were gazing up at the scene, which was vividly etched into the stone. Some of the original, vibrantly coloured paint – red, ochre and iridescent blue – was still visible in places.

'That's Ptolemy XII, and what he's doing is symbolically warning all of Egypt that he is not to be challenged. And you're quite right – the fellow he's about to despatch is an Egyptian – he was the governor of Nubia, but had grand designs on becoming Pharaoh himself.' He read the hieroglyphics. 'If I have things correct,' he said, 'this chap had been up to his ears in cheating Pharaoh out of money. More dangerously for him, he was also trying to amass a weapons stockpile to mount his coup against Pharaoh. After having his skull smashed, he would have been thrown into the sacred Nile, to be eaten by the sacred crocodiles. That's why the carvings are on this side of the temple – remember, the right-hand side is Sobek's – the crocodile god – a dark god.'

'May I ask a question please?'

'Of course you may, Mrs Lampton,' replied Rupert.

'You have been reading hieroglyphics for us all through our trip. What I do not understand is that sometimes you point from right to left as you read, sometimes left to right, sometimes up or down,' she said, 'how do you know where to start?'

There was a mutter of agreement from the rest of the party.

'The bird is usually the key to it,' replied Rupert mysteriously.

'The bird?' echoed Mrs Lampton, turning her head to look at the hieroglyphics Rupert had been interpreting.

'Yes, indeed,' chuckled Rupert. 'Find the bird in the text, see which way the beak is pointing, but be careful because you have to read the text towards the face of the bird or animal and not in the direction the face is pointing.'

Kormann was not listening to what Rupert was saying. Unnoticed by the others, he had stopped looking at the carvings and appeared to be deep in thought as he stared down at the sandy flagstones covering the courtyard.

'The Egyptians had a very simple legal system – brutal by our standards, perhaps, but very effective for their own times, nonetheless. As for this chap, well ... today, I suppose, we might call him an arms dealer,' smiled Rupert, as he looked around the little group, quite satisfied with his attempt to translate the images into words. 'Trouble for him was he got caught and...'

'That is where I have known this name before!' shouted the little Swiss, in an agitated voice. 'This Benschedler. My father – the police – I remember now.'

Grupfelder put a steadying arm on Kormann's shoulder.

'Steady, there, li'l buddy,' he said. 'What's up?'

'In the war – my father worked for the Swiss Securities Bank. There was a scandal. This Benschedler man ... he was very rich – an industrialist and famous hotelier in my country ... but he was also an arms dealer with the Germans ... a disgrace to all decent Swiss ... and he did many other wrong things ... My mother told me these things ... me and my little brother ... as we grew up.' He had started to sweat heavily, his glasses unable to mask the glint of triumph in his eyes. 'Now I remember ... he owned hotels all over Switzerland and he used them as a cover to hide all of his other illegal dealings ... and then ... the police ... one day ... they came to my father and took him away. With many others he was accused of helping in the deceptions of this Benschedler ... but my father was innocent – they were all innocent ... The government had found out – someone must have told them ... How else could they have known?'

All of this had been gabbled at considerable speed and, towards the end of his outpouring, he had lapsed into his native German. Kormann became more and more agitated, alarmed at these memories of the past, which he had hidden away as a very young boy. Now, with the key found and the door unlocked, they all started to flood painfully back.

'What was that you said at the end?' asked Grupfelder, a bemused look on his face.

'What? ... Oh ... pardon ... I speak in German because I think in German,' said Kormann, reverting once again to English and repeating the last part of what he had just said.

'The police, you say?' asked Ponsworthy.

Kormann turned to look at the Colonel, but his eyes were unseeing; his mind was cast back to a time, well over a decade ago, when he was growing up in Switzerland.

'The government said that Benschedler had compromised Swiss neutrality and had to be punished ... But there were also rumours of ministers in the pay of Benschedler ... There was much trouble ... My father and the others were made scapegoats, to restore the people's confidence in their government. My father was a broken man – a victim of the scandal which followed. He never recovered. And it was all because of *this man* and his *greed*!' He spat these words out with concentrated hatred, revealing a side of his otherwise placid nature, which had thus far been hidden.

'That's real tough, there, buddy. An you bein' just a li'l kid 'n' all,' said the burly American.

Suddenly, Kormann seemed to grow in stature, his glasses intensifying the burning in his eyes.

'And then he died!' he barked, focusing on the last, perhaps most important piece of his puzzle.

'Oh, I am sorry to hear that,' said Lydia Porter, expressing a genuine sympathy. 'It is very sad when a young lad loses his father, and it is...'

'*Benschedler killed my father!*' shouted Kormann, turning to look at the others, 'that was why my mother cried ... that is why I remember the name ... she said God would punish him ... for all those his greed had ruined and killed.'

He suddenly turned his gaze through the massive stone walls, in the direction of where *Khufu* lay, securely tied up to the little jetty. 'So, now we have this man, *Benschedler*... we have him on our boat. I have seen the passport ... it says he is a hotelier! *Where is he?*' he snapped, turning round on his heels to survey that part of the complex that was within his vision.

'Now that you mention it, I haven't seen him since luncheon...' said Colonel Ponsworthy, stroking his Kitchener moustache thoughtfully.

'And I don't remember seeing him when Mr Winfield was talking to us about our visit,' added Lydia Porter.

'Then I had better go in search of him,' said Kormann, in a voice that had taken on the attributes of a snarl.

44

Near Kom Ombo

Wadi Muhtadi – Mid-afternoon, Monday, 6th August 1928

The cohort of horsemen cantered down the bed of the wadi. Kicked up by the horses' flying hooves, clouds of sand rose into the still, hot air behind them. They had made good progress and were now approaching a section of the wadi where, on the Nile side, the wall of the dried-up riverbed reached up to a series of rocky outcrops that encircled a plateau.

'Sir, we must go up there,' shouted Hussein over his shoulder, as he reined in his horse. 'The way of our travel lies in that direction,' he said, waving towards the nearest of the rocks.

Ashdown nodded his understanding, as they all turned ninety degrees and began the short climb up and out of the wadi and onto the firmer ground of the plateau.

'Here you can take a little water, if you wish, Sir,' said Hussein. 'We must allow the horses to drink as well – they are working hard.'

Two of the policemen had quickly dismounted and were moving from horse to horse around the little column of riders with practised ease, each man filling a small metal bowl with water from their canteen at each stop.

'Not too much,' shouted Hussein, 'but we must make

sure they are looked after well. They are our only way of escaping the desert,' he said smiling, as he pointed round the horizon with a circular gesture.

Ashdown followed Hussein's pointing finger and gazed at the endless wastes of sand and rocky outcrops. Anyone lost in such an anonymous, pitiless void would not survive for more than a few hours.

'We do not have a long way to go now,' said the young Egyptian, opening his map and resting it over his horse's neck. Then, he unbuttoned and reached into a pocket of his tunic, drawing out his compass. After he had opened the leather lid, he held the instrument out in front of him for a few seconds, as he checked their position. Then, he looked once again at the map and turned to Ashdown, who had drawn up his horse alongside.

'We have travelled down Wadi Muhtadi and are here, where the rocks are shown.' Hussein pointed a finger at the map, which, Ashdown noticed, was British Army issue from the war. '*Muhtadi* means "Rightly Guided" in your language, Sir, and it has guided us well,' said the affable Egyptian, checking his compass once again.

'How much further to the river?' asked Ashdown, as he wiped his mouth with the back of his hand and then screwed the top back onto his water canteen. None of the others drank anything. Instead, they sat patiently in their saddles, waiting for the word of command to ride off again, their horses snorting and pawing the ground, as if to show that they, too, wanted to continue with their journey.

'We must leave the wadi now, because from here it will no longer guide us – it goes in the wrong direction.' Once again he traced their line of progress on the map with his finger. 'We will go that way,' he pointed off to the horizon, 'and we will find the river in, maybe, less than another hour, *insha'Allah*,' he said, smiling.

As the Major returned his water bottle to its place on his

saddle, he turned backwards to look down the wadi, in the direction from which they had come.

'Let us hope the wadi lives up to its name,' he said.

The young Egyptian watched, eyeing him intently.

'Many of our words have meanings which describe not only objects, or what we do, but also what they might signify. I, myself, have the name meaning "Little Beauty",' he said, as he closed the leather lid of the compass case and replaced it in his tunic pocket. 'My name is descended from the Prophet Muhammad, peace be upon him,' he continued, folding the map along its well-worn creases and putting it away inside his tunic. 'Do your English names have many meanings, Sir?' he asked.

That was something that would never even have crossed Ashdown's mind. To him, a name was simply a name. For the first time he wondered if his own name, Jeremy, had some associated meaning, but, as quickly as the thought entered his mind, so it evaporated as a total irrelevance.

'Some of them do,' he said vaguely, 'but most of them are just sounds meaning just the thing they represent.'

For a split second he suddenly felt inferior to this young Egyptian, who not only had fluency in both his native Arabic and the foreigner's English, but was also possessed of the ability to command an intellect able to question beyond the confines of his own world.

'I see,' said Hussein politely, 'but now, Sir, we must go.' And with that, he reined his horse to his right and galloped off in the direction of the river.

45

Kom Ombo

Temple of Sobek-Haroeris – Late Afternoon, Monday, 6th August 1928

With Grupfelder at his side, Eric Kormann set off at a determined pace, his face fogged with the mist of anger. His arms swung out, first left and then right, so that, despite his youth and small stature, he resembled a company sergeant major on parade. The others followed in hot pursuit, intrigued by what the Swiss had said as he stood in front of the ancient wall carving of the arms dealer about to suffer the full weight of Pharaoh's revenge. They straggled out from the temple and on down the incline in an oddly silent procession, as they made their way back to the gleaming steel security of *Khufu*. Not everyone had ventured forth to explore the wonders of the temple that afternoon.

'I say! That looks serious,' said Mr Rotherham, as he looked through the railings. From where he was sitting under the shade of the awning on the top deck he could see the little procession clearly. 'They seem to be in a frightful hurry.'

'Who does?' asked Mr Grassmere, in a whisper signifying a mixture of intense curiosity and hesitancy, lest his interest should awake his wife. Asleep in the chair next to his, with her jowls relaxed onto her chest, she could be heard snoring gently in the late-afternoon heat.

'*They* do...' said the owner of Rotherham's Patented Relish, pointing towards the returning group. '...And Mr Kormann seems to be very agitated about something. Look at the way he's walking!'

The two of them got up and crossed to the railings, from where they could get a better view of the little procession as it neared the tall sides of the ship.

'I'd say something is up,' said Rotherham, turning to the insignificant husband of 'The Lady 8', as he did so.

From the stern, a voice suddenly added to their speculation.

'That's typical – every man thinks he has something to say that is important. They make me sick!' said Ruth Kirby from her seat.

She had been sitting with her feet resting on the middle bar of the railings ever since she had refused Rupert's invitation to attend the pre-excursion talk. Her voice was heavily tinged with bitterness and derision. She spoke as if referring to men in general, rather than specifically to the young man, only just in his twenties, who marched resolutely across the sand at the head of the little procession on the riverbank below. In all probability she had not even seen either Kormann or the returning tourists. From the way she slurred her speech, it was also obvious she had succumbed to her addiction yet again. The two men turned their attention to Kirby as she delivered her anti-masculine diatribe, but, as the little procession below them reached the jetty, they quickly turned their attention back to Eric Kormann.

As he drew level with the white side of *Khufu*, the movement of the two men perched like two small pigeons on the top deck caused the little Swiss to look up and, catching sight of them, stop in his tracks. Shielding his eyes from the glare of the sky with his hand he shouted up to them.

'Excuse, please, where is Benschedler?'

'Who's that?' said Mr Grassmere, turning to the other

man. He was not usually aware of much, other than what it was his wife demanded.

'That other Swiss chap,' replied Rotherham, out of the corner of his mouth without taking his fixed gaze off Kormann. Even from their position on the top deck, it was obvious that something very serious had upset this quiet, usually placid man. 'You know – the one with the cane.'

'Oh... yes,' muttered Grassmere, who had, indeed, noticed the tall man with the ornate cane.

'Is he up there, please?' shouted Kormann.

'No, sorry ... I'm afraid it's just the Grassmeres and I. We haven't seen that other gentleman since before luncheon. We thought he must have gone off to the temple with you.'

'Gone to hell ... as they all should,' shouted Ruth Kirby, from the chair. She had made no effort to get up, as the two men had done, but rather stared out at the blue sky, lost in her own poisoned, twisted world.

Her outburst had caused Mr Grassmere to look in her direction, but Rotherham had ignored her. He found her rather crude and somewhat offensive.

'Why do you want him?' called down Rotherham, but his question went unanswered. The procession, with Kormann still at its head, had started to disappear through the door in *Khufu*'s side and was now assembling in front of the reception desk in the foyer.

'Excuse, please, but where is Benschedler?' asked Kormann.

Achmed, whose turn it was to man the desk, simply shrugged his shoulders in the traditional Egyptian manner.

'I am sorry, Sir, but I have not seen him since before luncheon was served.'

He turned to the other crewman, who was sharing the duty with him, and repeated Kormann's question, this time in Arabic. During the ensuing exchange, which could not have lasted for more than thirty seconds, there was much gesticulating and raising of voices. Rupert made his way to the front of the little crush and stood next to Kormann. With the exception of the four on the top deck, and the unaccounted for Benschedler, everyone of the group now filled the vessel's foyer, expectantly waiting for something to happen.

'Mr Kormann needs to talk to Mr Benschedler urgently,' said Rupert, as Achmed listened with one ear to his colleague's Arabic response to the repetition of Kormann's question and, with the other, to Rupert's English pronouncement. He raised his hand to his colleague in a gesture of understanding.

'Mr Winfield, Sir...' began Achmed, trying to silence his colleague, who was still talking and pointing towards the shore, '...the Benschedler gentleman, as I am told, was seen to go ashore during luncheon. Daoud saw him. He was walking the other way, away from the temple,' he pointed downriver. 'Daoud called out to him that it was most unwise to go walking away from the boat, as the desert is all around and there is no water, but the gentleman did not listen and just kept walking. We know this because Daoud then told Mr Mohammed, who told my colleague here before I came on duty...'

'What the hell has he gone wondering off for?' asked Stephen, 'there's nothing out there but desert.'

'There is a town and a railway station, Sir, but it is a long way to walk ... through the sand,' replied Achmed, 'so Mr Mohammed has placed Khatose on duty, out there on the deck, to watch for the gentleman's return. He said that if the...'

Kormann spun around on his heel and strode off once more, through the press of tourists and out through the entrance doors, across the deck and back down the gangway, onto the jetty.

'Damn it – this is just what we didn't want to happen,'

hissed Stephen, as he passed Rupert at the head of the gangway. 'What's he up to now, for God's sake – there's nothing out there but miles and miles of sand!'

'Perhaps he thought he could escape – cut across the sand and ... well ... I don't know – catch a taxi, perhaps?'

Rupert's attempt to lighten the seriousness of the situation fell flat.

'I really think that...' but Stephen was cut short by Simon Arling and Khatose, both of whom shouted out at the same time. They had spotted the dark shape, moving swiftly towards *Khufu* and without the aid of the heavy cane he carried. He was crossing the sandy ground which led from the crest of the ridge down to the water.

'There he is – come on!' shouted Kormann, as he, too, saw the figure approaching. Within a few brief minutes, the two parties met.

'*You murdered my father!*' Kormann shouted, stabbing an accusing finger at Benschedler. 'Answer me; do you not remember my father – Franz Kormann, the banker?' Kormann's voice was becoming ever more high-pitched as his anger reached dangerously close to the point at which it would erupt and boil over out of control. '*You*, who killed my father – *you*, who killed all the other innocents – *you*, with your filthy greed – *you*, who brought shame to our nation – do you have nothing to say? Do you not hear me!! *ANSWER ME!!!*'

Overtaken by the supreme emotion of the moment, the little Swiss seemed to have grown in stature far beyond his years, but the confrontation presented a potentially comical side – the diminutive Kormann, flushed red with uncontrolled anger, and Benschedler, the tall, icy, unmoved aristocrat, looming over him.

Although accosted by this unexpected outburst, Benschedler made neither effort to arrest nor alter his stride. He ignored the verbal attack delivered by Kormann, as if it were a minor inconvenience caused by nothing more important than an irritating sand fly, and strode on back towards *Khufu*. Excluding the four on the upper deck, the rest of the tourists had by now left the boat and were following closely behind the still-moving Benschedler and Kormann.

'Calm down, there, li'l buddy,' said the burly American, walking beside the little Swiss, who had gone even redder in the face, 'you'll do yourself an injury.'

Kormann said nothing. He turned towards the American, but his gaze was blinded by the release of years of suppressed and painful memories, blocked resentment and burning desire for revenge for what had been done to his father. Grupfelder, realizing that Kormann was fast approaching the point at which all logical action would cease to be a viable option, toyed with the idea of physically restraining the little Swiss before something very regrettable happened. When he caught sight of the hatred blazing in Kormann's eyes, he realized that nothing would be gained through such an action; Kormann had already past the point where rational, logical thought ended.

Benschedler, The Phoenix, strode on, his face thunderous, his expression fixed; the cane striding along with him in angry swishing arcs. His ominous, dangerous expression alone would have cleared a path for him through the thickest of crowds.

First there was that ambitious fool sent by Berlin and now this annoying little irritation, he thought, as he continued his undeterred progress back to the ship.

Behind the seemingly composed exterior, his mind was quickly assessing the threat that this ridiculous little man had suddenly presented. As he strode proudly and arrogantly on, he quickly realized that he was in a very dangerous situation, one which he had not anticipated. The first part of Kormann's tirade had been beyond earshot of *Khufu*. The sound of his voice, near hysterical with frustration at

Benschedler's cold, calculated indifference to his repeated questioning, had been lost amongst the sand dunes.

Now as the little procession tagged along behind Benschedler and the irate Kormann, the sounds of what little conversation there was reached the top deck, where Rotherham and Mr Grassmere were watching. Several of *Khufu*'s crew had appeared from the lower decks and now stood on the jetty between the rapidly approaching group and the entrance to the ship's foyer. When Kormann had stormed off across the short distance that had separated him from the approaching Benschedler, Khatose had run to Mohammed, telling him that Benschedler had been seen returning from the desert. Mohammed, mindful of what both Rupert and Stephen had told him of the situation, had taken it upon himself to station the larger members of the crew in a position where, if needed, they might possibly do some good.

Benschedler noted this wall of resistance strung out along the jetty preventing his access to the main gangway. Without modifying his stride, he slightly changed direction and advanced towards the ramp near the stationary paddle wheel at *Khufu*'s stern. What finally stopped his progress was the realization that Daoud, Khatose and the other crewmen, who had mirrored his change in direction and now formed a blocking group between the end of the jetty and the entrance to the foyer, made it impossible for him to reach the safety of the ship. With this realization, he turned to face Kormann, who was standing backed up by the other tourists on the sand, just below the foot of the jetty ramp. Still he said nothing, but just stood silently looming over the little Swiss. He was close to the edge of the jetty, with the blue of the Nile at his back and the white bulk of *Khufu* to his right, his hands, one on the other, resting on the heavy cane. Irritatingly, he still said nothing, but merely leered at the diminutive Swiss with a look of acidic disdain.

'Do you have no conscience?' shouted Kormann, his fists clenched tightly by his side in suppressed rage. 'Do you have no regret for what you have *done*? Are you even *human*?' he screamed. He had lapsed into his more familiar Swiss-German. '*ANSWER ME!*'

For the first time since the encounter began, in a quiet voice, which was very much in keeping with his aristocratic bearing, Benschedler spoke.

'What are you talking about, you stupid little fool? Of course, I do not know your father – why should I? You are a little worm and do not even merit being spoken to,' he said, not in Kormann's accented Swiss-German, but in the German of a Prussian aristocrat and confidant of the Kaiser.

'You are a murderer and must pay for your crimes – against my family and all the others!' shouted Kormann, still speaking his native tongue.

Grupfelder, who had understood nothing of this exchange, had finally decided to put a restraining hand on Kormann's shoulder, but this gesture of reassurance went unnoticed. Behind them, the rest of Rupert's flock, including Rupert himself and Stephen, formed a tightly packed semicircle. Somewhat incongruously, Stephen was still carrying his black medical bag and his walking stick.

'You are obviously quite insane. We have ways of dealing with such unpleasant irritations as you, my ignorant little friend,' continued Benschedler, his right hand tightening imperceptibly on the ornate handle of his cane. The white, claw like fingers were slowly draining of blood so that they resembled more a skeleton's fingers than those of a living being.

'What's he saying?' asked Marjory Cuttle, frustrated at not being able to follow the conversation.

'He speaks really excellent German, but what he is saying is very unpleasant,' whispered Simon Arling. 'It sounds as if he is addressing a servant or someone of a much lower status and it is definitely not what should be said in polite company. It is also a little confusing, but it seems that...'

'What's the blighter up to, then?' interrupted Colonel Ponsworthy, who had pushed his way to the front of the little group, slightly to the left of Kormann. 'What's he saying?'

Within the space of the few seconds which followed, Arling managed to translate only the first few words.

'This man has obviously had too much sun,' said Benschedler, in perfect English. 'He is suffering from the effects of delusion. I would suggest that for his...'

'*I am not mad!*' shouted Kormann, in English. 'This bastard murdered my father through his greed – and now, he must pay!' he continued, pointing angrily at the taller man.

Benschedler's eyes narrowed on the little Swiss.

'So ... we treat scum like you in the only way you understand,' continued Benschedler, reverting to German and towering over Kormann, like some terrible figure of retribution from the denouement of a grand opera.

In one swift movement, and almost before anyone knew what was happening, Benschedler twisted the ornate, phoenix-shaped handle of the cane, releasing the locking catch, and withdrew the stiletto blade from its scabbard. He stood facing Kormann, open hatred etched onto his face.

'What the hell is he doing? That's a sword, isn't it?' said Rotherham from the upper deck, grasping Mr Grassmere's arm and pointing down to the jetty below them.

At the same time, Mohammed appeared up the stairway, having been alerted to the activity on the jetty by Achmed.

'Come and look at this,' called Rotherham, as Mohammed ran across the deck, towards them. 'There is trouble down there – on the jetty.'

Mohammed looked over the rails and, within a split second, as he saw the blade flash in the sunlight, had realized that Kormann was in mortal danger.

'Quick, we must do something,' he said in Arabic, 'but what?'

In a flash of inspiration, he kicked the back support of a nearby deck lounger away from its locking cradle, which caused the chair to collapse flat on the deck with a bang. Then, with strength that belied his slight stature, he heaved the flat chair up into the air, clear of the end of the awning, and, holding it above his fez, flung it down over the rails with all of his might towards where Benschedler was standing. It crashed noisily, but harmlessly, down onto the jetty before bouncing backwards against the side of *Khufu*'s hull, and slid harmlessly down into the water between the ship and the jetty.

This attempt to halt the situation on the jetty by Mohammed, was unsuccessful as it neither halted Benschedler nor distracted him from his threatening behaviour towards Kormann. Suddenly letting out a deep-throated roar and taking everyone by surprise, he lunged forward towards the little Swiss: the ruby-red eyes of the silver bird flashing in the afternoon sun. Kormann stood rooted to the spot, transfixed, an easy target. Susan Lampton, seeing the sunlight glint on the razor-sharp steel blade, let out a scream and clutched the arm of Lydia Porter, who was standing next to her. Everything gradually deteriorated into a confused tangle of shouts and movement as the semicircle disintegrated.

Suddenly, there was the sound of a distant bang, like the popping of a cork from a good vintage of champagne. Benschedler, who had been about to hurl himself at the little Swiss, let out a scream and started to fall forwards, his right leg crumpling underneath him. Even before he had left the vertical, there was a second, far more deafening report, this time very close and sounding like a field gun being fired. Benschedler froze in mid-air and then, in a ghastly, slow-motion ballet, started to fall backwards, his feet leaving the floor of the jetty, his arms flung wide. From his chest flew scraps of clothing and flesh, as blood spattered in all directions.

The stiletto blade, which, a brief second before, had been destined for Kormann, now spun harmlessly away through the clear air, landing point first in the sand close to the water. The heavy cane, separated from its handle and blade, spun out of the lifeless hand which had held it and arced up and out across the river, before disappearing with a loud splash into the water. As it spun through the air a shower of round pebbles, the size of large marbles, was left in its wake. For a moment, each one hung motionless in the bright sunlight, reflecting the sun's rays and glowing in such a way as to reveal, even in this uncut and unpolished state, the promise of their true value.

Herr Graf von Hohenstadt und Waldstein-Turingheim, alias Benschedler, alias The Phoenix, turned a complete somersault before his head cleaved the shallow water, opening a path for his damaged body to follow. As the water closed over his inert form, the current reached for him and, almost as quickly as the body had splashed into the arms of the Nile, it started to drift away, heading out towards the middle of the river.

The whole incident had taken little more than a few seconds, but, to the people who stood watching, it seemed to have been an eternity. In the centre of what was left of the semicircle, Colonel Ponsworthy, his moustache bristling, stood staring straight ahead at where Benschedler had stood on the jetty a brief moment before. His right arm was still outstretched clutching his Webley service revolver, the barrel of which was still smoking.

'A nasty piece of work,' he said, in a tone of masterly understatement. 'Are you all right, Kormann?' he asked.

'I ... yes, thank you ... I,' but Kormann was in shock, still trapped between the world of his memories and that of the present.

'How did you know to bring a gun? Where on earth did you get that thing from?' demanded Marjory Cuttle, taking a step towards the Colonel.

'Years in the Army, dear lady, living with trouble and always expecting it.' He turned to Rupert and Stephen, who were standing together at the back of the group. 'You two made a good attempt at trying to keep things quiet,' he said. 'Always best to avoid panic,' he continued, returning the revolver to the holster which was under his armpit, concealed by his linen jacket, 'but it takes a lot to fool an old soldier.'

'Which, arguably, is more than can be said for you, my dear,' said Cuttle, taking Miss Eggerton by the arm. 'You really must complete your education and learn the difference between a revolver holster and a medical appliance!' she said in mock seriousness, before they both laughed.

'Something amusing you, ladies?' asked Simon Arling.

'Oh ... I do beg your pardon, Mr Arling ...' said Rebecca Eggerton, her hand held close to her mouth, trying to hide her mirth. 'A silly little private joke between the two of us,' she continued. 'You see, when we ...'

But Colonel Ponsworthy, realizing that for once he had an audience who might well be genuinely interested to hear what it was he had to say, was not about to give way.

'I thought something might be up. It was all a bit odd, what with that Printon fellow becoming a bit jittery after we left Abu Simbel and then this Benschedler chap being so off-hand and unconcerned at what happened on Philae Island,' he continued, starting to sound a little pompous, 'although I must say that quite how you two could possibly have anticipated this turn of events is a total mystery.' He looked at Rupert and Stephen, his Kitchener moustache still bristling with excitement. 'Still, it's as well to be careful, so I made sure I had my old friend with me,' he said, patting the holster through the jacket. 'We always travel together, you see.'

FATAL TEARS

Although he had suddenly become the centre of attention for a few minutes, the Colonel did not fully understand the circumstances which had given rise to events. He felt that there was something of a sense of mystery about the whole affair – a sense of mystery and curiosity that was shared by almost everyone else. He felt it was right for him to be informed of what exactly was going on. However, further speculation and questioning was avoided as, moments later, Richard Lampton saw Ashdown.

'Look, up there,' he said excitedly, pointing up to the ridge above them. 'Horses!'

Ponsworthy stopped talking and turned with everyone else to follow Lampton's pointing finger.

From their position on top of the ridge, the Major and his men had enjoyed a perfect view of the drama that had unfolded before them down at the water's edge. It had become obvious that some sort of confrontation was reaching its climax – they had seen that the moment they crested the ridge. There had been almost no time to think, other than to see the glint of steel and the threatening posture of the tall man who stood, ready to spring, close to the jetty. Ashdown had been forced to make a snap decision.

'Quick, Hussein, aim for the leg,' he had shouted, pointing at the tall man.

Ashdown had no doubt that he had given the correct order. It was not, after all, his responsibility that ultimately the fatal shot would be fired by someone near the jetty. The Major sought only to wound.

'Well done, Hussein,' said Ashdown, turning in his saddle to face the young Egyptian from their position on top of the ridge. 'Good shot!'

The young Egyptian said nothing, but simply smiled back, as he lowered the Lee-Enfield from his right shoulder.

'It was your order, Sir,' he said simply, turning to face the Major, '*insha'Allah.*'

On the top deck of the Nile steamer *Khufu*, Mrs Grassmere, who had been snoring in her upright, wicker chair, opened her eyes and, with some confused difficulty, began to rub her aching neck. She had been sleeping with her head drooped forward onto her ample bosom for far too long and now her overstretched muscles were objecting.

'Is it time for tea yet?' she asked, through an enormous yawn.

46

Kom Ombo

Temple of Sobek-Haroeris – Early Evening, Monday, 6th August 1928

Since the tourists had once again boarded *Khufu*, their talk had been of nothing else than the incident involving Benschedler and Kormann. Speculation had run riot, as had discussion of the enormous odds against two people – the avenger and the one against whom the vengeance would be meted out – being on the same trip in the first place.

In the forward observation lounge, most of the tourists had gathered for a late tea. They sat in excited little groups, talking animatedly. For a change, Mrs Grassmere sat subdued in a corner. She had snored through everything and, by the time her protesting neck muscles had dragged her back to consciousness, it was all over. She had seen nothing of the drama and so was unable to express an opinion on the subject, which, as Simon Arling remarked later to his wife, must have been something of a first. Her husband, on the other hand, was now engaged in animated conversation with Rotherham and Simon Arling. Kormann, subdued, vindicated, but restored to his usual self sat at a table with Grupfelder. The big American had been a rock-solid source of support for him, since they had all witnessed the justice that Fate had dealt out to the person whom Kormann firmly believed had killed his father by proxy all those years ago.

Within a few minutes of Benschedler disappearing under the water, Ashdown and his men had ridden across the short distance from the ridge to the jetty. Rupert, at Stephen's suggestion, had introduced him to the passengers as the commander of a police unit, which, by sheer good fortune, had just happened to be on routine patrol in the desert and in their vicinity.

'It was a fortunate coincidence that the Major and his men arrived when they did,' he had said, as everyone had gathered back on board *Khufu*. He had not mentioned the real reason for the Major's presence. That was not information for general consumption. 'The Major will travel with us to Luxor,' Rupert had continued, 'so that he can collect statements and prepare the necessary paperwork for when we arrive there.' Only a select few knew that this was not the only reason for Ashdown's presence. The pretence was maintained later still, as Ashdown stood on the sand alongside the jetty to bid farewell to the police patrol and to shake the young Egyptian police officer's hand: the very hand that had fired the rifle so accurately and the same hand that had been the last link in the quest that had taken him the length of the vast and unforgiving African continent.

'Thank you, and my thanks to your men for a job well done.'

The Major had been very impressed by the professionalism of his police escort and of Hussein in particular, but with everyone watching him, he felt that he had said as much as he could without compromising his cover. It had to sound as if he was simply ordering his patrol back to Aswan.

'*Insha'Allah*,' replied Hussein smiling back, before he and his men galloped off to retrace their steps over the ridge and back along the wadi, to where the train would be waiting to take them back down the line to Aswan.

With the approach of late afternoon, the tourists sipped

their tea and ate their cakes and sandwiches, chatting away in animated excitement.

Lower down in the ship, behind the reception counter in *Khufu*'s ornate foyer, Stephen, Rupert, Lampton, Mohammed and the Major were seated around the desk in Mohammed's office. This select party, at least, had some idea of the reality in which they now found themselves. Spread out on the desk in front of them was a line of marble-sized cloudy pebbles – 19 in total.

'So these are real diamonds?' said Lampton, a little disappointed that they looked so uninteresting in their uncut state, 'and they're worth a king's ransom? But they just look like lumps of glass.'

'They are the tears of the gods,' said Mohammed quietly.

'Indeed, they are,' repeated Rupert, picking one up and looking at it, 'and the gods have certainly had a lot to cry over, the last couple of weeks. Simon Arling had a more appropriate name for them,' he added, suddenly serious. 'He called them "fatal tears" that evening when Mrs Grassmere wore her diamond necklace at dinner.'

'I am now understanding what you told me about them, Mr Rupert,' said the little Egyptian. 'The ancient gods' tears fell from the sky and onto the sand... and for the tall gentleman having the black cane, they were indeed being the "fatal tears".'

Following the drama of that afternoon, Stephen had been quick to collect those of the stones which had fallen out of the cane and landed on the riverbank. He had done so, through applying the simple rationale that something which had been hidden from view in a heavy cane, was, in all probability, valuable. And he had been right. Daoud and Khatose, both of whom had been born on the banks of the Nile and had spent all of their lives learning its quirks and mannerisms, had swum out and dived to recover the cane, which still held thirteen more of the diamonds.

'Whoever your Printon was,' said Ashdown, 'he was probably involved with these, but it's all a bit vague at the moment,' he said, wondering if it would ever become any clearer with the passing of time and with further investigation.

'At least we are certain of one thing,' said Stephen, 'and that is that our Printon wasn't who he said he was. We have received word that the real Printon is in the police mortuary in Cairo. Our man was an impostor,' he turned to Lampton, 'which explains why he wasn't in the least bit interested in reminiscing with you about old times.'

'He didn't know anything about them,' replied Richard Lampton. 'Well, well. Do you think he was in with this Benschedler chap, then? Why else would someone assume a false identity and then go off on a tour up the Nile?'

'Certainly this Benschedler, whoever he really was, and possibly even our Printon were involved in smuggling these,' said the Major, pointing to the diamonds. 'I've been following Benschedler all the way from South-West Africa. Someone left a trail of bodies for us to follow and now, thanks to this' – he picked up the heavy cane and twisted the handle, withdrawing the stiletto blade – 'we know for certain that it was Benschedler who left them. It is a pity that we do not have a body to put a full stop on this affair,' said Ashdown, 'but we all saw him go into the river … and disappear.'

'The river has very strong force, Sir,' said Mohammed. 'The gentleman is already being on his way to Luxor by this very moment.'

'If the crocodiles haven't got him by now,' added Rupert. 'That would be quite appropriate, actually – an offering to Sobek – it was on his side of the temple that Kormann started things moving, after all.'

'As you say, Winfield. That would, indeed, be a sort of

justice,' replied Ashdown, as he carefully placed the stones into the velvet purse he had brought with him. 'At least, whoever Benschedler's masters are, they won't benefit from this little shipment. Well done, everyone. We've got the better of them this time around,' he said as he stood up.

'Who are "they", Major?' asked Lampton.

Ashdown flicked his eyes from Stephen to Rupert and then back, again, to Lampton.

He had no idea of how much these men knew of what it was they had become unintentionally mixed up in.

'Organized crime – and on a monumental scale,' he said mysteriously, avoiding giving anything away. 'Very unpleasant.'

He thought he saw something in Stephen's expression. It was a hint that this man, at least, knew more about things than he, the secretive Major Jeremy Ashdown, was prepared to reveal.

They had just left Mohammed's office and had entered the foyer, when their progress was halted by a voice from halfway down the passageway.

'J-e-r-e-m-y!' it said.

Hearing his name, Ashdown turned to face the direction from which the voice had come.

'J-e-r-e-m-y bloody Ashdown!' repeated the female voice, as the figure of Ruth Kirby approached, unsteadily, from the passageway. 'What a bloody marvellous coincidence, meeting you here, d-a-r-l-i-n-g!'

'Pardon, do I...' Ashdown stopped in mid-sentence, as the woman approached him.

'Fancy another quickie under the coffee bushes – like the last one?'

As she spoke, she continued tottering across the foyer, towards the little group of men. 'You took everything, the last time I was stupid enough to let you into me, but I forgot to give you this,' she said, as she swung her hand through the air and slapped him very hard across the cheek. 'You bastard!' she shouted, as Ashdown, involuntarily, reached up to calm his stinging flesh.

'Ruth … Ruth Kirby?' he asked, through a half-closed mouth. 'Is it you?'

'Of course it bloody well is me, you bastard!'

Ashdown had not noticed that the others had all moved back slightly, away from the confrontation.

'Ruth … I don't know what to say…'

'How about "sorry" for a start?' she shouted angrily. 'How about "I didn't really mean to leave you in the lurch" or, perhaps, "How did our son die?"?'

Everyone's attention was firmly fixed on the two protagonists in the centre of the foyer. No one saw the sparrow-like form of Miss Rebecca Eggerton emerge from her cabin at the top of the passageway. Following the earlier excitement she had found it necessary to take a half-hour nap and was now about to join the others for tea. As she lingered in the shadows, listening to the very loud and aggressive confrontation that was unfolding in front of her in the foyer, she was torn between a morbid curiosity to know more and an inbuilt sense of decorum, which told her that it was rude to eavesdrop on something that was, quite obviously, none of her business. She would go to the forward observation lounge by the back stairway, avoiding any involvement in the scene in the foyer. On the other hand, considering that the usually quiet Miss Kirby seemed to be in the middle of a diatribe, perhaps she should linger for just a few moments longer, until she had heard a little more of what the otherwise aloof Miss Kirby was shouting about.

Dear Miss Cuttle, although by no means a gossip, would like to be kept abreast of events, she thought, as she slowly began to retrace her steps to the back stairway. *Of course, it really is none of our business, but I'm sure Marjory would like to know. No harm can come of it because we will be careful to keep things between just the two of us.*

Miss Eggerton was unaware that in only slightly more time than it would take her to tell Marjory Cuttle about what it was that she had overheard in the furthest shadows of the foyer, her friend would have made Major Jeremy Ashdown's personal problems common knowledge to anyone who would listen, due to her inability to keep her mouth shut.

47

Nuremberg

Hotel Deutscher Kaiser, Königstrasse – Friday, 10th August 1928

The week had been a very successful one. Much groundwork had been covered in planning the Party's next steps. They were necessary if the Party was to continue building on its progress of the previous two years. The inner coterie had finalized the theme for the rally that was to be held the following year, once again in Nuremberg. They liked Nuremberg. It seemed to be a lucky city for them and their aspirations. Next year's event was to be even more spectacular than its predecessors. It was to be publicized as the '*Day of Composure*' and was programmed to be yet another step on the Party's path to rebuilding the self-respect of the *Volk* and its faith in the future, both of which had been lost since the disgraceful disaster of the Armistice. Careful steps would have to be taken to mask any reference to the use of force against the dissenting voices in Germany – for the moment, at least. It was vital to create the correct impression of a caring, united front.

The week had also passed without the sometimes unpleasantly acrimonious exchanges between certain members of this inner sanctum, which, of late, had become all too frequent at meetings. As power increased, so too did the need to present a politically stable, acceptable front to the *Volk*. Joseph had repeated this many times. If they could not present a vision of absolute stability and reliability, even if it meant pasting over the inevitable cracks in public, then they had little chance of seizing power on a wave of popular support. At best, they would simply present a different version of the same fumbling, incompetent, untrustworthy government in Weimar. And, more worryingly, he had been at pains to point out that the way things presently stood, they would never be able to totally count on the support of the army. And without the army – even allowing for Heinrich and his slowly developing, embryonic network of subversive forces – they would get nowhere. That remark had been one of the most contentious of the week. Hermann had taken exception to the suggestion that they would be able to achieve their goals without the support of the Air Force. The Navy, well what did that amount to in the bigger picture? But the Air Force – his pet pride and joy – that, under no circumstances, could be left out of their plans. In Joseph's opinion, the settlement of this argument had occupied far too much time – time which could have been much better spent on resolving the far more important issue of additional sources of funding.

'The winning over of hearts and minds is a very expensive business,' he kept saying.

Yes, the need for even more money remained a problem. Despite this omnipresent thorn in their side, it had been a very good productive week. At least, it *had* been up until that very morning, the day before they were due to leave for Munich. The three of them sat in Hermann's room, engaged in very earnest conversation.

'Well, I'm not going to tell him,' said Hermann. 'Fund-raising is not my job; I have other matters to attend to.'

'Like your aeroplanes and your art,' said Joseph, as he glared at the other, 'the purpose of which, in our greater scheme of things, seems to elude me...'

Hermann was about to make a suitably acidic response, when the third man in the room spoke.

'Perhaps you are the best one to tell him, Joseph,' said Heinrich, polishing his glasses yet again with a white cotton handkerchief. He was of a nervous disposition. The others had begun to wonder if this was not some sort of nervous gesture, the use of which had increased markedly in recent months. 'He likes your ideas and he listens to you.'

'A good idea, considering that your section, what with its rallies and expensive commissions for moving pictures, takes up a considerable amount of what resources we have,' said Hermann, a triumphant sneer on his face. 'Who knows, but it could well be your section that has to make budgetary adjustments in the short term... in light of present events...' he continued, as he fingered the arm of his chair. He did not look at Joseph.

'It is nearly time for him to wake up,' said Heinrich, looking at his watch through his newly cleaned spectacles. 'It looks to me as if you are, indeed, the best choice for such a delicate mission, my dear Joseph,' he said, in a self-righteous way.

'I will not forget this conversation, gentlemen,' said Joseph, as he stood up, 'I will not forget it at all. Your support in this unfortunate matter has left me...' he paused, as if searching for the most pertinent words with which to express his true emotions, '... almost speechless!'

And with that, he left the room, to climb to the next floor up and break the news to his Leader. In his hand he carried a telegram, which had been the cause of the heated discussion in Hermann's room. It was from the Cairo office of Kohler & Zehler, Importers of Fine European Gourmand Foods. The message itself, whilst appearing innocuous on the surface, had very serious implications.

FATAL TEARS

Cairo,
Thursday, 9th August 1928.
Regret to advise that latest shipment now postponed indefinitely.

Epilogue

Whitehall, London – Friday, 28th September 1928

The feeble rays of a dying autumn sun had long since ceased to fall across the impressively imposing carved façades of the government buildings in Whitehall. These buildings were meant to impress. They were the outward signs of a mighty Empire, from where entire populations and subcontinents were governed, and to where vast wealth accrued, as it had done for over two centuries, through trade and, sometimes, conquest. In the gloom of a London late afternoon, their very presence, even if shrouded by the onset of darkness, seemed to indicate to the world that all was well and that the unseen driving force behind the entire universe must, surely, be an Englishman.

'Well, my boy, we owe you a considerable debt of gratitude,' said the Uncle, as he raised his glass to his nephew. 'That was a fine thing you did, sorting out those diamonds.'

'Thank you, Sir,' replied his nephew, 'but I must say that it was more by luck than anything else, and it was most certainly due to several other people, without whose help it would have been impossible.'

'Well yes, my boy, and it goes without saying that we are really most grateful to them all – not that we can publicly admit to any of this, or even say thank you on a formal basis. National security, I'm afraid.'

FATAL TEARS

Stephen sat in a comfortable leather armchair, listening to his uncle recount the consequences of the recent events. As he did so, he idly fingered the handle of a heavy black cane, which he had propped up against the side of his chair. The glow of the fire that burned in the ornate marble fireplace danced and sparkled through the two ruby eyes that adorned the shape of a silver bird rising from the enfolding swirls of flame, which were cleverly designed to look like wings. The red flashes of the ruby eyes caught the Uncle's attention.

'So that's what the stones were smuggled in, is it? He just carried it all the way across Africa?'

'Yes, Sir,' replied the nephew. 'It's an extremely well-made piece of kit, if you'll pardon the Army parlance. It's a lethal weapon,' he continued, twisting the handle and withdrawing the stiletto blade for the Uncle to inspect.

'And this Major Ashdown, did he not want to keep it as evidence?' asked the Uncle.

'No,' replied the nephew, 'he said all he wanted was what it contained. Once he had the stones, he was quite satisfied that his job was done. So I thought I'd hang on to it as a souvenir. I also have to say that it helps with the old leg...'

The Uncle looked at his nephew with compassion.

'Ah yes, my boy, the leg. How is it?'

'We have our good days and our bad days,' replied the nephew, smiling, as he rubbed his leg, 'but, on the whole, we are managing quite splendidly.' That was not totally true, as he thought of the days when the throbbing in his stump was particularly annoying and uncomfortable. But he always remembered the others who had also been damaged in the war and who were far worse off than he was.

The glasses were refilled and the conversation continued.

'So, tell me please, Uncle, if it doesn't give too much away, who was this Printon chap – and this Swiss man, Benschedler.

'The first is the easier answer,' replied the Uncle, 'we have not the foggiest idea!' And he laughed, as he offered his nephew a cigar, which was refused. Turkish tobacco in a cigarette was one thing, but a full cigar was not to his liking. 'Of course, the real Printon was just exactly who he should have been. Poor chap – rotten bad luck to have been knocked down and killed in a Cairo street, after all he'd been through. Decorated for bravery, don't y' know!' He paused to draw in a couple of good lungfuls of smoke, as he held a flame to the end of the cigar. When it was alight, and burning to his satisfaction, he carried on. 'All we can surmise is that "*the enemy*", for lack of a better term, took the opportunity provided by Printon's death – which was purely a chance occurrence – to take his persona and use it as a mask for their own agent. As to exactly who this agent of theirs was...' he raised his eyebrows and shoulders, in a gesture of ignorance, '...we have nothing on him at all, I'm afraid. He was completely unknown to us.'

'I see, Sir,' said Stephen, quietly.

'Now, this Benschedler chap is of far more interest – at least we know who he was.'

'Really, Sir, do we?' said the nephew, sitting forward in his chair. 'You mean to say that he was the person he claimed to be?'

'Good Lord, no. That guff about being a Swiss national was a smokescreen. No, your man was actually the Count von Hohenstadt und Waldstein-Turingheim, and a rather nasty piece of work, too. Still, I suppose I don't have to tell *you* that do I?'

The nephew sat silently for a few seconds, digesting what his uncle has just said.

'But if Benschedler was not Benschedler, then that means Kormann didn't get his revenge, after all.'

'What's that, you say, my boy? Who's Kormann?'

For a change it was the Uncle who did not know something

that his nephew did. Over the next few minutes he was told of the events that had taken place at the foot of the double temple at Kom Ombo.

'Best to leave things the way they seemed, wouldn't you say, my boy,' said the Uncle, once he was in possession of the facts. 'At least this Kormann chap *thinks* he has finally avenged his father, and for that he can be thankful and, perhaps, can at last find peace of mind.' He drew again on his cigar. 'It wouldn't serve any purpose to disillusion the poor chap.'

'I suppose that you are quite right, Sir,' replied the nephew. 'He should never have to get himself so worked up over what happened to his father ever again – now that he believes he has put things to right and restored the family honour.'

'It is only a minor untruth in the broader picture,' said the Uncle, 'and, in the circumstances, it won't do any harm to anyone. No, my boy, this Count was quite well known to us,' continued the Uncle, steering the conversation back to the subject of The Phoenix. 'He had fared well leading up to the war – he travelled all over the place and had lands and estates everywhere. We first heard of him around '09, when he strayed off the social circuit and became involved with some, shall we say, less-than-honest business dealings.' He raised his eyebrows at his nephew, but he did not elaborate further. 'When the war came along, we lost track of him. Hardly surprising, really – everyone was busy fighting everyone else and it all became quite a mess. Then we had a stroke of luck – 1916, I think it was, when the Western Front had got bogged down. One of our friends spotted him in Geneva of all places. We found out that he'd moved most of his money there and – more importantly – he was trying to broker a deal with Benschedler – the *real* Benschedler – to buy arms for the Kaiser's army. The German war machine was beginning to show the strains of demand, so they must have thought that they could supplement their own production with stuff they could buy in.'

'But where would they be able to buy arms in those quantities, when the whole of Europe and Russia was in flames?'

'A good question, my boy,' beamed the Uncle approvingly. 'Now think, who was the one power with virtually limitless raw materials and the production capacity to match which was *not* involved in the conflict by 1916?'

'You don't mean...'

'I do,' said the Uncle, cutting him off in mid-sentence, 'but you didn't hear that from me,' he said, looking sternly at his nephew. 'Wouldn't do to upset our Allies, now would it?'

'Switzerland remained neutral in the war – so how was this Benschedler allowed to trade arms from a neutral, non-combatant country?'

'He wasn't,' replied the Uncle, his voice serious. 'It all became very unpleasant when someone ratted on the operation and the Swiss government stepped in. All hell broke loose, I can tell you. The upshot was a scandal of the most enormous proportions. This Benschedler ended up in prison and our friend, the Count, disappeared again.'

'Is Benschedler still behind bars, then?'

'No – he died, back in '20. They said it was from natural causes, but the rumour mill swung into top gear and claimed it was an inside job, paid for by the relatives of those innocents whom he had destroyed with his illegal dealings over the years – since before the war even began,' replied the Uncle.

'So, this Count masqueraded as Benschedler, using his name and passport...'

'...Which was a forgery. The unsavoury lot with which the Count threw in his hand – this Hitler chap and his new party – they're a dangerous crowd. That's why we had to stop the diamonds getting through to them – all we can do is to try and cut off their funding. Until those in office on this side of the Channel realize that there is a very real threat to us steadily building up on the other side of the water and they move to make it official government policy to try and stop it, there's nothing else we can do.'

'Isn't it rather odd, Uncle, that most of politics, or diplomacy, or whatever you want to call it, takes place in a state of denial? The reality of a situation hardly ever seems to enter the equation...'

'...And sadly, my boy, usually not until it's far too late,' added the Uncle. 'Nobody wants a repeat of the last calamity – there are too many open wounds still unhealed from that one. That aside, the current foreign policy of HM Government – and you didn't hear this from me, either – seems to be leaning towards doing anything to avoid another conflict. I mean *anything*,' stressed the Uncle.

'Surely you don't mean that Germany would try to...'

'There is a dangerous, pent-up resentment over the Versailles Conference amongst your average German. Resentment can be manipulated if you have the imagination and charisma to do so. Take the minds of a disgruntled nation, promise them what they think they want, fire them up to take on your ideas with some convincing rhetoric and you have them in the palm of your autocratic hand, m' boy.'

'You mean in Germany? Hitler? He has a criminal record and has spent time in prison. Do you really think the rest of them will follow him ... into another war?' asked Stephen incredulously.

'Stranger things have happened before now, my boy. Then again, the world really is an odd sort of place. This Major Ashdown – what did you make of him?'

Stephen was taken aback by the abrupt change in the

topic of conversation and had to think for a few seconds before replying.

'Very focused – a career soldier, or intelligence, or whatever department he's in. Quite tenacious ... but he has some personal matters that could get in his way if he's not careful.' He did not mention the domestic confrontation, which they had all witnessed in *Khufu*'s foyer.

'Oh ...?' said the Uncle, raising his eyebrows expectantly, but the nephew remained silent.

After a pause, which was indicative of the fact that his nephew was as capable of being secretive as was he himself, the Uncle continued.

'Well, my boy, whatever these personal matters might be, it seems as if Ashdown is very loyal to those whom, he says, have helped him in the furtherance of his duties. He has put in a request for a certain police inspector out in Nairobi to be promoted. Apparently the man was instrumental in the pursuit of the stones. There's an opening for a chief inspector coming up shortly down in Dar es Salaam, so we'll see what we can do.' They continued in amiable conversation for a further twenty minutes before the clock which stood in the centre of the marble mantelpiece started to strike six, echoing the distant chimes of Big Ben.

'Is that the time?' asked the nephew, glancing up at the clock. 'I must fly. Thanks awfully for the chat and the drinks. We're off to Covent Garden tonight – going to see *Aida*, of all things, would you believe?' he said, laughing, as he rose from his chair.

'Are you going with that archaeologist friend of yours?' asked the Uncle as he, too, rose from his chair.

'Rupert Winfield is his name, Uncle ... and yes, I am.'

'Why don't you bring him down for a weekend?'

'That's very good of you, Sir, but I think he'd be a bit uncomfortable. The full weight of the family can be terribly intimidating at times – even for family members.' He smiled and then added, 'Perhaps one day soon ... I'll see what he thinks about the idea.'

But the reality was that he wanted to keep his family separate from the life he and Rupert had started to make for themselves. There was also the question of family approval – or the withholding thereof. He did not want anything – including his family – to get in the way of the happiness he had experienced over the last few months.

'As you wish, my boy, but just say the word – you know you'll both be more than welcome.'

After his nephew had left, the Uncle, seated once again in his armchair next to the fire, opened that morning's copy of *The Times*. As he had an hour to kill before setting off for an evening at his club, he continued with his reading, picking up from where he had left off earlier in the day. There was a short report on a new talking film from America. It was called a cartoon and was hailed as a technical marvel where the pictures, which were all hand-drawn, came to life to the accompaniment of recorded sound. The Uncle never went to the cinema, but he wondered casually if there was any military use for such an invention. He made a mental note to contact the Ministry of Information. In Rome, the Chamber of Deputies had been taken over by the Fascist Party and their leader, Mussolini, had become Prime Minister at the invitation of the King. The Uncle had had reports on the strong-arm tactics Mussolini employed to achieve his political ends. It was quite possible that he was someone else who needed to be closely watched in the ever-shifting kaleidoscope of international politics.

He turned the page. There was an article about the continuing modernization of Turkey and the increasing use of a modern Turkish alphabet using Western characters, to replace the old Ottoman one written in Arabic.

Another modern state led by a strong-arm former military man, keen on flexing its muscles on the world stage, thought the Uncle, *and this president of theirs – Mustafa Kemal Ataturk – he was the one who got the better of us at Gallipoli, back in the war.* 'Another one to keep an eye on,' he muttered out loud, as he looked up from the page and stared into the flames.

The pages seemed to be full of mainly bad news from home and abroad. The international stage suddenly seemed to be crowded with a whole host of new players. It was all becoming far more complicated than it had been before the war. Back then it had been far easier to work out who was allied with whom and who was up to no good. 'Not that we were able to sort out the business in Sarajevo,' he muttered.

He returned his gaze to the newspaper. Next to the report from Turkey was another that caught his attention. It told of further difficulties arising over the future of Britain's interests in the new oil fields in the seven-year-old, British-protected Kingdom of Iraq.